Praise for Dreda Say Mitchell:

'As good as it gets'
Lee Child

'A great read written by a great girl'
Martina Cole

'Dreda Say Mitchell is right up there at the forefront of
British crime fiction'
Peter James

'Mitchell outguns Martina Cole for pure,
shocking East End gangster grit. ★★★★★'
Mirror

'Wonderful vivid writing and a truly original voice'
Peter James

'*Vendetta* is a fantastic thriller. I suggest you strap
in as you are in for a very bumpy and exhilarating ride!'
CrimeSquad

'An extremely well written fast-moving chase thriller. . .
Mitchell improves with every book' *The Times*

'The narrative t̶
and has a refr̶
Sunday

'Awesome tale fr̶
Sun

'The pace of this relentless thriller never falters . . .
it's fast, exciting fun' *Sunday Mirror*

Dreda Say Mitchell, who grew up on a housing estate in east London, is an award-winning novelist, broadcaster, journalist and freelance education consultant. For more information and news, visit Dreda's website:

www.dredasaymitchell.com
Follow Dreda on Twitter: @DredaMitchell

Also by Dreda Say Mitchell:

Running Hot
Killer Tune
Geezer Girls
Gangster Girl
Hit Girls
Vendetta

Death Trap

Dreda Say Mitchell

HODDER

First published in Great Britain in 2015 by Hodder & Stoughton
An Hachette UK company

1

A CIP catalogue record for this title is available from the British Library

Paperback ISBN 978 1 444 78945 4
Ebook ISBN 978 1 444 78946 1

Printed and bound by Clays Ltd, St Ives plc

Hodder & Stoughton policy is to use papers that are natural, renewable
and recyclable products and made from wood grown in sustainable forests.
The logging and manufacturing processes are expected to conform
to the environmental regulations of the country of origin.

Hodder & Stoughton Ltd
Carmelite House
50 Victoria Embankment
London EC4Y 0DZ

www.hodder.co.uk

To all my readers on Facebook and Twitter who have supported my books and spread the word, a massive thank you for your time and energy.

And to my agent, the amazing Amanda Preston, for all those fruitful brainstorming sessions.

one

Day One
6:40 a.m.

> **Madam B:** I am going to kill them.
> **se15:** How???
> **Madam B:** Machete. No axe to the head. Quick. Bloody.
> **se15:** Nah gotta be nice n sloooow. Waterboarding. Pure agony.
> **Madam B:** Hahaha. Should Kung Fu chop 'em up to DEATH.
> **se15:** Too much body contact. Your fingerprints everywhere ☺

Sixteen-year-old Nikki grinned as she stared at her iPad screen, dreaming up different ways to kill her parents. She sat crossed-legged on the bed, tablet in her lap, her trademark fingerless gloves covering her hands. She was on Yakkety-Yak, the latest social networking craze, chatting to user se15. Fantasising about how to take down her parents melted away some of the stress – bought that chill-thrill back into her life. Of course she didn't really want to kill them, but she was sick to death of them going on and on and on at her all the time like a pair of rabies-ridden dogs just waiting to sink their teeth into her.

You can't do that, Nicola . . .

You can't do this, Nicola . . .

And, of course, there was the classic,

We didn't do that in my day . . .

Nikki rolled her storm-grey eyes as the memory of her mum yelling that one at her – yet again – ricocheted in her mind, before she'd flipped a finger and banged out of the house yesterday evening.

But Nikki didn't have to worry about moan-fest Mummy at the present; she was safely tucked up in the best spot in town – the cosy bedroom on the top floor of the large house in Surrey: her pod of peace. As soon as she entered the room, her routine was always the same. Shut the door, drop the blinds, pop on the side lamp and then flip up the lid of her iPad to start chit-chatting to people who hid behind images of alter-egos and false names. Her lips pulled into a long, quick smile as she thought of another fantasy deadly deed to dispatch her parents permanently out of this life.

Madam B: Smother them with that mega size pillow they
    bought from Ikea . . .

Her fingers stopped moving when the door swung halfway open. A woman in her early twenties leaned her head into the room.

'Nicola, breakfast is ready,' she said in a gentle, Polish accent.

Nikki leaned back against the pillows as she answered Ania, the cleaner. 'It's too early too eat—'

'You know they have an urgent appointment this morning,' Ania smiled. 'Come on. And don't forget to take your gloves off.'

Then Ania was gone, but the door was left open.

Ping.

Hearing the sound, Nikki forgot about breakfast and went back to her Yakkety-Yak two-way conversation.

se15: Thought you wanted something nice n quick.
Smothering takes way too looooong.

Nikki's fingers got ready to answer, but her head hitched up and forwards when she heard a noise from downstairs; like something falling over. Then silence. She shrugged, thinking it couldn't be anything to worry about and turned her attention back to se15.

Madam B: Maybe I should cut out mum's tongue . . .

Her head snapped as she heard a crashing sound coming from downstairs.
Pop. Pop.
Her heartbeat kicked into high alert as she froze at the strange sound. Before she could try to figure out what the popping sound might be, two screams ripped through the air accompanied by shouting. Nicola jumped up, her iPad bouncing off her lap and onto the bed. Something was going on downstairs. No one yelled in this house, no one screamed. That's what she loved about it: the peace and calm, the way it made her feel like she was a person worth loving. Her body shook as quiet settled over the house again. But it didn't soothe her; something was terribly wrong. But what should she do? Stay here? Go downstairs?
Ping.
Nikki looked over at her iPad on the bed. Grabbed it up. Didn't look at the screen this time; instead shut the lid. Breathing way too high in her chest she moved towards the partially opened door. Stopped for a few seconds. Then used

the fingers poking out of her right glove to ease the door – really slowly – further back. Nikki took a deep breath as she stepped into the small landing.

No one there. Her gaze settled on the corner that would take her to the remainder of the landing that led to the stairs. Her hand tightened around her iPad as she started to move forwards, slowly. Forwards again, and again. She reached the corner, turned, and crashed straight into another person.

Nikki staggered back. Automatically opened her mouth about to scream . . . A hand slammed over her mouth holding the noise back. She stared up into the wild, terrified eyes of Ania.

'Shhh,' Ania whispered.

Nicola nodded back. The other woman pulled her hand away. She twisted away from the teenager as she wildly looked around. Her gaze stopped on the doors of the airing cupboard. Quickly she turned back to Nicola and gestured with her hand at the cupboard. The girl stared back in confusion, not under-standing what the cleaner wanted her to do. Her heartbeat pounded harder, and harder.

Ania grabbed her arm and hustled her towards the cupboard, which was opposite the room Nikki had previously been in. The double doors of the cupboard were the same height as the doors of the rooms around it, but with open wooden slats in the top half. Ania threw the doors open. The shelves were deep, with towels, bed linen and two duvets folded neatly on them.

'Get. In,' Ania shot out again.

Nikki once again started to ask, 'why?' but the sound of heavy footsteps on the stairs stopped her.

'Quick.' This time Nicola heard the desperation and tears in the cleaner's voice.

Nicola threw her iPad inside. Scrambled onto the middle

shelf with the duvets. Ania slammed the doors shut. Instantly Nikki was engulfed in dark and heat. The footsteps outside got closer, like they were now on the landing. Crouched low she slowly eased her head up and looked through the slats.

All she could see was Ania's back.

'What do you want?' she heard the cleaner shout.

Who was Ania talking to? Nikki couldn't see anyone else.

No one answered. Abruptly Ania staggered back, her voice high, begging, 'Please . . . No—'

Pop.

That's all Nikki heard. Blood spurted out of Ania's back, slashing high up against the slats in the airing cupboard door. Horrified Nikki felt blood slash against her lips and chin. Frozen with terror she watched Ania's body slump to the floor. And that's when she saw who was there.

A man.

Something strange covered his face and he wore black clothing. And he was standing over Ania with a gun in his hand.

Nicola wrapped a palm over her mouth to push back her sobs, but she couldn't stop the tears running from her eyes. The air in her chest was coming in strange, funny waves that made it hard for her to breathe. She'd never prayed in her life, but she wanted to pray now. Then she heard more footsteps. Her heartbeat madly kicked when she saw the gunman joined by another man dressed exactly like him. They stood staring down at Ania's body.

The one without the gun turned to the other and spoke. What he said Nikki couldn't hear because of the thing covering his face. The gunman answered him. She strained to hear what he was saying . . . then wished she hadn't when she heard his words.

'Let's make sure no one else is here.'

Oh my God.

Nikki knew she should move deeper into the cupboard but the terror held her still.

Move.

Move.

MOVE.

Finally Nikki started easing back, scared to death they would hear her. Her chest heaved, but she tried to keep her breathing down; keep it low. She stopped when she felt the end of the cupboard against her back. Panic gripped her again when one of the men started moving.

Oh God, he's coming towards the cupboard.

His black clothing blocked out the light sending Nikki into the darkest bowels of hell.

Please God. Please God.

He was getting closer. Closer. Closer.

Pleeeeease. Pleeeeease.

She kept the plea pounding in her mind to a God she didn't even believe in.

The man stopped, hovering just outside. Then he turned away to the side and started walking.

Just stay still until they go away.

Stay still.

Still.

Crouched like a caged animal, with a dead woman's blood drying on her skin, Nikki waited. The man who'd shot Ania joined the other one. They turned and started walking back along the landing. Nikki let out a soft and shaky breath of relief.

Ping.

Nikki looked desperately at her iPad.

The footsteps stopped. Started coming back.

No. No. No. NO.

The footsteps got closer.

They are going to kill me.

Going to kill me.

Kill me.

KILL ME.

two

As soon as Detective Inspector Rio Wray, of the Metropolitan Police Service, turned her car onto the street in Surrey she didn't need the address to ID where the killings had taken place. The place of murder was already taped off, local police stationed outside.

Number 3 The Lanes.

Sounded like something out of a Catherine Cookson novel, but the house was anything but. No back-to-back homes here in one of England's most des res locations, at least according to those 'where the super rich hang out' guides that were done every year that Rio was never asked to take part in.

The house was two-storeys, large and sprawling; bottom-half plain brick, top coated white. It put Rio in mind of a private school for girls (not that she knew anything about fee-paying education, having been to a rough and tumble inner London comp). It was set in its own grounds – low grass, mammoth trees, showcasing and sheltering it at the same time. Some would call it impressive, but to Rio all that green plain hurt her eyes, and the seclusion afforded by the garden made it the perfect place for murder.

Rio got out of the car, an ebony BMW, which she'd christened her Black Magic Woman. She finger-combed her twist-out Afro – or 'fro as she liked to call it – then approached the two officers on duty either side of the front door.

'Ma'am,' one immediately uttered when she reached them.

His tone was low, with a sideline in barely held back insolence that she didn't care for, but Rio left it alone. This situation was charged enough. The local police were in a tizzy about the presence of an outsider and her team running this investigation. One of the first acts of the newly appointed – and to some, controversial – Surrey Police and Crime Commissioner had been to shake up the investigation into the vicious spate of house robberies happening to wealthy householders living around London's greenbelt. She'd done the unthinkable – outsourced the case to the Met. A 'fresh-eyed, strategic approach' to solving the case was how she put it. B.S. management speak for 'you can't get the fucking job done.'

Rio could understand the heated resentment of the local police. Having another force come in to help clean up your house was not a good look. But then blood in your house was an even worse one.

Rio pushed the politics back and the policing up front. Over the last three months a group of criminals – infamously dubbed 'The Greenbelt Gang' by the media – had carried out audacious early morning and increasingly more vicious raids on affluent homes in the area in the last six weeks. In the last attack, fifteen days ago, a woman had been murdered and that's when Rio and her people had been assigned to the case.

Rio slipped on protective, forensic clothing and entered the house, registering the large, white tiles on the hallway floor, pastel green walls, occasionally broken by large paintings, and a wider-than-average staircase that curved seductively to a world upstairs.

A plain-clothes officer appeared from a room off the spacious hallway: DI Thomas Morrell. A top-heavy guy who'd learned how to carry his increasing weight around. He was bristling, just like the other times Rio had met him, his disapproval at her being assigned the investigation he'd once been the senior on out in the open. Rio didn't take it personally; she'd probably feel the same way if the situation were reversed.

'So, are we dealing with another Greenbelt?' she asked him getting down to business straight away. 'The privacy of the house fits their MO.'

The flesh on his cheeks wobbled as his mouth moved. 'That's not the only thing that fits. Paint-sprayed security cameras, French window at the back shattered by a single shot. No bullet casing to be found and the place a total tip as they searched for anything to line their pockets.' He pointed to the room he'd come out of. 'They made sure that no one was left standing this time.'

'Who discovered the bodies?'

'A local man who does the gardening. He turned up about an hour ago, couldn't get an answer, went around the back and saw a body in the kitchen.'

'We'll need to check out the gardener . . .'

DI Morrell twisted his lips in a way that Rio knew whatever he was about to spit out next was going to be nasty. 'If you were from around these parts you'd know that old Amos couldn't hurt a fly.'

Finally *it* was out in the open. *It* being he had a problem with her being black. She didn't have to be a genius to know that by 'around these parts' he not only meant Surrey but anywhere else in England. Colleagues questioning her abilities because of the colour of her skin was old news. She didn't have the time of day for some fat fuck of a detective who spoke in double meanings and didn't have the guts to say it plain and simple to her face.

'What's the body count?' she continued.

'Three. Male in the front room, woman in the kitchen and another female on the landing upstairs.'

Rio stepped into the main room, let her gaze roam around: a whirlwind of chaos. Typical Greenbelt Gang MO. So many things were dumped on the floor that it was hard for her to tell the shape of the room. Overturned cushions from the L-shaped creamy-beige leather suite, chunks of glass near an art deco style mirror, paper, twin discarded drawers of a dainty cabinet lying on its side. The lights on two small lamps, positioned on corner tables on either side of the French window, gave off an amber glow of softness and calm in a scene of total destruction. And the most brutal devastation of all was the body lying in the debris of the smashed glass table in the centre.

The victim was sprawled out like he'd just tipped over, one leg bent at an angle and the other straightened out. Dried blood circled the left side of his head. Not a perfect circle though, some of the blood had spread and leaked down the grooves between the wire-brushed teak floorboards. Rio crouched down beside him. With thirteen years on the job behind her, now aged thirty-five, she should've been a friend to death. But the air caught in the muscles of her throat as it always did. Rio just couldn't get why humans messed each other up. But then it wasn't for her to think about the why, but the who. Get the perpetrator off the streets and banged up behind walls so thick that the world soon forgot what their life-taking face looked like.

'Forensics are on their way,' Morrell said behind her. 'Looks like the poor bastard was shot with some type of pistol.'

Rio kept her brown gaze on the body as she pulled out a tiny torch from her pocket, displaying the faint, diagonal scar on her wrist. She shone it on the vic's head. The bloody grey-black strands of hair concealed the exit or entrance wound. She noticed a hole in his left hand: a defensive wound resulting from his hand stretched out in vain to stop the bullet coming at him. Rio guided the light against the clothing – black polo shirt with a white collar that was dipped in the stain of blood, dark blue tracksuit bottoms, and navy socks. The absence of footwear meant that the vic had probably been relaxing at home, having just risen for a day he had no idea was going to be his last. The clothing wasn't rolled or wrinkled which meant he'd fallen where he'd been attacked not dragged from anywhere else.

'Who lives here?' Rio asked, spinning on the flat of her feet to face the other detective.

'Married couple in their fifties. Maurice and Linda Bell. And from the descriptions given by the neighbours this is probably Mr Bell. His wife is in the kitchen.'

Morrell made it sound like Linda Bell was in the kitchen preparing a happy, cosy family breakfast. Rio stood up, torch still in her hand, and was guided by the other officer to the kitchen. It was a picture that she'd seen a hundred times. The ordinary domestic moment shattered by the interruption of a crime. The breakfast table had been carefully laid; this was no meal on the move while getting ready for work. There were fresh flowers in a vase, a coffee pot, toast in a rack, cereals in boxes, various spreads, all carefully laid out on a freshly ironed cloth. What stopped it looking like a breakfast buffet in a hotel was the blood – and the body.

'Gee-sus,' Rio let out, confronted by the violent streaks and spurts of blood on the floor and the white kitchen units near the sink.

And in a corner, slumped on the grainy flagstone floor, was the body of a woman. Her throat had been cut leaving a frozen, mini waterfall of dark red on the front of her sunshine yellow T-shirt. The only way to get a spray of blood from a wound like that was if the knife or sharp object had been plunged into the side of her neck and then sliced around the front; slice carotid artery; slice jugular vein; final slice through the trachea. Rio couldn't stop the image that flashed through her mind – standing in another kitchen, stunned as she watched the blood drain from the slit throat of someone she'd been tasked to take care of. The faint scars on her wrist throbbed as Rio shook off the unwanted memory. Rio didn't approach the body; best to leave that one to forensics.

She turned to Morrell. 'This gang are developing a taste for blood. You said there was another body upstairs. Did they live with someone else because the breakfast table is set for three?'

He shook his head. 'The Bells have a son and daughter and there's evidence that someone else was occupying one of the other bedrooms upstairs. Maybe it was the son or daughter, but there's no evidence of either of them being here now. They had a cleaner, but it's unlikely they'd be sitting down with the help at the brekkie table. Old Amos, the gardener, said she came in twice a week: Mondays and Fridays. Her name was Ania. The neighbours haven't a clue what her surname was. We think the body upstairs is the cleaner.'

Rio was glad to get out of the kitchen back into the hallway. She pulled in a few deep breaths and then wished she hadn't as the warmth in the air intensified the tang of death at the back of her mouth. Just as they started to walk up the stairs a voice behind called out, 'DI Wray?'

Rio twisted half around to find a man facing her at the bottom of the stairs. His stance was bold, legs braced slightly apart. Rio frowned; something about him was familiar and she had a prickly feeling at the back of her neck that the familiarity was not welcome. He looked somewhere between forty-five and fifty, with hair and the head-turning looks of what her closest friend called a silver fox, though the stubble on his chin looked more grizzly bear. He wore his formal suit and tie well on his six-two frame. Her gaze snapped back to his face as she remembered where she'd seen him. No way, her mind protested. DSI Newman would never hook her up with *him*.

'What are *you* doing here?' Her tone was hostile.

He answered, laidback and easy, with an accent that reminded Rio of her cousins who lived in Sheffield. 'I've been placed on the investigation team.' He took a step forwards. 'Jack—'

Rio didn't let him finish. Just breathing the same air as him further polluted the taste in her mouth. 'I know who you are and the day you're on *my* team is the day I've been sent to investigate Lucifer in hell.'

Rio swore softly as she turned her back on him and continued up the stairs. Jack Strong. Detective Jack Strong. Well, he'd better not follow her or she was likely to punch his lights out and send him tumbling straight back where he'd come from.

Still seething, Rio kept pace with Morrell as they hit the next floor, turned the corner, and stopped when she saw the female body lying face up not far from the door of a room or cupboard. She shook thoughts of Jack Strong from her mind as she approached the body. Attractive woman, the front of her top dried with blood. Eyes wide open. Hazel eyes.

The Greenbelt Gang had really gone ballistic this time.

'From the blood around her and the mess on her front I'd say she was shot once at close range.'

Hearing the voice behind her, Rio slowly turned, trying like hell to keep her temper down.

'I told you to get lost,' she threw at Strong.

'Yeah, well I've got orders to—'

Rio laughed with no joy. 'Orders? That's a strange word coming from you. As if—' Abruptly she stopped when Strong placed a finger against his lips in a gesture for her to be quiet.

Who the fuck did this should've-been-slung-out-of-the-force four years back think he was? Furiously she opened her mouth, but nothing came out because she suddenly knew why Strong was shushing her.

There was a sound, not too loud: a ruffling noise coming from somewhere. Still with his finger on his lips Strong moved forwards, eyes alert as he swung his gaze around. Then he passed Rio and kept moving towards the door behind the body. Rio followed.

They stopped near the door. The ruffling sound came again, then a sob. All three detectives jumped on either side of the door: Rio and Strong to the right, Morrell to the left.

Rio called out, 'We're the police, so whoever you are, come out with your hands held high.'

three

The answer was another sob, this one mixed with a few beats of open crying.

Rio hitched herself off the wall, eyebrows pressed down, the skin around her mouth tight.

'Come. Out. Now,' she repeated.

No response. The crying and sobbing stopped.

'Are you hungry, love? Need a drink?'

Rio was surprised to hear Strong's voice behind her, but before she could speak he set himself at the front of the cupboard. She couldn't believe he was putting himself in danger, so she mouthed, 'What the fuck are you doing?'

But he ignored her and carried on speaking. 'I've got a bottle of water in my pocket. It's yours if you want it.'

Silence.

Rio impatiently broke through the quiet with, 'Strong . . .'

But he leaned towards her and whispered, 'It's some kid. Sobs sound just like my Mary when she was upset.' He gave his attention again to whoever was inside the cupboard. 'We really are the police.'

'You . . . you could be . . . anyone.' They heard the voice for the first time. Female. Rasping. Weary. And yeah, Strong was spot on, young.

'Do you know what a warrant card is?' Strong continued.

Silence. Then, 'Is that the wallet thing that cops carry when they ID themselves?'

'That's the one.' Strong took an even step forwards. 'Why don't I take mine out, open the door and then you can . . .'

'Noooo.' The voice swung high, trembling in fear. 'Don't come in. Don't come in. DON'T. COME. IN.'

Rio quickly moved to stand closer to the newest member of her team. 'We should just drag her out.'

Strong looked at her and for the first time Rio saw he had blue eyes. Not just any old kind of blue, but the type that was intense and bright. Memorable. He leaned close into her again, his breath warm against her skin. 'Let me have one more go. If it doesn't work, we do it your way.'

Rio didn't like her commands not being carried through, but she needed to get the girl out into the open, and if that meant giving Jack Strong the floor she didn't have a choice. She briskly nodded back.

Strong started his persuasive dialogue again. 'What's your favourite music?'

'What?'

'Rihanna?'

'No way, she's light weight.'

Strong's lips kicked up into a grin. 'My girl loved dance music – couldn't get enough of it.'

'Loved? You said loved not love? Is your daughter dead?'

The smile slid from his face, but then he pulled it back into place. 'If we were going to hurt you lass, we'd have done it by now.'

The breathing inside the cupboard was audible now, frantic and heavy.

'I saw what they did to Ania.'

Strong's voice lowered a fraction. 'We're going to keep you safe. Make sure you're alright.'

Silence. Then a noise came from inside like she was moving around. Two eyes appeared at the slats. Wide, searching grey eyes. The girl's gaze jumped around as she checked out first Strong, then Rio. One side of the double door moved slightly. Both Strong and Rio eased a step back.

'You're alright girl,' Strong coaxed softly. 'We'll do this in your time.'

The door inched forwards, little by little. It kept moving until a hand, sporting lilac-and-black striped fingerless gloves, appeared. The fingers trembled and twitched. The girl's breathing shuddered as she halted the motion of the door, before shoving it wide-open, revealing herself for the first time. Crouched, eyes flickering with fear and at the brightness of the light, the colour of her face gave new meaning to the cliché 'as white as snow': as if her heart had stopped pumping blood above her neck.

Rio suspected that her shoulder-length hair was some type of blonde, but sweat had dyed it to a slick, tangled brown. Her grey eyes, a mixture of silver and bloodshot-weary, shone with the lost, wild look of a chained animal. Rio noted all of those things, but what she couldn't take her gaze off was the tiny, spot of red, or was it brown – maybe both? – that sat awkwardly just left of the centre of the girl's chin. If that was what Rio thought it was, then the girl had been peering through the slats in the door when the cleaner was gunned down, blood shooting backwards. Witnesses on the previous raids had been carefully controlled by the gang: terrorised, they had only seen what the gang had allowed them to see – which wasn't much. Now, for the first time in the Greenbelt Gang investigation, there was someone who'd inadvertently been given a front row seat to view the deadly action without the gang knowing.

A unique witness.

Rio stepped forwards, mouth curved into a reassuring smile, palms stretched upwards in a welcoming gesture. 'I'm Detective Inspector Rio Wray and you've been talking to my colleague Detective Jack Strong.'

The girl's eyes darted between them as if she still didn't believe their story. Then her hands braced, forearms shaking, against the shelf and she eased out of the cupboard. Her body swayed as soon as her feet touched the ground. Rio rushed forwards and wrapped her arms around the girl's waist. The girl's arms hugged Rio's shoulders as she pushed into the solid warmth of Rio's much taller body. 'I've got you. You're OK now, you're OK.'

The girl's T-shirt was damp, probably soaked through with sweat and the artificial heat from the airing cupboard Rio concluded. Despite all that heat the girl's skin felt ice cold.

The girl's body tensed and Rio knew what she was staring at. Gently Rio shifted her body, blocking the gruesome sight of the dead cleaner.

'Put your arm around my waist,' Rio gently instructed.

As soon as the girl's arm locked around Rio's middle she started leading her towards the stairs. But when they reached the top of the stairs the pressure of the teenager's arm increased, so Rio stopped.

'My iPad.' The girl spoke softly. 'I left it in the cupboard. Can you get it for me?'

Rio twisted her head and nodded at Strong. Then she turned back and said, 'We'll need to keep it as evidence, but you'll get it back.'

They hit the stairs. 'What's your name?"

'Nicola Bell. But everyone calls me Nikki.' Her voice was quiet and tight.

Bell. Probably the daughter that Morrell mentioned.

'How old are you?'

'Sixteen.'

'Well, Nikki, we're going to get you out of here . . .'

'I'm thirsty. The other cop . . . I mean policeman—' A girl with manners, Rio liked that. She didn't meet many kids in her line of work that put politeness at the top of their how-to behaviour list.

'We'll get you some water.'

As soon as they hit the hallway downstairs Rio guided Nikki towards the kitchen.

'DI . . .' Strong's voice was strident and urgent behind her.

Rio twisted her head to the side and only when she caught his gaze did she realise what he was trying to warn her about. But it was too late; they were already on the threshold of the kitchen. Rio tried to grab Nikki's head, but the girl had already seen what they didn't want her to.

Nikki's gaze was transfixed by the blood and body in the corner with its cut throat. She let out a horrified, choked scream as she slumped back in Rio's arms.

four

'I will only permit you to question her for a short period of time,' the doctor warned Rio. 'She's traumatised and needs rest.'

Rio stood with Doctor Melissa Green in the corridor of a ward on the second floor of Mission Hill Hospital. Rio had decided to take Nikki Bell to a hospital in London rather than one near the Bells' home in Surrey. The sixteen-year-old could break this case wide open, so Rio needed to keep her close.

'I've got an investigation to pursue and this girl is a key witness. I'm sure that you can understand Doctor Green how important it is that I speak to her now.'

The doctor's beeper went. As she pulled it out she replied, 'DI Wray, I know how you can get sometimes in your eagerness to find the truth. Just take this one gently.' She checked her beeper and started moving down the corridor, then looked back at Rio. 'I've got to go. Five minutes, that's all.'

Then, as Rio turned to the protection officer stationed at the door of Nikki Bell's room, the doctor paused for a second, flipped her head to the side and called out, 'Don't forget the match on Saturday. We're going to annihilate you.'

Rio responded with a cocky, raised eyebrow. She'd known Melissa Green for a good three years, through dealing with victims in the hospital. Two years ago Doctor Green and Rio had organised a netball match between the female medical staff and some of the female officers back at The Fort to raise money for the hospital's children's unit. The match had been a success, so every six months Rio 'Goal Attack' Wray faced Mel 'Goal Defence' Green on the field. Both teams were competitive and aggressive in their pursuit of winning, but The Fort Tigers were still leading in the 'we're whipping your ass' league table.

Rio put thoughts of the coming match from her mind as she approached the protection officer. Her superior, DSI Newman, had whinged on about restricted resources when Rio had made the urgent call requesting a protection duty of two officers. But Rio had played the high profile case card and if anything happened to their witness the heat was going to come licking back at his door. He'd eventually agreed, but when only a lone protection officer had appeared she'd felt mad enough to call her DS and pull a strip off him over the phone. But, of course, she hadn't done that. Rio was known for sticking by the book; she'd work too hard and long to let emotions get in the way of her ultimate goal – climbing the Metropolitan Police Service ladder as far as she could go. No way was she going to be booted out – not like disgraced, former cop Calum Burns.

Calum Burns, Jack Strong. Why did she always end up with the whiff of scum parked right beside her?

Rio dumped the bad thoughts when she reached the protection officer. 'No one, and I mean no one, comes into this room unless it's medical staff.'

As he nodded back Detective Jack Strong walked towards her. Rio had deliberately not been looking his way. He'd shown expert policing skills, talking the witness out into the open, but so what? That didn't put him in her good books. Or any of her books for that matter. As soon as she got back to The Fort he was history. Without acknowledging him, Rio quickly entered the room and shut the door firmly in his face. Turned her back. Waited. If he dared to enter this room he was going to quickly find out that she wasn't scared of verbally taking him down, even in front of the most valuable evidence in this case.

Rio gave it ten seconds. The door remained firmly closed. Good. Now she could get back to the case. The teenager was lying on top of the pale blue blanket that covered the bed. Nikki Bell was about average height, but she looked small and shrunken in the bed. After seeing her mother butchered in the kitchen the girl had started shaking and crying with such pain that Rio knew there would be nothing gained by talking to her straight away. So she'd let Nikki have some personal space and got her to the hospital as quickly as possible.

'I'm sorry about your mother,' Rio said as she walked towards the bed.

The February light coming through the single window was bleak and uneven. There was a chill in the air that even the central heating couldn't dispel.

'I'm sorry that you had to see her like that,' Rio continued when she reached the side of the bed.

Nikki didn't say anything; instead she dropped her gaze to stare at her fingers twisting tightly together. She'd refused to remove the lilac-and-black striped fingerless gloves from her hand, even when Doctor Green had wanted to feel her pulse. Maybe the gloves acted as some type of anchor to reality, Rio thought, or maybe they were a gift from her mother. Whatever the reason, Rio had told everyone to not make such a drama out of it. She needed this girl as steady and as grounded as possible to uncover every detail of what she'd seen.

'Do you mind if I sit down?' Rio quietly asked.

The teen shook her head, unleashing the natural bounce of

her blonde hair now the sweat had dried out. But she refused to make eye contact.

Rio knew she had to take this slow, but she was the first to admit she was shit with kids, especially the adolescent kind. All those hormones and moods clogging up the road towards the truth; she'd rather be busting the balls of some serial killer.

'I know this will be painful for you,' Rio started, 'but you're the one person who can help us because you're the only person who saw what happened. Do you think you can tell me what you saw?'

Rio hoped she'd got the tone right: didn't want the teenager to think she was talking down to her like she was some seven-year-old.

The girl didn't answer. Instead two of her fingers pulled up a small part of the blanket and started to rub the material together.

Take it slow, Rio warned herself, although instinct jabbed her to press on.

Finally Nikki raised her eyes to look at Rio. Her face wasn't so pale anymore. She had a bit of colour in her checks and on the tip of her nose. Her eyes had lost that silver shine, and were now brimming like soft clay.

Then she spoke. 'Can I have my iPad back now?'

'I explained earlier that we're keeping it for evidence.' Rio punched firmness into her voice. 'What happened, Nikki?'

The girl's gaze flipped away again. 'I don't remember.'

Was this kid playing her?

'Then why were you hiding inside the airing cupboard?'

Nikki swallowed deep, but kept her stare locked away from Rio.

'Ania made me get inside.'

'She must've told you to do it for a reason.'

Nikki shrugged. 'Dunno. She just told me to do it.'

'You don't come across to me as someone who would just do something without a reason.' Rio paused, controlling the irritation she heard in her tone. 'Do you want to get the people who did this?'

Nikki nodded.

Rio got out of the chair and eased down on the bed next to Nikki's hip. 'Then help me out.'

Nikki's fingers stopped playing in the blanket and she folded her arms over her belly.

'OK.' She raised her head and her light grey eyes stared at Rio. 'I was in the bedroom, on Hamlet—'

'Hamlet?' Rio asked, confused.

'That's what I call my iPad. Hamlet.'

Well at least this kid was getting a good education, not that Rio knew anything about *Hamlet* or any other type of Shakespearean play, except the unnecessary tragedy of *Romeo and Juliet*.

Nikki's arms tightened around her body. 'I thought I heard a noise from downstairs . . .'

'What type of noise?'

'Something falling . . . I don't know . . . Maybe a scream . . .' Her voice jerked with her memories.

'Then what did you do?'

'I got up . . .'

The door opened and Detective Strong pushed his head into the room.

The temper that Rio had been holding back came out full blast. 'I told you to stay outside.' She pointed at the bottom of the doorway. 'Not to cross the threshold.'

But he wasn't moving; in fact he dared take a step into the room. 'I need to speak with you—'

'Not now you don't.'

'Yes now.' There was a bite in his tone for the first time since

Rio had met him. Well screw him; she was the one calling the shots, not him. But just as she was ready to let another comeback fly he turned and strode briskly back into the corridor leaving the door wide open. Rio thrust herself to standing. If he wanted a punch up she was so ready to put her boxing gloves on.

Then she remembered Nikki. She plastered on a half-hearted smile of reassurance. 'Just try and relax and picture what happened. I'll be back.'

Rio found Strong in the corridor leaning casually against the wall.

'I don't like your tone.' Her gaze ran over him, slowly, from head to toe. 'Or the way you're posing against that wall.'

He slowly peeled himself off.

'Mind you, it doesn't matter because you're going to be off this case as soon as we get back to base.'

'In the meantime,' he answered, 'I'll do my job. I don't know who that girl is in there, but she isn't the Bells' daughter.'

That shook Rio up; she wasn't expecting that.

'She said her name is Nikki Bell.'

'The neighbours are saying the only daughter Maurice and Linda Bell have is called Leah. She's thirty years old.'

'She had to be in that house for a reason. Maybe she's their granddaughter?' Rio reasoned to Strong.

'Both the Bells' children are single without any kids attached.'

'Shit,' Rio let rip. She straightened her shoulders, turning to look with determination at the door of the room she'd just left.

'Go easy on her,' Strong gently advised.

Rio flung her gaze with contempt at him. 'Like you went easy on that lad four years back?' Strong tipped his chin up in defiance, but said nothing. 'Why don't you cash in your cards?

The Met doesn't need the nasty stain of cops like you stinking up its four walls.'

And with that Rio re-entered the room. She stared hard at the teen. The time for being gentle with the kid had passed. Swiftly she headed for the other side of the bed. This time when she reached the girl she didn't sit, but shifted her legs slightly wide, looming and looking down.

'Who are you, Nikki?'

The girl's tongue darted against her dried lips before she answered. 'I told you, Nikki Bell.'

'You see that's causing me a bit of a problem because the man and woman who lived in that house, who are now dead,' the girl flinched, 'didn't have a daughter your age. So whose little girl are you?'

The child whipped her head around to face the other side of the room.

'Look. At. Me.' Rio's slow, hard words had the effect she wanted: the girl turned back to her.

'There were four people in that house; three of them are dead. You're the only one alive, so you'd better start telling me who you really are.'

Nikki's teeth played nervously in her top lip, the skin on her cheeks splashing with a warm red. 'There were two of them,' she finally threw out, answering a question Rio hadn't asked her, but one Rio needed to know.

She leaned over and braced her hands against the blanket. 'What did they look like?'

Nikki lifted her slim shoulders in an anxious shrug. 'One of them couldn't–'

But before Nikki could continue, a commotion outside had Rio pulling straight again. Furious voices filled the air, one of which she recognised as Strong's. Rio rushed to the door and thrust it back. Stepping into the corridor, she found Strong pinning a man in a blue suit against the wall. His forearm pressed deep into the man's throat. A lone black rucksack lay tumbled on its side near the man's polished black right shoe. The protection officer was right by Strong's side.

'What the hell's going on?' she asked.

'This . . .' Strong looked the man insolently up and down, 'gentleman was trying to get into the room. When I told him he couldn't go in he didn't want to take no for an answer.'

He pulled the man, who was gasping for breath, slightly forwards. Then slammed him back into the wall again. And in a menacing growl, let out, 'Who are you?'

five

'Let him go,' Rio instructed Strong, but her eyes remained firmly fixed on the man against the wall. Unfortunately, she knew exactly who he was. Her mouth twisted in annoyance. This day was turning into a bellyful of trouble she didn't need. Rio wouldn't be surprised if Satan himself turned up to join the party.

Strong glanced at her from the side, those bright eyes of his brimming with questions. Rio was about to nod at him, but stopped herself. She was in charge of this operation, not him, so she stared him down. He turned back to the man and released him. The man pushed himself off the wall with a casual motion like he had done this before, which wouldn't have surprised Rio; he was someone who went looking for trouble. He flexed his jaw, ran his palms over his designer jacket.

As Rio walked towards him, she asked, 'What are you doing here, Mr Foster?'

Stephen Foster was tall enough to look down his nose at Rio; but she figured he was the kind of man who would look down his nose at anyone, no matter what his height might have been. The thought left a sour taste in Rio's mind as she waited for him to answer.

'I'm here to attend to my client. I'm the Bell family's solicitor and I'm here to look after Nicola Bell's interests.'

'And who is Nicola Bell?' Rio felt stupid having to ask him, of all people, who the girl in the room was.

He raised an eyebrow. 'Why am I not surprised you haven't verified who she is. She's Maurice and Linda Bell's niece.'

'Thank you for telling me.' Her words were grudgingly spoken. 'I'm Detective Inspector Rio Wray. I'm in charge of the investigation.'

'Is that how you take charge? Shoving innocent men against walls?'

Foster seemed to enjoy his jibe. But then cop bashing seemed to be Stephen Foster's part-time hobby, after minding the interests of his many rich and famous clients. Foster was notorious for taking on cases which embarrassed the Metropolitan Police Service even when there was no money in it for him. Civil liberties groups hailed him as a champion, the police a nasty, permanent thorn in their side. Rio had always found him an unlikely candidate for an enemy of the forces of law and order; everything about him screamed establishment with a capital E.

Voice as polished as his shoes, manners as elegant as his clothes; the exclusive and expensive worlds of public school and Oxbridge hung over him. Although he was obviously a paid-up member of the swanky posh set, this man was not afraid of putting on a pair of Mike Tyson-sized gloves, over his carefully manicured fingernails, to engage in a legal street fight; that included with the police. His mane of grey hair was a little too long and swept back in the style of an ageing rock star. And as far as Foster was concerned, he was a rock star in his sixties – but of the legal kind. With Foster on the case, Rio knew that she had to be careful, real careful; her superiors were not likely to forgive her if she thrust them in the ring, with Foster waiting for the ding-ding sounding the start of round one.

Foster looked at Strong with contempt and then back at Rio. 'This officer is on your team is he?'

Rio nodded. She didn't like Strong being here anymore than the lawyer, but she was loyal to her team to an outsider.

'Detective Strong was only doing his job.'

Foster looked over at the male detective. 'Jack Strong?' Rio wasn't surprised that he knew who the newest member of her team was. Probably would have been the lawyer assisting the family Strong had wronged if another solicitors firm hadn't got there before him. 'I see . . .' Foster said nothing else on the subject, but then his manner showed he didn't need to. 'If you could take me through to my client Detective Inspector.'

'How did you find out that Nicola Bell was in the hospital?'

He smiled cynically at her. 'I make it my business to know where my clients are.'

If he was going to play a cat and mouse game, Rio was more than happy to join in. 'I'm afraid the doctor's instructions are —'

But Foster cut across her. He wasn't loud – Foster didn't do loud – he was about hard-edged persuasion. 'I don't care what the doctor's instructions are, I will see my client—'

The sound of running feet, muffled sobs and cries of, 'Nikki? . . . Nicola?' stopped their conversation.

The two of them turned and watched as Strong stepped forwards and stood in front of a distraught middle-aged woman. Plump and small, wearing a bob haircut and a floral print dress. Three, chunky silver bracelets jangled around her right arm as she moved.

The woman wailed, 'Where's my baby . . .?'

Strong politely asked her to identify herself but not politely enough for the woman. 'I'm Nikki's – Nicola Bell's – mother. Now get out of our way.'

Foster walked towards her with authority. 'Mrs Bell, I'm Stephen Foster—'

'Hold up one minute,' Rio threw in quickly. 'You said that you represented the Bell family.'

Foster smacked his lips together. 'Meaning Maurice and

Linda Bell. They asked me to also look after the interests of their niece, Nicola, if she ever needed—'

'We should chuck him out of here,' Jack Strong suggested with menace, his northern accent becoming more pronounced.

But Foster wasn't intimidated. Instead he turned to Nikki's mother. 'You know what happened to your husband's brother and his wife. Your brother-in-law had been paying me a retainer just in case your daughter might ever need any legal help and advice. Of course it's your decision, but I would say that Nicola is in need of that help now.'

Indecision, mixed with grief and pain, were stamped on Mrs Bell's face. 'I don't know. My husband Frank isn't here. He's downstairs parking the car.'

Foster smiled as he laid a hand on her arm. 'Let me introduce you to Detective Inspector Rio Wray, who is heading up the investigation and Detective Jack Strong.' His hand gently squeezed. 'And this is Mrs Patsy Bell, Nicola's mum. Her husband Frank is Maurice Bell's brother—'

'Patsy? Pat? Where is she?' A man of average height, balding hair, wearing horn-rimmed glasses called out.

No one needed to tell Rio that this was Frank Bell. She had to grab back the high ground from the lawyer, so immediately stepped forwards to greet Nicola's father with an outstretched hand. 'I'm Detective Rio Wray—'

He ignored her hand. 'Where's my daughter?'

Rio made a wide gesture with her hand towards the room where the teenager was. 'If you step this way with me—'

'We should speak first, Mr Bell,' Foster smoothly cut in.

Frank Bell turned towards Foster. 'I know you. You're Maurice's . . .' His voice broke, no doubt dealing with the emotions of his brother's murder.

Foster nodded. 'Yes, I was his solicitor as you know. I would like a private word with you and your wife, if I may?' His gaze shifted to Rio knowing there wasn't anything she could do about his request.

All Rio could do, a few seconds later, was watch as he held a whispered, private discussion with Nicola Bell's parents. Two minutes later the parents and Stephen Foster made their way to her room. Rio strode after them. They were inside the room by the time she reached them. As she went to join them inside Frank Bell blocked her.

'On legal advice we've decided that Nikki is too traumatised to talk to the police at this stage,' he said. 'When she is well enough to speak we've decided that Mr Foster must be present as well.'

He closed the door in Rio's face and there wasn't a damn thing she could do about it.

six

'The Super wants to see you. Now,' the sergeant on the desk at
The Fort told Rio as soon as she stepped inside.

HQ, where Rio ran her squad of detectives from the second
floor, was known as The Fort by everyone, even the criminals,
because it had once been the site of a Roman Fortress and a
secure building during the Cold War.

'And this,' the sergeant reached for something under the
desk, 'arrived for you. I was going to leave it on your desk.'

She handed an A4-sized sealed envelope to Rio who pushed
it in her pocket, too preoccupied by having to see her superior
to deal with it at the moment. Inwardly Rio groaned. She
didn't need to hear the words coming out of DSI Newman's
mouth to know what he wanted to grill her about – the progress of the case. Mind you, she could use the opportunity to
talk to him about something else that was urgently on her
mind; her gaze shifted onto Strong who stood at her side. Rio
could barely bring herself to speak to him, but she did.

'Pull the team together.'

She left him, but that didn't stop her hearing his response:
'Yes . . . ma'am.'

The surly sarcasm in his voice was laced with provocation,
meant to slow her down. But she wasn't dealing with his shit

now. In fact she hoped to get Newman to toss him off her team. No point putting energy into something that wasn't going to be there pretty soon. She kept her stride long and balanced as she moved towards the lift. Pressed 3. Once inside, she straightened the collar of her jacket, smoothed her palms against the top of her black trousers, pushed her shoulders back and strong. Then she pulled out the envelope that had the Metropolitan Police Service official stamp on it. She opened it up and knew what it was instantly: her request for an annual firearms training refresher course. She had taken one each year since leaving the armed response unit ten years back. What she read in the letter did not improve her mood.

Request denied.
Reason: A need to prioritise strategic resources.

Cock and bull management chat for there was not enough cash in the kitty. Well there was nothing she could do about it; she'd just have to re-apply again next year. She pushed the letter back into her pocket and finger-combed her 'fro. Feeling more in control it took her a few seconds to walk from the lift to the inner sanctum of her superior's office.

'He's waiting for you,' DSI Newman's PA told her.

Rio nodded and opened the teak coloured door. But froze on the threshold of the room when she saw that Newman wasn't alone.

'Ma'am.' Surprise was evident in Rio's voice at finding Assistant Commissioner Pauline Tripple also present.

Everything about AC Tripple was smart: her formal uniform; her no-nonsense brown hair that tapered around the ears and neck with longer strands on top; her quick, logical mind that had helped get her nearly to the top of her profession. Rio had heard some other officers – always male – snidely call her Raspberry Ripple – a take on her surname, but also Cockney slang for nipple. Not everyone on the Force appreciated one of the top brass being a woman.

'Wray,' Newman ushered, waving a hand at the empty chair positioned on the side of the desk nearest to her.

The Super had the bulk of a brawler, but the reddened and deeply lined face of a man under much stress.

Rio took the seat in an office that was clean, bright and clinically white. Soulless. One of those minimal, paper-free affairs, the uplighters on the walls giving it the mood of a sanctuary of therapy rather than a place concerned with law and order.

Newman let out that unnatural half-cough he always did before having to say something awkward. Rio tensed; was she about to be booted off the case?

'Assistant Commissioner Tripple just wanted you to update her on the current case—'

'Are this morning's murders related to the incidence of house robberies in the Home Counties?' the older woman enquired over Newman. Her question blunt, her voice hinting at the city of Manchester she hadn't lived in for over twenty years.

'Looks like the same MO,' Rio swiftly answered. 'The bodies were discovered this morning by the gardener—'

'How can you be so sure—?'

It was Rio's turn to interrupt. 'There's a witness. Young girl: the niece of two of the murder victims. She's different from our other witnesses – the gang didn't know she was at the scene. But we've got a problem. The girl has a solicitor who has convinced her parents that she's too traumatised to talk at present. And when I do get to question her they insist that he be present.' Rio drew in a breath. Let it out. Paused. 'It's Stephen Foster.'

That pushed the AC to her feet, irritation pulling the skin tight around her mouth. 'That man ...' Her lips clamped together. 'Whatever you do make sure he does not have anything to come knocking at my door about. But do what you have to do to get that information from the witness. We're getting a lot of heat from some powerful people to get this investigation resolved. We need to get this gang closed down and behind bars, because some of the great and good of Surrey are starting to feel like they're living in downtown South-Central L.A.'

Her chin thrust out. 'I've assured Surrey's Police and Crime Commissioner' – there was something about the way AC Tripple said the title that showed she didn't quite approve of the role – 'that the person heading up this task force is one of my most competent and efficient officers.'

The appointment of Police and Crime Commissioners were seen by many as a way for the politicians to interfere in the work of the police; many inside the Force weren't happy, and it appeared that the Assistant Commissioner was among their number. She continued: 'You've been on this case for just over two weeks, so, with this new incident, I expect something drastic to happen, especially if you now have another witness who the gang knew nothing about. We can't afford any more murders. I trust you to get this job done quickly.'

And without another word the Assistant Commissioner headed for the door and was gone. Rio and her boss sat in the heavy tension left behind.

Newman broke the silence. 'Are you sure this case is related to the others?'

Rio nodded. 'What worries me this time is the level of violence used. The victims were the householders – Maurice and Linda Bell – and their cleaner. We still need to make formal IDs, but I've little doubt that their photos, which will have been patched through to us by now, will be joining the other victims of this gang already in the situation room.'

'You need to get this case cleaned up ASAP.'

'Then why give me Jack Strong as tag partner on my team?'

'Ah. Jack.'

Instead of continuing, Newman pulled open the top drawer of his desk and whipped out a packet of low tar ciggies. He stood and opened the window behind his desk. The surprisingly mild February air breezed into the room as he lit up, going against anti-smoking regulations. He leaned his face close to the window as he pulled in a deep shot of smoke and nicotine. His shoulders sagged and rose with the motion of smoking.

'I need you to look after him,' he finally said.

Rio instantly looked down at the faint scars on both her wrists, her face heating and her mind blurring with memories she'd fought hard to forget. 'Not that, sir. I can't do that again.'

There were four of them in the room now: Rio, Newman, Strong and the member of her team who was now dead, twenty-seven-year-old Jamie Martin. Murdered – throat severed, on her watch, when Newman had given her the task to mentor him in his first year as a detective. The fact that his attacker had also nearly killed her by slashing her wrists didn't give her the peace she was desperate to find. Everyone had told her that the grief would go and they were right. But what stayed with her every day, digging deeper when she shut her eyes at night, was the guilt. She should've protected him in that house in Camden and she hadn't.

'I'm sure you'll understand that protection is the last thing I feel towards Strong,' Rio uttered. 'With all due respect, sir, putting him with a black officer is not the wisest decision.'

Four years ago Jack Strong had been a Detective Inspector, the lead of his own team. He'd always been considered one of the boys, a bit of a loud mouth, but with old school experience and instincts that were much admired. That was until the day his team had stopped and searched an injured Somali teenager after a vicious mugging in South London. Instead of taking him to the hospital or getting him medical attention, Strong had detained him and slung him in a cell. Two hours later Yusuf Ishmail was dead. The Met had not only had to deal with the outraged cry of the black community but also that of the Muslim one as well, in the week leading up to Eid, the most important religious festival in the Islamic calendar. Turned out that the teenager had been attacked on his way home from Mosque by thugs who have never been found.

The Met Commissioner had spent the better part of the following year trying to regain the communities' trust at a time when young Somali men were complaining that they were twice as likely to be stopped by the police because they were both black and Muslim. Strong had been suspended but, to Rio's disgust, allowed to come back, with a demotion to the rank of plain detective. Plus he'd been made to undergo intensive 'race awareness and inclusion' training. Rio would've laughed at the last if the whole business hadn't been so serious. As far as she was concerned, once a bad cop always a bad cop.

Newman tipped his head to face her and she was surprised to see the wistful expression in his eyes. 'Did you know that me and Jack started out together?'

Rio merely folded her arms. Newman trying to drag her through a trip down memory lane wasn't going to move her.

'We did our training at Hendon and walked the beat for the first three years side-by-side.' He pulled in another puff of smoke and angled his head back towards the window. 'We were both ambitious, but in different ways. I wanted to be part of the decision makers, while Strong was happy to stay at the grassroots among the men . . . You know, rolling his sleeves up every day and getting stuck into the filth.' He flicked his butt out of the window. Closed it. Turned fully to Rio.

'He was a great cop. Then something happened to him that made him lose his way.'

'We've all lost our way every now and again, sir, but would we ignore the desperate pleas of a dying teenager?'

Newman didn't answer; instead he sat back at his desk.

'You know that I'm going to retire in a month's time,' he said quietly. 'Well, so is Jack. All he wants in his last month on the job is to be elbow deep in a case that gets his adrenaline racing.'

'I'm not hosting a fairground roller coaster called The Metropolitan Police Service Adventure Ride—'

'No, but you are under my command and will do what you're told.' Rio knew when it was wise to keep her mouth well and truly closed. 'Remember, Wray, that I'm on the cusp of putting your name forwards to take my place.'

Although Rio felt the pride that came with his words, she didn't like that the job came with strings attached.

'I thought you were doing that because you consider me the best person for the job.'

'I do. That's why I know you're going to make Strong's last days in the Force ones for him to put in his photo album.'

'If he slips up once . . .' Rio held up a finger. 'You're going to have to find someone else to provide fun and games for Jack.'

Rio got up to leave.

'And Wray . . .?'

Rio turned back around.

'You heard the Assistant Commissioner, so I don't have to tell you how high profile this case is. You need to get this job done. Quickly. If finding this gang proves hard you may want to think about enlisting some outside help.'

'Outside help? Like a CI?' Using confidential informants was common practice.

He shook his head. 'I'm thinking more of a specialist. A security consultant with his ear to the ground.'

Astonishment gripped Rio's face because she knew whose name he was going to slot into that role.

'Someone like Calum Burns.'

seven

Fuck! Fuck! Fuck!

Profanity was the only decent way Rio knew how to respond to hearing Calum Burns' name. Former cop. No: disgraced former cop, now doing his own thing in the world of security consultancy. Rio leaned the flat of her hand against the wall of the stairwell leading up to her office to stop the emotions burning her up. That's what Calum did to her: made her steaming, badass mad, and vulnerable; he was one of the only people who could make her think the ground wasn't beneath her feet.

Newman was wrong – no way could she ask Calum for a little bit of assistance on the side. Not because he wouldn't prove up to the task – quite the opposite, Calum was a man with his nose stuck in all types of 'wrong places' that could prove beneficial to this case. But what lay between them, thick and unresolved, was somewhere she wasn't going back to.

Rio hitched herself off the wall, got back on with her job. Less than a minute later she entered the operation room.

'Nicola Bell. Sixteen years old. A very special witness.' Rio's voice was confident and loud enough to get the full attention of her team.

Most of the team were made up of the six detectives she

usually worked with, but there were two others who were on loan from the original police squad working on the investigation in Surrey. And now there was Jack Strong. Rio saw him out of the corner of her eye, as she moved further into the room. He sat, arms folded, perched on a desk on the margins of the rest of the team. *Her* desk, committing one of the cardinal sins in Rio's squad – never, EVER invade her space, including thinking her desk was some kind of easy chair. But Rio let it alone . . . for now.

She stopped in front of the huge, freestanding whiteboard that had all the information relating to the investigation, using arrows to link photographs and writing about the previous raids in Surrey, and a large map with red lines and circles indicating key locations. Rio wanted to shake the team up so she pulled two photographs off the board and added three from a folder that was stationed near the board. She stuck them on the board.

'Murder.' Rio stabbed her finger against the gruesome image of Linda Bell, throat slashed, in her own kitchen.

'Murder.' She did the same to the photo of Maurice Bell.

'Murder.' Ania, the cleaner.

'Murder.' A gruesome shot of a woman with her face blown away.

The silence in the room was chilling – exactly what Rio wanted.

'That's what we're dealing with.' Her voice cut thickly through the quiet. 'A gang of men who, in the last six weeks, have graduated from robbery, terrorising people and holding them against their will to the ultimate crime – the taking of human life.' Rio zeroed her gaze onto one member of her team. 'Detective Richmond, outline for us what we know about this gang's MO so far.'

She could have used his first name but she wanted to keep

everything very formal to ensure that the gravity and urgency of their investigation remained in place.

Detective Peter Richmond was one of the Surrey officers, young, fresh-faced and – most importantly for Rio – keen. As he began to talk, Rio began to write the gang's pattern of brutal home invasion on the second whiteboard:

Targets: high-end properties that are secluded but have access to main roads a few miles away.

All raids within a 40-mile radius of London, so the press have started calling them Greenbelt Gang.

Arrival time: around 5 or 6 in the morning when all the occupants of the houses are still in bed.

Transportation: unknown. Obvious way is by vehicle but none of our witnesses have heard one. Assumption is they park up and walk the last few miles or maybe – a very weak maybe – use bikes although there's no evidence of that. They'd need adequate transport to carry stolen items away.

One member of the gang takes down any CCTV. Sprays the lens with paint from a can. Uses a paint gun for those mounted on poles. He's very accurate.

He's the only member of the gang we have photos of.

The team all looked over at the first whiteboard, which displayed two camera stills of someone dressed in black wearing a clown mask. The mask dominated the shot because the camera lens was looking down. And it was scary. Yellow curly hair, white, rubber skin, eyes painted demon black and red mouth set in an obscene wide grin, belching beige stained teeth and bumpy, enlarged bottom gum.

Detective Richmond started talking again and Rio continued to write:

Point of entry: Back of the house. Use silencers to shoot out windows to get in.

Collect spent bullets they've used.

Short the electrical supply. Disables any security. Keeps the house in darkness so as to terrify the residents.

High-powered flashlights to find their way around with the added bonus that the occupants can't see them properly.

Descriptions: black boiler suits and clown masks. Indistinguishable from one another.

Round up everyone they find in the house together.

Douse the most vulnerable person in petrol and threaten to set them on fire unless they're led to the valuables. Raid 3 they waved a lighter around.

First four raids, only one member of the gang did the talking, which we know from the voice picked up via the paint-sprayed security cams. Voice distorted by nitrous oxide so his voice was disguised and, of course, that effect frightened the residents even more.

What's taken? High-ticket items they've been shown. And then escape. Can't put an exact figure on the sums stolen. Estimate up to the value of a half million pounds.

No trace of anything from their haul has turned up on the radar yet.

Rio stopped writing as she interrupted the young member of her team. 'With raid five we know that things changed.' Richmond knew that was his cue to give Rio back the floor.

'On raid five, the victims were a newly married couple. The wife was shot point blank in the face while the husband survived.'

Rio moved to the other whiteboard and stabbed her finger

below the photograph of the corpse without a face. 'Her name was Rubina Ali. She'd been married for two weeks, worked as a financial analyst in the City and was planning to have her first child next year. That life has now been smashed because our gang of thieves decided to turn into a band of bloodthirsty men. She was home alone. What was picked up by the audio of the sprayed security cameras was that the shooter seemed jumpy and aggressive. There was no reason for the murder. The gang had the valuables. And there was the sound of a scuffle after the gunshot. Maybe the rest of the gang were trying to restrain the shooter.'

Rio stopped and let her gaze span her team. She got ready to ask a question, but a voice she didn't want to hear interrupted her.

Jack Strong: 'The shooter was probably someone who joined the gang for the first time.'

Rio ignored him. That was the best way to deal with Mr Useless who had been dumped on her.

So she carried on. 'This morning it appears that we have raid six. Three people are murdered. But we know something that the gang don't – there was a witness hiding, who they know nothing about. Her name is Nicola Bell: the niece of one of the victims, Maurice Bell, who owned the house with his wife Linda, another victim. He was shot; her throat was cut. We believe that the raid took place between six and seven this morning–'

'Around six forty-three a.m.,' Strong supplied.

A hush descended as every eye, including Rio's, turned to him. No one else spoke because her squad knew how she liked to run briefings – she'd go through the information inviting others to contribute as and when. No one called out without an invite to take the floor.

But Strong carried on. 'Nicola Bell's iPad shows that she

was on a social networking site called Yakkety-Yak. She was in conversation with someone and the last recorded time for that conversation was six forty-three so we can assume that this was roughly the time of the raid.'

The information he supplied was spot on, but Rio ignored him.

'What information have we got so far on Maurice and Linda Bell?'

'Mr Bell was fifty-nine,' another officer supplied, 'and made his money – a lot of it from all accounts – in property: residential as well as commercial. He also diversified into becoming a shareholder of the successful IT group XTC. I did some ringing around and he's worth millions. Linda Bell, on the other hand, was always a stay-at-home mum–'

'Have you got any intel on their two children?'

'All I've got,' the detective continued, 'are two names that we already know about from the neighbours. Leah and Cornelius. But I'm hoping to have some information patched through soon.'

'There was a third victim,' Rio continued. 'Ania–'

'It's a Polish name,' Strong joined in again, this time causing one of the veins in Rio's throat to throb. 'I did some calling around and discovered that her surname was Brown. She married a British citizen about two years ago. She'd been the cleaner for about nine months–'

'Detective Strong.' Rio let both words lie in the air. She knew she should just leave it alone, but she couldn't any longer. Newman might force her to babysit, but that didn't mean she had to let the baby puke and poop all over her squad room.

'I don't know how things were done where you came from, but here we have a system where contributions are made in an orderly fashion. That way each of us keeps track of what's going on,' she added, her tone becoming pointed. 'We follow *procedure* here.'

The bastard just lifted an eyebrow at her. Rio couldn't see his eyes clearly from where she was standing, but would bet her next pay cheque that they were a shade of mocking-blue. Rio jerked her gaze away from him and continued outlining the investigation so far.

'There were two different variations in the Bells' home compared to the other five raids. First, the blanking and painting of the CCTV wasn't as efficient as usual. Several of the cameras were left untouched – although we've got no film of the gang from those that weren't. Second, Nicola Bell only saw two members of the gang. We know from the other raids that there were about five or six members of the gang, so why weren't there other members of the gang upstairs searching for valuables?'

A scoffing sound came from somewhere but Rio couldn't locate where from. Then she found Strong. She nearly exploded because he was rolling his eyes, with a smirk on his face.

'Is there something you want to share with the rest of us Detective Strong?'

His leg stopped swinging. 'Do I have permission to talk?' No one in the room could miss the sarcasm loaded in his tone. 'I've got a theory—'

'Yeah, well,' Rio butted in, 'we're not dealing with blue-sky theories, we're dealing with facts. I know that this might be hard for you to grasp but we take crime seriously in this team, Detective Strong. If that's a hard concept for you to understand, maybe you should walk out of the room, straight up to the DS's office and get him to find you somewhere where they don't mind teenagers in their care bleeding to death in a cold, lonely cell.'

The air was thick. Tense. Damn! She hadn't meant to say

that, but this guy was ticking her off. Rio ignored the tiny part of her that was doing a victory dance at rubbishing and slapping him down in front of the others. It was an abomination – that's the word her mum would have used – that trash like Strong was breathing the same air as the others.

Feeling grounded and in control again Rio carried on. 'We still need to interview Nicola Bell more fully. At present her family lawyer is insisting that she be interviewed when he's present. Why he's insisting on this only he knows.'

'Who's the lawyer?' Detective Richmond asked.

'Stephen Foster.'

Rio was not surprised at the wave of unrest and disgust that filled the room. Foster was well known as not being a bosom pal of the Met's.

'But she was going to tell me something,' Rio continued. She pulled out her notepad and flipped it open. 'What she said was, "one of them couldn't" and then Foster arrived stopping all communication with our witness. What was it that one of the two members of the gang she saw couldn't do? So speaking to Nikki is our number one priority. In the meantime we have to go with what we've got. We've got a long list of suspects so far. Known names in the south-east blagging world—'

'You're missing the obvious,' Strong ground out.

Rio and everyone else looked over at him. She'd been so caught up in unpicking the Intel that she hadn't noticed that he was now standing.

Rio was fed up with this six-foot milestone around her neck. 'There's nothing obvious or simple about this case.'

Strong walked with a long, easy stride to join Rio at the front. 'Simple, no. Obvious, yes.'

Rio folded her arms across her chest, her mouth tightening. 'OK, Einstein, tell the rest of us – who've probably got fifty years of collective policing experience – what we've been missing.'

Strong faced the others. 'Robberies like this were common back in the nineties, just like bank and post office jobs. But that's all a thing of the past. And you know why?' His gaze spanned around. 'This type of crime is high risk, low profit. Who wants to get caught on a security camera and banged up for fifteen years? So why would this gang do such a high risk crime?'

There was an edge-of-your-seat quality to the way Strong spoke that had even Rio hanging on his every word.

'This gang, or someone in this gang – I suspect their leader – are only going to take this chance because they need cash quickly. So what do they do? Revert to what they know: going on the rob. Once they reach their jackpot the Greenbelt Gang will cease to exist.'

'But why do they need the money?' Rio asked, taking Strong seriously for the first time since she'd started the briefing.

'To invest in another crime. A crime where high rollers are only allowed to play. Something that's low risk, big profit.'

'What?' a member of the team asked. Their voice was filled with 'tell me now, tell me now' expectation. A few minutes ago this would have annoyed Rio, but now she grudgingly admitted to feeling the same.

Strong took in each face again, then stopped on Rio's: 'A big time drug deal.'

eight

'You know that I'm right,' Strong insisted as he stood in front of Rio in the corridor outside the operations room. He held a cup of coffee in his hand.

Rio didn't know if he was right, didn't know if he was wrong; what she did know was that she needed time to sort through his theory in her mind. This investigation was on a tight time frame and if she used valuable resources and took it down a blind alley there was going to be only one head on the chopping block – hers. And no way was her career going down the Suwannee because keystone cop here thought he had a light-bulb moment.

Rio gave him a hard look. 'You keep forgetting who's giving the orders here.'

Strong took a step closer to her, invading her space. 'You look like a woman who's about to get a load off of her chest.'

Rio expected his eyes to drift insolently to her breasts, but he kept his gaze fixed to hers.

'I don't want you on my team.'

'Pity you can't get someone to cuff me and haul me away, isn't it.'

'Since you're one of Newman's old kissing buddies I want you to ask him – ever so sweetly – to reassign you.'

Strong leaned into her, his heated breath brushing her cheek. 'And miss the way the invincible, *black* Detective Inspector Rio Wray swings a case? I don't think so.'

'You got a problem with the shade of my skin?'

'Got a problem with someone using it to rise in the ranks.'

This man was stepping way, way out of line. Rio pushed her face closer to his. 'People like you—'

'Should be hung, drawn and quartered? Made to stand naked on Oxford Street until their balls freeze off?'

Hot colour sizzled through Rio's cheeks. 'Watch your mouth.'

'The only thing I'm watching is my last case on the job. You going to begrudge an old timer that?'

'You start slinging arrows in the wrong direction and you'll find out what and how I begrudge.'

'I can't wait.' Now his blue gaze fell to her chest, making her breasts feel like tits instead. 'Sweet . . . heart.'

Rio thrust her face so close to his that they were nose-to-nose, eye-to-eye, bathing the other with ragged, hot anger.

'DI,' a voice called, reminding Rio where she was.

She pulled away from Strong and hitched her elbow deliberately up at the same time, catching the bottom of the cup he held. Coffee shot in the air, then sloshed down on his shirt.

'Oops,' was all she said too sweetly, as she fought to control the temper she knew could go into orbit if the wrong buttons were pushed. And this man had a way of poking her that was going to tip her over the edge.

Rio flicked her fingers once through her hair as she turned to find one of the female members of her team.

'We've located the Bells' daughter. Her name isn't actually Leah . . .well it is, but spelt Lia. It's short for Ophelia—'

Rio swore. 'Not the same Ophelia Bell—'

'Who's known to millions as Lady Clarissa Wilcott.'

nine

12:55 p.m.

'Freddy, I love you, not him. It was a mistake.'

'I don't believe you.' Freddy's voice was savage as he advanced on the woman crying in front of him. 'Finding this out as I'm just leaving to join the troops at The Front is destroying me. When I was in the hospital, after being gassed, all I could do was think about you. And to find out you've betrayed me . . .'

Abruptly, the woman fell on her knees in front of him, a lock of her hair bouncing free of the heavy black updo pinned to the back of her head. Her beautiful face looked up at him as she pleaded, 'No one knows, I swear it.' She tugged on the end of his military jacket as she sobbed, then looked back down at the Oriental rug she knelt on. 'Please, Freddy, I beg you. I beg you.'

Silence. Then Freddy's hand touched the top of her hair. Smoothed his palm against the silky strands as he arched his head back and briefly closed his eyes. Then he snapped his green eyes open.

'Come, my love,' he said softly. He moved his hand from her hair and held it out to her. 'I forgive you.'

The woman eagerly took his outstretched hand and rushed to her feet. Immediately she wrapped her arms around his neck in a tight embrace.

'*Do you really forgive me?*' Her strained voice was muffled against his skin.

His arms moved from his side. Kept going up as he replied, '*Yes. I forgive you. But if I find out you've been seeing him while I'm away fighting, you know what honour demands I do when I get back.*'

She jerked her face from the comfort of his throat to gaze up at him.

'*I'll have to kill you.*'

A voice yelled, '*And . . . Cut.*'

Rio and Strong stood on the edge of the indoor scene being filmed on the set of the TV drama *The Wilcotts*. The period drama, a saga about the ups and downs of an aristocratic family during the First World War, had first appeared in the daytime television schedule, but a growing audience had catapulted it to the nine o'clock primetime Sunday slot. The tabloids were full of whether stuffy James Wilcott, the Earl of Marchfield, would fall in love with Sally Grayson, plucky American divorcee cum Suffragette? What was young, gambling-addicted Lord Arthur going to do about getting the upstairs maid pregnant? Would Freddy Wilcott discover that his wife had been two-timing him with a fake Italian Count? Well, Rio now knew the answer to the last. Not that she watched the show – people prancing around in period costumes, like pantomime season was back in town, just wasn't her style. She was glad she wasn't a fan of the show because being on the set, with the cameras, the bright-loud lighting, the crew looking on, paraded something that was touted as spectacular, entertaining and art as just another ordinary job. Mind you, there was nothing ordinary about having a well-known TV face attached to the Greenbelt case. That was only going to ignite a fierce, new heat to the investigation; heat Rio could do without.

'I should be out there pulling in Intel on the drugs angle,' Strong whispered.

Rio ignored him as she watched Ophelia Bell, aka Lady Clarissa Wilcott, getting to her feet as the crew started chatting about what a great scene it was.

'Ophelia,' the young lad who had accompanied them to the set, called out. 'You've got visitors.'

Even from a distance Rio could see that Ophelia Bell was willowy and tall with one of those classic photogenic faces that took a stunning shot every time. The actress unbuttoned the top of her heavy, violet dress as she moved towards them. When she reached them Rio changed her assessment of her from willowy to painfully thin. The cheekbones stood out on her face like blades trying to burst out of skin and her collarbones caught the eye much more than the elegance of her neck. This was a woman in serious need of being force fed a week's worth of homemade cooking.

'You do know that this is a closed set,' Ophelia announced in what many would have named a cut-glass voice, but to Rio's ears was slightly pompous and a touch nose-in-the-air cold. 'The show's secrets and all that,' she finished.

Rio pulled out her warrant card. 'I'm Detective Inspector Rio Wray and this is my colleague Detective Jack Strong—'

The actress rolled her grey eyes. 'If this is about Connie, I don't know where he is. Nor do I want to know.'

'Is Connie your brother Cornelius?' Rio asked.

Ophelia's bony fingers opened a few more buttons on the front of her dress as she muttered, 'The rebel with too many causes; yep, that's my brother Cornelius.'

'Can we talk to you somewhere more private?' Strong spoke this time.

Ophelia swept the pads of her long fingers from the top of her throat to the base. 'Let's go to my dressing room.'

They left behind the set as they walked towards a large corridor in a grand Essex manor house called Whitlow Park. The show had moved to a non-studio based location once its ratings shot up. It was a house perfectly trapped in another era – wooden panels and elaborate staircases, rose cornice ceilings, showy framed paintings and floors that gleamed except where large rugs lay. Ophelia talked all the way to the dressing room.

'We just found out that the production company and broadcaster have done a top grade deal with the Americans to take it stateside. That's going to open up all kinds of opportunities for me. My agent said that it's only a matter of time before some big L.A. studios are knocking on my door with movie offers.'

Neither Rio nor Strong responded as she used the energy from her flagrant excitement to swing a door forwards near the stairs. The corridor that faced them was darker and narrower than the part of the house they'd just left behind. Finally Ophelia Bell opened the door of a small, sparsely furnished room.

'This was once the chambermaid's room. Gave the producer a mini thrill to pop Lady Clarissa in here.' She squinted at Strong noticing the stains on his shirt. 'Looks like you could use the help of our costume or props department.'

His blue eyes twinkled at her. 'Just a misunderstanding with my coffee, and some brown sugar.'

The scar on Rio's left wrist twitched, but she kept her irritation under control reminding herself what she was here to do.

Ophelia pulled off her wig to reveal paprika red hair cut into a short style; strands fell in diagonal lines across her forehead and straight lines on the sides. It made her look younger, but laid the bone structure of her face even more bare.

'So, what has good ole Connie been up to this time, detectives?' Ophelia threw the wig on to a small dressing table.

'You might want to sit down,' Rio offered as she pointed to the single chair in the room.

'I've had enough drama for one day so just tell me.'

'It's your parents—'

'Mum and Dad?'

'They were found dead this morning at their home. They were murdered.'

Ophelia's face turned scarlet as the skin below the sharpness of her cheekbones sank. She shook her head. 'No . . . Not Mum and Dad . . .'

She took a step towards Rio, but her leg shook so much she wobbled as her foot reconnected to the floor. Strong moved quickly towards her, his arms outstretched to catch her weight. Ophelia thrust her palm up at him, making him freeze and creating an invisible protective wall around herself. Rio and Strong remained where they were, giving this woman the time she needed to absorb news that no person expects to hear about their parents. Finally Ophelia moved, legs still shaking, towards the chair, her breathing an audible, erratic rhythm in the room. Instead of sitting down, her fine fingers gripped the back of the chair to steady herself.

Rio moved towards her. Then stopped to ensure the Bell's daughter still had her own personal space. 'I'm really sorry.'

Ophelia gazed at her, eyes a liquid grey and wide. Her voice was small. 'I saw them only a few days ago. Why would anyone do that to Mum and Dad?' Abruptly her head moved from side to side as her gaze darted around. 'God. I'll need to let Aunt Patsy and Uncle Frank know—'

'They've already been informed.' Rio stopped, thinking through what she was about to say next. 'Look I need to tell you something. What I'm about to tell you has to stay confidential.'

Ophelia nodded, but Rio couldn't be sure she was really hearing.

'The reason your aunt and uncle already know is your cousin, Nicola, was at the house as well.'

The other woman's hands flew to her chest. 'Oh God ... Nicola ... Nikki ... Nikki ...' Her voice lost its power somewhere deep in her throat.

'No,' Rio reassured her, knowing exactly what her mind was thinking. 'Nikki's OK. She managed to hide in a cupboard upstairs. But she's a witness because she saw who did it—'

Ophelia flung an arm wide. 'So why aren't you out there trying to find the murdering bastards right now?'

Rio ignored the pointed look Strong sent her way. 'Nikki didn't see their faces and has only been able to tell us some things, but not others. Your parents' lawyer, Stephen Foster—'

Ophelia's whole demeanour changed to someone ready for a tussle in the playground. 'What's that idiot got to do with this?'

'Have you got a problem with him?'

'What person likes a lawyer?'

But Rio sensed whatever the issue was ran much deeper.

'Your aunt and uncle confirmed that Nikki is his client. They don't want us talking to her unless he's present. She's in the hospital.'

The actress stretched her long neck with the arrogance of the character she was so well known for playing.

'He won't let you talk to her?' Her grey eyes were determined. 'We'll see about that.'

As Ophelia Bell got ready, Rio turned to Strong. 'I'll drive her to the hospital and you ...' Indecision made the rest of the words stick in her throat, but she didn't need to say them as Strong nodded, knowing what she wanted him to do.

But as he twisted around to leave Rio grabbed his arm. 'You put a foot wrong while you investigate this drug angle and you can kiss this case bye-bye.'

ten

'No one talks to her unless Mr Foster is here.'

Patsy Bell's voice was soft but determined as she spoke to her niece-by-marriage. Instead of the actress asking permission to speak to Nicola she'd arrogantly told her aunt that she was going to talk to her younger cousin. Nicola was in the attached private bathroom having a shower.

Rio had initially summed Patsy Bell up as a small woman who took the lead from her husband, but now she saw that she was someone who packed the grit to do what it took to keep her daughter safe.

'But why, Auntie Pat?' Ophelia responded. Rio saw the older woman wince at the use of the name 'Pat'. 'The sooner Nikki tells the police all she can remember, the sooner she can get home and be in the bosom of her mother.'

Patsy Bell bristled and Rio couldn't figure out what was happening here, but there was definitely something going on between these two women. Frank Bell remained silent in the chair beside his wife.

'Stephen Foster said he'd be back tomorrow morning and then we'll see if Nikki is ready to talk some more then.'

'And how would you feel,' Ophelia countered, 'if this gang

commits another murder in the meantime? I don't think Nikki's going to like the idea of having blood on her hands.'

Patsy shot to her feet. 'How dare you say something so wicked.' Her voice was no longer soft, but high and shrill with anger.

Her husband caught one of her hands. 'Come on, love—'

'No.' His wife shook her head. 'She needs to remember—'

The door of the bathroom pushed open and Nikki appeared, her face washed of the terror Rio had seen earlier, her blonde hair wet against the side of her face and shoulders. She saw her cousin and her face was transformed by a sheen of joy.

'Lia,' she let out with a smile. Then she rushed over and into the arms of her cousin.

Ophelia squeezed her tight, rubbed her cheek across her face.

'I wanted to help Auntie Linda and Uncle, but I couldn't,' the teenager said sadly.

Her cousin reassured her. 'Don't worry. I'm just glad that you're safe—'

'Ophelia.' Patsy's tone was sharp with the seniority of an aunt commanding her niece. 'Nikki needs all the rest she can get, so if you would allow her to get back in the bed.'

'Sorry, sweetie,' Ophelia whispered as she let Nikki go.

Nikki made her way to the bed, but Rio didn't miss the resentful look she threw her mother on the way there. It never ceased to surprise Rio how the dynamics of a family always came out during a tragedy. She knew it was wrong to rake up more trouble for the Bells but she needed Ophelia to get her cousin to talk. So Rio remained where she was, sensing if Ophelia was going to make this happen she needed to give her the space to do it.

Ophelia popped herself down on the bed beside Nikki. The girl gazed at her cousin with adoring, but shy eyes.

'All my friends are jealous that I've got a beautiful cousin who's on the telly,' Nikki finally said.

Ophelia suddenly turned her attention to her handbag. Its pink-red-brown interlocking woven print gave it a South Indian style. 'Look, I've got something new for your collection.'

Three tiny bells jingled at the bottom of her bag as she pulled something out and laid it on the bed. Nikki's eyes widened and shone with excitement as she gazed at a pair of lacy, fingerless gloves: black, elbow length and stylish.

'These are Lady Clarissa's,' Ophelia explained. 'She wore them in the episode when she attended the Duke of Hampstead's spring ball.'

Rio found it strange that Ophelia was referring to the character she played in the third person, like she wasn't the person that inhabited her skin. But what did she care, as long as the other woman got the information from their witness.

'Can I wear them now?' Nikki asked, turning her adoring gaze from the gloves to her cousin.

'No you can't,' her mother snapped. 'This isn't a catwalk, it's a hospital, and the reason you're in here is because something terrible has happened.'

'Your mother's right,' Ophelia agreed as she ran her palm over the lower half of Nikki's arm like she was touching silk. 'That's why you've got to tell me what happened.'

'Lia—' Patsy Bell warned.

Nikki looked over at her mother. 'It's OK, mum. I want to tell her.'

But Patsy wasn't looking at her daughter, she was gazing hard at her niece. Suddenly she got to her feet. 'I need to tell the medical staff about my daughter's nut allergy.'

For some reason her gaze lingered hard on her niece-by-marriage. Then she was gone.

There was a moment's silence after she'd left. Then Ophelia's husky tones filled the air. 'So, little lady, I want you to tell me everything you can about what you saw.'

Rio pulled out her notebook and pen. Nikki's head fell back against the pillow as she sucked in a strong punch of air.

'There were two of them. I already told her . . .' Her gaze shifted briefly to Rio.

'Did you see their faces?' her cousin asked.

Nikki shook her head. 'They were both wearing something strange on their faces—'

'Like clown masks?' Rio asked, speaking for the first time.

Nikki nervously rubbed her lips together as she shook her head. Her small hands fluttered in the air as she answered. 'They weren't clown masks. The faces were covered with a piece of . . .' She stopped, trying to get her words right.

'It's fine, hun,' her cousin reassured. 'Take your time. No one's rushing you.'

The girl's gaze skidded to Rio, then back to the woman she clearly worshipped. The tiny smile Ophelia gave her started her talking again. 'It looked like a piece of puffy cloth, you know, not fitting their faces very well. The cloth had two plastic things over the eyes. It looked really scary. And a trunk or hose thing—'

'Are you sure?' Rio asked softly.

Nikki nodded. Her cousin squeezed one of her hands.

'Could it have been a clown mask?' Rio persisted.

'Maybe.' Nikki shrugged again, her fingers twisting in the glove material. 'But I've never seen a clown face like that before because there wasn't any paint on the baggy material, it was just a sort of greeny-grey.'

Rio wrote in her notebook.

Description: raid 6 no clown masks. Covering faces=puffy material, plastic eye glasses (?) and a trunk/hose.

Whatever the gang had chosen to hide their faces on raid 6 was not something Rio could immediately identify. Maybe it was homemade. But why change their MO of clown masks to a strange type of face covering?

'Good girl,' her cousin reassured her. 'What about their height? Tall? Short?'

Nikki eyelids flicked down as if she was trying to remember the scene. 'One was about my size . . . I think . . . not sure. The other one was taller. About as tall as Ad—' Her voice cut off as she blushed. She sent her dad a furious and sulky look.

Rio didn't know who this Ad was and it didn't have anything to do with the investigation so she didn't go there. But whoever 'Ad' was had caused more tension to tighten in the room.

Rio's question cut through the strained atmosphere. 'Did you hear them speak?'

'A bit. One of them said they needed to check there was no one else in the house.' Nikki shook her head. 'I couldn't make out what they were saying. But one of them had a high voice—'

That fitted in with the nitrous oxide the gang used to change the tone and pitch of their voices. But what the teenager said next had Rio thinking something else.

'Like a woman.'

'A woman?' Rio jerked in, shocked. 'Are you sure about that?'

Rio scribbled in her notebook.

'No . . . Yes . . .' Nikki rubbed her forehead. 'Don't know. Although I couldn't hear what the other one was saying – his voice was high as well.'

Rio reasoned that the use of nitrous oxide could well make anyone think they were hearing a woman speak, albeit a woman auditioning for *The Muppet Show*.

'No,' Nikki bit out. 'They moved like men. I couldn't hear clearly in the cupboard.'

Rio scratched out a word in her notebook: *Woman*

Suddenly the tears of the teen crashed into the air. She was shaking. 'I can't stop seeing all that blood that came out of Ania. Red. Thick. It hit me in the face—'

'That's enough,' Patsy Bell shouted from the doorway. Everyone had been so focused on Nikki that they hadn't realised she was back. 'Get away from her.'

Patsy Bell strode towards Ophelia, raising her arm, and Rio was sure she was going to throw the two-toned brown-and-white polystyrene cup full of steaming drink into her niece's face.

'Mrs Bell,' Rio warned.

The other woman let her arm relax back, but her tone was furious as she addressed her niece-by-marriage. 'Leave. Her. Alone. Can't you see she's terrified? How difficult this is for her? She's not some character in a script.'

Ophelia tilted her head to gaze at her aunt and Rio was surprised at the cool absence of emotion in her eyes. 'I know who she is. And don't you forget it.'

Patsy's face grew pale. Rio stepped in. This was getting well out of hand.

'Let's all cool down—'

'After the other one shot Ania,' Nikki suddenly interrupted, 'and they started looking around, the other one sort of slumped against the wall. I could hear his breathing, ragged and loud. His hand moved. I think he was holding something. Not just the,' she gulped, 'gun.'

Rio thought quickly. Breathing difficulties. Holding something.

'Did you see what he was holding? Was it an asthma pump?'

Nikki shook her head. 'I don't know.'
Rio wrote quickly in her notebook.

Gang member with breathing difficulties on raid 6?
Medical problem? Asthma pump?

eleven

2:30 p.m.

'You don't look like the type of woman who would burden herself with a family,' Ophelia said to Rio. Then she drew the half-gone ciggie between her thin fingers to her cherry painted lips. Her cool grey eyes were hidden behind Ray-Ban midnight green, tinted shades.

They stood around the back of the hospital, near the bins, in an unofficial smoking zone. A man and woman stood not far away, heads together as they puffed on a fresh batch of nicotine. After Nikki's recollections about the gunmen her mother came over all protective lioness again and blocked any further questioning. Rio had invited the actress to join her in the canteen to find out more about her parents but Ophelia had shaken her red head saying she wasn't in the mood to be recognised, or as she put it, 'be part of a finger-pointing sight-seeing tour for the public.' Rio got the impression that she usually loved the whole fame game, but not today. Not the day she'd found out her parents had been brutally butchered. But she'd consented to have a smoke and talk in a place where she was anonymous.

'Just a brother,' Rio answered the other woman's question. 'My parents are both gone. My dad cut out on us when I was five and my mum passed away three months ago.'

Ophelia took a few more lazy puffs and, with smoke drifting with her words, said, 'How did you deal with it?' She didn't need to tell Rio what 'it' was. Death.

Rio's eyebrows shuffled together. 'I was lucky enough to know both my grandparents. My dad was from Trinidad but my mum came from the neighbouring island of Grenada. When my grandmother in Trinidad died we all went down for her funeral. My grandmother's mother was from the Punjab and I think my gran still held on to some of her Hindu beliefs.' A tiny smile creased Rio's lips. 'There was a bit of a tussle between her African blood and her Hindu relatives about what her send-off should be. But in the end they all agreed that whatever it was, whatever it looked like, it had to be a journey of peace. I never forgot that word when my dad died. My mum died. Peace. Peace.'

Ophelia pushed the ciggie to her lips and sucked hard. She shifted her gaze and head away from Rio. Smoke clouded around her face, leaving a hazy mask that dulled the glossy red of her hair. Rio had an impulse to wave the smoke away; this woman had had too much dirt thrown at her recently.

Ophelia turned back to her. 'Why did you become a cop?'

'Why did you become an actress?' Getting people to talk was one of Rio's specialities. Over the years she learned that sometimes the best way of doing that was by going an indirect route.

The other woman flicked the butt on to the ground, then folded her arms reminding Rio how skinny she was.

'Don't get me wrong. I had one of those blissful childhoods – attentive parents, top of the range schools, lived in a neighbourhood that had style mags gagging. But I always found myself wanting something else. Someone else's life I suppose. At uni I got involved in the drama society and it just seemed that the natural progression would be to attend drama school.' Her cherry lips twisted.

'Your parents didn't approve?' Rio pulled out an ener-gy-protein bar from her jacket. She offered it to Ophelia, but the other woman wrinkled her nose as if she was being offered poison.

Rio ripped the wrapper as Ophelia started talking again. 'It was Dad really. He wanted me to become part of the business—'

'And what business was that?'

'Aren't you Ophelia Bell?' a voice interrupted.

Both Rio and the actress turned to find the couple who'd been smoking nearby, less than a metre from them. It was the man who spoke, his cheeks high-red with excitement.

'No. Now push off.' Ophelia's cherry lips snarled fiery peppers style.

'But that's you up there isn't it?' the man persisted, pointing.

Both Rio and Ophelia looked at what he pointed at; a poster on the wall advocating the work of a charity called, 'Love Yourself' which was having a week's awareness about eating disorders. One of the charity's patrons was photographed on the poster – Ophelia Bell.

'Can you please leave us alone?' Ophelia's voice was harder, but Rio noticed that her cheeks had pinked over as soon as she spotted the poster.

But the couple weren't going anywhere. The man peered closer like the actress was an exhibit in a shop window adver-tising sales. This time when he spoke his tone was scornful. 'You're her alright; I'd recognise that voice anywhere. And that show you're in is crap, love, and you're crap in it.'

Rio stepped in. Showed her warrant card. 'Maybe you want to talk a bit more about your own personal crap in Interview Room Number One down at the station.'

Her threat got the couple rapidly moving along.

'See what I have to put up with? Every little tosser's a critic these days.' Ophelia pressed the sunglasses closer to her face. 'I suppose you're wondering now if I've got an E.D?' Seeing the confusion on Rio's face she added, 'Eating disorder.'

'It's none of my—'

'Well I have,' the actress carried on as if Rio hadn't spoken. 'Or had. It's no big secret. It was years back when I was a teen. When "Love Yourself" asked for my help I gave it.' She took a deep breath. "Now, where were we? Ah yes, Dad's business. The honest God truth is I don't really know. I think he had a partner before I was born, but I'm not sure. When I was young I think he made his money in property, but once again I'm not sure. Whatever it was he sold up and diversified into something else. Something more lucrative.'

'What could be more of a money spinner than property in a place like London?'

'Who knows? I didn't much care. He just wanted to make lots of money and I wanted to entertain people.'

'He must've been proud when he saw you on the telly, especially when *The Wilcotts* became such a success.'

Ophelia removed her Ray-Bans. Her eyes were bright and glassy. 'I like to think he was. He belonged to a generation that didn't really open up about their feelings.' She shrugged, a small one that was more continental than British. 'He did pat me on the back last year when I was nominated for the National Television Awards. He didn't say anything, just touched his palm to my back.'

Ophelia shivered and Rio knew she was feeling that loving touch on her back all over again. She placed her glasses back on her face in an action that was more a fumble than a sure move.

'In the last few days, did your parents mention seeing anyone out of the ordinary near where they lived?' Rio then took her first bite of the bar. It tasted just as it always did – like wood shavings mashed together with glue – but it kept her energy levels going.

Ophelia ruffled the front of her hair with her fingers. 'The last time I spoke to them was a few days ago. It was Mum's birthday and I was meant to go over, but then a rehearsal came up.' She shook her head. 'They didn't mention seeing anything strange. Mind you there were always weird goings-on at the home nearest to them: that pop star living with his wife, mistress and two adopted kids from Cambodia.'

'And what about your brother? Cornelius? We haven't been able to locate him because we don't have any contact details.'

'I don't have a clue where he is or a number for him. Nor do I want one. He doesn't appear to understand the concept of work but fully understands the role of a full-time parasite. The last time I saw him he looked like he needed a good hose-down to clean up his life.'

'Would your parents' lawyer, Stephen Foster, know where he is?'

Ophelia face screwed up fiercely. 'Foster?'

Rio remembered the repulsion the other woman had displayed earlier when his name was thrown into the conversation in her dressing room. 'You don't like him?'

'I hate that man.'

'Why?'

Ophelia pulled her neck long. 'I don't have time to talk about Stephen Foster when I've got to think about burying my parents.'

She twisted around, walking hurriedly away, leaving Rio alone among the smell of smoke and trash. Rio gazed up at Ophelia Bell on the 'Love Yourself' poster.

*   *   *

'The parents still inside?' Rio asked the protection officer when she arrived back on the ward.

He quickly explained that Nikki's parents had gone to the canteen while a partner from Stephen Foster's law firm had just arrived to speak to Nikki and didn't want to be disturbed. Rio scoffed when he told her Foster's associate had said that the lawyer was indisposed for the next few hours. She couldn't believe that he had a vulnerable client, who'd witnessed a woman being murdered, and he was off doing God knew what for the day. Probably glad-handing some of his celeb clients.

'What was it like speaking to Lady Clarissa?' the officer quietly asked her.

'You a fan?'

'Me and the missus watch it every Sunday.'

Rio remembered the man abusing Ophelia outside. 'I think that it's one tough business.'

'She should try arresting drunks on a Saturday night. Now, that's what I call a rough business – not dressing up and reading autocues.'

Rio looked over at Nikki's hospital door. 'Did you double-check the identity of the guy from Foster's?'

'Sure.'

'You're certain about that?'

The guard appeared slightly put out. 'I rang Foster's office. He's OK.'

Just as Rio raised her hand to lightly tap on the door, her mobile rang. She checked the caller ID.

Calum Burns.

Rio froze, like she wasn't in the hospital ward anymore but being dragged back into the past. What did he want? They hadn't crossed words with each other in three years. Maybe DSI Newman had given him a bell and told him to contact her?

The saliva in her mouth started drying up. The phone kept ringing.

Rio took the call. 'Don't phone me again.'

She cut the call. That was easy. Then why was her heart pumping like it had just learned to beat for the first time?

'Detective Inspector Wray.'

Rio looked up to find Stephen Foster striding towards her.

'I thought you were indisposed?'

'Indisposed?' He gazed at her confused.

'Yes, that's what the associate you sent over to speak to Nicola Bell told our protection officer.'

'Hang on a minute, I was going to send a colleague, but I decided to come myself. I never told him—'

But Rio was gone, racing over to Nikki's door. The blind was down, the door locked. Rio didn't hesitate; she kicked in the flimsy door. A man, sporting a black Kagoul coat, hood up, stood over Nikki holding a syringe.

twelve

The man jerked to face Rio, the raincoat zipped to his nose, hood low down on his forehead. The only part of his face on display were light brown eyes and a touch of white skin.

'Put it down,' Rio shouted.

She stayed where she was, just inside the doorway, knowing that any move could force him to plunge the syringe into the teenager's neck. Nikki's head was still, her eyes wide with terror.

'Back. Off,' Rio continued yelling, stretching her arms wide and frantically waving her palms behind her to keep the protection officer and Foster outside.

The man's hands moved quickly; one flipped the syringe around so he now held it like a dagger while the other pulled out a slim pistol fitted with a silencer. He jammed the silencer against Nikki's temple. A strained, protesting noise came from the back of the sixteen-year-old's throat, but she still didn't move.

Shit.

Rio took a step forwards. 'Put the gun and the syringe down.' She kept her voice calm. Even.

But he ignored her, instead shouting, 'You two gentlemen behind her, please join us inside.'

Confident, professional, and polite: that's what Rio noticed about his voice and tone; all he was missing was the briefcase, suit and tie. Another policeman in the room would work to Rio's advantage, but another civilian? No. That was going to make things messier. But she could do nothing as the protection officer – Officer Drake (his name was suddenly really important to her if anything happened) – and Stephen Foster followed the gunman's instruction. Rio felt the body heat of both men as they stood close behind her right side.

The gunman addressed Officer Drake. 'Drop any weapons on the floor.'

Rio could feel her colleague's gaze shift sharply to her for guidance what to do, but she couldn't look back, couldn't take her eyes off the gunman and Nikki.

'Do. It,' she ordered.

While the officer dropped his taser and CS gas, Rio mentally jammed as many facts in her mind about the gunman's physical characteristics.

White-olive skin.

Skin only visible around the eyes.

Five ten to eleven

Light brown eyes. Can't see if they had another colour mixed in with them.

Defo English accent, but a slight roll in some words. West Country?

Black Kagoul. Black tracksuit bottoms. No distinguishing marks on tracksuit. Black trainers, no marks on those either.

Right-handed from the gun in his hand, but using his left hand with equal confidence.

'You next, lady cop,' the gunman continued his instructions.

Rio eased her taser out and let it drop on the floor.

'And the gas,' the gunman's voice held heat in it for the first time.

Rio shook her head. 'No CS. Search me if you doubt my

word.' She said the last deliberately, hoping he would take the
bait to come into her personal space, which would give her the
opportunity to attack. The material of the raincoat under his
eyes moved and Rio realised that he was smiling. No, this man
wasn't fool enough to fall for that trick.

'You.' He now addressed Foster. 'Lock the door.'

But instead of following the instruction, Stephen Foster
started running his mouth like the overpaid shark he was.
'You'll get at least ten years for threatening behaviour, five
more for carrying a firearm . . .'

'Shut the fuck up.' It wasn't the gunman but Rio who spoke.
'Do what he said. Shut. The. Door.'

'The lock is broken—'

Rio just did it because she was frightened what might
happen next if this legal prick kept sounding off; swiftly she
twisted right and belted Foster a stinging open palm across his
cheek. As his head rocked back in shock, Rio faced the gunman
again, her palms in the air.

'We're OK,' she offered quickly. 'The door.'

Foster finally did what he was told.

'Both you men sit down and face the wall near the bathroom. Hands flat on the floor behind you.'

As Foster and Drake faced the white wall Nikki let out a tiny
moan. The paleness of her face worried Rio.

'Why don't you let the girl go?'

But he wouldn't play her game; the only game he wanted to
play was his own. 'If you stay rational, we can avoid any
bloodshed.'

'Why are you after the girl? Are you a member of the gang?
If you—'

'Come here.'

Rio held her ground for a few seconds. Then approached
him. As soon as she reached him, in one swift move, he pressed

the gun to her forehead. Nikki slumped even further into the softness of the bed. He put the syringe in his pocket and then ran his spare hand up and down her suit like a nightclub bouncer. Satisfied that she was clean his next words chilled her.

'Down on your knees facing the other way.'

Nikki's soft sobs tore through the air.

Maybe Rio was the one who needed bitch slapping now because she refused to move. He increased the pressure of the barrel firmly against her skin.

'I mean it and you know that.'

Yes she did, so she started to move.

'What the hell's going on? Where are the police? Where's my daughter?' Patsy Bell hysterically yelled outside.

That's when he made his mistake. His eyes jumped to the closed door. Rio grabbed his gun arm the same time Nikki scrambled off and under the bed. He fought back just as Officer Drake leapt to his feet. The gunman kneed Rio in the stomach as he slammed his arm back down. Rio swallowed the pain as she drew every ounce of strength she had to try to bring his arm up. Taking Rio by surprise he abruptly relaxed his arm. What the heck . . .? No, Rio's mind screamed when she realised what he was doing – lining the aim of the gun directly with Drake.

Pop. A bullet slammed into the other officer's shoulder toppling him backwards. Rio took advantage of the gunman's diverted attention – bent her knees and yanked him across her shoulders before throwing him to the other side. The gun clattered and skidded along the floor. Rio flung herself on top of the gunman's body, letting loose a one-two combination of punches to his head.

She twisted her head to Foster, who still remained on the floor, but was now crouched by the groaning, fallen policeman. 'Get help,' she yelled.

A powerful jab smashed into the side of Rio's head. Stunned, she hit the ground. Dazed, pumping oxygen madly to her lungs, she saw the gunman heave himself to his feet. Something fell from his pocket as he rushed for the gun. Rio tried to get up, but the heaviness in her head kept her pinned down.

Get up. Get up. Get the fuck up.

But she couldn't. Her position on the floor gave her an excellent view of Nikki, lying in a protective ball under the bed and what had tumbled out of his pocket – an odd shaped, lethal looking knife. Her gaze jacked back up when she realised that the man was back. This time standing over her with the gun pointed at her head.

3:14 p.m.

'Help! Help!' Foster finally shouted.

The gunman looked over at the lawyer, then twisted around and headed for the open window. As Rio finally managed to sit up, two things happened at the same time: the gunman disappeared through the window and the door slammed open. Detective Jack Strong rushed over to Rio. His hands touched her, but furiously she shook him off.

'He's escaped out of the window. Get to your car and see if you can head him off from the ground. I'm going after him on foot.'

Rio stood up, gave herself a few seconds to control the spinning in her head. As she belted for the window she heard sobs coming from Nikki's bed; at least the girl was still alive. Outside of the window Rio saw the gunman about a metre below, fleeing from the rooftop he'd obviously dropped onto. Without hesitation Rio scrambled out of the window and made the drop.

The roof was flat but scattered with gravel like stones that were evenly spread. Where the stones had been disturbed it was possible to see where her gunman had fled. She ran to the edge and placed her hands on the waist-level rail that skirted the edge of the roof. Rio instinctively tilted backwards when she saw how far down it was – four or five floors. No, he hadn't escaped that way. She heard squealing wheels below and saw Strong come round a corner on a service road in an unmarked saloon. He slowed and leaned out of the window, looking upwards. Rio shouted, 'Cover all the exits . . .'

Strong cupped his hand over his ear indicating he couldn't hear her, so Rio pointed down the roof in the direction the assassin had fled. Far below, Strong raised his thumb to show he understood and set off slowly, scanning the roof.

Rio followed the marks in the stones, but the roof was complicated. Blocks of hospital rooms seemed to have been added on top, along with chimneys and small brick buildings. All served as access routes, which meant plenty of cover and a variety of escape routes.

Rio twisted around when she heard a swishing of stones and footsteps. She moved close to the blind side of a chimney. With teeth gritted and clenched fists, she took some deep breaths and then swung round the chimney to confront the would-be killer. He was gripping a pole and looked up in alarm as Rio raced forwards. She landed a solid right full in his face. Only as he fell backwards did she realise that he was wearing overalls and the pole in his hand was in fact a rake and he'd been running it over the stones. Not her target.

Shit.

She leaned over the prone man and shouted, 'I'm a police officer, have you seen a man up here, running?'

Only when the bewildered workman began refocusing his eyes did Rio realise what a hopeless question it was to ask. She set off in pursuit again. But then she stopped, doubled back and picked up the man's rake, 'I need to borrow this . . .'

Rio began to prowl the roof, unclear where she was going. There were too many windows and doors butting onto the roof to plug. She went over to the edge again and looked down. Strong's car was crawling on the service road below in a low gear. That's when she heard it: a knock, like a blunted hammer. A second knock, then a third. Gripping the rake Rio rushed off in the direction of the noise.

Bang. Bang. Bang.

She turned a corner. The gunman was in plain sight.

He was using the butt of his pistol to try to knock off a padlock on an access door.

She raised her rake like an axe at the same time the padlock hit the roof floor. Rio charged as he wrenched the heavy door open. The sound of her feet on the gravel alerted him; he swung around in her direction. The rake swung towards him and caught him a glancing blow on his arm. He toppled backwards, banging his back against the open door, slamming it shut again. His gun spun a few yards away. Rio flung down the rake and raced over to where the gun lay, bent over to swipe it up.

The sound of a gun's hammer made her freeze.

'Leave it . . .'

Slowly Rio straightened up and turned around. The man had a second gun – a smaller one, but no less deadly. Rio knew she had made a mistake by not beating him unconscious when she'd had the chance.

'Back off,' he growled.

Rio eased back as he moved forwards. She watched as he picked up the fallen gun. He waved it, indicating that she was to back off. He picked up the other weapon, did the same to the rake. Rio quickly swung her body into a defensive position, but he was already on her. The wooden pole struck her head. The force and pain made her fall to her knees. She tumbled sideways.

Another blow had her crying out as she instinctively folded her body into the foetal position. Then she was moving and realised that the man was dragging her by the collar. Blackness started to swallow her vision.

Don't black out.

Don't black out.

She fought it, head swimming, body bursting with pain. But the blackness wouldn't go away.

DON'T BLACK OUT.

Rio forced her eyes wide.

The rail at the edge of the roof was above her and a pair of light brown eyes that seemed to be floating in a sea of material that obscured the rest of the man's features.

In a demonic whisper he said, 'You're not afraid of flying are you?'

What? Only when he grasped Rio under the shoulders did she understand; he was going to push her under the rail and over the edge, five floors down to her death.

Desperately she tried to fight back, but her muscles refused to work. Her body was sliding closer. Closer . . .

'Help!'

A man's screeching voice lit up the air.

'Murder! Help!'

Strong? No.

Rio almost blacked out again.

Her vision came back and Rio's gut clenched wildly as all she saw above her was endless grey sky. The world was the wrong way around. Her neck hurt. Her breathing collapsed inside her as she realised that her head was hanging over the edge. All he'd have to do was one more push.

'Murder! Murder! Murder!'

No, it wasn't Strong, but the workman. Rio never knew where she got the strength from but she raised a foot and kicked the gun in the shin. It pushed him back. She heard feet crunching in the gravel.

'DI Wray? Rio?'

Strong. Jack bloody Strong.

'Looks like your flight has been cancelled,' the gunman said somewhere above her.

Then Rio heard a crunch on the stones, and the rusty hinges of a door being opened.

She tried to move, but couldn't. Her head started throbbing; her vision blurred.

'DI?' Hands were pulling her back.

Don't black out.

Don't black out.

If he gets away he'll come back for Nikki.

Rio blacked out.

thirteen

4:06 p.m.

The first person Rio saw when she regained consciousness was Jack Strong. He stood looking down at her and that's when she realised she was lying on a bed. The right side of her face and head hurt like someone had tried to stamp her to death. Images flashed through her mind:

Nikki's head slumped to one side.

Man with a raincoat.

Gunman . . .

That pushed Rio up. Her fingers gripping the bed for support, the pain increasing with a crazy intensity.

'Take it easy,' Strong said.

Rio swung her legs over the side, her breathing pulling in and out of her body in rapid spurts. 'No time for taking it easy.' Finally she stood on shaky legs. 'How long have I been out?'

'About forty minutes.'

'Shit.' Wrong word; its intensity doubled her pain, forcing a long groan from her lips.

'Shall I get Doctor Green?'

Rio waved Strong's question to the side as she rode the wave of pain until it eased back. 'We need to check the hospital's security cam—'

'Already done. No joy there. As a cost-cutting exercise the

hospital alternates each day on having its cameras on different sides of the hospital—'

'Don't tell me,' Rio cut in. 'No cams this side today.' Rio almost let rip with more swearing, but thought about the pain and let the cursing alone. 'But he couldn't have turned up pretending to be from Foster's firm wearing a raincoat zipped to his mouth. Someone must have seen his face, especially Officer Drake.'

Strong nodded. 'I've already got someone onto checking CCTV and traffic cams. We might get an ID for him if we catch him getting into a vehicle and trace it.'

Rio nodded back, deep breathing at the same time to get some stability. Then she looked at Strong. 'But he did leave a knife behind. It ended up somewhere near Nikki's bed. We can use it to pull off prints and maybe DNA.'

'We checked the room.' Strong shook his head. 'No knife.'

Rio frowned. 'I saw the blade fall out of his pocket. Find it. Ask the medical staff, one of them might've picked it up by accident mistaking it for one of their surgical ones because it had a slim shape, with a curve at the end.' Rio rubbed her head. 'I don't get what's going on here. Do you think he's a member of the gang? And if he is, how the fuck did he know she was here?' Rio uttered the last as if talking to herself.

Rio slowly moved towards the door. 'Well, at least we have Nikki safe . . .' Her voice dribbled away as she saw the look on Strong's face. 'What's going on?'

'Mr and Mrs Bell took their daughter home.'

'What?' Rio couldn't help the roar the word became.

'Said that on the advice of their legal counsel, they did not feel that their daughter was protected in the hospital.'

'Foster.' Rio swore, no longer caring about any possible pain. 'If the gunman found her here he could find her at her home. Get a protection unit—'

'They refused to have one.'

'Let me guess: on the advice of their legal counsel.' Rio paced, trying to think her way through this one. Her mobile rang. Annoyed at the interruption Rio pulled it out of her jacket.

'What?'

'I hear they've been a few problems at your end.'

Rio squared her shoulders immediately despite the pain. 'Yes, ma'am. We've been—'

'Why don't you tell me all about it back at base in fifteen minutes.'

The line went dead.

'Don't worry about Raspberry Ripple, she's just blowing off steam.'

'Don't call her that,' Rio growled.

Strong's mouth jerked up at the side. 'Oh I forgot, all you feminist cops like to stick together.'

'I wish I had time to tell you what a disrespectful, nasty pig and the other ten adjectives I've got burning in my brain to describe you, but I don't. A girl's life is on the line. Drop me at The Fort and then go to the Bells' and discreetly keep an eye on everyone.'

Strong nodded, but added, 'What about the info on the drugs deal I've picked up?'

But before Rio could answer her mobile rang again. She checked the ID this time.

Calum Burns. Again.

Furious she punched the connection to the call. 'I already told you—'

'Is she dead?'

'What are you talking about?'

'That little girl you're looking after.'

'I'm not discussing this case with you.'

'Cool. Fine. No need to tell you about the Wanted poster with Nicola Bell's face on it.'

Wanted poster? Nikki? The image imprinted itself on Rio's mind. The pain started throbbing like a razor blade slicing over and over through her skin.

'What's going on, Calum?'

'There's a professional hit out on your girl.'

The line went dead.

fourteen

The Hit: Day One
4:35 p.m.

'What the hell went on?'

Assistant Commissioner Tripple's words bounced around inside DSI Newman's office as Rio stood rigidly in front of her desk, the bruise to her head throbbing. But Rio could tell from the set of the AC's face she wasn't finished speaking.

'You have the only credible witness in your custody, with a protection officer guarding the door, and what happens? Someone manages to get to her and almost kill her on our watch.'

Rio took every word on the chin. No arguing, no defending herself. The AC was right: that was her watch and a young girl had almost died.

'There's a contract hit out on the girl.'

For the first time ever Rio heard her superior swear. 'How do you know?'

'A source.' Rio quickly added, 'A confidential source.' She didn't need anyone asking any questions about Calum, although Newman had given her the go-ahead to see him. She wasn't planning to have Calum attached too long to this case.

'Reliable?'

Calum reliable? If you were talking about their relationship, no way, Rio thought bitterly, but Calum was a man with his ear to the ground, so if he said there was a contract out on Nikki Bell it was probably the truth. Rio nodded.

AC Tripple waved her hand at the empty chair Rio stood in front of.

Once she was seated, the other woman said, 'You know that I've always thought that you were the one who was going to make a difference. The one who was going to finally mark out a place for women and ethnic minorities in the force.'

Not many people realised that Rio's relationship with the Assistant Commissioner went much further back than when the other woman had taken up her post as one of the leading officers in the Metropolitan Police Service. Pauline Tripple had taken Rio under her wing during Rio's three-year stint in the armed response unit, sacrificing personal time to give her advice and show her the ropes. Tripple hadn't had an easy time during her steady climb up the career ladder and she was determined that other women entering the force would not have to deal with the level of hostility she'd had to go through. She'd recognised Rio's ambition, determination and strong will. Rio was thankful for her help, but wasn't sure about being the double poster girl for gender and race equality in the Force.

'I gave you this case because I know you can solve it,' the other woman continued. 'You're special. You've got the smarts that we need at the top. The Met is going through a very rocky patch, as you well know. Public confidence in us is not where we would want it to be at the moment. We need to become a twenty-first century police service and the twenty-first century looks like you, Rio Wray. I know you don't like that – see it as some type of burden, just want to get on and do a stellar job – but the reality is if we don't have people like you at the top there's only one way we're going to go: backwards.'

'Got a problem with someone using it to rise in the ranks.'

Jack Strong's words came back to Rio. That's what she hated the most: people assuming that she only got where she was going because someone powerful was opening doors for her, not because she was talented and bloody good at her job.

So Rio dared to say something that she knew might be seen as rank disrespect. 'Ma'am, you know that I've always been grateful for the time you've invested in me, but I don't need someone holding my hand.'

The AC's mouth tilted into a bittersweet, lopsided smile. 'Do you know how many times I wished someone – just one person – had stretched out their palm to me, when I was coming up? It was rough back then. I had to work twice as hard as any man to show I had balls big enough to do the job as well. But do you know what I started to realise? I don't have balls; don't want them either. I had something different that pushed me on and up. I take pride in some calling me Raspberry Ripple, and you know why? Because I made it, and that's why I'm going to recommend you for DSI Newman's post when he retires.'

Rio couldn't help the way her chest punched out in pride. 'Thank you, ma'am.'

The chummy friendliness left the Assistant Commissioner. 'But that's not going to happen if you muck up this case. I know you don't want any special favours so I'll tell it to you straight – if you don't solve this case within the next two weeks, I'm going to pull you off it. And that promotion will disappear before your eyes.'

When Rio got back to the operations room she stared at the e-fit picture that had been made up of the witness descriptions of the hitman. Nothing special about him; he looked like any other ordinary bloke. And there was no joy with a match to anyone else on their database.

5:00 p.m.

Rio approached Strong's car, stationed on the opposite side of the road to Patsy and Frank Bell's home. He rolled the driver's window down, but Rio went around to the passenger side and got in.

'Everything's been quiet,' he told her. 'Did the AC give you the usual blah blah about being taken off the case if you didn't solve it pronto?'

Rio refused to engage with him on this subject and kept her face looking straight ahead.

'Or did she wind you up by dangling that promotion above your head?'

Now Rio turned to him, her cool brown gaze dressing him down. But he kept up his insolent chat. 'Pauline Tripple was a real goer back in the day. Bet she never told you about—'

'Tell me what you've got on the drugs deal angle,' Rio calmly cut in. She was tired, body still stinging, and she didn't have the reserves to sing along with the nasty tune he was humming.

With a small, cynical tip of his lips that would usually get her temper in motion, he pulled out his mobile. That surprised her; she thought he'd be old cop style, like her, with his notebook or a file. Strong used his thumb to scroll down his mobile screen. He silently read for half a minute and then looked back up at her.

'I spoke to the drugs boys and a couple of trafficking analysts and asked them if they had any info that could help us. In particular, if they knew of any consignments that were being held up while the investors over here raised the money or if they knew of anyone new on the scene, anything unusual, you know . . .' His finger tapped against the screen. 'They did turn up a couple of cases that might fit our bill and this one is the best of the bunch.'

He passed her the phone. Rio gazed at a photo of two men sitting in what looked like a bar.

'This came from a police surveillance team in Brussels,' Strong explained as he leaned closer to her. 'The man on the right is Frank Decker, who used to act as the middle-man between a major Turkish drug supplier and a big syndicate in London. But the thing is we picked up the London end of the operation six months ago, which left our Turkish friends with no one reliable to sell to and they're looking for new partners.'

Strong's finger touched the screen. 'The guy on the left is Terry Larkin who comes from South London and whose family have been small time, bit part players, in the underworld for years – nothing too serious but they're always around, you know? The thing is that about ten years ago, Larkin was the running mate of a leading member of the syndicate that's just been taken down and there's a suggestion that maybe Larkin's been offered the chance to take over the London end of the operation. The word is that he may have had a partner in crime at one stage with significant cash to inject, but they fell out or something . . . Anyway, it sounds like the partner left him high and dry, so he'd need to raise some serious dough and as far as anyone can see, he hasn't got it. So he might have been a candidate for a Greenbelt style operation.'

Rio sighed. 'Might have been?'

Strong took the mobile from her and used his fingers to enlarge the photo so that the bottom, right-hand corner was prominent. 'Yeah. As you can see from the time and date on that photo it's the same date as the fourth Greenbelt raid, which rules out Terry Larkin from being there. However, we know Terry's made a number of trips to Belgium on false pass-ports but he never goes the same way or uses the same methods. Plane, boat and train, he uses them all. We also think that the

Turks have got a container full of gear sitting somewhere in a warehouse in Antwerp and they're not moving it, which suggests they're waiting for the London end to be sorted out. And even though Terry can't be a Greenbelt guy on raid number four, he comes from a family that includes other candidates who might be. Like this guy, for example . . .'

Strong got another photo on screen: a mug shot. Name: Gary Larkin.

'Terry's younger brother – Terry's older than him by about ten years. Convictions are mainly mid-range, including a failed prosecution for firearms possession and a conviction for an armed raid on a post office. He served time in prison for the post office offence and other terms for burglary and violence. But the last of his convictions was five years before. There's nothing to suggest this is a man who could be responsible for anything on the scale of the Greenbelt raids.'

Rio took the phone and studied the photo. It was of a man who had once been handsome but was now heading into middle age with greying hair, wrinkles and jowls. And that had been five years previously. He seemed too old already to be running around the countryside raiding homes and killing people.

'What about his medical history? Any signs of chest complaints or breathing difficulties?'

Strong admitted, 'He's registered with a doctor who's very discreet about his criminal client's illnesses. You know the type – if he comes in with a bullet wound, the quack puts it down as a sore throat. I've got the feeling that anything medical that might help ID Gary Larkin won't be on his records . . .'

Rio focused on the photo. Gary Larkin looked like what his record said that he was: a small-time crook whose best days were behind him.

'And Rio, there's another interesting thing about Gary–'

Her gaze flicked up at him. 'DI Wray. That's my title and that's what you will use.'

'Whatever you say, home girl.' Rio didn't rise to the provocation, but let him continue. 'Gary Larkin is on our list of convicted criminals we want to bring in to interview – just to eliminate them from our inquiries. All our other potential suspects have airtight alibis. Larkin's very low down on the list, I'll admit, but nevertheless . . .'

'Look at this photo.' Rio pushed the mobile at Strong. ' What does it tell you?'

Strong looked at it for a while and said, 'I don't know.'

'He's got loser stamped all over his face. A drugs deal might be his last chance to make something of himself before he fades away – but he hasn't got the money–'

Rio was looking into her suspect's eyes, 'Let's pay him an unannounced visit and ask him if he'll help with our inquiry. Did you do any digging about other members of the Larkin family?'

Strong tapped away at his mobile again and then passed it to Rio. She couldn't fault the detective next to her; he'd done a quick and efficient job of finding out everything they had on the Larkin brood. Gary was the only one with convictions for violence and firearms, although the entire family seemed to have been picked up for something at one time or another. There was even a cousin who had skipped town and decamped to Cyprus years back rather than face questioning about an armed robbery.

Terry seemed to be the brains behind the outfit. His convictions were for the cleverer type of crimes – fraud, gambling and numbers rackets. It made sense . . . but only just. What if big brother Terry organises the importation of narcotics while Gary raises the cash?

And Terry's seventeen-year-old son, Samson – stupid

name – already looked like a handful. He had a string of convictions for sadistic, unnecessary and unprofitable violence.

'I see that young Samson has caught your eye,' Strong said. 'After his last offence, an unprovoked attack on a girl in a bar, Sam – that's what everyone calls him – was warned by the court that he was looking at a custodial sentence but that was pending reports. They sent the kid for psychiatric tests and the shrink concluded that he has an unhealthy obsession with guns and violence and needed urgent and prolonged treatment. The psych – get this – thinks the kid's a bit of a genius.' Strong scoffed, 'Like anyone in that family has more than two brain cells to put together. Anyway the court put him on probation and ordered him to attend anger-management counselling.'

'Let's see if we can land unannounced on his doorstep as well,' Rio said, the excitement of knowing that they may have the lead she'd finally been after giving her an energy boost.

'That's where our problems start. A couple of weeks ago, Samson began skipping appointments with the doctor and probation service so the local police went round there to see what was happening. According to his father, Terry, the kid had gone abroad and got a job but they had no contact details for him. According to Dad, he's in Spain. But the local cops have been keeping an eye on the family's phones and there are no calls from Spain or anywhere else. So there's a warrant out for Samson's arrest.'

'When did he disappear?'

Strong smiled. 'All the evidence suggests he did a runner a couple of days after raid number five, when the newly wed was killed. Let's target Gary Larkin because I suspect he'll be the easiest one to break. He doesn't sound anywhere near as savvy as his big brother.'

'Do we have an address for him?'

Strong shook his head. 'I'll get onto it. Then we can pick him up.'

'We're going to do this properly—'

Strong stared at her, not able to hold his anger back. 'I'm getting a bit sick and tired of you implying I'm some kind of loose cannon—'

Rio grabbed his arm. 'Shut up and listen up. We don't have any solid evidence. Sure, we've got a lead, but we need to play this by the book. And prioritise. Priority number one is making sure that Nikki and her family are safe. I need to persuade them to have a protection duty. Then I need to talk to my CI.' She knew Calum would hate being pegged as a confidential informant after his years being an officer, but she wasn't ready yet to let anyone know he was her source. 'To see if he's got any other info on this hit.'

Strong hitched up his eyebrows. 'I know it's not my place to ask who your CI is—'

'You've got that right,' Rio snapped. Just thinking about Calum filled her head with the image of her in a cream dress holding his hand. She got rid of the memory as quickly as it had come. 'And double-check again with the hospital about the knife.'

Rio got out of the car. Before she shut the door, she hesitated, then half-turned to Strong and muttered, 'Good work.'

'Speak up, I can't hear you.'

Rio slammed the door, his dry laughter following her as she walked towards the Bells' front door.

fifteen

5:11 p.m.

Rio hesitated before knocking on the Bells' front door because of the raised voices she could hear inside: female voices – Nikki and her mother. She couldn't make out what they were saying, but their voices were getting higher and higher.

She pulled the knocker back. *Bang. Bang. Bang.* Three knocks should get their attention. Silence, then the sound of feet coming towards the door; Patsy Bell opened the door.

Her face was a deep red, like she'd been running a race, and there were dark circles carved under her eyes.

'We've been advised not to speak to you.' Patsy Bell's voice was clipped, anxious; her fingers pale as they clutched the door. No chunky bracelets this time.

'Please,' Rio responded softly. She couldn't help but feel sympathy for this woman, but she had a job to do. 'A few moments of your time is all I'm asking for.'

Indecision played across the other woman's face. Then she pulled the door open and stepped back. Rio walked inside. The Bells' home was on a much smaller scale than her dead brother-in-law's. And the scattering of footwear in a corner of the slim hallway and the jumble of coats on a wooden rail mounted on the wall gave it a more lived-in feel. Rio followed Nikki's mother into a lounge where Frank Bell sat tense on a comfy single sofa, his facial skin the shade of someone who'd been living in the dark for a week. Nikki sat, back bent forwards like a cat ready to spring for freedom through any opened door, on a matching two-seater.

Frank Bell got to his feet. He didn't have to open his mouth for Rio to know he wasn't pleased to see her.

'We can't talk to you,' he said, repeating his wife's words.

Rio caught Nikki's eye. Then the teenager dropped her gaze as her back slumped and she seemed to shrink further into the settee.

'Can we talk?' Rio lifted her chin slightly in Nikki's direction. 'In private?'

A worried look passed between the other two adults. Then, arms wrapped around her middle, Patsy spoke to her daughter.

'Honey, we need you to go up to your room.'

The girl's face tilted defiantly to the side. 'Why?'

'Don't argue with me, young lady, just do it.'

Nikki threw her legs over the front of the sofa, but made no move to follow the instruction. 'It was me some guy slapped around in the hospital, so I've got a right to hear what she's got—'

Her mother stepped threatening towards her. 'If you don't do what I've just requested, I'm—'

'What?' Now Nikki stormed to her feet. 'You going to slap me as well?'

'Nicola.' Her father's tone was hard.

The teenager swung her gaze between all the adults in the room, finally settling on staring daggers at her mother. 'Auntie Linda always said that you treated me too much like a baby.' Her chest heaved. 'I wish she was still alive and you were—'

'Don't say it,' Rio cut in gently, but with enough threat for the girl to understand she was crossing a line.

Nikki's cracked breathing sounded high in the room. The heat of her emotions flushed her face. She gave her mother one last long stare, then swept out of the room.

'I'm sorry about that,' Patsy said looking embarrassed.

'Nicola's behaving in a pretty understandable way considering all that's she's been through. Is it Stephen Foster who's instructed you not to speak to the Police?'

That look passed between the other two again. This time the answer came from Frank. 'He says we just need to be really careful because . . .' He inhaled deeply before carrying on. 'You might accuse our daughter of being involved—'

'Whoo!' Rio said in alarm as she placed her palm flat in the air. 'There's no suggestion that Nikki had anything to do with this.'

'But Mr Foster says he's had cases like that before,' Frank carried on in a strident voice. 'Where the innocent end up as the accused.'

'Please,' Rio interjected. 'We know that Nikki isn't involved because the way the crime happened points straight to the Greenbelt Gang. Plus someone tried to kill her in the hospital.' Rio was a straight talker, so she told them most of what she'd found out. 'I think there's a hitman trying to kill your daughter.'

The girl's parents both gasped.

'Why?' Patsy's voice shook.

'The gang obviously didn't know she was there—'

A two-beat knock sounded from the front door. Frank Bell started to leave the room, but Rio's voice stopped him. She placed a finger across her lip, demanding silence. Then she slowly moved close up to Patsy Bell.

Whispered in her ear, 'Can I get to the front of the house from the back?'

The other woman nodded. 'Through the dining room.' She pointed to a door in the far corner of the room.

The knock at the door came again. Harder. Louder.

Rio rushed into the dining room, bypassed the long table, towards the closed French doors. Turned the long, brass handle which opened into the conservatory and moved quickly to the set of doors at the end. Opened. The cold air bunched in her face as she stepped out into the garden. The garden was covered in the growing dark of a February day turning into early evening and the scent of roses perfumed the air. The ground wasn't soft beneath her shoes. Hard with grooves; probably some type of decking she guessed. Rio placed her hand on the grainy, bumpy brick of the wall. Slid it along as she moved. Stopped when she hit the corner. A faint light from the neighbours gave her a dim view of a long walkway, with a brown recycling bin midway down. Silently she lengthened her stride as she headed for the wooden door at the end, reached it and with the pads of her fingers lifted the black, cold latch and pulled back.

The breath caught in her throat when she was confronted with the silhouette of someone standing right in front of her. Without hesitation, she unleashed a power punch to the throat, then backed it up with a right hook to the face. The person crumpled to the ground.

Nikki sat on the last step of the landing on the second floor listening.

'You could've broken my nose. You've used violent force against me once already today.'

'Thought a lawyer like you would be used to taking a jab or two.'

The lawyer and the cop were getting into a hissy-fit with each other.

'If you had been as attentive in your duty to protect my

client at the hospital no one would have been able to attack her right under your nose.'

'This family need around-the-clock twenty-four-seven protection. If someone tried to attack Nicola today you can bet that they're going to try to finish the job.'

Gasp. Sounded like Mum. Nikki felt a bit bad for laying into her before. She knew that Mum only wanted to keep her safe.

'So why aren't you out there on the streets trying to apprehend them?'

'My team is. I wanted to make sure that this family remains safe. I've reassured Nikki's parents that she is not under suspicion. Mr and Mrs Bell, the only way we can do that is to give you protection.'

'Like the guard you posted at the hospital?'

The lawyer was getting in the cop's face again.

'I don't take my orders from you, Foster. These parents want to keep their daughter out of harm's reach and they know that our protection is the only way.'

Silence. Nikki inched her head out further.

'OK.'

Dad this time.

'Stephen, she's our only child and we waited a long time to have her.'

'I fully understand. But Detective Inspector I'm going to make it my business to make sure you're removed from this case.'

'Do what you've got to do. Mr and Mrs Bell, make sure your daughter doesn't speak about this to anyone.'

Nikki jumped up when she heard the footsteps in the hallway downstairs and slipped quietly into her room. These adults were getting on her nerves, big time – wanting her to do this; wanting her to do that. Always pushing and pulling her this way and that, until she thought her life was way out of her control. That was some messed-up shit with the guy in the hospital. Freaked her totally out. But she wasn't scared anymore; she could look after herself.

Nikki moved across the bedroom to the black bureau where she kept her undies and accessories. She pulled open the second drawer, took out the pair of fingerless gloves cousin Lia had given her earlier and put them on. Nikki admired them on herself for a few seconds, then moved to the cabinet near her bed and grabbed her mini iPad; the cops didn't realise that she had a second one, which she called Baby Hamlet 2. Then she reopened the door and propped herself, cross-legged, near the radiator in the corridor under the attic door. For some reason she'd always found this spot in the house a place she could think. She flipped the iPad's lid up and was on the Yakkety-Yak site in less than a minute.

Madam B: Someone tried to kill me today.
se15: Yeah sure and my name is Leonardo Di Caprio.
Madam B: Well Leo – hahaha – this is for real.
se15: What's going on?
Madam B: Can't say. But some guy packing needles and a shooter tried to take me down in the hospital.
se15: Hospital!?!? ☹
Madam B: I'm ok. ☺

Nikki's fingers stopped typing.

'*Make sure your daughter doesn't speak about this to anyone.*'

Her teeth played in her bottom lip. She knew she shouldn't say anything . . .

Madam B: Aunt and uncle dead. Cleaner as well.
se15: Stop messing me around.

Madam B: Blood everywhere.

se15: Hot mess up. You OK?

Madam B: Yeah. I'm a big girl. Some kickass lady cop
watching my back. And she's getting cops to guard the
house . . .

As Nikki typed she didn't noticed the attic door above her head
slightly open, then quietly ease back into place.

sixteen

6:33 p.m.

Rio's Black Magic Woman entered a part of London that was filled with personal ghosts. Happy, youthful memories of nights spent clubbing that always seemed to end munching a Jamaican patty while waiting for an early morning cab, and disturbing ones of the man she was about to see. Brixton was full-on and London to the max – big roads, big lights, big noise from the people perpetually on its streets. Rio swung the car past the Ritzy Cinema into a quiet road, parked up, but didn't get out. Instead she sat in her car outside the butcher's shop in Brixton, psyching herself up for something she didn't want to do.

She'd rather be watching an autopsy than enduring the inevitable, personal, razor-sharp cuts from the tongue of the man in the office above the butcher's. But then Rio had never run a case that involved a hitman. She'd investigated family murder, drive-by murder, stranger-on-stranger murder, but never, ever, a murder for hire. Rio needed help if she was going to keep that girl safe.

I can do this. I can do this.

I. CAN. DO . . .

She pushed opened the door of the car, hauled in a deep slice of evening air. The air didn't taste pleasant in her mouth, but she knew it was a damn sight more pleasant than the scene she was about to face. A closed sign – red bubble writing, white background – hung on the butcher's door, but there was a faint light coming from a room upstairs. So *he* was in. Before she lost her nerve Rio walked down the narrow street that ran along the side of the building, until she found a heavy, black door. Hi-tech bell and intercom system. Round lens at the top. Camera.

Shit.

Probably wouldn't let her in once he clocked her face. Rio debated whether to go back around the front and break into the shop and make her way, unannounced, upstairs. No, the bastard probably had the whole place nailed with an alarm system. She was going to have to front this out and persuade *him* to let her in.

As she raised her finger to press the bell Rio was surprised to hear a long buzzing noise. Then a click as the lock was released from the door. The bastard must be watching her through the camera. That nervous itch was back, crawling under her skin, but at least she didn't have to do some song-and-dance pleading routine to get him to let her in.

She pushed the door and entered a dark, tight stairwell. It was slightly dusty but not too unpleasant to breathe in. She took the stairs, her nervous tick becoming a thin film of sweat along her hairline. She was about a third of the way up when she heard a sharp click behind her. Rio half-twisted around then breathed easier as she realised it was the door closing securely back into place. She continued up until she reached a small landing then peered around and found two doors – one partway open, the other closed. A beam of light shone beneath the latter.

Screw this. No more playing around.

Rio pushed her emotions into neutral as she strode

confidently to the first door, grabbed the brass knob and thrust it open. No one inside, just a desk, a black swingback chair and steel cabinets propped on the wall halfway to the window. The empty glass on the desk showed someone was here.

'Well, well, well. If it isn't Ray Gun.'

His voice behind her almost made her jump. But she maintained her position, kept her nerve, slowly eased around. Then she lifted her head so she could stare him straight into his corrupt green eyes.

Calum Burns stared back, relaxed, as he said, 'I told you to stay the hell away from me.'

Stay away from me.

Rio flinched as the words echoed in her mind. The exact same words Calum had flung in that letter he'd sent her three years ago.

Stay away from me.

I don't need you anymore.

It was that last line – the final one of the letter – that had hurt the most. A line that reinforced the line that had come before, it screamed she should stay away; don't knock on his door; keep moving and never look back, girl.

Rio, Calum and John 'Mac' Macdonagh had been as close as three friends could be as they trained at Hendon Police Academy. They'd carried that friendship through their first ten years on the job. Then each had gone their different ways – Rio to serious crimes, Mac undercover and Calum to counter-intelligence. Although they'd still remained thick as thieves, ambition, life and tragedy had started to get in the way. Rio was the first to admit she was a career cop, a go-getter.

And Calum? He was the charming cop who everyone wanted to work with; the man who made women feel like it was truly raining men. Good looking; a star officer – if a little rogue sometimes – and just plain great old-fashioned fun to be with. There had always been that tiny sizzle between them. The type of free-spirited feeling where sex held two hands out inviting them, with a wink, to grab a hold so it could whip them around the corner and take the plunge. But they'd never done it – never taken the plunge. They were mates first and buddies didn't go around banging each other.

The day she'd found out that her dad – the man who had ditched any type of father role with her when she was five – had died changed all of that. Rio hadn't expected to feel such a gutful of aching emotion: a crippling wave of needing to be held, to feel grounded. Numerous bottles of beers later Calum had done the honours and they'd been smooching between the sheets like two teens who'd wanted to find out if all that stuff about the birds 'n' bees was true. No, they'd never made it to bed that night. They'd fucked on the Turkish rug in her lounge; her on top of the kitchen counter, slammed up against the passage wall with Humphrey and Ingrid gazing at them from the large, framed *Casablanca* movie poster.

That should've been the end of it, but they'd just kept going at it, day after day, month after month. Their secret; one they didn't even share with Mac. Until the day they'd taken it too far . . . and then, five days on, whatever *IT* was was finished: dirt beneath their feet – goodbye, *adios*, *auf wieder*-fuck-ing-*sehen* baby!

Rio finally broke the heavy silence. 'If you didn't want me to come knocking at your door you shouldn't have given me a bell earlier on.'

Wrong thing to say. Rio didn't have time to go tripping down a way-too-twisty memory lane. *Stick to the script.* 'I need your help.'

Calum didn't move from where he lounged in the doorway

– didn't answer – gave Rio the time she needed to assess his face hoping to find some new lines, some loosening of the skin, anything to show that this man's life hadn't been easy in the three years since they'd seen each other. No, two years, Rio corrected herself. The last time had been at the funeral of Mac's son, two years back. She'd kept her distance from him that day, just like his letter had laid out. The only signs of ageing in his face were two faint creases twin-set around the corners of his mouth. His dark brown hair was neatly placed around his paler face giving him a monochrome shading that was spoilt by those vibrant green eyes of his.

Calum straightened his tall frame and made his way to the other side of the desk, keeping well out of her space. Rio noticed his limp, the awkward movement of his right leg, just like she had the day of Mac's boy's funeral. She knew he'd probably damaged his leg in the car accident she'd heard he'd been involved in three years ago, when they were still– Rio shook the thought off and strayed into another unwanted territory instead: trying to see him in the hospital. She'd tried every which way she could to see him in the hospital, but he wouldn't see her. By the time his letter arrived she'd found out he was in a private clinic somewhere. And then it was too late. Calum had been branded as dirty and kicked out of the force. What he had done the top brass weren't saying and she couldn't ask a man who had treated her like Typhoid Mary.

His leg wasn't her business. Nikki Bell was.

'You going to throw me a lifeline or not?'

He still didn't answer her, didn't miss a step as he rounded the desk and eased down into the swing chair making it squeak. He reached over and fingered the empty glass. He tilted his head to the side and ran his gaze slowly over her, from twist-out 'fro to just below her clenching stomach muscles. But he didn't speak.

Well she had enough words for both of them, Rio decided, as anger bubbled in her bloodstream. Rio rounded the desk and was in his space in less than five seconds. Calum's head moved slightly back, like he was enjoying a touch of unexpected sunshine, but his expression didn't change.

'You think you can ignore . . .' Rio rasped as she bent over him, then her palm was like a missile thrusting hard against his chest, 'Me?'

Calum's chair skidded across the floor.

She followed him. Reached him.

'You think you can push me . . .' Slam. Her hand was back hitting his chest. 'Away?'

His chair skated back and hit the wall by the window.

Rio kept her distance this time, pulling herself straight. But she wasn't done with him. 'Better people than you have tried to shoo me off, shut me up, tell me point blank to my black face that I don't belong.' Her chest rose with the impact of stuff she tried not to think about anymore. 'But you've got a different style – pen and paper. Next time have the guts to say it to my face.'

Rio turned and headed for the doorway. The fury was so powerful inside her she wasn't even sure she was walking a straight line.

'Thought you wanted to find out about the hit on that little girl you've got tucked away somewhere?'

His voice made her freeze, one leg in the room, the other out. Rio felt the tremors of anger rippling through her body. Slowly she turned back to find Calum on his feet. The tension tightened between them as he headed for the filing cabinet, his once-upon-a-time sinful swagger replaced by an uneven gait. Good. She hoped his leg was fucking killing him.

'Where did you hear about the contract on Nicola Bell?' she finally asked, her voice calmer, but she remained near the door.

Instead of answering, Calum pulled out a bottle of Cognac from the drawer, left the drawer open as he retook his seat and poured a decent amount into the empty glass. Rio rarely drank; anything that got in the way of her thinking straight was off limits.

Calum drank deeply. Then said, 'A contact of mine. Don't bother asking for a name because you know that's not the way I work.'

Rio took a step into the room, then another. 'Did this person say who's behind the hit?'

'This isn't a Mickey Mouse contract where the guy with the money meets the hired gun. It's a professional hit, which means there's never any face-to-face, just instructions: get the job done, wire the cash and walk away.'

Rio moved closer to Calum until the natural barrier of the desk was between them. 'Is there a name in the frame for who the hitter is?'

'It's an anonymous business full of faceless people. I could find out, but why would I do that for you?'

Rio pressed her lips together. 'Because a girl's life is in danger.'

'Not my problem.'

'Then why contact me to give me a heads-up?'

He said nothing.

'I don't get it.' Rio bent and leaned her palms against the desk. Major mistake – seeing Calum's face in close-up reminded her that he was still one of the hottest males she knew. 'You were one of the best officers I ever knew. And now I see before me a man who doesn't give a crap.'

'You know what crap is?' Rio heard anger in his voice for the first time. 'Being kicked out of the only job you ever wanted to do in your life while you're lying in hospital—'

'Are you saying that those rumours that you were covered

from head to toe in filth weren't true? That there's a different reason you were made to leave?'

'Why I was *made to leave*,' he parodied her. Then let out a short laugh that sent nasty shivers down her back. 'You make it sound like the commissioner thanked me for my service, shook my hand at the portal of Scotland Yard and then told me to piss off.'

Calum thrust his face forwards. He opened his mouth, but bit the words back. Grabbed his glass and drained it. Placed it back on the table with a firmness that said he was back in control. 'I meant what I said three years ago – stay away from me. And the way I hear it, it's not like you've kept your body sanctified and pure for my return. Phil Delaney ring a bell?'

So what if she'd been involved in a shag fest with Mac's boss: the head of the Research Unit, Phil Delaney. Calum lost all rights to tell her where to put her vee-jazzy-jay when he issued his marching orders in cold, black ink. Not that Phil was getting access to it either these days.

Rio straightened back up, but felt like what she was about to say was putting her on her knees. 'I need you to help me find out who has ordered this hit and who's trying to carry it out.'

Calum folded his arms. 'No-can-do.' Stretched his mouth into a nasty mini smile. 'Unless you've got the readies.'

It stuck in Rio's pulsating throat to tell him she'd been sanctioned to involve him in the investigation if she needed to.

Rio twisted her mouth in disgust. 'Is that what your life's all about now? Money? The highest bidder, including those with blood on their hands, gets your services.'

Instead of being insulted, Calum laughed. 'So you want me to put my neck on the line for old times' sake? That ain't–'

The buzz of the intercom sounded. Calum pressed the button on his desk without getting up to check the security camera. Rio heard footsteps on the stairs.

'We're done,' Calum announced.

Now it was Rio's turn to throw out smiles that had nothing to do with true laughter. He'd uttered the two words that gave her every right to ransack her way through his life. The sting of red creeping under his cheeks made it clear he knew he'd made a big league mistake.

'No, we're not done,' Rio said softly. 'You want me gone for eternity then you know what you have to do.'

'Am I interrupting?' a voice asked behind Rio, halting any comeback from Calum.

Rio turned to see the last person she expected to bump into – Stephen Foster.

'What are you doing here?' Rio swung her gaze back to Calum. 'What's going on?'

'Bye-bye, Ray Gun,' Calum answered.

But Rio didn't move. Instead her mind started buzzing. Why would Foster come to see Calum? Maybe they were associates and dealing with an on-going issue? No, Calum wore the face of a man who'd got one well and truly over her. Why was he so pleased? It must have something to do with the case.

'Let me guess,' Rio started with mock drama, 'Foster has asked you to use your security consultant expertise to find out who the Greenbelt Gang are.'

'Let's just say that Mister Foster has the type of instant cash that I understand and doesn't call my integrity into question.'

Rio grilled her brown gaze into Stephen Foster. 'If I find out that you're interfering in this investigation, I'm going to make sure I'm the person reading you your rights.'

Rio strode past him and hit the stairs. She was almost at the bottom when she heard Calum's voice at the top.

'The money up for grabs is half a mill, to take out the kid in five days. That means the clock's already ticking.'

seventeen

6:55 p.m.

The Bells.

That's all Rio could think about as she sprinted to her BMW. A feeling of dread inched up her spine.

Half a mill to take out the kid in five days . . .

Although there was a team keeping an eye on their home, stationed in a car across the road, there were many different ways of getting into a house: via a neighbour's back garden; the roof; underground . . . Rio knew her brain was going into overdrive, but she needed to see Nikki's family with her own eyes before she could breathe easy again.

She slammed into the driver's seat, phoned the Bells' landline – no one picked up. Rio contacted the protection team guarding the Bells.

'I want you to check the house. Now. The back, the roof, and then knock on the front door. Report back to me immediately.'

Rio waited.

One minute.

Three minutes.

Five.

They got back to her on the seventh.

'The back and roof are clear. Mrs Bell opened the door. Everything's calm.'

'Keep watching. You see anything out of place ...' Rio paused. 'Don't be afraid to use your weapons.'

Rio didn't say the last lightly. The Met had recently been involved in two high-profile cases where firearms had been discharged. Although both inquiries had upheld the police service's actions, the last case had been touch and go. The Met was still trying to rebuild its reputation with the public over that one.

Rio twisted the ignition key to be greeted by the stuttering noise the engine made when it refused to start. Bollocks. She should've whistled bye-bye to this car years back, but it was her beloved Black Magic Woman.

'Come on,' Rio chanted as she tried again, and again.

She slapped her palm with frustration against the steering wheel. The feeling crawling along her spine grew worse. If anything happened to the Bells—

Rio tried the car one last time as she did something she hadn't done since she was a kid: prayed.

Heavenly Father . . .

The engine clicked into gear. As the car roared down the street she used one hand to switch her mobile onto speaker-phone.

'Strong, I want you to meet me at the Bells now.'

The car lurched into a sharp right.

'I've trawled all the camera footage and our guy from the hospital is on screen, but I couldn't ID him; he's not in our system,' he said.

'Where did he go?'

God if he was anywhere near the Bells . . .

'Last image was from a traffic camera. The hitter going down the rabbit hole of the Tube system.'

'Just meet me there—'

'You think something's going down?'

'Just do what I say.' Rio couldn't help the volume her voice rose to.

She terminated the call. Put her flashing lights on. Sirens blazing she turned the speed dial to seventy in a forty zone.

7:05 p.m.

Patsy Bell quietly closed the bathroom door and breathed. Really breathed. She hadn't felt like she was breathing since hearing about her brother-in-law's and his wife's murder. Not that she'd liked Maurice, because she hadn't. He'd bullied her Frank about his career as a history lecturer; that type of job just wasn't good enough for a Bell.

'You should be in the City making a pile of money for the security of your family. Like me . . .'

Me, me, me; money, money, money – that's all Maurice had gone on about. Frank had told her the tales about how his brother had sold his soul in the pursuit of riches. Well fuck living-Maurice and dead-Maurice. And as she was handing out overdue fucks, fuck Ophelia too. If it was up to her Nikki would never see Ophelia again, but Frank said . . .

Patsy shrugged off her bathrobe as she stared at the filled bath, just glad for the time to forget for a while that someone was trying to kill her daughter. She inhaled the sweet scent of the Fizzy Lizzy lavender bath bomb Frank had kindly popped in earlier for her. He'd even lit two tealight candles sitting on the edge of the bath. How her Frank had come from the same womb as Maurice she would never know.

Suddenly she smiled as she heard music drifting from downstairs. Her favourite piece: Bach's Violin Concerto in E Major. She loved the fire in it, the pace, the upbeat tempo. Good ole Frank always knew how to cheer her up.

'Frank – my back!' she yelled. There was nothing better in

the world that the feel of her husband rubbing and soothing the stress away as he scrubbed her back. Patsy slipped into the water.

Umm . . . Heaven.

The water caressed her body and the soft aroma of the candles seemed almost to be running its fingers along her skin. Her body, heavy with fear and fatigue, became light and her eyelids began to droop.

She heard the door gently open and close but she was in the twilight world where sleep seems to be only a few wisps away.

Eyes still closed, she whispered, 'I think after all this is over we should send Nikki to stay with my sister in Kent.'

Frank didn't answer. Instead she felt his soft hand on her head. Patsy let out a sigh of contentment.

Umm . . . Heaven.

A hand jammed across the lower half of her face. Tightening. Squeezing. With one strong, seamless movement, she was plunged beneath the water.

7:30 p.m.

The traffic on the motorway was hell. Despite the siren, Rio was backed up in a line of traffic that stretched far into the distance. Boxed in: no way forwards, no way back. Rio punched her horn. She had to get out of here. She pressed down the passenger window. Looked across at the driver in the flash soft-top alongside her in the left-hand lane and yelled, 'When the traffic starts rolling again, don't move.'

Less than a minute later the traffic was back moving. The driver followed her instruction creating a gap big enough for her to manoeuvre into. The BMW kept going until it swerved into the hard shoulder. Rio racked up the speed.

=

7:34 p.m.

Finally some peace in the house, Frank Bell thought.

'Pat?' he called out of the front room as he pressed the replay button to start Bach's Violin Concerto in E Major again. Couldn't stand all that hysterical violin shrieking himself, but his Pat adored it, which was good enough for him: bought the roses back to her cheeks when she was feeling a bit off.

'Pat, honey, shall I come up and do your back now?' he called out, the same time the violins kicked in.

No answer. His niece, Ophelia, thought her aunt by marriage didn't like being called 'Pat' because she hated her name being shortened, but the truth was it was his special name for her and that's why she didn't like anyone else using it.

Frank walked back over to the sofa and picked up the photo of Nikki he'd been looking at before – his little baby girl, ten days old, all screwed-tight eyes and tiny features. Innocent. The snap had been taken in this very room the first day they'd bought her home. God, how he wished she'd never gone over to his brother's yesterday; how he wished he'd put his foot down for a change and made her stew and sulk her troubles away in her room. But he hadn't and now some madman was out there trying to kill her. But Nikki was safe now; in the place she was meant to be. They might have troubles like any other family but underneath it all they loved each other.

Frank got up and placed the picture back on the mantelpiece as the music swayed in the room. He ran a palm lovingly across his daughter's picture and then turned his attention to his mobile phone. He needed to make sure it was charged up in case Stephen Foster or that detective contacted them. He placed the phone at an angle on the floor near the wall socket and plugged in the charger. *Ping.* As he straightened he frowned thinking it was strange that Pat hadn't answered him. Probably crying herself silly in the bath. Poor love.

'Patsy?' he called out again as he exited the front room.

No answer.

The violins grew faint as he took the stairs and called out to her again. The first thing he noticed when he reached the landing was that the bathroom door was slightly open. Frank tensed; why was the door open? Maybe Pat had gone into the bathroom and then left to get something in their bedroom? Frank quickly walked to the bathroom, pulled the door completely back, walked in ... He staggered back when he saw what was in the bath. His wife staring at him, eyes wide, hair drifting around her face under the water. He couldn't stop his chest heaving as his breathing wheezed high and loud from his mouth.

Oh God. Oh God.

He shot forwards, jammed over the bath as his hands dived into the water. Awkwardly he grabbed Pat under the arms and dragged her upwards. Gritting his teeth, he heaved her wet, dead weight from the bath and lay her tenderly on the tiled floor. He felt the pulse in her neck.

Nothing.

Felt again.

Nothing.

He rubbed his hand anxiously against his soaking shirt.

Oh God. Oh God.

Then he remembered ...

Nikki.

He shouted his daughter's name.

No answer.

He ran for her room. Thrust the door back.

No Nikki.

Can't breathe. Can't breathe.

It was like someone had shoved a plastic bag over his head.

Frank twisted around and belted for the stairs. Ran. Almost fell just before he reached the bottom. He had to get help. His gaze skid crazily around.

Phone. Phone.

He remembered his mobile charging in the lounge. He staggered into the room and back into a world of violins. He shook his head remembering the two protection officers in the car outside. And that's when he felt it; someone else was in the room.

'Nikki?' he cried out as he turned around.

But it wasn't his beloved daughter.

7:47 p.m.

Siren still going, Rio slammed hard into the Bells' road and skidded to a halt behind another vehicle parked outside the house. Next to it stood Jack Strong.

'What's up?' he asked as soon as she reached him. 'The protection guys,' a nod of his head indicating the other officers in the car across the road, 'said everything's quiet.'

'The hit out on the girl is for five hundred grand and to be done within five days.'

Strong's face turned icy and hard. 'They'll have to get through me first.'

Rio might not like the guy but he sounded like a man up for the job.

'You think something's going on?' he continued.

'Just a feeling I've got. Once we've made sure that the situation is secure I'm going to have a chat with her parents because I want Nikki under my full protection.'

Rio turned to the car parked across the road and raised her hand to signal she wanted the protection officers to remain in place.

'I don't want to go in mob-handed and shake the family up if there's nothing out of place,' Rio explained to Strong.

But when they reached the front of the house, the way Rio hammered the knocker against the door was enough to wake up the dead. No response. Rio didn't try a second time, just moved out of the way so that Strong could kick the door in. Three solid kicks later they were in.

The house was still: a stillness Rio didn't like.

'Mr and Mrs Bell?' Rio called as she moved cautiously forwards.

Silence.

'I don't like this,' Strong whispered. 'Shall I check upstairs?'

'No. I don't know what's in that room. I need you by my side.'

Their eyes held for a fraction of a second acknowledging this was the first time that Rio had admitted she needed his help. As soon as they entered the main room, Rio saw Frank Bell's prone body on the floor. She crouched by it and felt for a pulse, then turned to Strong and shook her head. Turning back to the body she noticed something thick wrapped around his neck, some type of black lead. She peered closer and noticed something small, rectangular and silver hanging off the end of the lead. Rio quickly figured out what she was seeing – a USB attachment. Her eyes scanned the room and stopped when she saw the phone near the electrical wall socket. Whoever had killed Frank Bell she suspected had strangled him with his own mobile phone charger.

'Get the protection guys in here and call for backup and an ambulance,' Rio said to Strong as she stood up.

She ran back out into the hallway, yelling, 'Nikki, Nikki . . .' She rushed from room to room to see if there was any sign of the girl but she found none downstairs.

She took the steps two at a time, frantically shoved opened

the first door she came to: master bedroom, no one inside. The next room, a bathroom.

'Shit, shit shit,' Rio fiercely cursed as she was confronted by a naked, wet, still Patsy Bell, lying face-up on the cold floor.

Rio twisted out of the room. 'Nikki. Nikki!'

She kept up calling the girl's name as she hit the next room. The room with the picture of a teddy bear on the front. Rio inhaled a deep breath bracing herself for what she might find inside. Finally she opened the door. Empty. Mini iPad on the neatly made bed, the temperature was cold with the night air coming in from the half-opened window. Open window? That's where the girl's body was likely to be, broken on the ground outside. But when Rio looked down from the window, there was no sign of a body, only the roof of the conservatory. Back facing inside, Rio called the teenager's name again, hoping that she might have had the wits to hide again. So Rio checked the built-in wardrobe and under the bed.

'DI?' The other detective poked his head into the room. 'You need to see this.' He disappeared back on to the landing. Rio followed him and found him looking up. She followed his gaze to find the attic wide open.

'That's probably where he was hiding,' Strong explained.

'Probably came straight here when he escaped from the hospital. No wonder the protection guys didn't notice anything strange.' Rio threw her hands up to stop herself punching the wall. 'But where's Nikki?'

'Two possibilities,' Strong supplied as the sirens screamed outside. 'Either she got away through that open window in her bedroom, or the killer took her with him.'

eighteen

8:00 p.m.

Rio stared at the zipped body bag containing Frank Bell's body as it was wheeled away. The blue and red lights of the ambulances and police cars blurred in the hard-hitting rain as Rio stood outside. Despite the activity of her colleagues, an unsettled, dark quiet circled around her. And guilt. Once again she felt that she'd let down someone in her care. Detective Martin's young, eager face flashed in her mind. Then the image of how she'd last seen him, throat savagely cut . . .

'No point doing that.'

Rio tilted her wet face to find Strong in front of her.

He continued, his silver threaded black hair sleek in the rain. 'You followed procedure—'

'I should've checked the house thoroughly when I was here earlier.'

'But you didn't.' A shadow passed over Strong's face. Rio knew that he was remembering the death of the youth that had placed him squarely in the unforgiving spotlight. For the first time she wanted to know his side of the story; but wanting to know and going there were two different things.

'What we have to deal with,' he continued, 'is where we are now: a missing girl who might have done a runner, or been taken.' He tunnelled his fingers through his damp hair. 'I've

spoken to the neighbours and no one saw anything. The people
on the left said they heard raised voices earlier, which appar-
ently was no unusual thing. So maybe the kid cut out before
all this carnage happened.'

Rio shook her head. 'But the footprints in the garden were
fresh and two different shoe sizes.' She flexed her right fingers
as her thumb rubbed along her wrist scar. 'What I don't get is
why take her and not kill her at the scene instead?'

'But she might be out there,' Strong persisted, 'with someone she feels safe with. I'll get in contact with the actress
cousin because they've obviously got a tight relationship. If
she isn't there Ophelia Bell may know where she might be. Go
back inside the house and see if you can find an address
book . . . anything that can put us in touch with people who
may know where she's gone.'

Abruptly Rio stared hard at him. 'Don't forget whose
running this show.'

Strong just raised an eyebrow. 'Like I could do that, brown—'

'You call me brown sugar again dickhead and you're in the
next body bag leaving here.'

With that Rio stomped back towards the house. Made sure
she put on gloves and new protective footwear before going
inside. Instead of going straight to Nikki Bell's room she did
what she always did – a careful walk-through of the crime
scene. She took each room downstairs in turn, checking
cupboards, drawers . . . looking for any type of paperwork that
had a name, an address that could lead to the girl. She found
plenty of stuff about the mother and father – paid bills, golf
club membership, results of a smear test, more paid bills, but
nothing hinting about where or who Nikki might turn to on a
cold, wet night.

Rio took the stairs and walked into the master bedroom.
Painted a peaceful green with a three-door built-in wardrobe

and a king-size bed with an ornate iron headboard and foot-board. Two towel robes – blue and white – were neatly laid out on an easy chair by a simple dressing table. But Rio headed for the chest of drawers.

Just before she reached it, her phone pinged. Text from Strong.

Cousin not answering. Found anything?

Rio answered.

No. In parents room.
Checked the girl's room yet?
No.
I'll do it.

Rio punched off. Got back on with searching the chest of drawers. The first two drawers were full of underclothes: the first drawer those of Patsy Bell's and the second belonging to her husband. The third drawer got Rio's surprised attention. It was filled with photographs. She couldn't see them too well so she grabbed the whole drawer out and placed it on the bed. Lots of photos of a baby – a little cutie with blonde hair and soft eyes that hadn't yet made up their mind whether they were blue or grey. Rio guessed they were Nikki. But why keep them tossed together in a drawer somewhere like a shameful secret? Rio raised her eyebrows as she remembered where she kept the one and only picture she had of her dad: beneath her mattress. Made her remember him every night she got into bed, but she didn't have to look at his sorry arse every day. Whatever the Bells' reasons for tucking their daughter's baby image away wasn't helping her find who the girl might have gone to, if that's what had happened.

Rio picked the drawer up and as she started to slot it back

in its place the photos swerved to the side and a bunch of folded white papers appeared. She pulled them out. Unfolded. Read.

An adoption form. From the correspondence and letters Rio had found downstairs she recognised that it was filled in with Frank Bell's handwriting.

Adopted child's name:	Nicola
Age:	10 days old.
Name of adoption parents:	Patsy Anna Bell. Frank Stanley . . .

Frank had scratched out the next bit of the writing, obviously realising that he'd made a mistake.

Clou

Then written Bell.

Birth mother's name:

There was no birth mother's name. Or birth father's.

So little Nikki was adopted. Rio wondered if the girl knew? Was that why this house was so filled with tension and disagreements? Had Nikki found out and wanted to find her birth parents?

'Detective Inspector. Found something.'

Rio's head came up as she heard Strong's shout. She folded the adoption papers and tucked them into her bag, headed for Nikki's bedroom. She found Strong with the girl's iPad flipped open next to him on the bed.

'Think we've hit the jackpot,' he said as Rio reached him and sat down.

'Should've clicked to this one a lot sooner. My daughter was always on her mobile and living her life online.' He continued. 'Nikki is no different. Look.'

He pointed at the screen. Rio read.

Madam B: Got to get out of here!*!*
se15: Let's meet up.
Madam B: Text me where.

Rio looked up at her colleague. 'Shit, she's taken her phone. At least we know she's with someone she knows.'

But instead of affirming what she'd said, Strong scrolled up the page of Nikki's virtual conversations with se15.

'Maybe not. Read this,' Strong said quietly.

Rio again read. Her breath caught in her throat.

'She's been telling someone all about the case and that she's a witness. Stupid girl. Probably a friend of hers?'

'We can't say that because I can't load any conversations that they may have had earlier today. What if she's been communicating with the hitman and of course never realised?'

Rio swallowed hard. 'The hitman comes here and kills her parents, but before that he makes careful arrangements for her to meet him. That doesn't make any sense. Why wouldn't he have just finished the job here?'

'Who's meeting who?' Another person asked in a commanding voice.

They both looked up to find the Assistant Commissioner standing in the doorway.

Rio was back outside with Strong and the AC. The rain was as sharp as the words Pauline Tripple battered Rio with.

'Give me one reason why I should keep you on this case?'

Rio tipped her chin defiantly. 'Because you taught me to make sure I saw an investigation through to the end. You told me that there are no loose ends, no excuses: just get the job done. The only family you have are the victims in your case. You don't sleep, don't eat, don't shit, don't piss until you know how it's going to end.'

Tripple frowned. 'I don't think I used the words shit or piss.'

'Yes you did, ma'am.' Rio pulled in a heavy breath. She knew what was coming – she was off the bloody case.

'A father died in that house. And a mother . . .'

'I know, ma'am,' Rio cut in softly. 'We put all the proper procedures in place. We weren't able to do this earlier because Stephen Foster had built a wall between us and the family. As soon as more Intel came to me about the hit out on the girl I acted straight away.'

'And is the girl safe?'

Rio pressed her lips together. Once the AC found out that Nikki was long gone, probably making her way to her death – if she wasn't dead already – Rio would be lucky if she wasn't stripped of her stripes.

Rio opened her mouth, but Strong got there before her. 'Yes, ma'am.'

WTF? Rio jerked in astonishment to look at him.

'Where is she?' the older woman carried on in her clipped tone.

'A safe place.' Strong continued. 'If you'll excuse me, ma'am, but myself, the DI and the team guarding her are the only ones in the know. And we want to keep it that way for now. So, no disrespect, but that information is of a sensitive nature, which means we won't be able to tell you where she's located.'

Tripple gave him a sharp look. Then nodded. 'OK.' She switched her intimidating gaze back to Rio. 'Tomorrow at nine, on the dot, I want to personally reassure her that everything is being done to find her family's killers and that we are going to make it priority number one to keep her safe.'

Knowing she was deep in a lie not of her making, Rio nodded.

'I hear that you may have a new angle on the case. Something about a possible drug deal? That's the type of work that keeps my confidence in you, DI Wray. But tread carefully, follow procedure; we can't afford to have any more law suits on our hands.' Then she swung her gaze between both of them. 'Good work getting the girl to a safe place.'

As soon as she was gone Rio twisted in fury to face Strong. 'What the fuck did you say that for?'

He moved closer to her, his blue eyes stormy with emotion. 'You tell her Nicola Bell has become a ghost and you are off the case.'

'And why would you,' Rio's gaze snapped all over him, 'give a crap in hell about that?'

'Has it occurred to you that I want to make sure Nikki is safe as well? And that I think she'll be safer if you're on the case.' There was a sadness in his face that she remembered seeing when they'd first met Nicola and she'd asked him, with an honesty so many children had, if his daughter wasn't alive anymore. Rio didn't even know if he had kids. But what if there was something in his background that made him need to find the girl?

But Rio didn't mention any of that as she replied, 'No one said that *you* were going to be shoved off the case.'

He pushed his head slightly forwards, something other than the rain making his eyes glimmer. 'Maybe I like the touch and feel of coffee spilling all over me.'

Heat rose high in Rio's face. Two questions stormed into her mind. Was this man, of all men, hitting on her? But by far the worst question, was she enjoying it? *Down girl!*

Rio got her mind back on the dilemma in front of her, remembered what she had a reputation for. 'No. We can't do this. I don't cut corners. I play everything by the book. She wants to see the girl in the morning for fuck's sake. What are we going to do when she arrives?'

Strong moved his head out of her space. 'Your sense of duty can wait. This girl can't. We've got a lead – se15. If that's the killer –?'

'I've already said that that doesn't make sense.'

'Can you think of anyone else it's going to be?'

Rio found herself nodding like someone was pulling a string attached to the middle of her head. Then she started throwing out orders.

'Let's see if we can track her movements through her mobile phone.'

nineteen

'Well, well, well,' the woman said as her eyes lazily ran all over Jack Strong standing in the doorway with Rio. 'If it isn't Detective Jack . . .' her hooded eyes rested on his face. 'Strong in all the right places.'

Rio wasn't sure whether to roll her eyes or chuckle because the woman in the Information Bureau looked like she was about to celebrate her seventieth birthday any day now. The Bureau was on the second floor of a building that was about a mile away from The Fort. Its workers were a small team of admin staff, not police officers, and their job was to obtain information from the three main telephone towers. Rio and Strong's big problem was that any use of outside agencies was going to cost and that meant a paper trail that would show up their lie. Accessing mobile phone records was no different. So Jack had told Rio to let him do all the talking.

'Sylvia.' Strong's lips eased into a long, cheeky grin.

Strong propped himself on the end of her horseshoe-shaped workstation.

The woman watched Rio instead with a twinkle in her eye. 'Looks like I've been kicked to the kerb and you're stepping out around town with a new lady friend.' She flashed Strong a mock-sultry look.

'I wish I had the time to sweet talk you back into my arms . . .' Strong's face became serious as he dropped his voice low. 'I need to track when and where a mobile phone has been used in the last couple of hours. But I need you to keep it off the books.'

Teasing vanished from the other woman's expression. 'Since all that newspaper hacking business, things are a bit more tight around here. The higher uppers are so paranoid I think they're going to ask us soon for paperwork every time we visit the toilet.'

'Sylvia, I really need this one. Someone's life is on the line.'

The woman pursed her lips, turning the creasing around her mouth into worry lines. Abruptly she turned back to face her computer screen as she said, 'OK, let me have the number.'

Strong gave her the information she needed. Sylvia typed away as Rio and Strong anxiously waited.

'Here we go,' the older woman said, as information filled her screen. 'One call, two hours and fifteen minutes ago. Placed just outside of London.'

Rio thought that fitted in with Nikki still being at home.

'Next call was to the same number she contacted earlier. This call is placed at about one hour later near London Bridge Station. And then she texted the same number thirty-three minutes ago.'

'What's the text say?' Rio dived in.

Sylvia turned to look at her. 'No words, just a smiley face.'

'Can you find the name and address of the person she's been calling?' Strong clipped in.

Sylvia went back to her computer and a minute later said, 'Adeyemi Ibraheem. Twenty Beacon House, Peckham.'

'Of course,' Rio said. 'I should've guessed. SE15 is the post-code for Peckham.'

Rio halted at the sudden paleness on Strong's face.

'Is this address known to you?'

But instead of answering her he leaned down and kissed Sylvia on her cheek. The skin on the older woman's cheeks screwed up in pleasure.

'Can we access the PNC from your computer?' he asked her, the colour back in his face.

Sylvia swung out of her chair, stretched. 'I need to make a cuppa. But not too long.'

Strong was in her seat as she walked away. He typed away for a few minutes.

'Bingo,' he said.

Rio leaned in close and saw a photo of a young black man. 'Adeyemi Ibraheem,' she read aloud. 'Twenty years old. Juvvie record for shoplifting when he was sixteen – got community service and put into a mentoring programme. But no other . . .' Her voice stopped again before she read on. 'But he's got a much older brother – Chiwetel Ibraheem - who has done time for breaking and entering, robbery and gang affiliation. You think they could be part of the Greenbelt Gang?'

'It seems to add up, but no one said they were black.'

'No one could see what colour they were.' Irritation drew lines across her forehead. 'And if they'd spoken how would anyone know they were black? Maybe our gang were all meant to be singing Bob Marley's "One Love" in between telling their victims how they're going to set them on fire if they don't do what they're told?'

Ignoring her sarcastic words Strong said, 'And Twenty Beacon House is on the Bonnington Estate.' Abruptly he jerked out of the seat as his face grew pale again.

'You'll have to go without me.'

They were back outside in the dark, Strong leaning against the brickwork of the building that housed the Information Bureau with Rio facing him. Silence lay for a few seconds between them. Rio could see whatever he was about to tell her was serious. And she wasn't going to like it.

'That case I was involved in,' Strong quietly started – Rio could hear something in his voice; it wasn't remorse, but she'd swear it was grief – 'where the teenager died in the cell. He lived with his family on the Bonnington Estate. I can't go back there. Can't do it.'

Rio knew this wasn't the time or place to ask him what had happened, but she could see that he was having a massive fight with his emotions. She didn't know this man, didn't know what to say. So she did what Rio Wray did best, kicked the emotions aside and got back on with the case.

'I can't go on my own—'

'Don't you think I know that?' Strong's response was savage and loud. He pushed off the building. 'I can't go back on that estate. All I ever wanted to be was a cop. Plain and simple,' he said, his voice more gentle. 'Sure, I'm a bit rough around the edges, but that didn't mean I went out of my way to do a bad job. I was one of the best.' His palms rubbed together as he said the last with pride. 'Then one messed-up day—'

Strong looked away from her as his nostrils flared. 'I can't help you . . .'

Rio let out a long breath. 'Then I'm going to need to find someone who can.' She thought instantly of John 'Mac' Macdonagh. She was reluctant to contact him, knowing he'd had his own troubles recently, but what choice did she have? 'There's another officer I could ask who will keep his mouth shut.'

Rio pulled out her mobile. The line connected with Mac's. Rang six times. Voicemail. She snapped off the connection. The only option left to her was one she didn't want to take. Nikki Bell's face planted itself in her mind reminding her that she had to use any options she could.

Rio dialled another number. 'Listen . . .' Her voice grew louder. 'You cut this call and . . . Meet me . . . You heard right, meet me. I'll be parked up by the entrance to the Bonnington Estate in Peckham. Fifty minutes. Be there.'

Her heartbeat was pounding in a way that wasn't healthy.

'Who are you meeting?' Strong asked.

Face grim, she didn't answer him as she walked away.

Sylvia watched Jack Strong and his colleague being swallowed up by the darkness as they moved away from the building. She turned away and moved out of the office to the drafty corridor near the top of the stairwell. Pulled out her mobile.

'They were here. About five minutes ago . . .'

twenty

The north Peckham that Rio's BMW parked up in was very different from the one she'd remembered policing years ago. The residential skyline dominated by miles of walkways, that had once been the notorious North Peckham Estate, was gone. In its place were low-rise homes that weren't jammed one on top of the other, but with spaces that gave residents privacy and maybe that chance to breathe more easily.

The homes on Bonnington Street were half-hidden in the semi-light of two lamp posts and the moon which was round and strong above. The quiet unnerved Rio as she looked through the windshield trying to find the person she waited for. She checked her watch.

10:12 p.m.

He was late. Maybe he wasn't coming, which wouldn't surprise her. Bollocks, she might have to do this one on her own. She might—

Two rapid taps sounded on the glass of the passenger-side window. Rio's hand reached for her baton as she looked across. Her hand relaxed.

Calum.

Rio released the lock on the door. He slid inside, taking care with his right leg. Shut the door. The air closed in around

Rio; she felt the heat coming off his body. It felt good. It felt bad.

'I take it you haven't asked me here for a quickie in the back seat?' Calum asked, his mocking green gaze looking straight ahead.

'Nicola Bell's parents were murdered this evening.'

Calum swore.

'I wouldn't be here with you if I didn't have any option, so—'

'Yeah, yeah, yeah, you're not telling me anything I haven't already figured out.' Now he looked at her with a sideways glance. 'I gave you a heads-up about your girl, which doesn't give you the right to start stalking me.'

'Which begs the question what are you doing here? Why come running to the woman you told to stay the hell away?' His gaze shifted away from her, confirming what she suspected was his motivation. So she told him. 'Whatever you've cooked up with Foster means you need to stay near to this investigation and what better way to do it than to remain cosy and close to the detective leading on it. So let's agree to drop the bullshit drama.'

She expected some outraged denial speech in response, but what she got was silence as he hitched his stare back at her while his green gaze lingered on her face.

'What do you need me to do?' Calum finally said.

'First thing is, leave our past in the past. We don't go there. This isn't about you and me, it's about a young kid who's probably in danger.'

'So the girl cut out on you.' His expression became stern. 'After what I told you earlier, you should've been sitting on her twenty-four-seven—'

'I think someone is holding her in one of the houses on this street—'

'So why haven't you got an armed response vehicle with you? What the heck are you doing here on your own?'

'Because as soon as someone knows I let her slip between my fingers I'm off this case.'

Calum smiled. 'Never thought I'd see the day when Ray Gun would be going all Lone Ranger.'

Rio's hand curled into a fist. Sometimes this man just made her want to . . .

'You deck me, baby,' Calum warned softly, 'and who's going to get you out of this mess?'

Rio's hand fell flat.

Calum's gaze scanned the street. 'Which house are we talking about?'

She gave him the address and the name of their target.

'You tooled up?' Calum asked.

'The usual – CS, taser and baton.'

'You might need one of these.'

Rio couldn't help but gasp when he pulled out a revolver, reminding her of her stint in the armed response unit.

'No guns,' she told him firmly. 'This needs to be done quick and quiet and clean. We knock at the door and take it from there.'

Calum's response showed his frustration. 'If the girl's alive and we knock on the door it could lead to her immediate death.'

'We do this my way, which means no gun play.'

Rio knocked on the beige coloured door as Calum waited half a step behind and to the side of her. The house was well kept from the outside and the mini-garden in the front appeared well loved and cared for. Rio tensed as she heard the slap of feet from inside. Her warrant card was already in her hand.

The outdoor light came on. The door partially opened, a

security chain holding it back. Rio saw half of the face of an older black woman, a black, satin nightcap on her head.

'Yes?' The woman's voice was soft, Nigerian and edgy.

Rio showed her warrant card. 'I'm Detective Inspector Rio Wray. Are you Mrs Ibraheem?'

'If this is about Chiwetel, he doesn't live here . . .' Her voice cracked. 'Has something happened to him?'

'If I could come in, please.'

The woman unhooked the chain and opened up. She stepped back as Rio and Calum entered. The scent of food cooked earlier lay thick in the air. The woman was large in both height and size. She clutched the ends of a bright red dressing gown. Her dark face was sad and mournful as if she had been in this position before.

'We need to speak to your son Adeyemi.'

Suddenly the woman straightened her back as her arms dropped to her side. 'He's not here.' She shifted her body so that she stood almost in the middle of the hallway like she was trying to protect the rest of the house.

Rio inched closer. 'I think that you're lying to me—'

'No.' Mrs Ibraheem gazed over Rio's shoulder. 'He's good boy—'

One of the doors leading off the hallway opened. A young man stepped outside. As soon as he saw Rio he twisted around and started running. Calum was already after him, bolting past both women. He lunged forwards and grabbed the man by the back of his T-shirt and flung him face first against the wall.

'Leave him alone,' his mother cried. 'He's done nothing wrong.'

But Rio ignored her as she strode towards Calum and his captive. The man shifted his face so that only his profile was pressed against the wall. His breathing was ragged and hard.

'Are you Adeyemi Ibraheem?' Rio asked.

'Of course he is,' his mother called out. 'You think I let strangers sleep in my house?'

'Where is Nicola Bell?'

The eyelid that Rio could see flickered as he replied, 'Don't know no Nikki Bell.'

'She didn't call her Nikki, Dumbo.' Calum slammed him hard against the wall again. 'Tell us where she is?'

'No, I—'

But he never finished as the door of the room he'd come out of was flung open. Nicola Bell stood in the doorway and yelled, 'Leave him alone. He's my boyfriend.'

twenty-one

10:20 p.m.

Nikki Bell sat shaking on the camel-brown sofa in the living room, wrapped in the arms of her boyfriend. To say that hearing about her parents' death had knocked her for six was putting it way too mildly. Her legs had gone from underneath her as the shock and tears came. Adeyemi had carried her into the family room, while Rio sat opposite and Calum and Mrs Ibraheem hovered in the doorway.

The sixteen-year-old looked across at Rio. Her skin was pasty in contrast to the golden-blonde hair that hung over half her face. She flicked her hair impatiently aside.

'They didn't want me to see Ade, just like they didn't like me seeing cousin Lia. Not because he was black and his parents are Nigerian, they didn't have a problem with that. They hated that he's Muslim. What did they think he was going to do? Blow up their conservatory? Not all Muslims are terrorists.' Her voice broke. 'I wish they were still here so I could tell them . . .' Her voice fell away as her head moved in a bewildered side-to-side movement, fresh tears spilling from her mournful, grey eyes.

Her boyfriend's arm tightened protectively around her as he spoke for the first time. 'Is that why her parents are dead? Did someone go to her house to kill her? That man who was in the hospital earlier?' Although he spoke with anger there was a natural gentleness in his tone.

'I'm sorry,' Rio answered, 'I'm not able to divulge details about the investigation—'

'For fuck's sake—' He exploded back.

But his mum's voice stopped him in his tracks. She spoke rapidly in a language Rio couldn't understand and then finished up in English. ' . . . It's best for your *friend* to go.'

Ah, so there was trouble on the home front. Mum didn't approve of Nikki.

'How did the two of you meet?' Rio asked, her tone softening.

The lovebirds gazed at each other and shared a private smile. It was Ade who answered.

'I've been studying up at Oxford. Part way through my second year.' His hand moved up and down against his girl-friend's arm, not a rub more a comforting shuffle. 'We met at a sixteen to nineteen student conference last year—'

'She's not right for you,' his mum jumped in, her opposition out in the open. 'Do you know what they call children from Peckham? Thugs. Criminals. Animals. One son is already lost to me. But not my Ade.' A bittersweet smile curved her lips. 'He's made me proud. Oxford University.' Her chest pushed proudly forwards. 'That girl is no good for him.' She made that tutting sound that most black people called 'kissing your teeth' and bustled past Calum out of the room, her back slightly bent.

The couple on the sofa wore new strained expressions as if another death had occurred in their lives. Rio wasn't going to get involved in this family drama.

'Nikki, you can't go back to your home.'

'Can I stay with cousin Lia?' Her face lit up for the first time. 'I used to stay with her on the day of my birthday, but then Mum and Dad said I couldn't anymore.'

More family drama Rio didn't need to know about.

Rio pointed at Calum as she stood up. 'This is my friend Calum Burns.' *Friend? Yeah, what a joke that was.* 'I just need to talk him.'

She moved past Calum into the tight passage and he followed her.

'So how are you going to look after your young cub, Mommy Bear?' he asked. He leaned more on his left side.

'I should organise to take her to one of the safe houses,' Rio whispered.

'Too obvious. The hitter might already be on that trail. He found out about where she lived pretty quickly, so there's no reason he can't do the same for a safe house. It needs to be somewhere totally off the radar. A place only a few people are going to know about.'

Rio leaned closer to him. 'Yeah, but if *you* know you're going to go blowing it into Foster's ear.'

Calum shoved a mock-shock look onto his face. 'You're the one, sweetheart, who said to leave the bullshit drama outside the door.'

'I ain't your sweetheart.'

He leaned his mouth close to her face, his heated breath coating her skin. 'Think the law might have something different to say about that.'

A stubborn silence rose between them, each mentally daring the other to step through the door he'd banged wide open.

Calum pulled his head back, firmly closing the door again. 'OK, cards on the table about what I'm doing for Foster: he wants me to use my contacts to find the gang and it seems to me that your suggestion that we team up is the best way for that to happen.'

Rio reared back like boiling water was heading for her face.

'This is an official investigation which will be done officially . . .'

'Like going into a potentially dangerous situation in downtown Peckham without backup?'

Rio twisted her lips. 'That was a one-off, which paid off.' Her glance slid to the room where her traumatised charge was. She needed help; couldn't do this on her own. But Calum? With so much crap strewn between them, was she crazy to even think of him? But Stephen Foster had already involved him. So had she. If she kept him in plain sight she'd know every move he was making. What was that saying – oh yeah – keep your friends close and your enemies even closer.

'Deal. We'll both keep her safe. The only other people who will know where she is are DSI Newman and Jack Strong—'

'Jack "boys only" Strong?' Calum looked incredulous. 'You are kidding.'

'Wish I was. It's a long story I'll tell you when we take Nikki to a place she'll be safe.'

'Which is where?'

'Somewhere even you don't know about.'

11:30 p.m.

Nikki's place of safety turned out to be a house in one of London's most expensive districts: Notting Hill, West London. It wasn't one of those plush, grand old houses that the area was well known for, but a three-bed mews house tucked around the corner from the All Saints Road.

'You going to tell me where *this* is?' Calum asked. Nikki was sandwiched between him and Rio outside. The girl held a black, lime-green handled holdall that she'd packed when she'd taken off to her boyfriend's.

As Rio opened up she answered, 'My mum's home. Now

mine and my brother's since she passed away three months ago.'

Calum whistled. 'If I knew that you were sitting on a pile of cash I might've . . .'

His words dribbled away at the hard stare she threw him. Although the place had been empty since her mum's death Rio came over once a week to keep it dust free. People kept telling her to sort through her mother's things as quickly as possible after the funeral, but she hadn't had the heart to do it, so the home Ruthie Wray had loved so much remained untouched.

Rio popped the small hallway light on. She soaked up the emotional warmth of the house, as she always did. The red-leaf wallpaper resembled tacky wrapping paper and the green flowered carpet was an interior designer's nightmare, but to Rio they were filled with memories of happy times.

As Nikki let out a long yawn Rio told her, 'You can have my old bedroom—'

'This I have to see,' Calum interrupted.

'No, this is a girl thing,' Rio quickly got in. 'Wait in the kitchen. You'll find the coffee in the cupboard near the cooker. I take mine—'

'No milk.'

Rio stared after Calum as he made his way to the kitchen in that precise, even step movement he'd developed from what-ever damage had been done to his right leg. He'd remembered about her being lactose intolerant, which meant – she realised with an involuntary thrill – that he hadn't been able to push her completely from his mind in the last three years.

She reached the bedroom with Nikki. She hadn't wanted Calum to see the room because it was too personal: this was the small space where she'd grown up, crafted herself into the woman she was today. Who knew what Calum would figure out about her if he popped his head round the door? The room wasn't too big, wasn't too small, just the perfect size for a girl learning how to spread her wings.

Rio shook off the comforting nostalgia as she turned back to Nikki. 'I'll get you a towel, show you how the shower works and then it's beddy-bye time for you my girl.' Rio paused, looking deeply into the girl's eyes. 'I'm really so very sorry about your mum and dad.'

Nikki's teeth played nervously against her bottom lip. Then she swiftly moved her gaze from Rio to the mahogany chest of drawers near the single bed. The teen didn't speak. Sorrow was such a killer of an emotion. Abruptly Nikki started to move towards the chest of drawers, then picked up the solitary item that rested on top of it.

Shit. She'd meant to stash that away.

'Is that you with your mum?' Nikki asked as she held out the small picture frame.

Rio moved slowly forwards. When she was close enough she peered at the photo the frame held.

Mum. Her: twelve years old. And . . .

She didn't even want to look at the other person; that meant becoming intimately involved in a past she'd long let go.

'Yeah. That was taken in the sitting room a couple of days after I turned twelve.'

'Did your dad take the picture? Is that why he's not in the photo?'

Rio pulled the photo gently from the girl's hand. 'Nope. He wasn't the stay-at-home type of dad. He was long gone by the time that snap was taken.'

'And the little boy in the picture?'

Rio refused to look at the photo. Instead she opened the top drawer of the chest of drawers. 'That's my younger brother.'

'What's his name?'

Rio placed the photo very gently on the bottom of the lavender scented drawer.

Rio didn't feel like lying this time. 'Frederick.'

She slammed the drawer shut.

Fifteen minutes later, Nikki was tucked up in bed and Rio was sitting at the small table in the kitchen facing her one-time good friend and fleeting lover, a mug of milk-free coffee between her palms. Her bag lay carelessly thrown on the floor by her leg.

'How many people know about this place?' Calum asked. His green gaze appeared sleepy, his skin more pale than usual, as if he were in pain.

Rio rubbed the pads of her thumb along the smooth hardness of the mug. 'Just the people who I told you officially need to know, that I mentioned earlier, and a handful of my relatives. Most of my people live in Sheffield, so there won't be any surprise calls.' She hesitated a few seconds before speaking again because she knew what she was about to say wouldn't go down well. 'I'm going to need someone here all of the time—'

Calum's eyes widened as he shook his head. 'Nooo waaay. Babysitting is defo not part of the services I provide. Assign Jack Strong to hand-holding patrol.'

Rio had thought of that; it was the perfect way to keep him out of her hair. But it was a no-can-do situation because Strong was helping her work the drug angle.

'You're the one who said we should team up, remember,' Rio pushed. 'Plus if I ask another officer to do it, it's one more person in the chain who knows where Nikki is. The only person I can trust is someone who's more hardcore, more ruthless than a hitman.'

'Is that how you see me?' His question was husky. Unexpected.

Rio fought for words, surprised that she might have hurt his feelings. 'Not on a personal level, but professionally you're known as one of the best freelance consultants around. You set up your stall and reputation in a pretty quick timeframe, which couldn't have been easy with your accident – whatever that was.' She couldn't help chucking the last tartly in.

And she couldn't help what came out next.

'Why wouldn't you let me see you?' Rio moved her hands away from the warmth of the cup and lay them flat against the coolness of the table.

Calum sighed. 'Don't do this, Rio–'

'Do what? Ask the question I have every right to ask after three years.' Her vocal chords ceased up in her throat. *Why is this still so effing painful?* 'I tried to see you three times. *Three times.* Every time I was turned away. Told, only relatives allowed.' A sharp look passed between them. 'I came one more time and was told that you weren't there anymore. I tried your place.' She shrugged. 'Where did you go? On holiday? Another woman? Turn your back on me–'

Calum swore. 'It wasn't like that–'

'That letter you sent says it was.'

He leaned across the table. 'You want the truth?' Suddenly he shoved away from the table and staggered to his feet. He pulled a cutting breath in, filled with pain.

Seeing his pain Rio too stood, filled with remorse. 'OK, that was out of order. Wrong time, wrong place.' She took a step closer to him. 'Do you need some painkillers?'

He just looked at her, then started laughing. It was the first time she'd heard him laugh all day and she wished it wasn't. This wasn't the laugh she remembered. The one that turned cheekiness and an outrageous joy for life into memorable sounds. No, this laugh hacked up the type of noise it was best not to remember.

'I told you to leave this alone,' he said simply.

Rio swallowed. 'Forget about me, but you can't leave that girl sleeping down the hallway alone. When I think of how close Nikki came to meeting her death tonight . . . You're the only one who can protect her when I'm not here.' Rio moved quickly back, bent down and started rummaging madly in her bag. She straightened as she pulled out Nikki's adoption papers, and handed them over.

She gave Calum time to absorb what he was reading before saying, 'The Bells gave this girl a great start in life and I'm going to make it my business to make sure she keeps living the good life they had mapped out for her.' Rio stepped back from him. 'You'll be helping Foster out by keeping his client safe.'

'Still as bossy and bullish as ever, Ray Gun.'

Usually she hated his use of that name but his teasing was a welcome intrusion.

'OK. I'll do it,' he finally agreed. 'I'll be back here at nineish in the morning.'

He left and it was a good few minutes that Rio remained alone in the kitchen. Then she spoke to the dark emptiness Calum had left behind him.

'Thank you.'

twenty-two

'Meat is murder.'

Rio gritted her teeth at Nikki's words the next morning. The teen was staring down at the bacon breakfast Rio had got up early to specially make for her. The girl had woken up like she'd had a night sleeping with a nest of bees and sporting a pair of gloves her mother would never approve of – fishnet, fingerless, except for the garter-like pink lace around the middle finger. That's if her mum wasn't dead, Rio quickly reminded herself.

Why is it so cold?

Why don't you have Netflix or Amazon Instant?

Why can't I have Hamlet and my mobile?

Moody, rude and downright disrespectful – that's why Rio had never thought about having kids; she didn't fancy spending the rest of her life answering the monotonous question 'Why?' But she had to give this girl some significant slack; four people in her family, including her parents, had been murdered yesterday.

'I bet you didn't check to see if it has peanuts in it?' Nikki carried on.

'Are peanuts murder as well?' A silly image of a row of peanuts facing a firing squad invaded her mind.

Nikki's eyes snapped. 'I've got an allergy to them. If I eat even a trace I'll end up in the hospital.'

'I need to tell the medical staff about my daughter's nut allergy.'

Rio heard Patsy Bell's voice in the hospital. She should have remembered.

Nikki flicked the two rashers of bacon onto the table. Stared back at Rio with 'I dare ya' eyes.

Rio didn't rise to the challenge. Instead she leaned over to grab the bacon when her phone rang. She twisted away and moved to the counter near the window and grabbed the phone up.

As she passed Nikki she said firmly, 'You're in my house now, my rules, so eat the rest of your breakfast.'

In the hallway she answered the call. 'DI Wray.'

'Sounds like you didn't get much sleep last night.'

Hearing the brittle tone of Assistant Commissioner Tripple Rio squared her shoulders. 'Good morning, ma'am. I was just about to ring you so that you could come and see Nicola Bell.'

'I don't think that there's much need for that. Not now that you've found her.'

Stunned Rio couldn't speak. Then the words were tumbling from her tongue. 'Ma'am ... um ...' Shit, where were the words when she needed them?

'You looked too surprised when Detective Strong said that you had the girl safely hidden. I trusted you to get her back, but just to keep you on your toes I told you I needed to see her this morning. And of course the first place a good officer starts when looking for someone is tracking their mobile phone. When one of my contacts at the Information Bureau, who was also my PA many years ago, had alerted me that you had a good trace on her I relaxed.'

'Yes, ma'am,' was all Rio could say.

'But I'm warning you, Wray, don't let it happen again.'

'No, ma'am. I'm following up a significant lead this morning.'

'Good. I'll leave you with a warning about something else.' Rio waited. 'I know that you want to rise up in the ranks, probably aiming to be the first black, female Commissioner. Then you've got to learn that when you're stretching the truth, keep the emotion well hidden on your face.'

Rio stood there for a full minute after the call had ended, slightly shaken, but also pleased that the lie was in the open now. The Met's mission to be seen as honest and transparent was one she took to heart.

When Rio got back to the kitchen, she sighed with relief when she saw that the girl had finished all of the food on her plate, the bacon still abandoned on the table.

'Mr Burns will be here soon to look after you—'

Nikki's lip curled 'I don't need looking after. I'm not some baby; I can take care of myself.'

Rio played it like she hadn't heard her. 'Go get yourself washed up.'

'I'll shout when I need you to put my nappy on,' the girl muttered smartly as she left the room.

Rio leaned against one of the walls. *God, what have I done to deserve this teen hell?* The doorbell went. Trying to shrug off a feeling of total harassment, Rio walked out to the hall and towards the door. Standing on the doorstep, with a heavy looking black holdall bag in his hand, was Calum. He appeared fresher this morning, his hair gelled neatly back and his skin more evenly toned.

'So how's our girl today?' he asked as he moved slowly inside.

'Driving me nuts.' More nuts! Gee-sus.

Calum lifted the corner of his mouth with pity. 'Any girl

who names her iPad after a dead Danish prince is not going to be easy.'

'What?'

'Hamlet. Must be something going on in the Bell family about that play.' Seeing the look of confusion on her face he added, 'Ophelia. She's Hamlet's crush.' He stumbled slightly as he moved.

'Are you getting whatever is going on with your leg seen to?' For the first time Rio felt comfortable enough with him to ask. She didn't like seeing her own one-time crush in pain.

But he made no reply, moving towards the cute-sized sitting room. Rio mentally shrugged; if he didn't want to talk about it that was his business. By the time she got to the room he was already unzipping his bag and pulling out a laptop.

'I'll need to be working while I'm here.' He didn't look around at her, instead drew out a plug and lead.

'If there are any problems you call me straight away. Oh yeah, Nikki's allergic to peanuts, so watch what she eats.'

He looked up at her. 'Sure thing, Ray Gun.'

'And get her to draw a picture of what she saw the gunmen wearing over their faces. I asked her to do it for me, but she wasn't playing ball. Maybe you'll have more luck.'

After Rio gave him a detailed description of the killers' disguise her mobile went off again. Jack Strong.

'We've located Cornelius Bell. A place called The Rebels' Collective . . .' Rio listened and took the details.

Before she left she spoke to Calum one more time. 'You text me on the hour, every hour, to let me know that Nikki is safe.'

twenty-three

9:40 a.m.

'Wait here,' Rio told Jack Strong as he started to exit her BMW parked on the road facing The Rebels' Collective.

'We work the same way the animals were herded onto Noah's Ark, lass,' he answered. 'In twos.'

'Not this time. It's better if I tell him about his family on my own.'

Strong leaned back in the passenger seat. 'You're the boss.'

A few seconds later Rio stared up at the building that housed The Rebels' Collective, one of the many abandoned and forgotten pubs that were littered all over London. Three-storeys high, it stood on the intersection of two streets, as if it had once been the cornerstone of the community. The ground-floor windows and door were lost behind graffiti and poster-splattered wooden boards and corrugated sheets. But upstairs, different coloured bed sheets doubled-up as curtains, giving the upper building a rainbow flag feel. The only grandness it might have once held was in its faded pub sign: The Lady's Love.

Rio moved to stand in front of the large corrugated sheet that blocked the main door. No knocker or bell in sight, so she pounded her fist against it three times. She heard a noise shifting somewhere close behind the door, but no one spoke, no one opened up. So Rio slammed her fist twice more.

'What do you want?' Male voice. Irritated with strains of weariness.

'I need to speak to Cornelius.'

'What for?' The voice was stronger this time as if it was directly behind the door.

'I'm a police officer. I need to talk to him about a serious matter.'

Silence. Then, 'He isn't here.'

Now it was Rio's turn to become very irritated. 'If you don't open up I'll be back and this time I won't be on my own, the drugs squad will be right beside me.'

More silence. Then a loud thud, a click, a scraping noise as the corrugated sheet was shoved forwards. A man appeared – strapping build; mid-twenties; white; dark hair, that was a number one cut all over. His nose was pierced and he displayed a multitude of badges on the top half of the T-shirt he wore. Rio couldn't read any of the taglines of the badges from where she stood, but taking in the way the man glared at her, she guessed they said stuff like 'Death to the Pigs'. Only when Rio caught the fluffy, pink slippers at the end of combat trousers and the way the T-shirt slightly pushed out at the chest did she realise that she was dealing with a woman.

'I need to speak to Cornelius urgently, so I'd rather check out for myself that he's not around.'

The woman didn't move; instead her expression became more defiant. 'You're betraying your race by becoming a puppet of the institutional racist cop system.'

Oh, I'm dealing with one of those.

'And you'd know all about racism against black folks, being black yourself,' Rio countered back. 'Well some of us don't have a trust fund to look forward to when we're thirty to help us forget our troubles.'

The other woman's face pinked up. In Rio's experience,

these trust-fund liberals were always so easy to pick out. Always the ones sprouting the most shit about how they were going to save the oppressed of the world with their bare hands. They didn't know dick.

'I don't have time to debate why you're still using the term "race" when it doesn't exist because it's a social construct made up by the Victorians,' Rio carried on, bored. 'But if you're a member of the *human race*, like the rest of us, you'll let me in because what I've got to tell Cornelius is going to hit him hard.'

The woman looked shaken by Rio's know-it-all speech. Finally she pushed the makeshift entrance wider and stepped back and to the side. 'He's on the second floor, first room near the stairs.'

Rio pressed her lips tight as she entered and was immediately hit by the stench of recently puffed skunk. The place wasn't the wreck she was expecting. It showed the signs of too many people sharing such a small space – a few items of clothing scattered around, a sleeping bag neatly folded on a wooden bench with a plush-red cushion back – but it was clean. The wooden bar gleamed and the windows were stained glass that showcased eye-grabbing shades of green. The floor wasn't floorboards as Rio expected, but red, quarry tiles. They were chipped and broken in places, but Rio could almost feel the footsteps of past generations who must have come here to drink and ease off the stresses of life.

Rio felt eyes upon her, twisted her head slowly and found a man lying on another red-cushioned bench giving her the evil eye.

'We don't call each other he or she here,' the woman who'd let her in announced behind her. Rio didn't turn, but waited for her next life lesson. 'We don't use gender barriers to stereotype or make assumptions about people. We use their name or–'

'I get it,' Rio abruptly cut in. Beneath her breath she muttered, 'Yeah, we're all Martians from another galaxy.'

She knew she shouldn't be funning with someone else's political beliefs and actually saw some merits in what Miss Pink Fluffy Slippers was going on about, but all she could think about was telling a son that his parents were dead.

Rio passed the end of the bar and hit the stairs. These hadn't been as fortunate as the bar area: the bannister half-gone and steps with holes. Carefully she made her way to the first floor. Saw the closed door to the room she was after. Knocked.

'We're sleeping.' Woman's voice, high and muggy.

Rio opened the door and walked inside. The air was high with skunk. A see-though, blue bong was on the floor, near where a couple lay beneath a duvet on a mattress. The woman – more a girl really – was white, with short, electric-blue dreads, and the man's face was buried beneath the duvet with only his hair visible – one of those man-buns that some of the young white guys were sporting nowadays. The woman's pink nipple peaked just above the duvet, but she didn't seem too bothered about it.

'I'm Detective Inspector Rio Wray. Are you Cornelius?' Rio addressed the man.

'No. Connie's in the room at the end.' He pulled the duvet over his head.

Rio closed the door behind, took long strides to the room facing her at the end of the landing, knocked. No response. She didn't bother politely signalling she needed to come in, instead she grabbed the handle and opened. Frowned. This wasn't a room, but a store cupboard. Why would the guy in the other room have said . . .?

Rio snapped around and ran back to the room she'd just been in. She shoved inside the room. The woman was alone now, sitting up with the duvet wrapped around her. But all Rio saw was the makeshift curtain flapping at the wide open window. Rio rushed over, looked down, saw the man who she now knew was Cornelius Bell, naked, except for a pair of boxers, jumping onto the iron balcony below on the first floor.

Rio knew she had to get around the back quickly. She hooked her leg over the window then froze when she saw that the thin side street that Cornelius Bell was heading for was blocked by a high-wall at one end and an open exit at the other. That meant the only route for his absurd getaway led to the front of the former pub.

'Leave him alone,' his bed mate squealed as Rio jerked her leg back inside.

Rio ignored her as she rushed out of the room and bolted down the stairs that creaked and whined with her unsteady weight. The man and woman downstairs were both on their feet when Rio reached the bar area. They looked agitated, ready for a fight.

'Stay out of my bloody way,' Rio stormed as she picked up speed and rushed past them.

She used her shoulder as a battering ram, guessing that Pink Fluffy Slippers hadn't locked the corrugated sheet behind her. The makeshift door gave with a crash. Rio sprinted into the daylight. First thing she saw was Detective Strong bolting out of her car.

'Stay back,' she yelled at him.

Rio twisted her gaze onto her target, and caught the back of Cornelius as he motored along the street. She used everything she'd learned as her school's former female one hundred metres champion to follow. But Cornelius was no pushover, maintaining the distance between them. The burn of rising blood and adrenaline kicked into every muscle that Rio had. Her mouth gaped wide as she pumped in oxygen helping her to accelerate even more.

Cornelius swung around a corner. Five seconds later Rio did the same. The distance between them started closing. He was tiring, while her strength was only getting stronger.

'Cornelius,' she yelled out.

He flicked his head over his shoulder and she saw his expression was like a terrified rabbit bang in the middle of headlights. He stumbled. Rio didn't. He crashed against the side of a parked car and slumped to the floor. Panting Rio reached him. Stopped. Running footsteps sounded behind her.

'Leave me alone,' Cornelius desperately let out between harsh, uneven breaths. 'I haven't done anything wrong.'

Rio softened her voice. 'You're not in trouble. I've got bad news.'

'DI, you alright?' Rio didn't answer Jack Strong; instead she kept her attention fixed on Cornelius Bell.

He gazed up at her like he still didn't believe her.

'It's your mother and father.' Rio took a steady breath. 'I'm afraid your aunt and uncle as well. I'm sorry but they're all dead.'

Maurice and Linda Bell's son's face crumbled. Lying in the road, in his underwear, he bawled like a newborn babe.

Cornelius's head was bowed as he sat on the mattress back in his room at The Rebels' Collective. He now wore a pair of shorts, oversized T-shirt and his man-bun looked like it was about to fall apart. His girlfriend's arm wrapped protectively around his shoulders. Rio realised that his companion was much younger than she'd first suspected. Although she was thin, she had all the puppy fat on her face of a teenager who hadn't yet reached eighteen. And the skittish expression in her eyes that Rio had seen on too many runaways.

'How can they have been murdered?' Cornelius raised his head to look at Rio. His eyes were bloodshot and glazed.

Rio leaned back against the wall, near the box that was a makeshift table covered with a yellow cloth and a photograph of a young boy. Jack Strong was stationed near the door. 'Our investigation is obviously still ongoing, but the evidence we have so far suggests that this may be the work of what the press are calling the Greenbelt Gang—'

'Who?'

It hadn't even occurred to Rio that he might not be in touch with the latest news – probably too busy enjoying the high-life with his skunk and smooching with his lady friend beneath the sheets.

'Connie, you know, that crew who've been out on the rob and killed that woman who'd only been married for a couple of weeks.' For the first time the girl spoke. Brummie accent and soft, Rio heard the care and comforting way she spoke to her boyfriend.

'I remember,' he answered, but confusion still lit up his face. 'Did anyone see anything?'

Rio stalled. The less people who knew about Nicola the better. But she was his cousin and his sister was bound to tell him anyway.

'You're not telling me something,' he continued, judging the way she suddenly tightened her lips. 'Ophelia will let me know—'

Rio pushed herself off the wall. 'Your sister said that you don't speak to each other.'

Cornelius dropped his head again and muttered, 'We don't. Well, not since she hit the celeb Z-list and doesn't want everyone to know that her bruv is living in some hole in South-East London. Probably asking her agent how to best play this all out for maximum PR exposure.'

His words were bitter and harsh. No, not much love lost between this brother and sister.

'What I'm about to tell you, you have to keep to yourself,' Rio said, but her gaze flicked to the girlfriend.

'Cookie's OK. She won't tell anyone. She doesn't feel comfortable talking to other people, even the others here when I'm not around.'

Connie and Cookie. If this had been any other situation Rio would have laughed.

Cookie dropped her arm from his shoulder and got to her feet. She was tiny and small-boned, a white girl with blue dreads. Her hair rocked as she shook her head and spoke directly to her boyfriend.

'No worries, babe, I'll be downstairs.'

When she was gone Rio told him about Nicola. His reaction was more explosive than his sister's. He shot to his feet and stared out of the window.

'You're joking. Nikki saw . . . Ania being murdered—'

'We're still trying to clarify exactly what she saw, but whoever did this didn't know that she was there.'

He shuffled around and stuck his hands in the pockets of his shorts. His hair floppe over his forehead giving Rio a glimpse of the boy he had once been. 'She's a good kid. A bit nutty every now and again, but it can't have been easy for her to see what she did. Where is she now?'

'In the hospital—'

'Why? Was she hurt?' Alarm raised his voice.

Rio shook her head. 'She was traumatised when she saw the bodies—'

'Bloody hell.' He wiped the back of his hand against his mouth. Rio saw that his hand was shaking.

'Put some clothes on. Get some food in your belly. Then ring your sister.'

He wrapped his hands around himself as he nodded.

Rio turned and signalled with her head at Strong who

opened the door. His phone rang just as Rio decided to face Cornelius again with a question that had been bugging her. It didn't have anything to do with the investigation, but she hated loose ends.

'Your sister doesn't appear to like your parents' solicitor, Stephen Foster. Why is that?'

'I don't know.' She could hear the threat of tears back in his voice. 'I've never even met this Stephen Foster. All I know is that my mother and father are dead.'

Rio left him to his grief and turned back to Strong who just punched off his mobile.

Once they were outside the room he said, blues eyes gleaming, 'Next stop is Gary Larkin. I've just got his location.'

10:00 a.m.

Rio didn't kick-start her car once they got back inside it. Instead she anxiously waited for Calum's text message. Five seconds later it came. A single word:

Safe

twenty-four

10:55 a.m.

Road works had made the journey to South-East London much longer than they'd expected. Rio and Strong drove in silence to Gary Larkin's address in a rundown suburb of South London, the ideal place for a criminal down on his luck. His home was a small brick-block of flats surrounded by a square of unkempt grass and a few weather-beaten trees. They identified his flat from the outside: top floor, curtains closed although it was still daylight.

'Are you sure we can trust Calum Burns to look after the girl?' Strong asked.

She'd filled him in on the safe house situation as they made their way across the capital. Strong had said nothing, obviously using the journey to figure out what he wanted to say to her.

'I trust him, that's all you need to know.'

Strong raised his chin as he turned to stare at her. 'You know why he was booted out of the Force then?'

Rio pulled the keys from the ignition. 'He's not the only officer who should've been given his *adios* orders.'

A slow, sour smile turned up the right corner of Strong's mouth. 'And there was me thinking we were becoming best friends.' He turned the smile into a short twist of his lips. 'All kind of rumours went around at the time as to why Detective Burns was shown the door. Not that it's got anything to do with anything but I heard he got hitched—'

'Married?' Rio turned swiftly to face him. 'Where did you hear that?'

Strong tapped a finger twice against the side of his nose. 'Now that would be telling.' He turned the conversation as he gazed back up at Gary Larkin's home. 'He doesn't want prying eyes from neighbouring properties . . .'

'Yeah, but we're going to need a bit more than that. Leave the talking to me.'

Just as they got to the lift, Rio's mobile pinged. Urgently she pulled it out. Checked.

Safe

Hearing from Calum eased some of the tension as she rode the lift with Strong to the top floor. Larkin's front door was in one corner of the landing, the letterbox sealed off. Rio didn't see a bell or knocker so she rapped her fist against the door.

No answer.

Her next knock was louder.

Still no answer.

The door of a neighbouring flat opened, bringing the background sound of Ella Fitzgerald's mournful vocals on 'Cry Me A River' out on to the communal balcony. An older woman peered out, sporting half glasses, liquorice-dyed hair and a mauve tracksuit with silver glitter running down the seams that was designed for someone at least twenty years younger.

'You looking for Gazza?' She slipped her glasses partway down her nose, squinting her sharp eyes at Rio.

'Yes.'

'Are you mates of his?' The woman's eyes shifted to Strong and her gaze started dancing, obviously liking what she saw.

'That's right,' Strong answered taking a step forwards,

missing the tightening of Rio's lips at his disregard for her order to let her do all the talking.

The woman's brown-pencil lined eyebrow rose some more at Strong. 'You'll find him down the bookies, that new one that opened last month on the high street.'

Strong pulled out one of his most charming smiles as he took another step towards her. 'We haven't seen him for a while. How's he doing?'

Larkin's neighbour's eyebrow dropped down as her mouth puckered. 'Not good. He's broke and he can't get a job and I don't think he's a well man either.'

'Not well?' Rio jumped in. 'What's wrong with him?'

The woman shrank back behind her door. 'Are you sure you're friends of his?' She didn't wait for an answer, slamming her door and zipping the chain in place.

Rio tilted her head angrily at Strong. 'I thought I told you who was going to be the mouthpiece.'

But, as usual, the man wasn't seeing it her way. 'Yeah, well she wasn't responding to you now, was she. Probably lonely and liked chatting with a fella.'

'Well she'd have to bloody be lonely to figure you for her knight in shining armour,' Rio muttered, but loud enough for him to get the message.

As they went downstairs Strong whispered, 'That doesn't sound promising. He's broke and he lives part-time in a betting shop.'

'On the contrary, it confirms he needs money and it sounds like he's ill.'

The high street had seen better days. Most of its shops were pawnbrokers masquerading as part-exchange electrical and digital goods stores, sunshine-yellow painted money lenders, anything for 99p stores and, of course, bookies.

'Reckon this is it,' Strong said, staring at the lavender and white sign for 'Betcha'.

Rio told him, 'You go in; you look like a gambler. I look too smart. Check he's in there, place a bet and then come and fetch me.'

Strong laughed. 'Too smart? You don't know much about gambling do you?' He went through the door and Rio caught the sound of horse racing on TV monitors before it closed again. A few minutes later Strong re-emerged.

'He's in there. He was keeping a close eye on the door and watched me as I filled in a betting slip. Only when I got it right and placed a stake at the counter did he lose interest. He's definitely on the lookout.'

Rio nodded. 'Let's find out if Mr Larkin wants to help our inquiry . . .'

Strong swung the door back open and they entered. The shop smelt of despair and hopes being desperately clung on to. Rio didn't need to look for Gary Larkin. He turned around on the opening of the door, a pen and slip in his hand. His appearance had gone further downhill since his mug shot five years earlier – more grey in his hair and a face so hollow it seemed life was slowly ebbing away from him. But his eyes were steely.

When he saw Rio and Strong come in, he seemed to murmur under his breath. He let his betting slip drop to the floor and put one of the free pens provided by the shop in his pocket. He waved goodbye to the cashier and began to leave the shop.

Rio got in his way. 'Gary Larkin?'

The man she confronted looked into her face. 'You know full well who I am, love. Now if you wouldn't mind getting out of the way, I've got some business to attend to.'

He began to leave again but Rio laid her hand on his arm. 'My name is Detective Inspector Rio Wray and this is Detective

Jack Strong. We're investigating the Greenbelt Gang raids and I was hoping you'd agree to answer a few questions that might help our inquiry.'

Larkin looked down at her hand, his mouth curling at the sides. She let her hand drop away.

Larkin looked up again. 'Presumably, you've read my record? If you have, then you'll know that me and mine don't do friendly chats with the filth.'

'Not even when it's a matter of innocent people being murdered and terrorised in their homes? We're not accusing you of anything; we'd just like your help. Other figures from your world are and we're hoping you will too.'

Gary looked at her with contempt. 'Very moving plea, Inspector, now if you don't mind . . .' And with that he walked out.

But Rio wasn't going to let him get away that easily. She caught up with Larkin on one side, and Strong flanked him on the other, matched him step for step. He ignored them and kept going. He seemed to be heading back to his flat but then he clearly thought better of it and did an about turn. When it was clear they were going to get no joy from their man, Rio tried another tactic.

'Gary – have you got a phone number for Samson?'

Larkin's stride faltered on hearing his nephew's name: he stopped, turned around. He didn't look so confident anymore, his eyes blinking way too many times. 'Samson? What Samson?'

'Samson Larkin, your nephew. You talked about me and mine a minute ago so I'm assuming you have heard of your brother Terry's son.'

'Funny,' he said sarcastically. 'I don't have a number for him . . .' He hesitated slightly before adding, 'What do you want to speak to him for?'

Rio gave nothing away as she answered, 'He's been skipping meetings with his probation officer. You know, just
routine . . .'

'That's sounds a little too routine for the attention of someone who's heading up the Greenbelt inquiry?'

'Ordinary police work has to go on. And we thought, as we
were speaking to you, we'd ask after Samson's whereabouts.
But that's OK; we'll find him ourselves.' She watched his
expression closely but could read nothing in it. 'Look, Gary, if
you change your mind about helping us – you know, anything,
rumours or gossip about Greenbelt, your own pet theory about
who's doing it, anything – give us a call.' She reached into her
pocket, took out a card and offered it to Larkin. 'Or better still
come with us now.'

He ignored the card. 'Oh yeah, and why would I bloody well
do that?'

'Eliminate yourself from the case. If you've got nothing to
hide you're going to be fine. However,' Rio let the word ride
between them, 'if your name ends up in the frame we're going
to come back here mob-handed. Now an innocent man
wouldn't be worrying so much.' She held up her palms. 'It's
your decision.'

'You're not listening are you? My family don't talk to
coppers . . .'

'Tell you what, Gary,' Rio continued, her tone light and even,
'why don't you give your brief a bell and we'll be in the car
waiting outside your block. If you change your mind in the next
ten minutes you know where to find us. If you don't . . . well,
who knows what will happen in the next twenty-four hours.'

She put the card back in her pocket and signalled to Strong.
They walked back down the high street. As they turned into
the road leading to Gary Larkin's home, Rio looked back the
way they'd come. Gary Larkin had disappeared.

As soon as they got back in the car outside the block of flats Rio confidently said, 'I predict he'll be back in five minutes—'

Strong turned to her. 'No way. Let's make a bet. I say Gazza's back after five minutes.'

Rio didn't do bets: brought back memories of too many arguments between her mum and dad when she was growing up and her father lost the mortgage money in some loser gambling game. But she was tempted . . . so tempted.

'Alright, you're on,' she agreed.

'Forfeit?'

Now that was easy. 'You do everything I tell you to for the rest of this investigation.'

Rio's heart lurched as she waited for him to name his price. 'OK,' Strong said slowly. 'A kiss when and where I choose.'

'Flip off, old man,' Rio scoffed. 'Ain't going to happen.'

'What you worried about? That you'll like it? It isn't like you're connected to anyone, from what I hear, so why don't you give those lips of yours a day trip out, lass?'

Not connected to anyone. Rio thought of Calum. He didn't own her; she could do what she liked with any part of her body.

And that's why she said, 'OK, you're on. But you're going to lose.'

He chuckled. 'Better get those lips of yours ready for an outing.'

Four minutes later Rio grinned as she spotted Gary Larkin walking towards the car in the rear-view mirror as if summoned by an invisible hand of justice.

'Thou must obey thine senior officer,' Rio whispered to Strong triumphantly.

Larkin got closer and closer to the car. Rio reached for the door handle but froze when her person of interest walked straight past the car. Strong let loose a chuckle as Gary approached his block. Rio was in silent despair for two reasons.

Strong leaned across. Whispered, 'Better get those lips nicely turned out . . .'

Rio pulled back when she saw Gary Larkin reappear. Checked her watch.

'Still fifteen seconds on the clock.'

Come on, Gary.

Strong looked over at the red-lit digital clock on the dashboard.

Come on, Gary.

Gary was within an inch of the car when the clock struck the next minute.

'Your lips are mine,' Strong said sweetly as Larkin reached the vehicle.

Rio wound down the window getting back on with the job. 'Hello again, Gary.'

He gave what sounded like a prepared speech. 'I've been having a think about what you said. And I'm prepared to talk to you. Know why?'

Rio raised an eyebrow. 'Because you want to clear your conscience?'

'Nah. Coz I'm innocent.'

Rio smiled. 'Let's take the rest of our discussion down the station.'

While Strong accompanied their person of interest into the back of the car, Rio sent a text message to a member of her team:

Get everything ready.

twenty-five

11:16 a.m.

Adeyemi – Nikki's boyfriend - pretended to enjoy the company of his friends and the soft music in the background inside the café style bar of the theatre that had once been a shoe factory in Peckham. But he wasn't listening; hell, he couldn't stop thinking about Nikki. He was worried about her. No, he was frightened for her since her uncle, aunt and parents had been murdered.

His mum disapproved of Nikki. 'You need a girl your own age,' was all she said, but the worry lines on her face told him she always meant so much more than the words leaving her mouth.

And as for his brother . . . well, Chiwetel only ever chatted about him studying hard to get a decent job, a one-way ticket out of the not-so-hip part of London SE15. *Not like me,* his brother often said with regret, *I'm part of the university of the street.*

His family didn't get it, didn't understand how he and Nikki had just clicked on that student conference six months back. Best of all she made him laugh . . .

'Earth to Ade, earth to Ade.'

He parked his worries about his girlfriend to the back of his mind – not too far though – as he looked across the small, round table at his mate Chrissie. She was pretty, ballsy, mixed white-black heritage, the type of woman his mother would welcome with open arms.

'Are you with us, my friend?' she blew over to him, her small twists dancing around her face. His two other friends sat looking at him with grins on their faces. 'So are you coming with us to the all new urban production of *Henry V* set on a council estate here next week?'

Ade didn't much fancy going out and about while Nikki was in such a fix.

'I—'

His mobile pinged. He pulled it out. Text.

I'm at Peckam Rye station. Now. Come get me.
Nikki

Both rattled and relieved Ade pushed out of his chair. 'Got to go.'

He didn't even wait to hear the surprised comments of his friends as he hurried out of the bar, jumped the stairs two at a time and then hit the exit. And immediately bumped straight into a man . . . The man gripped his arms to stop them from falling.

'Sorry, sorry,' he said, but was soon on his way with no time to lose. Finally he was going to see Nikki, to see with his own two eyes that she was alright. Elation built inside him as he reached the main road. Two things puzzled him though – why had she signed the text 'Nikki'? She never signed off her texts. And strangely, her number hadn't come up like it usually did.

He reached for his phone the same time he turned a corner. But he never took it out because everything around him started to blur, tilt. He rubbed a hand against his eyes. His legs might be moving but they felt like they were wading through quicksand. He shook his head, but the world around him didn't come right; it got worse. The colour of the doom-toned sky and buildings started to blend into one. He needed to stop or he was going to fall down. Ade didn't understand what was going on. Maybe he had that bug that was doing the rounds? As he raised his foot instead of going forwards he tilted back against something hard.

'Easy does it,' a voice breathed into his ear. 'You're OK.'

'What?' Ade could hear the bustle of the main road receding into the distance as whoever had spoken to him steered him someplace else.

'Where ... are ... you ... ?' But he never finished as the world dropped away.

The last thought he had was that he had to get to Nikki.

twenty-six

Midday

'I'm not saying nothing until my brief gets here,' Gary Larkin insisted as soon as his bum hit the seat of the chair in Interview Room Number Two.

'Why do you need your solicitor if you haven't done anything wrong?' Rio responded.

Larkin's lip curled. 'Because I don't trust you lot.'

Without a word Rio left him alone with the uniformed officer in the room and quietly closed the door.

She quickly checked her phone and read Calum's on-the-hour text; things were good at his end. The calm she felt was immediately replaced with urgency as she headed for Interview Room Number Four. She could already smell what was going on inside before she opened the door. Rio coughed slightly as she entered the room filled with light smoke. Strong and the two officers on loan from Surrey inhaled and exhaled quickly on cigarettes.

Strong pulled the cigarette away from his lips grimacing slightly with the expression of a former smoker. 'Why are we doing this?'

'You'll see . . .'

Rio stopped speaking as the door opened admitting another member of her team carrying the vacuum cleaner that belonged to one of the Fort's cleaners and an envelope under his arm.

'You do know that this is against health and safety rules?' Strong said, smoke mingling in the air with his words.

'Like you care about rules,' Rio replied, more with camaraderie than annoyance as she bent down near the vacuum cleaner. She pulled it apart until she had the dust bag in her hands. Unclipped it and spread a light sprinkling of dust around the room. She then moved to Strong with the opened bag.

'Right, drop your ciggie end in here.'

'Is this some type of strange ritual you guys do at The Fort?' he asked as he followed her order.

But Rio didn't have time for questions as she walked towards the two officers who dropped their cigarette ends into the bag.

'Get this out of here,' she said to the officer standing near the vacuum cleaner. Rio took the envelope from him and turned to the two Surrey officers. 'Thanks for doing this. If anyone asks you about this say nothing, just refer them to me.'

Once they were gone Strong walked over to her. 'DI what's going on here?'

But before Rio could answer the door opened. The desk sergeant popped her head around the corner. 'Gary . . .' She covered her mouth as she started coughing. 'Larkin's solicitor is here.'

Rio turned to Strong. 'Bring Larkin and his brief in here.'

Strong frowned. 'But I thought we were questioning him in Number Two.'

'So does Gary.' Rio allowed herself to smile. 'Just get them in here.'

Once she was alone Rio allowed herself to take a steady, long breath and regretted it instantly when dust particles entered her throat. She swallowed, pushing them down and out of the way. What she was about to do wasn't strictly

illegal, not really bending the book: just being strategic with
the resources she had available. Rio placed herself on one side
of the bare rectangular table, the envelope in front of her, and
waited.

When Larkin and his solicitor, Ben Catley, walked into the
interview room, accompanied by Strong, the young man of
law recoiled, coughing and took out a hanky. 'Have you been
burning bodies in here, Detective Inspector Wray?'

'I'm sorry about this, but our last interviewee was a heavy
smoker. Of course, we should have asked him to stop but he
said he was stressed out and needed a smoke.'

From behind his hanky, Catley told her, 'Well, we can't
possibly conduct an interview in a room like this; you'll have
to find somewhere else.'

Rio sounded innocent. 'I'm afraid I didn't realise that the
room I'd placed Mr Larkin in was already booked.' She allowed
herself to look at Gary Larkin for the first time. 'You don't
mind do you, Gary – I'm sure you're used to smoky
environments?'

Larkin looked pale, the bob of his Adam's apple working
overtime.

As he sat down Rio pressed on with the caring cop routine.
'Are you sure you're OK? Do you suffer from asthma or any
other respiratory conditions?'

Rio caught Strong's hooded eyes as he sat beside her and
saw that he finally realised what she was doing. Nikki Bell's
words lay between them: *One of them couldn't breathe
properly* . . .

Gary Larkin puffed out his chest. 'Nah, I don't suffer from
asthma. Got lungs of steel.' But the splutter he let out at the
end maybe told another story.

Strong put on the electronic recording equipment. The
interview started.

But before the questioning began Ben Catley said, 'I would like to make a quick statement on behalf of my client.' He coughed, then started up again, 'I object, in the strongest possible terms, to the harassment of my client who has not been involved in any criminal activity for many years . . .'

But Rio wasn't listening to him; she was only interested in keeping her gaze glued to Larkin's face. A film of sweat shone around the side of his nose and below his receding hairline. His features were rigid – trying to keep himself under control, or just nerves at being questioned? Rio knew she would soon find out.

A belching cough from Catley announced the end of the statement.

'Have you finished, Mr Catley?' Rio kept her eyes on her person of interest as she asked the question.

'For now.'

'Good.' She placed her forearms on the table and laced her fingers together. 'I'm sure you understand, Gary – I can call you Gary?' But she didn't wait for his response. 'That just to keep the books straight and to completely eliminate you from this inquiry, it would help if you could tell me where you were during any of the Greenbelt raids, so we can categorically confirm you weren't involved?'

Gary smiled at her. 'I can tell you where I was for all of them.'

Everyone was surprised, even his solicitor.

'All of them?' Rio's fingers tightened together. 'How can you possibly know where you were for all of them?'

Gary coughed once. He didn't put his hand over his mouth, Rio thought, definitely a man who wasn't brought up right. She didn't like the way the sweat on his face was drying up like he was feeling confident.

He threw his head slightly forwards. 'Because whenever a

big crime goes down, I make a note of where I was in a book, just in case you lot try and pin it on me later. A lot of the guys do that.'

'But according to Mr Catley, you haven't been involved in the underworld for years?'

His head inched back. 'I haven't. But that hasn't stopped you lot from bringing me in for Greenbelt has it?'

'So where were you at approximately at five forty-five on the morning of January the eighth?'

Larkin didn't even blink. 'At home, with the wife, sleeping.'

'How can you be so certain of this?'

He reached into his pocket and produced a small book, with a padded black cover like a diary. 'I've been checking while I was waiting for Catley here to turn up.' He looked in his book. 'Snoozing like two babes we were.'

'And if we talked to your wife she'll back you up?'

His chest puffed out slightly, but this time he spluttered and wheezed.

'Mr Larkin,' his solicitor asked, 'Are you OK to continue?'

A few softer coughs left his mouth. Rio noted that the rest of them had got accustomed to the smoky atmosphere in the room; the only person who hadn't was Gary Larkin.

'I think we should suspend this questioning—'

'No.' Gary waved his hands stopping his solicitor. 'I just want to get this over and done with so that I can get back to my Maria and the girls.'

A beloved husband? A devoted father? Yeah, and my name's Michelle Obama, Rio thought.

'Must feel good knowing that you're married to a woman who's taking care of your back,' Rio said, once the man opposite had his lungs back under control.

Catley softly jumped in. 'My client has given you a full account of what he was doing at the time and date you requested. So shall we move on to any other dates you wish to explore with him?'

And that's what Rio did.

January 11th?

Sleeping.

January 21st?

Kipping on the sofa at my brother Terry's. Me and the missus had a barney.

February 1st?

Watching a live wrestling match on Sky from America. Wrestlemania.

February 14th?

Valentine's Day. Want to hear what me and the wife were up to beneath the sheets?

'A woman was killed on that raid,' Rio said. 'She hadn't been married long. Had her whole life ahead of her.'

Gary Larkin ran a finger under his nose as he sniffed. 'I heard. Hope you catch the bastard who did it.'

Then Rio asked about 22 February; the day before yesterday.

'Twenty-second?' Larkin's question was filled with puzzlement.

Rio's shoulders tensed as she leaned forwards. The moisture was back on his face.

Rio's voice punched across the table at him. 'That's right. Yesterday. A gang entered the home of Maurice and Linda Bell, murdering them and a third occupant, their cleaner. Surely you don't need your book to tell you that?'

He was clutching his book as if looking for support. 'Sure. I was at ... sleeping ...' His eyes flicked around. 'I think I was sleeping–'

'You think?'

'Yeah.' He nodded twice. 'Yeah.'

Rio explained, 'It's been in the papers, Gary. Maurice Bell

was shot in the head. Their cleaner was shot in the back. Linda Bell was found in the kitchen. Do you know what happened to her, Gary?'

By now Larkin's face was bleached white. The sweat was rolling down his face. 'I didn't have . . .' It was like he couldn't find his breath. 'This is crap. I've had enough of this nonsense. Catley tell her . . .'

Rio pressed on. 'Her head was almost cut off. Someone took a knife and sliced it right across her throat. Was that you, Gary?'

Rio pulled out something from inside the envelope on the table. A photograph. With a single finger she spun it around to face Larkin. It was the gruesome image of Linda Bell's bloody corpse slumped in the kitchen.

Larkin's other hand desperately searched inside his other pocket. 'That's not my style and you know it.'

Catley shoved his voice between the two. 'I think we're about done here Detective Inspector Wray. My client has clearly demonstrated he couldn't have been involved in these tragic events.'

But she ignored him. Kept her intense brown gaze slammed against Larkin. 'This is your chance, Gary, to tell the truth—'

He shook his head as his laboured breathing took over the room. 'Couldn't have been me. Know why? I was getting ready to go to the bookies—'

'That's a bit early for the bookies. And I thought you were sleeping? Or was it dossing down on your brother's sofa?' Rio twisted her mouth at him. 'You're not convincing me here.'

He stared back at her, his mouth half opened like a fish that knew its days were up because it wasn't going to be seeing water ever again.

'Gary, you don't look well.' Strong spoke for the first time. 'Do you need some water?'

But the other man just waved his hand and spoke, words so faint they could barely be heard. 'No . . .' Deep gulp of air with a wheeze caught up in it. 'Just got' – another huge intake – 'a cold.'

But all that mattered to Rio was solving this case, keeping Nikki Bell alive. So she pressed on, determined not to leave her fish dangling high.

'You were at the Bells weren't you? Who else was with you?'

Gary's lawyer jumped in. 'You don't have any evidence to support that, Detective Inspector.'

But Rio didn't answer as her gaze was firmly fixed on Gary. His face was now nearly wet and had gone waxen with a tinge of blue. Abruptly Gary Larkin slumped back. The rasping from his chest sounded like his lungs desperately needed an oxygen machine.

Now Rio was concerned. She turned to Strong. 'Get the desk to call an ambulance.'

Gary raised his head looking horrified. He shook his hand as if forbidding her to do so. Then he slowly slid off his chair and fell unconscious to the floor.

twenty-seven

12:30 p.m.

Something was badly wrong. Ade knew that as soon as he woke up. His head hurt, from his right temple right across to his left. He felt stiff and achy all over. And it was dark. That's when Ade realised that he didn't know whether it was light or dark; something was sticking and pinching the skin over his eyes leaving him with only visuals in his mind – images that were quickly taken over by full-blown terror. He'd been on the main road on his way to . . . to . . . He couldn't remember.

Remember.

Remember.

Ade saw her text. Remembered.

Nikki.

That's who he'd been going to meet, up at the train station. So what was he doing here? He tried to call out, but his voice was muffled as a piece of material sucked down to his tongue and out again as he exhaled. Then he realised that the material covered his face, from his hairline to just below his chin. Now he started struggling, but he couldn't move; his arms stretched downwards, secured to something, and his legs lay straight and were held down. He was flat on his back in a tunnel of terrible black.

Then he heard the footsteps: heavy and dragging, as if the

person wanted him to know they were there. The footsteps stopped by his right side. The person's body heat sent new chills through Ade. A sharp, whirling sound came from somewhere above, like a plane passing in the distance. Ade flinched, screwed up his face as he waited for something to fall on him, crush him to death. But it never came; instead he heard a snap. The person leaned over him and stuck something sticky across the material under his chin, binding it to his skin. That's when Ade knew that the sound he'd heard was tape being released from a roll and then torn off. The person did the same to the material on his head.

Water hit his face. It came out of nowhere. Weighed down the material on his forehead, his cheeks, beneath his mouth. But it felt like the water touched every pore of his skin, a huge wave that was headed straight for his mouth.

Nooo.

He couldn't stop it from going deep into his throat.

Please, please, don't let me drown.

His tummy muscles convulsed as they fought to keep the water from his lungs. He was no longer wet with just water; sweat leaked all over his body. A tsunami-style wave was coming straight at him . . .

Abruptly the tape was peeled away from the material under his chin. The cloth hitched back from his mouth so that it lay just below his nose. Ade gulped in oxygen, a lifeline to staying alive.

'That didn't feel good did it?' The voice was male, light, its calm more threatening than a shout.

'What . . . do . . . you . . . want?' Ade asked between ragged breaths.

'Where's Nicola Bell?'

'Did you drug me? Were you the man who bumped into me outside the theatre?'

The man laughed. 'You're smart. You love her very much, don't you? So just tell me where she is.'

Ade was reeling with all the information coming at him. 'I. Don't. Know.'

There was a slight shuffle of footsteps. 'Did you feel like you were drowning? Like the water was deep inside your body?'

Ade was too terrified to respond.

'I didn't put any water near your nose or mouth. See that's what happens when the water touches your face, twists your mind so much that you think you're battling for your life in the biggest ocean you've ever seen.' Ade felt hot breath against his chin and lips. 'What's it going to feel like when I do pour water over your nose and mouth? When it's filling up your guts and lungs—'

'I don't know where Nikki is.'

The hot breath disappeared. The cloth was stuck back down. Water directly hit his nose, his mouth. Funny how he'd only been joking with Nikki yesterday about using waterboarding on her parents as they chatted on Yakkety-Yak. And now some madman was using it on him.

Don't breathe in.

Don't breathe in.

But Ade couldn't hold his breathing for long. As he let out a shattering breath a finger prodded hard into his solar plexus. Ade went under. He fought it with his mind, but he couldn't stop the images that blasted over him. Not an unknown ocean this time, but the memory of not been able to get out of the cupboard under the stairs when he was playing a game of hide and seek with his brother when he was eight. It was dark. Suffocating. The lock wouldn't move, jammed into place. Tears rolled down his face as his tiny fists banged against the door. He screamed:

Mum.

Chiwetel.

Mum.

Chiwetel.

But no one came. He was going to die.

The cloth pushed back. Ade sucked in air again, this time with a weak up- and downwards movement of his chest.

'Tell me.'

He couldn't even answer.

'Tell me.'

Then something strange happened to Ade. He was back inside his memory, not inside the cupboard this time, but just outside it, being held in the comforting hug of his big brother.

Never cry. Always stay calm, find peace. Then be logical and think through what you have to do to survive, Chiwetel had told him.

And that's what Ade did now. Calm. Peace.

'If I knew where she was I wouldn't tell you. You better let me go or my brother and his friends will hunt you down.'

'Not cool, Ade, not cool at all.'

Ade tensed, waiting for the water, but it never came; instead he heard his tormentor start speaking.

'He doesn't know a thing. Don't worry I've got a few more leads.'

No more words, just heavy footsteps coming back towards him.

twenty-eight

Strong was nearly as worried about what Rio had done as he was about Gary Larkin, who'd been wheeled out of The Fort on a stretcher and taken to A&E with an oxygen mask on his face.

'You're taking a risk. Setting Larkin up for an asthma attack – he could have died. Even that idiot Catley might get you for this.'

Rio sounded innocent. 'He hasn't got asthma, according to him, but it matches one of the gang having some type of chest-breathing complaint. I had to test this theory . . .'

'He was confident about answering questions about the first five raids but when it came to the one at the Bells' he wasn't prepared. Don't you think that was strange?'

Rio ran her fingers through her 'fro as her brain ticked away. 'That did seem to be the point where he toppled over the edge. Maybe he was the one who killed Rubina Ali on the fifth raid and so the gang decided he's a liability and didn't take him on their next murderous job. Or maybe it was seeing the handy work of the gang in the photo of Linda Bell that was his tipping point. Being confronted in full colour with your crime is never easy.'

'What about the alibis?'

Rio was contemptuous. 'Alibis? He's written down where he was in a book? If that isn't a criminal preparing to bust his way out of trouble I don't know what is. We're taking this to the next level. We'll get warrants to search his flat and then his brother's place. And we need to do it fast; the paramedics told me he could be back out of hospital as early as tomorrow.'

Strong was doubtful. 'We haven't got any real evidence. He might not even have asthma; it could have been flu or something. He's got alibis. His brother is on film with the drugs guy in Brussels but Gary isn't.'

Rio's mobile pinged. She took it out.

Calum: **Safe**

'DI?'

Rio turned to find Detective Richmond holding a folder in his hands.

'Autopsy report has come back on Frank and Patsy Bell.'

As soon as he handed the report over, Rio started reading. It confirmed what she'd already suspected – Mr Bell was strangled and Mrs Bell was drowned. But it gave another piece of information she hadn't known – Frank Bell was probably immobilised by some type of stun gun, like a taser.

Rio closed the file and looked up at Strong. 'Gary Larkin is involved. I know he is and he was prepared to risk his life to avoid us finding out. We're going to his flat and if they won't give us a warrant, I'll go burgle the place myself. I've got a sixteen-year-old girl whose life is on the line.'

1:35 a.m.

It took Rio half an hour to persuade Judge Wilkinson that she needed two warrants. She suspected he was pissed that she'd managed to track him down at lunch at his club. But as soon as he heard the words 'Greenbelt Gang', he issued search warrants for both Larkin brothers' homes.

2 p.m.

As Rio got a 'safe' text from Calum, Gary Larkin was having a desperate talk with his brother.

'It's over. I'm going to have to skip the fucking country and it's all you – and your fucking kid's – fault . . .'

After he'd vented his anger on his brother Terry, Gary Larkin was so unsteady on his feet that he nearly collapsed. Instead, he slowly sank down in the public phone box that stood a few yards from where he lived, until he came to rest, crouching and leaning on the box's structure. He'd skipped out of the hospital as soon as he'd got his hands on an inhaler, but the stench of urine and stale alcohol in the booth made him realise that his lungs were still on dodgy ground.

His brother tried to calm him down. 'Alright, Gazza boy, just cool it will you and tell me what's happened.'

Gary resented the way his brother always remained cool, never descending to cursing and swearing. He still had that cultured voice from going to that smart Church of England boys' school – the one that Gary hadn't got into.

Gary squeezed the words out of his wounded lungs. 'I was picked up by the cops for some *friendly* questioning over the raids. That bitch inspector tried to trip me up by filling the fucking interrogation room with fag smoke that had my breathing going into overdrive. She knows something. I had an attack and ended up in bloody 'ossie.'

'So you've got asthma – so what? Millions of people have got it.'

Gary's voice was a mix of asthma and panic. 'Yeah – but millions haven't got a record like mine. And as soon as they've got a warrant, they'll be straight round to rip my place apart–'

'But you haven't got nothing incriminating at yours have you?'

Incriminating. There his brother went again with his flash talk.

Gary hesitated. Then, 'Nah, of course I ain't.'

Terry went into that big brother mode that Gary hated. 'If you're lying to me—'

'Wouldn't do that, Tel, now would I? If only you'd kept your partner sweet—'

'Don't mention that dirt bag to me,' his brother yelled back. Terry got real touchy when anyone mentioned the man he'd once been in business with. 'So they pulled you in for some questions. So what? Everyone's going to be pulled in at some stage over this; it's not a problem. They've got nothing or you'd have been arrested. My kid's gone. They probably won't even be able to get a warrant. They're just trying to push your buttons. Stop panicking . . .'

For a few moments, Gary's head began to clear. He rested his head on the phone box, his tight grip on the receiver relaxing slightly. Terry was right; there was no need to lose it. The cops had zilch on him. Dickhead Samson was gone and he had the wife to back up his alibis. He began to feel slightly ashamed. He was a professional. 'I'm not panicking – but I am angry, I shouldn't have been put in this situation.'

'It happens. Go home and sort yourself out. Rest up and stay calm.'

Despite the condition he was in Gary remembered, 'And the bitch cop started going on about yesterday . . .'

But he never finished; he saw blue lights reflected around him and then a police car followed by a BMW, followed by another police car. There were no sirens but the convoy was in a big hurry. The cars mounted the pavement outside his block and officers began getting out. Gary looked on in disbelief, before whispering, 'Fuck, they're here already . . .'

He let the phone drop and straightened up. Thrust out of the phone booth. As he approached, he realised that Bitch Cop was standing amid a group of uniformed officers throwing out instructions. He saw the look of surprise on her face when she saw him.

'I'm no doctor, but I rather think you should be in hospital . . .' she greeted him.

He drew a breath accompanied by some wheezing and told her, 'What me? I'm as fit as a fiddle. Never felt better.'

Bitch Cop pulled a paper out of her pocket and handed it over to him. Gary read the search warrant, hoping her haste meant there was a mistake in it; there wasn't. He crushed it in his hand and threw it on the ground.

'It would save us a lot of time if you could point us to anything hidden in your flat that might help with our inquiry. Save us all a heck of a lot of time, plus we don't want any unnecessary damage to be caused in our search.'

Sarky cow.

'You won't find anything in my place, with or without any unnecessary damage.'

2:09 p.m.

'Are you going to open up or not, Gary?'

Rio stood next to Gary at the door to his flat. Behind them was her search team. Larkin seemed to be fumbling and looking for his keys before announcing, 'I haven't got them. Must've left them at the hospital.'

'Can someone get Big Momma?' Rio told Detective Richmond, using The Fort's nickname for one of their battering rams.

But Big Momma wasn't necessary; Gary magically found his keys and opened up. The flat was much more spacious than it looked from outside.

'Mr Larkin, I'd like you to accompany Officer Blake into the main room.'

Rio didn't hear what he muttered under his breath, but knew it wouldn't be complimentary.

'Let's get started,' she told her team.

They began with the bedrooms. Beds were stripped, wardrobes emptied, linings felt and carpets pulled up. An electronic device was checked for concealed cavities in the wall. When her people emerged from the bedroom, Rio told them to carry on with the kitchen and then the bathroom.

'You're wasting your time. There's nothing here,' Gary Larkin yelled from the main room.

Rio ignored him and entered the kitchen. She rang Strong, who was leading the search at Gary's brother's home. 'Anything?'

'Nope. And judging by the look on Terry's face, we won't be finding anything either. No sign here of where his kid's gone . . .'

'Keep looking.'

When she'd finished her call Rio went to check on Gary. The main room had the imprints of a female touch – a girly gossip mag on a sofa, family photos framed on the wall and a small, battery-operated massager on the floor near the armchair Gary sat on. A flashy fish tank with three fish swimming happily in their home was behind him. His face was lit with a smug smile. He raised his hand sarcastically. 'Please Miss, can I go to the toilet?'

'Officer Blake will have to go with you.'

'Oh, come on—'

'You know the drill, Gary.'

Gary was outraged. 'What's your fucking problem? I'm entitled to some privacy here. What do you think I'm going to do? Leg it out of the window? We're on the top floor. Frightened

I might have a dead body in the bath panel? You're wasting your time here, Wray. If I had anything hot in this flat, I'd have turned tail and run. Timewasters . . .'

Rio thought carefully before saying, 'OK. But leave the door unlocked.'

When Larkin was gone a colleague whispered, 'He's right, he'd have run for it.'

'Yes,' Rio said, not happy at one of her team saying out loud what was staring her in the face. 'I know . . .'

When Gary came back he said, 'Maybe you want to check my underpants?' He smiled as he made a lewd gesture towards his crotch.

But he wasn't smiling when one of the team said a few minutes into the search, 'Boss, come and have a look at this.'

Alarmed, Gary got out of his seat with a shout of 'Planting something on me now are you? I thought you were supposed to have given all that up.'

Rio and Larkin went over to the fish tank under which one of the team had found a small plastic bag with a sticky brown substance inside it. Rio took it.

'What's this?'

'It's a few grams of cannabis resin for my personal use – I like a smoke – you can put the cuffs on me if you want, but I thought you were supposed to be hunting for a bunch of gun-slinging desperados?'

The officer started to slip the resin into an evidence bag, but Rio ordered him to put it back. Larkin could have his smoke. 'Although you shouldn't be smoking anyway with asthma.'

'What are you, my flipping mum now?

Gary resumed his seat while the search continued. Rio could tell from the look of satisfaction on his face that they were going to find nothing. When they were finished, Rio looked around the flat and then ordered her team, to their obvious dissatisfaction, to do it all again from the beginning. Gary said nothing. When Rio called Strong she discovered that the search at Terry Larkin's had revealed nothing that could be considered as having any connection at all to the Greenbelt murders. They'd reached a dead end.

Forty-five minutes later, a second and then a third search were over. Despite having his flat turned upside down, Gary seemed to enjoy escorting the police from his premises. Before closing the front door on them, he sneered, 'Greenbelt Gang? You people couldn't catch a bus.'

When they were gone, Gary hurried over to his kitchen window and pulled back the curtain slightly in anticipation of watching Bitch Cop and Co. drive away. Instead he saw them move up the street, in a horizontal line formation, searching in gardens and bushes on the route that he'd taken when he'd got back from ringing Terry.

He let the kitchen curtain go and rushed off to the bathroom, leaving the light off and opening the frosted window a fraction to see what was going on below. He could hear the voices of the cops as they went backwards and forwards. Lungs wheezing again, Gary went back to the kitchen and watched the cops group together around one of their cars having another one of their conferences. His lungs tightened. Although he was desperate to continue, he was forced to go back to the living room to get his asthma pump. He looked everywhere, but he couldn't find it. He clenched his fists in despair and, taking deep breaths, went back to the kitchen to see what was going on outside. The conference had broken up, but there was no sign they were leaving. Instead the filth were leaning against cars and chatting. He heard some laughter. He let the curtain fall once again and whispered, 'What the fuck are they up to . . .?'

The silence in the flat was broken by a hammering on his front door and Bitch Cop's shout of, 'Open up.'

When he did so, he found her and two officers standing there. Without saying a word she raised an evidence bag, which had a battered pistol inside it.

Bollocks. Terry said stay calm.

'Never seen that before in my life. Did you get it out of the boot of your car?'

'No, we found it outside on the grass where you threw it when you were in the bathroom earlier. Isn't that right?'

'Wrong again, Wray. As you'll discover when you finger-print test it. And by the look of it, that gun hasn't been fired in years.'

But she was having none of it. 'You're under arrest for possession of a firearm.' The bitch turned to one of the other coppers. 'Mr Larkin seems to be looking unwell again. Make sure we've got a doctor on hand back at The Fort this time.'

twenty-nine

3:30 p.m.

Rio, Strong and their person of interest were in Interview Room Number Two this time. No smoke or dust clogging up the atmosphere, just clean and clear for Rio to see the truth. Rio and Strong sat on one side of the table, Gary Larkin on the other. Rio had deliberately placed a closed file in front of her on the table. Closed files were always a good prop in an interview: kept suspects nervous, on the edge of their seat wondering what was inside.

'Are you sure you don't want a solicitor, Gary?' Strong asked.

Larkin had refused to see a doctor and now he didn't want legal representation as well. If he was happy to play this two against one Rio didn't care, but she did not want a legal technicality to mess up the case if she had her man.

Gary was all bluster. 'You can't connect that gun to me. And as for this Greenbelt thing – do me a favour. You can call me a cab, Wray, I'll be out of here in time to pick up my kids from school.'

'The pistol was found under your window, Gary. Are you saying someone else put it there?' Rio placed the pad of a finger on the file knowing his eyes couldn't help but follow her movement.

Gary shrugged, eyes remaining on the file. 'So you say – but personally, I reckon you put it there. You're not putting me on trial for that gun; a decent brief would have you for breakfast. But then you're not really interested in that old banger of a pistol are you? You want to talk about Greenbelt. So go ahead – fire away. I've got rock solid alibis. You've got nothing.'

There was a knock on the door. An admin officer came in and passed Rio a piece of paper on which were the results of the forensics on Gary's gun. No match to the Greenbelt killings or any other crime. No fingerprints either. Indeed, it was in such a bad condition that it was possible that it wouldn't fire at all - or if it did, it was more likely to injure the person pulling the trigger. Rio put the paper down without showing it to Strong. Instead she made a big drama of slowly opening the file and placing the forensic report inside. Rio closed it and pushed it slightly further in Gary's direction. His eyes watched her every step of the way. Rio wasn't surprised to see him fold his arms across his chest; she'd seen that reflex action from suspects, the need to keep their hands pinned down in fear of lunging across the table to grab the file and find out what was inside.

'Why did you get so upset when we talked about the murders of the Bell family?'

He sneered, 'How about I didn't have anything to do with it.'

'But your explanation for where you were was a bit confused.'

'I was tucked up in bed.'

Rio placed her palms flat against the file. 'Come on, Gary, you can do better than that.'

There was impatience in his voice when he answered. 'If I'd been out shooting people, I'd have a story for you wouldn't I? Are we about done here?'

Rio drew the file towards her. 'How well do you know your nephew?'

Gary blinked in a way that Rio now recognised as a nervous tick. 'Which nephew? I've got several.'

'Your brother Terry's boy – Samson.'

'I've seen him around, at family functions and what have you. But my brother's family and I aren't close.'

Rio picked up the file and leaned back in her chair. 'Bit of a psycho isn't he?'

A film of sweat appeared on Larkin's forehead. 'Is he? I wouldn't know.'

Rio finally did what Gary Larkin was desperate for her to do – opened the file. She didn't speak, just took her time running her gaze over the information and then turning the page. Rio flicked her gaze up at her interviewee. Yes, the sweat was spreading, giving his face a sickly, glossy skin. She'd read somewhere that sweat was said to purify the body, well she hoped that Larkin was ready to cleanse the deadly secrets of his soul.

Finally she stopped reading and looked up at Larkin. 'Do you know what I've just been reading?' Her suspect remained stubbornly silent. 'Samson's life of crime: battery; assault; GBH. The medical report on the young woman he attacked in a bar doesn't make pretty reading. Stitches, bruises, fractures – she has flashbacks, nightmares, undoubtedly permanent psychological scars.' Rio flipped a page. Looked up again. 'The psychiatrist's report paints a picture of a young man who no self-respecting father would let near their daughter. And if you don't believe me, you can read it for yourself.'

Rio placed the single page summary report on the table and flipped it so that Gary could see. He unfolded his arms and picked it up, squinted his eyes and read. Rio gave him a full minute before speaking.

'You didn't know about any of that, did you, Gary?' Her voice was soft, quiet.

He looked stunned, his hand trembling as he lay the report back on the table. 'No'.

'When was the last time you saw Samson?'

'Dunno. Christmas maybe?'

Rio shook her head, so Larkin admitted it might have been more recently.

'Is that why the killing started on the fifth raid? Samson lost his cool and decided to flex his out-of-control muscles?'

Gary didn't answer.

'Is he on the run then?'

No response.

'If he was a pro – like you – he wouldn't say anything and would have alibis all lined up. But he isn't a pro; he's a disturbed eighteen year old. And you know what they're like in interviews, Gary. They lose their temper; they say all kinds of stuff, trip themselves up, point the finger at other people – that's of course if they don't break down and make a full confession.' Rio carried on with a lie. 'We know where Samson is and when we pick him up how long do you think he will last before spilling his guts?'

Gary closed his eyes, but not before Rio saw the despair in them.

'Don't let yourself be dragged down by something your nephew did and maybe you couldn't control. You're no killer, are you, Gary? You help us and maybe we can help you.'

Gary reopened his eyes as he took a deep breath. 'OK. There is something I'd like to say . . .'

But he never finished his sentence; the admin assistant came in accompanied by a well-dressed man.

'Not another word, Mr Larkin,' said Stephen Foster.

*   *   *

Furious, Rio stood up. 'What are you doing here?'

Foster walked over to Gary and placed a hand on his shoulder. 'Don't worry, Mr Larkin, we'll sort this out in a jiffy.' He sat down next to his client, forcing Rio to reluctantly retake her seat as well. 'Can you tell me what on earth you think you're doing, Detective Inspector? Interviewing my client without myself being present? That's an extremely serious matter.'

Rio's voice was leaden, 'Mr Larkin waived his rights to legal representation. Isn't his solicitor Ben Catley?'

Foster ignored her question and turned to his client. 'Would you like to confirm that I'm your solicitor?'

Gary looked as shocked as anyone to see Foster, but he nodded. 'Yeah.'

'Good enough for you, Detective Inspector Wray?'

Rio, who looked like a child whose Christmas present had just been stolen, insisted, 'Gary said he didn't want a solicitor present for this interview.'

'Yes, of course he did. He's a sick man who you bullied into it. But we'll deal with that later. The more immediate question is this firearm offence. Have you got any evidence that this gun belongs to Mr Larkin?'

'It was discovered under Mr Larkin's window where he threw it during a search of his home.'

Foster raised an eyebrow. 'I don't care if it was found on his front-door step. I'm asking if you have any evidence that it belongs to my client?' There was silence followed by another question. 'And you're using this bogus possession to blackmail my client into admitting that he had something to do with these Greenbelt raids despite the fact you've got no evidence for that either?'

After another silence, which he milked for all it was worth, a triumphant Stephen Foster got to his feet. 'Come on, Mr

Larkin; let's go back to my office for a chat. We'll decide what legal cases we want to bring against the Metropolitan Police Service.'

With that he swept towards the door with his beaming client. Calmly he opened the door and said to his client, 'If you'd just wait outside a moment.'

Gary Larkin didn't need to be asked twice, quickly escaping from the room.

Stephen Foster partially drew the door back and then looked directly at Rio. 'Since I'm not able to talk to my *other client* directly, can you or someone in your team present Nicola at my office at five this evening. She needs to be present for the will reading of her uncle and aunt.'

Then he left. But Rio wasn't letting him off that lightly. She stood up to follow him, but Strong grabbed her arm, rising to his feet as well: 'You might be bringing a wagon-load of trouble to the Met's door and Tripple isn't going to like it.'

Rio shook him off and rushed to catch up with Foster. She found him near his client at the reception desk.

'A word if you please, Mr Foster.'

With a cynical twist of his lips he joined her.

'What's going on here?' Rio asked, voice tight.

'I'm doing my job.'

'But how can you represent a suspect who may have been involved in the murder of former clients of yours and hiring a hitman to kill another? Surely that's a conflict of interest.'

Foster sighed. 'There's no conflict of interest, because currently Mr Larkin, as I understand it, is merely a person helping with your inquiries.' He let loose with one of those smiles of his that got right on her nerves. 'But if there is a conflict of interest I'm sure I can resolve it to everyone's satisfaction.'

'Yes, I'm sure you could.'

The smile slipped from his face as he lowered his voice. 'And let's be clear about one thing – carry on harassing Mr Larkin and I will make sure he sues the pants off the Met and you personally.'

thirty

Samson Larkin pushed half of his chips onto red number 18: the same number as his birthday. He watched the roulette wheel spin as he held his breath.

The first week of life on the run was a holiday for the eighteen year old. His father had arranged for him to be flown to France in a light aeroplane, no questions asked. From there, he'd gone on to Italy and caught a ferry to Turkey from where he'd moved on to North Cyprus, all on a cousin's passport. There was a family resemblance but it didn't matter, no one was looking very closely anyway. He was expecting it to be a breeze; it was hardly likely Interpol would be looking for a Londoner who was in violation of his probation.

When he got to the small village up the coast from Kyrenia – the holiday home of an older cousin he didn't remember but had been told had done a runner from Britain years back – he collected the keys from the estate agent who held on to them on the cousin's behalf. His cousin was currently sunning himself up in Florida on an extended holiday. *Lucky bastard.* The estate agent hadn't asked any questions either, which was just as well; Samson didn't like being asked questions.

For seven days, he got up at lunchtime, topped his tan up

on the beach, went to bars and tried to pick up a hot-body bitch; but the girls weren't taking to his chat-up lines.

Now Samson was fed up; bored. He didn't like the food or the constant sun and he'd already spent most of the cash his father had given him to tide him over for the next few months. Yesterday he'd rung his father, via his dad's neighbour, and said he wanted to come home or, failing that, needed another couple of grand sent down.

His dad went ballistic. 'You can't come home; you're staying put. And you aren't getting any more dough either. Don't ring here again – and keep your nose out of trouble.'

'But I'm broke.'

'Get a job then; sell candyfloss on the beach or something.'

And that's when he figured out he could make some quick cash gambling at a casino further up the coast. So, an hour earlier, he'd decked himself out in his best suit and shades and got a cab there, with the few hundred pounds worth of local currency he had left stuffed in his pocket. The place was upmarket and Samson resented the way the security on the door seemed to be implying he wasn't flash enough to come in. After they finally waved him through, he steadied his anger by buying a couple of cocktails and then posing at the bar for a while before going to join a game of Blackjack, which he'd heard was just like Pontoon. He lost a hundred quid in ten minutes. Getting up from the table, hissing that the 'house was fixed', he went over to the roulette table.

Samson had only the haziest idea about how the game was played but he watched how the other punters put on their stakes and then pulled up a chair.

Now he watched the wheel turn and turn and turn. Stop. The ball rattled to rest on his number. Bang on! It was his first punt. The croupier pushed Samson's winnings over to him. He'd already made more than he'd brought to Cyprus in the first place. A blonde sitting opposite – kitty-kats on display, golden tan from her hairline down to her aquamarine blue glitter painted toes – smiled at him with admiration.

Roulette was easy.

He pushed all his winnings and what was left of his other chips onto the number of his birthday, only on black this time.

He sent the blonde a flirty-dirty smile while the wheel turned. She raised her hand. Crossed her fingers for him. To Samson's disbelief, the ball came to rest on red and a completely different number. The blonde gave him a sympathetic shrug while his stake was raked away. Unsure what he was supposed to do next, Samson got out of his chair and went round to the other side of the table and took the blonde's arm.

'Come on, babe, this place is bent; let's exit this dump and get a Sex On The Beach somewhere else.'

The woman's smile vanished as she pushed Samson away with alarm. Before Samson could react a man, who was standing at another table, came up and confronted Samson.

'What you doing with my woman?' the man growled.

Fuck this shit.

Samson threw a punch at the man who swerved to one side so Samson didn't make contact. A second punch hit the man but not cleanly, so Samson tried again. But before he could do so, he was hit in the face by a fist, which felt like a bag full of nails, and he tumbled backwards onto the roulette table where the gamblers were running for cover, shouting and screaming. The boyfriend was standing over Samson. Unable to get to his feet, he grabbed the man's leg and sank his teeth into his ankle, biting as deeply as he could. He held on hard while he was kicked repeatedly with the other leg, until finally, he was pulled off by two bow-tied security staff.

As he was dragged to his feet, he screamed, 'I'm a gangster, I've killed people; you're all dead! You're all fucking dead!' But rather than take him away, the bouncers held him up straight. The boyfriend was right in front of his face and asked 'Are you English?'

Samson's head was hanging slightly and he said nothing, so the man merely nodded and said, 'I thought so.'

Then he punched Samson senseless.

thirty-one

4:15 p.m.

'If you were on the run, where would you go?' Rio asked Calum.

She stood propped against the wall in the main room of her mother's house while Calum lounged back, mug of coffee warming his hands, on the russet coloured armchair that had been her mother's throne. Nikki was in the bedroom getting herself ready for the trip to Foster's office to hear the reading of her dead aunt and uncle's will. Strong was waiting in her BMW outside as backup in case the hitman was hiding out, ready to strike, somewhere near Foster's. If the hired gun tried anything, both she and Strong would be ready for him.

Calum gazed back at her looking the most relaxed she'd seen him since re-entering his life. 'Straight into your loving embrace,' he answered with a chuckle.

Rio's mouth quirked into a 'oh yeah' smile. It felt *so* good to be laughing with Calum again. If only she could turn the clock back and make it right between them. God, how many criminals had she heard say that exact same thing?

'There are rumours that you got married,' she informed him softly, 'to the wrong woman.'

He hesitated before he answered, 'Is there ever a right woman to marry?'

Rio let go of that line of questioning and got back on to the first. 'So where would you hide out?'

'Are you talking domestic or international?'

'Not sure, but I suspect it's abroad.'

Calum leaned forwards and placed the cup on the small side table. 'It all depends on who I am and what I've done? And, of course, who or what I'm running from?'

Rio pulled off the wall and folded her arms. 'I am eighteen, violent and don't want the cops to find me.'

Calum studied her, his green eyes becoming thoughtful and ever so slightly dark. 'Who are we talking about here?'

Rio clammed up. Calum might be helping her, and he'd kept to his side of the bargain letting her know that Nikki was safe every hour, but she was still keeping all information given to him on a need-to-know basis. And did he need to know Samson Larkin's name?

Rio made her decision. 'Have you heard of a South London crime family called the Larkins?'

Calum frowned as he rubbed his forefinger and thumb against his jaw. 'Only Larkins I know are three brothers – Martin, Terry–'

'And Gary,' Rio finished. 'I didn't know there was a third brother.'

'Martin, the oldest, was the one who managed to get away. Last I heard he was some well-known academic specialising in – get this – criminology.'

Rio let out a little puff of surprise. 'You're not talking about Professor Martin Larkin?'

'One and the same. The way I hear it he stays well away from South London. Not many people know about his blood connections and the only reason I know is because of my dealings with the family. Plus he's a friend of my mother's–'

'The Dame?'

Calum rolled his eyes heavenward at the name everyone called his mother. She knew it needled him so shouldn't have said it, but she was too shocked to hold it back. Dame Maggie Burns was the high profile and very vocal CEO of a leading campaign group that advocated on behalf of women who had suffered domestic abuse. People listened to her, even the government. Some men called her – behind her back – a ball breaker, while others hung a halo over her head. Whatever, she scared Rio shitless. She'd only met her once, that third time she'd turned up to see Calum at the hospital three years ago.

'*Stay away from my son.*' Five words uttered so softly but with such an electric edge of retribution that Rio hadn't even argued, had just turned and walked away.

'How did she end up hooking up with Martin Larkin?'

He shrugged. 'He was a trustee for years on one of her charities.'

'Why the hell didn't you tell me you knew the Larkins?'

'Because you never asked. And you know why? You still don't trust me.'

The momentary peace between them shattered. Rio felt angry: at herself and because Calum was right, despite what she'd told Strong earlier about trusting him. He had knowledge of the dirty goings-on across this city, so should have been one of the first people she drew on for Intel. And what had she done? Let all her personal baggage get in the way. She had such strong feelings for this man. Was it love? Hell, she didn't even know. But what she was sure about was it was time to trust him.

'I picked up Gary Larkin as a potential suspect in the Greenbelt case . . .'

Rio told him the whole of it. After she finished, Calum said, 'The drug deal makes sense, but I never pegged Gary as a violent criminal. He's the baby of the Larkin brood – Terry's junior I think by ten or eleven years. He's low level, an opportunist really. And if they need money to get an in on a drug deal where would they get half a mill to pay a hitman?'

'That has been on my mind as well. But you know what the underworld is like. There are all kind of deals going on. Maybe Gary and Terry Larkin agreed to pay their killer once the deal comes through and they have access to a steady stream of cash.'

Calum thought for a few seconds. 'Maybe. But it's not the usual way these bounty hunters set their terms and conditions. Once the job's done it's cash-in-hand.'

'The eighteen year old is Samson Larkin, Terry's son. Did you know him?'

Calum shook his head. 'He was a kid when I knew the family, so he wouldn't have been on my radar.'

'He hightailed it out of town while on probation. Family claim he's in Spain working like any decent man. But there's no trace of him there. So where do you think he might have gone?'

Calum thought about it. 'Well, obviously, it would have to be somewhere with no extradition treaty, so that's most of Europe out. Then it would have to be somewhere that an eighteen-year-old Brit would feel reasonably at home, so that's most of the rest of the world out. So it's likely to be somewhere comfy and cosy; either the family or a friend has to stash the kid so he won't have to start filling in forms for accommodation or registering with the local cops.'

'So where does that leave us?'

'The Turkish Republic of North Cyprus—'

'Hold up a minute.' Rio quickly took out her phone. Clicked on the file containing the Intel about the Larkin family Strong had gathered. Rapidly scrolled down. 'There's a cousin who has a place in Cyprus, but it doesn't say whether it's the north or south. Doesn't say what the cousin's name is either.'

'It's the ideal criminal des res. No extradition treaty with Britain and not too far away. Unlike the Greek side of the island, which does have an extradition agreement.' He cocked an eyebrow. 'Now trusting me wasn't too hard, was it?' His eyebrow dropped as one side of his mouth lifted into a sleepy smile. 'We used to be such a great team – me, you and Mac. Taking on the world. Thinking we could spin bad into good.'

Rio couldn't help the feeling of nostalgia that swept her. Memories of the three of them, heads close together, in their favourite café, batting and dissecting information on a case. God they were so young, so foolishly idealistic.

'I know you're also here to dig up anything you can on this gang for Foster,' Rio said, easing her mind away from the past, 'but I've been upfront with you about the Larkins, so I think it only fair you tell me anything you find out about them too.' Rio ran her brown eyes across his face and held out her palm. 'He might be able to offer you money, but I'm offering a price-less friendship.'

Shiiiit. That made her sound like some bloody, floppy-haired poet.

'No touching, babe. Don't forget I might be a married man.'

Their gazes fixed together. Then they started laughing – really laughing – filling the room with human music that was catchy in-drawn breaths, gasps and air that waved in and out of their throats. And then they stopped. Quiet. Their eyes remained meshed together.

Calum broke the silence, voice barely audible. 'Last time I heard that sound coming out of you, Ray Gun, was when you wore that cream dress.'

Her face fell like he'd reached across and scratched and dragged down her skin. She stood up, ran her palms down her thighs. 'I threw *that* dress away. Gave it to the local charity shop. Did you get Nikki to draw what she thought she saw the gunmen wearing?'

Rio kept her tone sorta icy, as usual not quite pulling it off; she had way too many hot emotions swimming just below her surface to stray into cold waters.

Calum reached for a piece of paper near his laptop and handed it to Rio. The drawn image put her in mind of the Elephant Man. That she couldn't break the chain of what this was was really starting to mess with her head. *Damn loose ends.*

'Do you like it?'

Both Rio and Calum turned when they heard Nikki's voice in the doorway. They both reacted with surprise and spoke at the same time when they saw *it.*

'What the heck?'

'That's different.'

It was Nikki's homemade haircut. Her shoulder cut was gone, replaced with a brutal short style that hugged her head.

Nikki self-consciously flicked a few stray strands sideways onto her forehead at the same time modelling Lady Clarissa's long, lacy, fingerless gloves her cousin had given her.

'Do you think Lia will like it?'

That's when Rio realised that the teen had tried to replicate her cousin's hairstyle.

'It looks . . . good.' Rio's response was slow; there was something troubling about the girl's appearance that she couldn't figure out. It wasn't just the new hairdo, there was something else . . . As Nikki turned to the side, displaying her profile, the truth gripped Rio. Or at least what she thought might be the truth. Rio saw Nikki's adoption papers in her mind, still tucked and folded safely away in her bag.

Not your business. Nuthin' to do with the case. Let the might-be-truth drop.

As soon as Nikki was in the back of the car Rio got back on with her job and whispered to Strong, 'When we reach Foster's I want you to make contact with the High Commission in the Turkish part of North Cyprus. Give them Samson Larkin's description and find out if they've heard of him. The one thing we know about Samson Larkin is that he can't stay out of trouble.'

thirty-two

5:04 p.m.

Foster's office wasn't in the City where many of the top legal firms were based, but in a beautiful town house in Kensington. It gleamed a stunning white that looked like it had been painted the day before, with a glossy black door with accompanying large, bold brass knocker and a simple plaque that read 'Foster'. No associates, which didn't surprise Rio; Foster had always portrayed himself as a man who didn't appreciate sharing the limelight with anyone else.

'You OK?' she asked Nikki, who stood beside her. Rio still couldn't get over the haircut.

'I still don't get why I need to be here. Why can't Mr Foster just let you know and you can tell me?' The teenager's expression was confused and frustrated – probably just wanted to spend the day doing virtual chat on the Internet; well that's if she had an Internet to access, which Rio made sure she didn't.

'Your aunt and uncle probably left you a little gift or something,' Rio explained.

She pressed the intercom button. A woman's voice came on, efficient and clipped. 'Can I help you?'

'It's Detective Inspector Rio—'

But she didn't finish as a long buzzing sound unlocked the door. Rio and Nikki stepped inside a world that was as gleaming and sterile as the brickwork. Chequered black-and-white floor tiles, lawn-green, carpeted staircase, with a deep curved, wooden bannister and pure white walls. The only thing out of place was the shade housing the light in the ceiling: an ugly imitation-chandelier made of folds upon folds of blue paper.

'That gets people every time,' a voice said from the top of the stairs.

Both Rio and Nikki looked up to find Stephen Foster standing there, relaxed in a sombre, navy suit and spit-polished leather shoes. Rio couldn't help how her mouth tightened; she just was never going to click with this man.

'It was a gift from my first celebrity client. A long-forgotten actress from the 1950s who didn't have quite enough for the fee so she gave me the light fitting to make it up.'

'Didn't think you did charity work,' Rio said.

He just lifted the corner of one side of his mouth in a smile that put Rio more on edge.

His smile bloomed as he switched his attention to Nikki. 'Good evening, Nicola, it's good to see you again. I hope they're treating you well in the place you're staying.'

'I'm staying at—'

Rio grabbed the girl's hand and squeezed. The teen closed her mouth.

'Let's get on with this shall we?' Rio said tightly.

He waved them both upstairs where they walked through a slim corridor and into a large room that was obviously Foster's office. Inside were Nikki's older cousins, Ophelia and Cornelius. Rio saw Ophelia draw in a stiff breath when she saw her young cousin's hair, but Nikki did not notice. Rio suspected she knew what was going through the actress's head.

Not your business; stay well away.

Nikki ran across the room and threw herself into cousin's embrace.

Her cousin held her tight as she said, 'I've missed you.' Ophelia ran her hand over Nikki's hair. 'Hey, like the cutie hairdo.'

Nikki giggled self-consciously.

Rio noticed that Cornelius stayed tight to his seat. He'd obviously tried to make an effort for the meeting, dressing in loose, black linen trousers and a jacket that was a size too big. The man-bun was gone with his hair neatly combed to his shoulders, but the red blotches on his cheeks showed he wasn't comfortable being here. In contrast, his sister had all the poise of the actress the public had come to adore, but if it were possible she appeared even thinner to Rio.

'Let's all take a seat.' Foster waved at the two chairs, waiting for Rio and Nikki.

Once they were seated he began. 'These are always sad occasions because it means that one of our loved ones has passed away and unfortunately in this case it's two people who I had come to know very well and admire over the years—'

Ophelia let out a scoff. 'Skip the homily because frankly I don't need to be in your presence any longer than I have to.'

Foster didn't even look at her, instead he opened the leather-bound black folder in front of him and took out an envelope. 'Maurice and Linda Bell asked me to make sure that their will remained sealed until it was time for it to be read.'

He opened the envelope, pulled out a single piece of paper and started reading. 'This is the last will and testament of Maurice and Linda Bell, March the fourth, 2009, who resided at Number Three, The Lanes. We revoke any wills and codicils previously made by us. We bequeath our home, its contents, our shares and businesses to our niece Nicola Bell—'

Cornelius slammed out of his seat. The back of the chair hit the floor. 'You've got to be kidding, man. No bloody way—'

'Connie,' Ophelia cut in sternly, remaining calm and seated.

Nikki's gaze swung between her two cousins. 'I don't understand.'

Ophelia responded, her voice cool, but slightly detached. 'Your uncle and auntie left everything to you. You must not feel bad about it. This is a good thing because they loved you—'

'Screw that,' her brother raged. 'I'm their blood, while she's—' He pointed his finger at Nikki making her shrink back in her chair. Tears gleamed in his eyes. 'Fuck. This.'

He slammed out of the room leaving behind a smothered, electric tension.

'He'll get over it,' Ophelia said, her gaze staring sharply on Foster. It was like she wanted to say more, but she kept her cheery painted lips firmly in place.

'I don't want it,' Nikki violently said. 'You can have it all, Lia—'

'Don't worry, darling,' Ophelia started. Then her hand flew up. 'Excuse me, but where's your bathroom?' she asked Foster as her hand covered her mouth. She was already on her feet as he pointed to a room that adjoined his office. A few seconds later the sound of her gagging and retching could be clearly heard in the other room, reminding Rio of the woman's past battles with an eating disorder.

Rio sat there shocked. She'd never been to a will reading where there was this much drama. Why would the Bells leave all their worldly goods and possessions to their sixteen-year-old niece? But if what she suspected was true . . . Whatever the reason, it was already causing a shit storm of tension between family members who would soon be organising the funerals of four people.

As Rio took Nikki's hand to reassure her, Ophelia reappeared in the room. She might look pale, but the way she held herself was back to perfection. And then she spoke to her younger cousin and all Rio could think about was the one time she'd seen the character Lady Clarissa on the telly.

'Mum and Dad left all their beloved things to you because you're young; not like me, I've already begun my life. They want to make sure that you get the best start possible. To make sure you're on the right road for the rest of your life.'

'Maybe we can share it?' Nikki looked at Foster. 'Can I do that?'

'You can do whatever you want.' Foster then turned to Ophelia. 'But not at the present because everything will be held in a trust until you're twenty-five, except six hundred thousand, which you can use anytime you want to. In the meantime I will be the administrator of that trust.'

Losing none of her poise Ophelia said, 'I always thought you were a total tosser.'

Rio had never been so pleased to hear her phone ring; a heaven-sent excuse for her to escape the tension in the room. She excused herself and hit the landing.

Checked the ID.

Calum.

'You're going to be tonguing me for the rest of your life, bay-bee,' he said in his usual overblown fashion.

'French kissing you can't be any worse than what I've just witnessed.'

'Well I'm about to turn around your day.'

'The only thing that can do that is Stephen Foster getting killed in a freak manhole explosion?'

'I've got something way better than that.' Calum paused.

Anticipation swelled in Rio as she waited.

'I've discovered where the Greenbelt Gang are holed up.'

thirty-three

Rio eagerly placed the three photographs of the same house on DSI Newman's desk. At her superior's side sat the Assistant Commissioner.

'I've had a tip-off that this is the hideout of the Greenbelt Gang. It's an oast house in Kent—'

'Where did the information come from?' AC Tripple interrupted.

Rio looked sharply over at her DS. 'Calum Burns. You did say that I could use his cooperation?'

Newman nodded. 'But we need to be careful that Burns isn't dragging us down a hole we won't be able to get out of.'

'Of course, sir.' Rio was feeling the heat; what she wasn't telling her superiors was that Calum refused to divulge his source. All he would say was it was someone who owed him big time.

'Calum's intel only included where the gang are hiding,' Rio continued, 'not the identities of the gang members.'

'Not even Gary Larkin?' Newman said.

Rio shook her head. 'Calum Burns was adamant that this just doesn't fit Gary Larkin's MO. The house is owned by a front company based in the Cayman Islands, so it will be hard to find out who owns it. This is the strongest lead we've had in this case. I want to take an armed response team down there and investigate.'

The AC gazed intently into Rio's face. 'But all you have to go on is an anonymous tip-off. I'm not sure that will be enough to instigate a gold-level operation.'

Rio played her final card. 'Calum's source also said that he believes the gang are getting ready for another raid.'

A look passed between Newman and Tripple. Finally the Assistant Commissioner turned back to Rio and simply said, 'Please can you wait outside.'

Once outside Rio couldn't sit down on the chair that Newman's PA offered her; she was too pumped up to remain still, so she paced, ignoring the silent, disgruntled puckering of the PA's lips, who probably thought she was disturbing the calm energy of the room. Rio knew that sanctioning an armed operation was a serious thing, especially with the heat that the service was still feeling over two armed incidents that had gone badly wrong. But if this operation didn't take place . . .

Rio abruptly stopped pacing when the door opened. She wasn't invited back in. AC Tripple just said, 'Make sure you apprehend this gang. And everything - I mean everything - is played by the book.'

8:10 p.m.

Body armour.

High-tech stab and bullet-proof vest.

Taser.

Incapacity spray.

Telescopic baton.

Speed cuffs.

Torch.

Rio checked herself in the mirror in the locker room. It

bought back all her memories of being in one of the Met's ARV (Armed Response Vehicles) ten years back. And just like then, every time she donned the specialist clothing and its lethal sidekick weapons, she felt the same – a strange power mixed with fear. You could take another life, lose your own; you never really understood the situation you'd find yourself in until you were in the field. The only items Rio was missing were a self-loading Glock and Heckler-Koch assault rifle. She would be the only member of the armed response team who wasn't armed; shit, she still saw that lousy letter denying her annual firearms refresher training.

'You look like one mean machine. The response unit are here.'

Rio turned to find Strong admiring her just inside the doorway. She drew in a deep breath as she gazed back at her reflection. 'Who's heading up the team?'

'Specialist Firearms Commander Billy Jenkins.'

Rio allowed herself a half smile. 'Good. He was my CO when I worked in his unit.'

Strong moved further into the room. 'I think we might've lucked in with the High Commission in Cyprus. The North Cyprus police notified them that they have a British national fitting Samson Larkin's description. He was arrested after a disturbance at a casino, but was travelling on a false passport so we can't be sure that it's him.'

Rio reached for her blue cap with 'Police' written on it, but she didn't put it, instead turned it in her hands. 'No matter, the important thing is that we think he's in lockdown.'

'But without extradition how are we going to get him back?'

'Well let's hope that tonight nets us the gang, which means we can think about Samson Larkin after.'

Strong took a step closer. 'There's one other thing. Remember Nikki's boyfriend, Adeyemi Ibraheem? His mother's at the front desk demanding to see you—'

Rio turned back to face him. 'What does she want?'

'She said that her son's disappeared.'

Rio placed her cap carefully on her head. 'I can't deal with that now. Tell her to come back tomorrow or give a statement to one of the other officers.'

As she swept past him Strong caught her arm. Rio partially twisted around to face him. Her brown eyes caught his intense blue. He let go of her arm.

'You still owe me a kiss,' he said softly.

'What?' Then Rio remembered their bet as they waited outside Gary Larkin's home. 'Look—'

But Strong's head was already moving. His lips touched her skin, but not where she was expecting it. His mouth grazed her forehead.

'You look after yourself,' was all he said.

Rio couldn't speak; there was something thick lodged in her throat. All she could do was nod before she walked away.

The atmosphere in the operations room was highly charged and thick with focus and tension as everyone listened to Officer Billy Jenkins outline the strategy for the operation. Rio stood by his side in front of a board, which had maps and photos attached. Most prominent among the photos was the oast house itself that the gang were reported to be hiding in. Once used for drying hops, the building resembled a stone farmhouse with an inverted funnel-shaped stone tower built into the structure. The tower in the photo had small windows built into it at the top. It stood on a small hillock, with commanding views of the surrounding countryside. Jenkins didn't bother to tell his armed officers that the place was a natural fortress and that a lookout in the tower could see anything coming or going. It was too obvious.

The only cover that could be used for approaching the

house was a number of hedges that divided up the neighbouring fields. The only way up to the house was on a gravel drive
that ran up from a lane, which was a quarter of a mile distant.
Jenkins continued to explain that he was going to divide the
team into two sections. They'd approach in the two, armed
vehicles down the lane, headlamps off and park up, out of
sight of the house. One team would use the hedgerows as cover
to get to the back of the property. The other would go down on
the verge of the gravel drive to the front of the house. When
everyone was in place, Jenkins would give a signal and stun
grenades would be thrown through the windows and explosive
charges would take off the front and back doors. At the same
time two four-by-four vehicles, with arc lights, would come
down the drive to illuminate the scene. The two units would
then gain access by the windows and doors and detain anyone
inside.

Rio asked, 'What if the windows are reinforced and we can't
get our grenades in?'

Jenkins was curt. 'Shoot them out. Of course that doesn't
include you, Rio.' He addressed the whole group. 'Although
Detective Inspector Wray will accompany us she will remain in
the armed vehicle once we reach the scene.'

Rio nodded. But she added, 'This gang are dangerous. Only
shoot to kill in the most extreme situation because our ultimate goal is to take them in alive.'

thirty-four

The two specialist firearms vehicles and four-by-fours gathered in the forecourt of a disused garage, two miles from the oast house. After a final run through to ensure everyone understood their roles, and a weapons check, they set off, Rio beside her former commanding officer. A mile down the road they turned off into the lane that ran up to their target. It was narrow, and trees and bushes brushed and rattled against the doors as they drove down. Once on the lane, they'd turned off their headlamps and slowed to ten miles an hour.

As they went down, Rio could see the house, with all its lights turned off, as a black silhouette against the night sky looking more like a medieval castle than a house. Her hand rubbed against the place where she would have kept her Glock if she'd been allowed one. Another half a mile down the lane the convoy came to a halt. Rio looked at her watch.

9:23 p.m.

Jenkins gave Rio a grave look. 'Let's hope this doesn't take too long.'

Then he jumped out into the night. She watched as the inky figures set off. One team used the cover of a hedge running along a neighbouring field, while Jenkins' group inched back down the lane to the gravel drive that led up to the house. The end of Rio's nerves felt like they were giving her a static charge as she sat by the radio to await confirmation. She knew it would take a while for them to get to their allotted points. It always did.

'In position.' The voice of the officer of the team camou-flaged by the hedge flickered into life on one of the radios in use. One was a direct link to the officer in charge, the other was set to the main police frequency.

'Any sign of life in the house?' Jenkins spoke back

'No. The curtains are all closed and it looks dead in there.'

The radio went silent. Rio looked out into the darkness. The moon was behind clouds and she could see nothing. She didn't like sitting in a van. A rapid patter of rain set up a beat against the vehicle almost matching the racing of her heart. She stared hard at the radio. Nothing.

Come on.

Come on.

Rio checked her watch again.

9:33 p.m.

Ten minutes had gone by and still there were no more commands on the radio. Rio cursed under her breath knowing that even the simplest of operations could go wrong in the dark. She desperately wanted to go up to the house herself . . . but protocol dictated she stayed put.

She looked out of the window at the outline of the house that was nearly obscured by the night, wind, mist and rain. Why wasn't Jenkins back on the radio?

Come on.

Come on.

COME ON.

The sound of gunfire from the oast house tore through the air.

Rio broke protocol and got on the radio.

'Boss? Boss?' Her voice was frantic. 'Jenkins? What the hell is going on up there?'

Finally he came on. 'I don't know. There's shooting coming from somewhere; I'm trying to get round the front to see if it's our people. I can't see anything up here.'

'Is it coming from inside the house?'

'Can't tell . . .'

Another burst of gunfire. Then another. The rat-a-tat of automatic fire: a Heckler & Koch, or another type of submachine gun? Rio jumped out of the command vehicle and entered the unnerving dark. She ran down the lane in the driving rain. More gunshots beat out as she turned onto the gravel drive. Crouching low, she was conscious of the crunching of her feet against the gravel as she drew closer to the house. She drew up to a stone wall and breathed easier when she found several of Jenkins' men aiming their guns at the house.

'What's going on?'

Jenkins swore. 'God damn it, Rio, what the hell are you doing?'

'I heard gunfire. Is it coming from inside?'

'We thought we heard gunshots from inside, so one of my men opened fire.'

'So what are you doing?'

'We wait.'

Rio rapidly shook her head with disbelief. 'I can't let them get away . . .' Rio pulled a Glock from one of the officers who held an assault rifle.

'What are you doing?' Jenkins was furious. Even Rio couldn't believe what she was doing. 'You're not authorised and I'm not going through six months of a disciplinary to explain why—'

But Rio didn't wait for him to finish, just said, 'I'm going around the back.'

Rio set off, skirting the stone wall. She could hear the squelching of Jenkins' boots in the mud as he followed her. The scene was now silent except for the wind, which was ripping across the hill. As they came round to the back, Rio was sure that she saw a figure moving across the grounds at the rear of the property. She squinted and pressed her head slightly forwards. Yes, there it was again, someone in the dark. Someone was out there. Whoever it was they were hugging the ground like an animal.

She yelled, 'Stop – armed police!'

There was a flurry of movement. Rio let loose a fusillade of shots over the top of what she thought she'd seen. Her gunfire was answered as if in a call and response by gunfire from the police at the front of the building firing over the roof.

'Did you see that?' Rio said breathlessly to Jenkins. 'I saw someone.'

But Jenkins shook his head. 'I didn't see anyone.'

How couldn't he have seen it? She definitely saw someone.

'Come on,' Jenkins commanded.

Rio and Jenkins moved into position at the rear of the house by an outbuilding.

'Have you got any of the stun grenades?' Rio could feel the anger still vibrating from the firearms commander. 'Look, I'm already here, so let's see if we can catch the bastards.'

After a few tense seconds Jenkins nodded. He passed her the grenades.

'I'll go in; you keep your gun trained on the building.'

Rio felt no fear as she ran across the courtyard. When she reached the wall of the house, she felt her way along but instead of a window, she found the back door. It was slightly ajar. She raised the Glock to her shoulder and pushed the heavy door open with her foot. Sank to her knees, pointed the firearm high and peered inside. If the landscape was too dark to see anything, inside the building it was black. She took her torch and illuminated a corridor. It had rooms opening off it and what seemed to be a staircase at the end. She heard footsteps behind and to the right of her. She flicked off her torch and rolled onto her back, pointing her gun upwards. Three shadows seemed to be closing in on her; she shouted again, 'Armed police; raise your hands!'

'It's me! Officer Blake!'

The figures threw themselves to the ground when several were pumped in their direction. Lumps were chewed out of the brickwork and glass shattered and scattered across the courtyard.

Rio yelled, 'Jenkins, ceasefire.'

Rio, Blake and his men now all hugged the wall.

'Sorry, boss, we got the wrong place. The hedge we followed went down into a hollow,' Blake explained breathlessly, 'so we couldn't see the target anymore. We followed it along, turned right along the next hedgerow and found ourselves at the oast house – only it wasn't the right one, it's the next place a couple of hundred yards away. When we heard the shooting, we tracked back.'

'Radio?'

'No signal in the hollow. When we got back within range, I radioed the command vehicle but you were gone. Where's the gunfire coming from?'

'Not sure. Let's use some grenades and go and clear the ground floor.'

Rio threw the grenades. Flashes, vibrations and smoke shook the air. Rio and the team rushed inside, guns raised. The place was silent.

Inside they flicked switches by torchlight to get lights working but nothing happened. No electricity. They moved gingerly down the corridor. Paused by the first door they came to.

Blake whispered, 'There's no one in here DI Wray. I think all the shooting came from our side.'

But Rio kicked the door back. She levelled the Glock up and around. No movements; no sounds. One of the others shone their torch behind her striking the room with a vein of light. She went inside. A kitchen. The room was empty, except on a long oak table, as if set out for inspection, were knapsacks and holdalls. Rio let her gun drop and went over to the table. She opened one of the bags. Inside were silver plates, figurines, jewellery and other valuable items. Blake was by her shoulder. 'What is it?'

'I don't know for sure, but I strongly suspect that it's some of the gear that was stolen by the Greenbelt Gang.'

'They were here then? They must have got away.'

'Maybe. Let's clear the house.'

They left the kitchen. Some of Jenkins' team were now congregating in the corridor. They were ordered to search the rooms one by one. Rio took the upstairs alone.

The stairs groaned under her feet. On the landing at the top were various rooms with their doors closed. But one door was slightly open. Silence was interspersed with shouting – 'Armed police' – from downstairs, and doors being kicked open. Rio kept her gun up and her torch breast-high in her other hand. She kicked the door further back, breathing heavily in her nose. There was already a small light in the room; the orange glow of a cigarette and the stub of a cigar on a side table. Sitting next to it was a tumbler of booze with ice still floating in it. When Rio shone her light around the air caught in her throat; illuminated was the pale, astonished look of a man slumped in an armchair. Further down, two large holes gouged by bullets were soaked in blood and jagged flesh. Rio's torch moved on. Another man, also dead, by a window shattered by gunfire. He was lying contorted on the floor, his head half blasted away.

'Jenkins? Billy? Sir?' Rio roared.

No response.

She called again. Silence. She knew she should wait for someone to join her, but she didn't. Rio hit the stairs to the next floor, stopped when the torchlight shone onto the feet of another dead man dangling on the landing above. Probably gunned down trying to escape upwards into the oast house's tower. He gripped the bannister tightly, his lifeless fingers holding on more powerfully in death than they'd been able to in life. His face was frozen in terror and two shots blasted open his chest.

Rio couldn't get her head around the scene of death around her. If this was the Greenbelt Gang, why had someone murdered them? Rio picked up a trail of blood with her torch that led into an attic bedroom. Inside was another victim. He lay face down on a bed as if taking a demonic nap amid the terror. This body had taken more punishment than the others. He'd been shot multiple times. Riddled with holes in his right arm and leg. Another bullet had hit his shoulder and the shot that had probably finally killed him had gone through his heart. In his hand was a grey object, which was being held by the victim like a talisman. Rio knew what it was – an asthma pump.

She grabbed the victim's jacket and pulled the body over. Shone her beam into the dead man's face.

Gary Larkin.

thirty-five

'This is one hell of a mess,' Billy Jenkins told Rio angrily as they entered the operations room back at The Fort.

No one else spoke. There was none of the feeling of high elation of a job well done. Four men were dead and someone was going to have to pay the price.

Rio answered as she pulled off her stab-proof vest. 'I'm telling you that they were already dead—'

'But you weren't meant to have a gun for fuck's sake.'

Hearing Commander Jenkins turn the air blue, everyone stopped and looked openly at them. Billy was one of the coolest leaders of any unit in the Met, one of the reasons he'd been especially chosen to manage an arms response unit. He had the deep respect of his team and superiors, led by example not by insult and cursing.

Rio strode towards Billy as if being nearer to him would make the truth of her words sink in. 'Someone else killed them. You were there when I saw someone outside.'

Jenkins shook his head in disgust at her. 'I told you at the time, I didn't see anyone—'

'Then how did they all die?' Rio threw back. Then she saw the look on his face, which made her gasp and rock back. 'What? You think *I* pulled the trigger? I—'

'Rio, are you alright?' Heart still beating badly she turned to find Jack Strong striding towards her. His face was tight and slightly red with confusion, eyes deep blue with concern.

'I just heard what happened,' he continued when he reached her. Then his large palms were sliding up and down her arms as if to make sure she was really there.

'I'm fine.' But she knew she wasn't.

Their gazes caught and held.

'Out,' a strident female voice commanded.

All eyes turned to the doorway where AC Tripple and DSI Newman stood. Tripple looked furious, while Newman's face was stamped with annoyance and worry.

'You and you,' the Assistant Commissioner continued, pointing a finger first at Rio, then at Billy Jenkins, 'stay put. The rest of you, out.'

Strong gave Rio a reassuring squeeze before he let her go. No one hung around and soon the room held only four people. Rio knew she was about to get the bollocking of her life, so straightened her back ready for the battering. She didn't have to wait long as her former mentor reached her in clipped strides.

'Tell me the reports of you handling a firearm are *not* true, Detective Inspector.'

Rio dipped her head. 'I'm sorry, ma'am—'

'Look at me when I'm addressing you.'

Rio instantly raised her head, but didn't dare look the older woman in the eye.

'You silly, silly . . .' Tripple railed, shaking her head as she tried to find the words. Then she turned her head in fury towards Billy Jenkins. 'How the hell did she manage to get hold of a firearm? You were meant to be organising that team with absolute precision—'

'It wasn't Billy's fault—'

Tripple swung back to Rio. 'Don't. Speak.'

The tension tightened with the tautness of an elastic ready to snap as the AC paced backwards and forwards, forwards and back. It gave Rio the space she needed to realise that her actions had jeopardised not only her own position but that of the whole team. Billy was a man who had taught her so much when she'd been part of his team and it hurt now to think that her behaviour might mean he'd earn a strike in an exemplary career.

AC Tripple finally stopped pacing. The expression on her face was back to the one Rio associated her with – professional calm.

'You're suspended.'

Rio rocked back. 'What?'

'Commander Jenkins, I want a full report on my desk in two hours. Now please leave us.' Billy nodded once, then made for the exit.

'That includes you, DSI Newman,' the other woman added.

Seconds later Rio and the woman she'd admired above everyone else were alone.

Rio wasn't someone who could keep her mouth zipped when there was something that needed saying, even to a superior officer, so she spoke. 'This was no one else's fault but my own. I decided—'

But Pauline Tripple cut over her. 'If anyone asks, you're to say that you were defending yourself while you were being attacked.'

'Ma'am?' Rio was startled by the suggestion.

'And that you took your firearm's refresher training this year—'

'No,' Rio responded with fire in her words. 'I can't do that. I come from a community that always feels that the police are colluding and twisting the truth against them. Do you know how many times my friends were stopped and searched by the police when we were growing up? I was stopped? The police weren't the police, they were cops roaming the streets like any other gang, except they could do what they wanted because they had the law on their side. One of the reasons I joined was to change all that. I need to be able to look the people I serve in the eye. So, with respect, ma'am, don't stop me being able to do that.'

'But you're part of another community now as well. *Our* community. *Our* rules. *Our* ways of working together. You broke those rules so you've put at risk everyone in our community. You decide to walk a straight line on this then we're all going to be walking right on behind you, except the rest of us will be falling one by one as we're crucified.'

The other woman stared at Rio with a determined glint in her eye, waiting for her to say the magic words. But Rio couldn't do it. Couldn't lose that one part of herself that had remained pure and true – her integrity. People could point out other shit she might have done, but her understanding of right from wrong? No fucking way – no one was going to take that away from her.

'Then be prepared,' Tripple said softly seeing Rio had made her decision, 'because you might go down. I'm not going to be able to protect you from those who've just been waiting for a chance to say "I told you so about that Rio Wray. Got where she was going because of some positive, ethnic and gender monitoring initiative, not on her own merit."'

Rio tipped her head back. 'They're already saying that, so let them now come out of the hole they're hiding in and tell me point blank to my black, magic woman face. I learned integrity from you and I'm not about to let you down.'

An emotion crossed the other woman's face that Rio found hard to identify. Pain? Sorrow? Regret? Whatever it was it made Rio's belief in herself grow.

'I only took the gun because I saw someone – whoever that

person was gunned down every last one of those men. I was trying to protect them. Trying to make sure that they stayed alive to face a fair trial.'

'So there's clear evidence that they were the Greenbelt Gang?'

Rio nodded, shedding some of the weight that had been clinging to her since the end of the disastrous raid. 'There were firearms and other items that will easily be tied to the crime scenes. And our main person of interest, Gary Larkin, was among the deceased.'

'Well, we'll be able to use that to deflect from everything else. Knowing that the gang are no longer active will keep the public on our side.'

'But something's not right here. Why would someone kill the gang?'

The AC looked at her sternly. 'Our business is to make sure that the crime was solved, which is what we've done. Anything else can be sorted out. Obviously you're still suspended pending an internal investigation—'

'But if there's something we're missing here, a hitman could still be on the trail of Nikki Bell. Something's not right here—'

'You're suspended Detective Inspector Wray. As far as the service is concerned, the perpetrators have been identified and no longer pose a threat. That's the story I'm going to tell, Commander Jenkins will tell and you better be telling too. If there's a contract killer still out there we will find him, not you.'

'What's going to happen to Nikki?'

'The girl's not your concern anymore. It's already late so best to leave her with Calum Burns for the remainder of tonight. I'll send a unit over in the morning to get her. You're to stay away from her.'

She moved her face closer to Rio and menacingly whispered, 'If you go anywhere near this case while you're suspended, you're finished.'

thirty-six

The Hit: Day Three
Midnight

The last time Rio tried getting drunk was three years back; the night she'd found out her dad was dead. And look how that had turned out! Shagging Calum and doing one of the craziest things in her life. Now here she was – playing crazy again – willing herself to get smashed out of her head, in a low-lit bar where the patrons were interested in only one thing – the volume of liquid in their glass. Neat, dark rum, that was her poison – booze her mum had called the Devil's Juice. The only problem was, she hated the taste of spirits. Disgusting stuff. How anyone became a slave to it she would never understand. Rio sat at a stool at the bar, facing the twin shelves of drinks housed in bottles so colourful she thought they were fireworks standing to attention, getting ready to blast off. Just like her career exploding before her eyes and she could do fuck all about it.

Rio knocked her head back as the glass touched her lips. She grimaced, wanting to spit rather than swallow. Thirty per cent alcohol burned a path down her throat, but still wasn't strong enough to stop the shit swirling around her head. She wasn't just off the case, she was out in the cold.

Suspended.

No warrant badge.

No Detective.

Just plain old Rio Wray born in Notting Hill, West London.

God, it hurt. Really hurt.

'I got a pretty mellow Glenfiddich at home, DI.'

Hearing the words whispered close to her ear, Rio slo-mo turned her face to the side to find Jack Strong beside her. Strange thing was, she zeroed in on those eyes of his – a kind of sparkling, magical blue, probably the brightest thing inside this dark dump. She mentally shook her head – no, the brightest things were the bottles tempting her to consume more.

She turned back around as he spoke, surprised that her words were rock steady. 'Haven't you heard? I'm not a detective inspector no more.' She lifted the glass again and pressed it against her lips. Tipped it back. Fire hit her belly. Slammed the glass back down.

'Let's get you out of here,' Strong continued, his hand touching her shoulder.

Rio violently shook him off. 'No. Like it here.' She twisted her whole body around, almost tipping off the stool. But she didn't notice, only intent on talking. 'Know why? Because I think every last person in here has fucked up as well.'

The man beside her made no response; instead he slid his arm around her waist and heaved her up. Her feet didn't feel like they were on the ground.

As Strong gently started to lead her away, Rio mumbled, 'You believe me, don't you? Someone killed those men before I got there. Someone else was inside that house.'

'Sure I do.'

Strong kept her moving, not letting up until a nasty blast of cold air shook Rio up. She gulped in massive bands of air, each inhalation making the world come more into focus.

Rio started talking again. 'No more red-eye when we get to your place. Just chuck a bucket of cold water in my face.'

Rio gasped for breath as the unexpected water blasted her in the face.

'What the hell did you do that for?' she stammered, gasping at the water clinging and dripping on her face with the power of Greenland ice. 'I didn't really mean it when I said dump water on me.'

She'd been half-slumped in a high-back chair in Strong's kitchen. Now she was ramrod straight after he'd heaved a large glassful of cold water in her face. She glared up at him. He grinned back.

'You need waking up. Plus I still owe you for that coffee trick you played with your elbow.' Then his face became serious. 'Never thought I'd have to shake up the mighty, all-powerful Detective Inspector Rio Wray.'

Rio used her fingertips to swipe some of the water from her skin, her expression intensifying. Everything above her shoulder hurt as the booze pushed her head into a spin. 'What do you want me to do? Get a bloody mega-phone and stand on the rooftop of The Fort preaching "Some bastard dunnit!" to the world.'

Strong swung a chair out and shoved himself into it with such urgency the top half of Rio shuffled back slightly. Her head was back thumping again. His eyes held hers with the force of being pinned to the floor. 'I want you to follow the truth.'

That made Rio start sobering up. She licked her dry lips. Spoke. 'The only way to do that is to not go by the book. I don't bend the rules, don't break them, I just follow them. I rattled the rules one time today and look at the awful mess I left behind.'

Frustrated, Strong flung his hands in the air. 'The first thing I learned as a boy in blue was to listen to my gut instinct. And your gut is shouting at you that something in that house wasn't right. If that's true, you know what that means? There's still a hitter out there gunning for that girl. Probably killed the gang as—'

'Don't you think I've told myself that?' Rio winced as she yelled, but couldn't hold it back. Who the hell did he think he was, getting in her face and reciting what she already knew? 'If I start down that path I'm going to end up like . . .' Rio clamped her mouth shut.

But she didn't need to say it because the man opposite said it for her. 'Like me.'

The silence in the small room was no silence at all, its power a huge pane of glass shattering around them.

Suddenly Strong looked exhausted as he leaned across the table. 'You want to know what happened four years ago?' Rio said nothing, just stared back, some of the anger draining away from her. 'I got it wrong, that's what happened. Not the way you think.' He inhaled deeply. 'I wasn't there.'

Confusion quickly followed by surprise changed Rio's features. 'What do you mean—?'

'I should've been there, but I was laying flowers on my wife and daughter's graves. They died in a road accident six months earlier and tore my world apart. I was a mess; didn't know if I was coming or going.' The unevenness of his breathing touched Rio somewhere deep in her chest. But she remained quiet, letting him talk. 'I got to work that evening, but couldn't stop thinking about them. You know, thinking about the last time I saw them frozen forever on a slab inside a black body bag. So I skipped out of the office, without telling anyone, and went to their graves.' He smiled. 'My Debbie was the same age as Nikki – sweet sixteen. Gorgeous girl who had the best future waiting for her.'

The smile dropped away. 'Got back to base to find a shit storm waiting for me. There was no way that the top brass were going to admit that the senior officer - me - wasn't there. And they were right; I should've been there. The buck stopped with me. I owed that family an apology.' His head flipped up, the belligerent Jack Strong she'd come to know back in place. 'But I didn't owe no accounting to this black group, ethnic minority watchdog, Islamic whatever they were calling themselves—'

'But we're part of the public service and that means we serve the public. How the heck are they going to have any confidence in us if their sons and daughters end up taking their last breath inside a prison cell?'

'I am what I am. I know what I did was wrong, but what about you, Rio? You going to continue letting a wrong be a wrong, while you sit around bleating about playing it by the book? While Nikki Bell's life's still at risk?'

Rio shoved out of her seat. Started pacing. Where was another Devil's Juice when she needed one? Rio knew he was right . . . but so was she. When she'd joined the police force she'd signed up to all the rules and regulations, all the processes and procedures. They were there for a reason: to be fair; to keep order, so everyone, including the bad guys, knew exactly what to expect. Start breaking that cycle and chaos reigned supreme. Hadn't she just seen that in action when she'd gone against orders on the raid? But no matter how she tried to convince herself, Rio couldn't get Nikki's face out of her head.

Nikki crying.

Nikki smiling.

Nikki sulking.

Nikki dead?

'I . . .' Rio swung back around to find Strong almost on top of her. His gaze was intense, so was hers. Without really thinking what she was doing, Rio clasped her palms around his face and drew his face down to hers. Strong jerked out of her hold. They stared at each other breathing heavily.

Rio spoke first. 'For God's sake don't say you think of me as a daughter.'

'No,' Strong uttered softly, 'I think of you as a mate and mates don't break that unwritten rule.'

Rio looked up as she shook her head. 'If only you'd been by my side three years ago with that advice.'

There was a moment's silence before he said, 'You – friend – need to get some shut-eye. Spend the night. I've got a spare room.'

Less than a minute later they were in a room that Rio suspected had once been his daughter's but she kept that to herself. Instead she stared at the neatly made single bed.

'I'll leave a towel for you in the bathroom—'

'Thank you . . . for coming to get me.' Rio didn't turn around as she talked.

The only answer she got was the quiet click of the door as it closed. Now alone, Rio moved towards the bed and sat heavily on it. She flopped back into its softness as her mind came to terms with her new status in life and started figuring out what she was going to do about Nikki Bell.

thirty-seven

1:04 a.m.

Rio checked her watch. She hadn't been able to sleep. Couldn't stop thinking about Nikki.

1:30 a.m.

Rio still couldn't sleep. Couldn't get rid of the thoughts that might turn her world upside down.

1:49 a.m.

Rio got out of the bed that Jack Strong had offered her for the night and went to the bathroom. She took her mobile phone.

1:55 a.m.

'Are we agreed on this?' Rio's tone was quiet, but rushed and urgent as she spoke to Calum on her mobile.

She stood in Jack Strong's unlit bathroom. Chill clung to her half-open blouse and the floorboards drove cold through the bare soles of her feet. She'd been speaking rapidly to Calum for the last five minutes. Her breath almost hurt in her throat as she waited for his answer.

He kept her waiting another half minute before saying, 'OK. Are you coming over now?'

Rio shook her head. 'No. I still need some massive thinking time—'

'Rio?' Her gaze bounced up at the door as she heard Strong call out her name.

'Got to go,' she hurriedly whispered to Calum as she heard Strong's movements in the corridor.

'Was that another voice?' he asked. 'Who's with you?'

The handle to the bathroom started turning.

'I'll see you at your office later on.' The words came out quickly.

The bathroom door opened as she cut the call. Rio wrapped her hand around her phone as Jack Strong appeared in the doorway. They looked at each other. Neither moved.

'You OK?' he finally asked.

Rio's palm tightened around her mobile. 'Yeah. Couldn't sleep. Mind just keeps moving. Can't get it to stop.'

'I make a mean chamomile tea—'

'Jack Strong and herbal tea?' Rio let out a low laugh. 'Now that's a combination I never thought I'd see.'

The side of his mouth flicked up. 'My Rachel loved the stuff. I always keep a box in the cupboard.'

Rio moved towards him. Looked in his eyes. 'Never thought I'd say this but I do believe that you're a good man.'

Before he could answer her she left him. A minute later she found herself back on the bed. This time she didn't lie down, but fixed her hair into medium-sized twists. She needed an as-perfect-as-she-could-get twist-out afro for the day she was about to face.

2:10 a.m.

'Nikki. Nicola. Wake up.'

Dazed Nikki felt the hand against her shoulder as she lay on her side, facing the wall, in bed. She groaned. Didn't want to move. Didn't want to move.

'Calum. Too tired.' She wrapped her hand around the duvet and pulled it closer to her chin.

'No-can-do, little lady. We need to get out of here now.'

Nikki groaned some more as she finally turned to face him. He looked bigger than usual, looming over the bed. She scrubbed a fist over one eye and then uncurled her hand and ran her fingers through her Ophelia-styled shorn hair.

'It's still dark outside,' she said as she sat up.

'I know. But there's good news. The people who murdered your family aren't going to be a problem anymore.'

'What? How?' She pushed her legs over the bed and stood up.

Calum placed his warm palm against her shoulder. 'That doesn't matter at the moment. What you need to do is get ready.' His hand fell away. 'I thought you wanted to see your cousin Ophelia?'

Nikki couldn't hold back the pants of excitement that escaped her. Lia. She'd be with cousin Lia again. Just the thought of being held in her cousin's arms made the world seem right again. A place where no one could hurt her anymore.

'Where's my bag—?'

'Don't worry about that, I've packed up all your gear.'

'But I need my gloves – the long, lacy ones that she gave me. I want her to see me wearing them—'

'We need to move. Now. You can put the gloves on in my car.'

Calum was already out of the room by the time she started scrambling into her jeans and trainers. Her hands shook as she threw on her jumper. She couldn't believe it – she was going to see Ophelia again. She wanted to laugh. Jump. Punch the air. Do some stupid dance where she rocked out to a made-up tune called 'Ophelia'.

Nikki grinned as she joined Calum in the narrow, dark corridor. He stood by the door holding her black, lime-green handled bag. She liked the way he smiled at her as she joined him. One of those big, easy smiles that made any existing tension inside her disappear.

'Will I get to see Rio again? I'd like to thank her.'

'Yeah, you'll get to thank her kid.' His smile dropped away. 'The car's already open. Take this.' He handed her bag to her. 'Put your bag on the backseat. I'll be out as soon as I put on the alarm.'

'Alarm?' She stared up at him. 'I didn't know that the house had one.'

He smiled again. 'There's a lot you don't know, kiddo.' He waved his thumb at the door. 'Go on, hop it.'

And that's what she did, opened the door and felt the cold blast of safety and the early morning at the same time. The Notting Hill street was dark, still. The solitary street light shone bright, much further down the road, but Calum's car was parked in the shadows. Nikki hummed the theme tune to *The Walcotts* as she moved to the car. Kept up her humming as she pulled the back door open. Swung her bag . . .

A hand clammed over her mouth from behind. The shock froze her. Her head was jerked back. She slammed into a body. The tick-tock of her attacker's heartbeat pulsed against the side of her neck. Then her world became truly black as something was shoved over her head.

A voice growled deep and hard into her ear. 'Do everything

I say. *Everything.* You don't want to find out what's going to happen if you step out of line.'

2:57 a.m.

'Let me out,' Nikki screamed for what felt like the millionth time. She thumped her small fists against the door, then leaned back and let fly a kick that hurt her more than the door.

She was frightened, scared of what was going to happen to her now. One minute she'd been standing outside the safe house, waiting for Calum, and the next a hood had enclosed her in a nightmare of darkness. Then she was bounced in the back seat of this car taking her on the ride from hell.

She had felt so disorientated that she couldn't say how long they drove for. But when the car stopped, she was taken out, not roughly, but with a gentleness that terrified her even more, and guided up stairs to someplace that felt flat beneath her feet.

'Turn around in thirty seconds,' the same voice had instructed.

Then the hood had been whipped off her head and something slammed behind her. Nikki didn't wait thirty seconds, but immediately spun around to find a door shut behind her. Instantly she had gone for the brass handle, but the door wasn't moving. So she'd banged, yelled, screamed – but no one came. There was no window, only a single bed and a free-standing black lamp in one corner.

Now she slumped to the bare floorboards exhausted, almost broken. She didn't want to end up dead as well.

thirty-eight

7:56 a.m.

Rio was already dressed, ready to go as she stared at her mobile phone in her hand. Rain tapped against the window almost matching the rhythm of her beating heart. Today was going to take her down a path she never thought she would go down.

The mobile rang. She took a breath. Then calmly answered.

'Detective Insp—' She clawed the remainder of the word back, remembering she was suspended. 'Yes? . . . What?' She nodded. 'I'll be right there.'

She terminated the call, left the room and strode with ease towards the front door.

'Who was that on the phone?'

She turned to face Strong who waited just outside what she assumed was his bedroom. 'That was the Super. He needs me at The Fort. They can't find Nikki.'

8:05 a.m.

Greenbelt Gang Die in Gun Battle with Cops . . .

A rain-soaked Cornelius Bell stumbled as he heard the breaking news headline coming from a car that had stopped at a red light near him. The headline made him feel sick, so he pulled even harder on the spliff as he found shelter from the aggressive rain huddling in the shadow of a closed shop door-way. He felt the three crack rocks in his jeans' pocket and the desperate urge to indulge in something stronger than weed to take him to a place where reality wasn't crowding in on him. His reality was that he needed to decide whether he was going to talk to that cop. But what was he going to say to her? How was he going to explain?

He felt the cold and the wind around him as he scurried into an alleyway. The pain was back: sharp this time, almost unbearable, as if he were drowning, lungs filling with his own self-inflicted torment.

The Greenbelt Gang were dead.

He pulled out his pay-as-you-go mobile. Called the number the cop had left with him. The phone connected, started to ring.

Come on, come on . . .

But no one picked up; just voicemail: *This is Detective Inspector Rio Wray of the Metropolitan Police Service. Your call is important to me, so please leave a message after the tone.*

The beep sounded harsh and too loud in his ear. He hesitated. Didn't want to leave a message, wanted to speak to her directly. But he spoke, his words worked up by weed.

'Cornelius Bell here . . . I need to speak . . . to talk . . . Now . . . Ring me back . . .'

The phone made a fussing sound Cornelius knew well – out of juice. He threw it as hard and as far as he could, but was so high on dope and his troubles he didn't hear it clatter and smash in the distance somewhere. *Shit. Fuck.* He rarely cursed, even in his head. His mother had taught him that no matter how bad the situation you always minded your manners.

Mum.

Why wouldn't her face leave him alone?

He thought about that girl at The Rebels' Collective, who had come on to him a while back, right in front of Cookie – which had so embarrassed him – pushing her Canary Wharf high boobs and chat about karma in his face. Maybe she was right and all he needed to make everything right was some karma.

Yeah, right, the reading of the will had been some kinda karma.

The crack cocaine started to burn up in Cornelius's pocket.

Why had he thrown the phone? He needed to call that cop. Or had he just done that? No, he couldn't remember doing it; he needed a phone. He moved out of the shadows, into the savage rain, and hurried down the street. As he passed the shrouded railway station he looked over his shoulder, convinced he heard footsteps: no one behind him. He pushed only one thought in his head – get a phone. When he hit the high street he noticed several cars waiting outside a kebab shop. Cornelius hurried over to one and tapped on the door. The woman inside lowered the window a fraction.

'Hello, I'm Cornelius Bell. My parents were murdered by the Greenbelt Gang. Could you lend me a couple of quid to make a phone call? I'll give it you back.'

The woman recoiled in horror, hastily closed the window and locked the doors. Cornelius started banging against the window with the flat of his hands. 'I just need some cash for a phone call—'

'Oi!' a commanding, deep voice yelled. Cornelius turned to find a big, burly man looking at him. 'Get away from my motor, you stinking junkie . . .'

Cornelius started running and running, his mind spinning, his thoughts churning. He ignored the looks he was getting until he reached The Rebels' Collective. He bashed his fist heavily against the corrugated sheet door. He was let in by a face he didn't know, and as soon as he was inside Monica, self-styled leader of the group, cornered him.

'We're setting off in the van for the anti-fracking demo at ten, so we can be there by late evening, and for the rest of the week. You are joining us, of course.'

She sounded like his dad, always telling him to do this crap, that crap. Always telling him he just wasn't cutting it as a Bell.

'Frack off,' he roared. His eyes roamed wildly around the room at the others: 'The lot of you. Get out of my face.'

Monica pushed herself into his space. 'We've been talking about you, Connie, having doubts about your commitment to the cause. We all understand about your parents, but if you don't pull your shit together soon, you're out.'

The crack was eating away at his skin.

Without answering, he pushed past her, almost making her fall.

'Sorry,' he mumbled, remembering his mum's advice, and rushed up the stairs. Once inside his room he leant heavily against the door, his breathing high and erratic. He was glad Cookie wasn't here; she didn't like seeing him like this. He reached for the belt in his trousers. Funny how wearing a belt was the one thing from his past life that he couldn't let go of. Dad had impressed on him from an early age that belts were a man's way of showing the world he was smart, decent, respectable, someone to be relied on.

When he'd left home the first thing he'd promised himself he would do was to stop wearing the belt – like he was sticking all that crap straight back into his father's moralising face. He'd tried to do it, but couldn't. Sure he got off his face every now and then, but maybe he wanted people to see him as a decent and respectable guy.

But he didn't feel either of those things anymore. And he didn't have a phone. He moved further into the room and stopped at the cardboard box that masqueraded as a table with its peaceful yellow cloth that Cookie had put over it. He stared at the framed picture of the small boy, Cookie's brother, and almost started to cry.

The rocks in his pocket burned deep into his brain. He dropped on to the bed, took out the crack and laid his belt neatly, like good memories, next to him.

thirty-nine

9:04 a.m.

Rio spotted a frantic Ophelia Bell as soon as she entered DSI Newman's office. Strong had come back to The Fort with her, but he'd gone to the operations room while she'd come upstairs. The actress appeared haggard, her skin pale as if it hadn't received any nourishment for a week. She was all bug-grey eyes and veins standing tall on her neck.

'Tell me what's happened?' Rio asked as she took the seat that Newman waved her towards.

But it was Ophelia who dived in. 'They can't find her. I came here as soon as they called to tell me they would be releasing Nikki into my care, but they said they couldn't find her.' Her bony fingers weaved the air with her every word.

Rio turned to Newman. 'I don't understand, she was with Calum.'

'Whose Calum?' Nikki's cousin asked, confusion deepening on her face.

Newman answered, with a nervous little cough as an introduction. 'Calum Burns is a private security consultant that we sometimes use. He's one of the best and has been making sure that Nicola was kept safe—'

''But I can keep her safe,' Ophelia burst over him with anger. 'She needs to be with family now.'

'We all need to calm down,' Rio said gently. She turned to her superior officer. 'What happened?'

'Calum said that she went missing early hours of this morning. The fool should have contacted us straight away, but said he was sure he could find her.'

'Do you think someone has taken her?' Ophelia asked, then her teeth twisted into her bottom lip.

Rio looked over at her superior officer who shook his head slightly. They hadn't told Ophelia about the hit out on her cousin and Newman obviously wanted to keep it that way.

Rio's next words were meant to reassure her. 'What we know is that Nikki has a history of taking off. Her boyfriend's mother was here yesterday–'

'Ade's mum?' Seeing Rio's surprised expression, she continued, 'She told me all about Ade, and that Uncle Frank and Auntie Patsy tried to keep them apart. She trusts me.'

'Ade's mum came here yesterday to report him missing. Nikki and Ade probably cooked up some scheme and are safely together somewhere. Or maybe she's gone to a friend, so what I suggest you do is call anyone you can think of who she may have gone to–'

'But you'll help me do that?'

Rio switched her gaze slowly back to Newman who was looking very uncomfortable indeed. Rio could see that he wasn't going to help her out here so she turned back to Nikki's desperate cousin.

'I'm taking some personal time now that the case is closed, but we'll make sure that finding her is a top priority. We'll have her back with you in no time.'

The expression on Ophelia's face became fierce. 'I bet that bastard Foster has got her nice and snug somewhere.'

'Why would you think that?' Rio asked.

The other woman let out a full-blown scoff. 'Oh come on,

you were there for the will reading. She's his client and now worth a zillion bucks. Nikki's not a vulnerable kid to him anymore; she's an investment. He's going to spin her so many different ways she won't be able to tell north from south, and while he's doing that he's going to make sure he helps his greedy little self to as much of her money as possible. That's what really gets me, not that Mummy and Daddy left me out in the cold, but that that detestable man will be sitting pretty and flush for the rest of his money grabbing life.'

Ophelia's words left the air polluted with ugly animosity. Whatever foulness lay between this woman and the Bell's solicitor, Nikki was the one who was going to end up in the muck, Rio thought.

'I'm not letting that creep get away with it. I'm challenging the status of the will as soon as possible.'

Rio wasn't surprised to hear this pronouncement. 'For whatever it's worth, Miss Bell, Nikki said that she was more than happy for you and your brother to share it with her.'

'You don't get it.' The words were so biting and cold they forced Rio back in her chair. Ophelia screwed her lips together as one of her hands came up to pat her hair. 'I'm sorry. I'm just so anxious about Nikki's whereabouts.'

'If Stephen Foster has her,' Newman spoke again, 'at least we know that she's somewhere safe. As her next of kin you can talk to her about him and what she wants to do next. The important thing is that we find her and I've no doubt that with your assistance we can do that sooner rather than later.'

Ophelia absently nodded as she grabbed her handbag and stood up. 'Can I find a coffee somewhere before I start making those calls?'

Only when she was on her feet did Rio see how much more weight she'd lost. How she was standing on legs that appeared more like poles Rio would never know. It compelled her to say, 'You need to get some food into you as well. There's a vending machine at the end of the corridor where you can get a snack and a drink.'

After she was gone Rio stood up and looked at DSI Newman. 'I've been warned to stay away from the case, so if anything else crops up—'

'I tried to persuade the AC to consider giving you a desk job while the internal inquiry is underway, instead of a complete suspension.'

Rio let out a long puff of air. 'I didn't need to hear you say that – I knew you'd try everything you could to help me.'

'It's hard times for the Met at the moment. We've had two firearms incidents that have got everyone on edge. We can't police this great city of ours if the people don't trust us.'

Rio nodded, then asked, 'Have you brought in Terry Larkin for questioning?'

'We had a little chat with him at his home. He was at a party during the incident, so he's got plenty of witnesses to confirm he was nowhere near Kent.' Newman shrugged. 'And of course he knows nothing about anything. So what will you do with your time?'

Rio hesitated, then answered, 'Catch up on life, I suppose.'

In the corridor on the way out, she bumped into Ophelia, who was having a tussle with the vending machine.

'It's a touch temperamental,' Rio said softly when she reached the other woman. 'Let me.' She gave the machine a thump on one side and a Kit Kat lurched and fell.

But the other woman didn't reach for it; instead she turned her gaunt face to Rio. 'She is going to be OK, isn't she?'

Rio sympathised with the naked pain printed on her face. 'Your daughter—'

Her lips clamped together; she hadn't meant to say that.

Ophelia reared back, any trace of blood left in her skin flowing away. 'My what?'

'Sorry.' Rio held her hand up. 'Not my—'

'It's OK.' The other woman sighed. 'It was bound to come out some time. How did you know?'

Rio pulled out the adoption papers from her bag and handed them over. 'I found them in your aunt and uncle's home after their murders. I didn't know what the score was about whether Nikki knew or not, so I kept them. It was only after she cut her hair,' Rio smiled, 'to look like you that I saw the resemblance.'

Ophelia pushed the papers in her pocket. 'I was fourteen, mucking around with some boy and not even realising what was going on. Maybe if my parents hadn't sent me to that strict convent school I might've figured it out; we weren't even Catholics for God's sake. No way was my father going to have people know that his daughter was in trouble.' Her voice softened. 'And truth be known, I wasn't up for being anyone's mother. Uncle Frank and Auntie Patsy had been trying for years for a kid . . . so that's what we did: gave Nikki over to them. The only thing I asked was that when she got a bit older that she spend a couple of hours each year on her birthday with me.' Her voice now shook. 'But a few years back they decided to stop her from coming. They never explained why . . . maybe they thought Nikki was getting too close to me.'

The explanation for the tension between Pasty Bell and her niece in the hospital was suddenly clear to Rio: two mothers vying for the affection of their daughter. *Family. The people you don't choose but who you are stuck with for life.*

Rio touched the other woman gently on the shoulder. 'I won't say anything to her; it's not my business. You need to get some rest. And eat. With your history . . .'

'My eating disorder is a lifelong battle.' Ophelia smiled, a bit too brightly. 'But I'm fine. I'll be back to my normal self once I know that my child . . . that Nikki is OK.'

Rio left her and two minutes later found herself hovering outside the operations room on the second floor.

You shouldn't be here.

Just a little peek . . .

That room was practically her whole life, where she'd staked out her ambitious for all to see. And now it might be out of her reach . . .

'Thought I might find you here.'

Rio turned to find Jack Strong behind her.

'Any news on Nikki?' he continued.

Rio shook her head. 'Her cousin's going to check out any contacts she has. But she's probably with her boyfriend—'

'Should I contact his mum?'

Rio shrugged. 'Can't help you with that one, I'm suspended remember.'

He took a few steps towards her. 'Newman and Tripple want me to head up a small unit looking for the hitman – that's if he's still out there. Cornelius Bell left a message in your voice box. He sounded weird. Said it was urgent. Maybe Nikki's with him?'

'Doubt it; he didn't seem close to her. Probably just wants to find out about Nikki. I'll go over . . .' Rio stuttered to a stop. She couldn't just visit Cornelius Bell. She was suspended. Meant to stay the hell back from this case. Nikki's stubborn face took up pole position in her mind. The Assistant Commissioner might not agree with her but her first duty was to that girl.

'I'll pay him a visit now,' Rio said quickly. 'Although, of course, I'm no longer part of this investigation'

'Of course.' A knowing look passed between them.

'But you might want to see this.' Strong continued as he

took out his mobile phone and passed it to Rio. On the screen was a mug shot of a young man she recognised as Samson Larkin.

'It just came in from the authorities in Cyprus.'

Rio handed the phone back to him with a grateful nod.

'You know where I am if you need me,' he told.

Rio didn't want to implicate him in anything she might do, but having someone on the inside would prove to be useful.

'Keep me briefed about any evidence found at the house.'

He didn't say anything, just gave a single nod.

As soon as she was back in her car she got onto her mobile to Calum.

'We cool?' she asked.

'We're cool.'

'I need to check on Cornelius Bell first and then I'll be straight around. Any problems—'

'The only problems we'll have is when you get here.'

Rio knew he was right. But she stood rock solid behind the decision she had made.

'There's one more thing I want you to do . . .' she said.

9:25 a.m.

Nikki lay on the floor, knees tucked tight to her chest, her arms wrapped around her shins, trying not to think about what was going to happen to her next. But the same terror-drenched words that had taken over her mind as she hid in the cupboard at Uncle Maurice and Aunty Linda's beat in her head.

They are going to kill me.

Going to kill me.

Kill me.

KILL ME.

forty

Rio wasn't surprised to be stonewalled at the entrance of The Rebels' Collective by the same woman she'd had a verbal ding-dong with two days ago. The woman wasn't doing pink, fluffy slippers this time, but a pair of black Dr Martens that were splattered with squiggly, bright-coloured patterns that looked like they'd been painted by local graffiti artists as practice before they did the real stuff on some council-owned wall.

'Well if it isn't the woman who sold out her brothers and sisters by becoming the agent of an oppressive regime. The cop who beat up Cornelius—'

'I didn't touch him. I had a job to do, which was to give him the regrettable news about his parents' deaths.'

'Monica,' a voice shouted from inside. 'We've got to get on the road now or we won't make it to the demo.'

Monica? Rio stared at the woman in front of her. She decided sarcastically that the name was too soft, too whole-some for the next leader of the free world.

'Look,' Rio said, 'he called me and left a message saying he needed to speak urgently, so here I am. Now – are you going to let me in?'

'Have you got a warrant?'

Rio was about to tell her that she could go and get one until she remembered that she couldn't do that anymore, 'No. Do I need one? He called me.'

'Why don't you call him back then?'

'I did, but there was no response.' Rio could feel her irritation growing. 'Why don't you go and get him if you don't believe me?'

'OK.'

The makeshift door slammed in Rio's face. Less than a minute later Monica was back, but this time she didn't open the door.

'He's here but he's not answering his door. He's probably sleeping; yesterday was a rough day for him. I'll get one of the others who are staying to tell him you called in the morning. I won't be here to tell him.'

Irritation boiled over into anger and Rio kicked the door. Did it a second time and said, 'I think he's worried about something.' A third kick. 'I'm going to keep this up until I get to see him.'

'OK, OK, for fuck's sake . . .'

The door started opening . . . Rio kicked it again and it banged back. Monica jumped inside the room. Rio strode in, her gaze quickly taking in the small group of people, some with rucksacks on the floors, others with them on their backs. A few didn't have any bag.

Rio turned stern eyes onto Monica. 'From the amount of luggage you and your friends are packing it looks like you're taking a long trip to save the world, so let's make a little deal, me and you; you stay out of my business and I'll stay out of yours.'

Rio turned her back and went up the stairs. Once she got to Cornelius's room she tapped against the door. No answer.

'Cornelius, it's Detective Inspector Rio Wray. I know you want to talk, so let me in.'

No answer. This time she hammered against the door. Nothing.

Rio leaned her ear against the door. No sounds. That worried her. She could feel it in her bones that something was wrong. She started kicking the door with the same force she'd used downstairs.

'That's all you people know.' Rio half-turned to find Monica on the end of the landing. 'Kicking and stomping on others to get what you want.'

'How was Cornelius the last time you saw him?'

Monica's expression changed to something Rio would swear was either alarm or guilt.

'He looked a bit fucked up to be honest. I would never have bugged him about . . .'

The voice tailed off. Even more alarmed, Rio turned back to the door and booted it in with an almighty motion that shook her from head to toe. The door crashed back and she rushed inside. And stopped. Behind her there were gasps, muffled cries and whispered words of horror from the people in the doorway.

A belt had been tied to a pipe that led from the ceiling and the other end formed into a noose. An overturned chair was nearby. Cornelius was hanging, neck red and stretched, face purple and his tongue obscenely poked out of his slack mouth.

Monica's broken voice asked, 'Shall I call an ambulance?'

Rio sighed and said nothing. Cornelius Bell didn't need an ambulance.

He was dead.

Rio inspected but didn't touch the body. She looked at Cornelius's fingernails: torn and bloody. She looked up at the ceiling. Fresh scratch marks flecked with blood. In his death agony, Cornelius had clearly clawed at the ceiling, trying to save himself, but he'd left it too late.

Rio turned to look at the stunned crowd that had gathered by the door. 'Can you tell me anything?'

The members of The Rebels' Collective were in shock and said nothing, apart from one girl with purple hair who offered, 'He hasn't been himself since his parents were killed.' She turned an accusing eye on Monica. 'And while some of us wanted to support him, others wanted to kick his arse out into the cold.'

Monica's neck inched back in a defensive motion. 'We all agreed—'

'Only because you kept on bullying us,' the woman with the purple hair accused. 'He was a brother of the collective. And we let him down.'

'Someone needs to call an ambulance. And the police,' Rio said.

Monica looked at her sharply. 'But you're a cop.'

Rio knew she was in difficult position; what she was doing could be interpreted as the 'investigating' that the AC had warned her to step back from. But she was covered to the extent that Cornelius had called her and asked to talk . . . Then again she didn't have to needlessly put herself in the spotlight.

'Call the police . . . I need everyone to go downstairs to give me some space.'

'Yeah,' the purple-haired woman answered, before adding, 'Maybe this will give us time to decide whether we want to talk about the leadership of the group when the rest of you get back from the demo.'

They took their troubles away and left Rio with the biggest one she had hanging in the room. It didn't seem dignified to leave Cornelius Bell up there, but she dared not touch him. What was Cornelius going to tell her, and could this and his suicide be linked? Careful not to touch anything, Rio started looking for clues that might answer her question. And that's when she saw the envelope placed near the photograph of a small boy.

Rio Wray.

He'd written her name on it; left her a message about what he wanted to tell her. As she slipped the envelope in her pocket she felt a presence in the open doorway.

Cookie, Cornelius's girlfriend stood there gazing up at his body. Grief and shock froze her into place.

By the time Rio got Cookie back downstairs she was struggling and cursing like a person who had lost their soul. But Rio wouldn't let her go and eventually managed to get her into a chair. The other members of the collective stood on the periphery as if coming any closer meant catching a contagious disease.

Rio got down on her hunches, her hands wrapping around the younger woman's wrists pinning her to the chair.

'I'm sorry.'

Cookie's head swung from side to side, electric-blue dreads flying in the air as tears made continuous watery tracks down her face.

'I know that doesn't help you at the moment . . .' The sound of a siren tore up in the distance outside, giving Rio her prompt to leave.

She looked around at the others. 'I know that some of you are leaving, but will one of you look after her?'

The siren got closer.

Rio rose and without a backwards glance left the collective. She twisted in the opposite direction from the ambulance blaring its noise into the street, walked a couple of streets and when she was safely out of range pulled out the envelope Cornelius had left her. A small, folded flyer advertising a gig by a band called 'Stop n Search' was inside. She flipped it over. His handwriting was shaky. No punctuation:

I take the blame for everything nikki nikki save

And that was it. Rio struggled with her disappointment that Cornelius hadn't spelt out what he'd meant.
Blame for what?
And why was he so preoccupied with Nikki?

forty-one

11:52 a.m.

nikki save.

Part of Cornelius Bell's last recorded words stayed with Rio as she eased her BMW to a halt outside of Calum's office above the butcher's in Brixton. Was he just worried about his younger cousin because a hitman was – or still is – on her tail? But Cornelius hadn't known about the hitman. And what did he blame himself for? Did it have something to do with the case?

As much as she twisted and turned the last question in her mind, Rio couldn't find an answer ... Unless Cornelius had somehow been inside the house with the Greenbelt Gang and pulled the trigger ending all their lives. Revenge? No, she dismissed it instantly. No way would Cornelius have known where the gang was; plus he'd been hooked on the type of gear that didn't keep a mind straight. Maybe that was all his suicide note was? The ramblings of a junkie's wired brain.

Rio got out of the car and walked up the stairs to Calum's office after being buzzed in. She halted briefly outside the first door on the landing upstairs and then moved on towards the next room, Calum's office.

'Thank God you're here,' Calum said as soon as he saw her.

He was at his desk, one leg on it, his bad leg on the ground, with a glass of – she assumed – Hennessy's. The front of his dark hair stood up in tufts with the pattern of fingers that had been thrust through it many times. His face was creased with tiredness, which didn't surprise her knowing he would have been up most of the night.

'Been that bad?' Rio offered sympathetically, remaining in the doorway.

Calum drained the glass and slapped it down on the desk. 'Of course it's been effing bad. I'm not happy with what we've done.' He dropped his leg and stood up, rolling the muscles of his shoulders. 'Are you sure you know what you're doing?'

Rio didn't hesitate. 'Yeah. I wouldn't be able to sleep at night if I stood back and did nothing. Plus, I've just seen Cornelius Bell hanging from his own belt. Dead.'

Calum whistled as he lifted his eyebrows. 'Suicide?'

'Looks like. He left a note saying that he was to blame and rambling about saving Nikki–'

'What does that mean?'

'Dunno, but it just confirms what I've been thinking – something else is going on here and I'm going to find out what it is.'

Calum moved towards her and started speaking again in a hushed voice. 'You think Cornelius had something to do with the gang?'

'I've got three pieces of a puzzle. But the connecting piece that fits them all together is missing. The first piece is that the Greenbelt Gang were all murdered by someone. Maybe they needed shutting up ... and if they needed to be silenced I suspect that means Nikki does too. Which leads me to piece number two: the hitman, who I still think is out there trying to get a bullseye on Nikki. Now I've got a new piece: the suicide of Cornelius Bell.'

Calum tilted his head, his green gaze piercing Rio: 'Never

thought I'd live to see the day the all perfect brown-eyed girl of the Met got suspended for putting a foot out of place.'

Rio thought he would be crowing and gloating about her present situation, but he wasn't. She'd always felt that he was just waiting for her to put a step out of line so he could jump in her face and mockingly sneer, 'Now you know what it feels like.' Rio wouldn't go so far as to say he looked sympathetic, but he wasn't taking the piss out of her either. Then he did something she wasn't expecting – he rubbed the pad of a finger along her cheek. It made her remember who they were, other than former friends and colleagues. And she hated it; there was no space for emotion with a hitman on the loose trying to get his job done in the fastest time possible.

'I've done what I've done,' she finally responded, stepping back slightly so his finger fell away. 'So are you going to help me?'

'You talking about us or the case?'

Now he was the one pissing *her* off. 'Just answer me.'

The old jovial Calum slid back into place, one side of his mouth perking up. 'Sure. But just remember what I said, your whole career could go pop if you carry this out.'

Midday

Shaking and tired, Nikki managed to scramble up off the floor when she heard the footsteps again. She hadn't heard them for at least the last hour. She was done with screaming and crying; it was clear no one was coming to her rescue. Nikki tried to remember what she'd been taught at that girls'-only physical defence class she'd taken when she was fifteen.

Relax.

Get your defence pose ready.

Strike.

The footsteps got closer. Nikki rushed towards the door, but stopped about one leg length away and got into a fighting stance: body at a forty-five degree angle, left leg forwards, hands up in the on-guard position with the right elbow down protecting her liver.

A key thrust into the lock. Click. The lock turned.

I can do this.

I can do this.

Nikki kept the chant going around her head, even though she felt her leading leg begin to tremble, her balled hands shake.

I can do—

The door thrust open. But instead of leaping forwards, Nikki stumbled back when she saw who stood in the doorway.

The cop Rio and the man she'd come to trust so well, Calum Burns.

forty-two

Nikki's back was pressed tight against the wall as she accused them. 'You kidnapped me.' Her grey eyes possessed the wildness of a stormy sea. 'Why? Why?' She placed a shaking palm just below the base of her throat. 'I thought you were going to kill me.' There was an audible sucking sound as she pulled and twisted the air back into her chest. 'You're not going to kill me are—'

'Of course we're not, sweetheart,' Calum softly cut in.

Rio moved to stand in front of the trembling girl. She stooped with enough space between them so the teen didn't feel crowded. Calum held himself back in the doorway.

Rio decided that if they left this much longer Nikki was either going to descend into shock overdrive or scream the place down, so she told her the one thing that might make her listen.

'There's a hitman out there trying to kill you.'

If Nikki's body could get any stiller it did in that moment. Except for her chest, which was rising and falling.

Rio pressed on. 'That's why the police have been guarding you. The man who attacked you in the hospital is still out there trying to finish the job off. The reason he wants to kill you is because you're the only witness to what took place in your aunt and uncle's home. The killer on your trail has been given five days to execute . . .' Rio deliberately used the word so the girl was in no doubt about the danger she faced, 'the job.'

The teenager finally spoke as her palms came flat against the wall on either side of her. 'But I thought the cops had caught that gang—'

'They have,' Rio interrupted softly. 'But I still think that man is out to kill you—'

'But why drag me over here with something over my head like I'm some kind of animal? Why would the cops do that?'

Rio took a shallow breath. 'I'll be upfront with you. My colleagues are easing up on the operation, now the gang's out of the way. They're still looking for the man after you, but I know for a fact they've only put a small unit out there to try to find him. My boss believes that now the gang are out of the way the hitman will abandon his mission because why would he continue to do a job if there's no one around to pay him now.'

Nikki rapidly blinked. 'That makes sense—'

'It should, but there's something about this that just doesn't add up. I can't tell you all the ins and outs, but I can tell you this – if that man got to you I would never be able to forgive myself.'

The girl's breathing started to settle down. 'If you've known this all along, why didn't you tell me from the get-go?'

Calum joined the conversation for the first time. 'Maybe we should've, but at the time we had to think quickly and couldn't take the chance you might not go along with our plan.'

Nikki looked at him with eyes of deep betrayal. 'You got that right. You nearly scared the knickers straight off me.' Her lip trembled. 'I liked you. I thought you were my friend.'

Calum took a step into the room. 'I like you too, sweetheart, that's why I'd do anything to make sure you don't get hurt. I know that you want to go and stay with your cousin Ophelia,' he raised his hands, 'and I'm not going to stop you if that's what you decide to do. You're right; we should've been letting you make some of the decisions for yourself.' He took another step closer. 'But what if you go to stay with Ophelia and this killer finds out? That's going to put her in danger as well, isn't it? And I know the last thing you want is for Ophelia to get hurt.'

'Like Calum says,' Rio added, 'I'm going to put the decision for this in your hands. If you want to go, we won't stop you. I'll drive you over to your cousin's myself. But all I'm asking is that you give me four more days, including today, to sort this out. If that time is up and I'm no closer to sorting this out you're free to leave. That's all I'm asking for, Nikki. But the decision is yours.'

Silence. Rio kept her gaze on the girl and watched a range of emotions cross her face – fear, confusion and, finally, exhaustion.

Nikki peeled her body off the wall, but didn't move forwards. 'OK, I'll stay. But only if you let me call Lia to let her know I'm alright.'

Rio didn't need to look around to know that Calum was smiling. 'Good girl. But you can't tell her where you are. I'll give you a throwaway phone with a jammed signal just in case anyone tries to track down the number and our location.'

Nikki's eyes lit up. 'What? You can do that? Will you teach me how to do it?'

Rio heard the admiration and almost hero worship in the sixteen-year-old's voice, reminding her of the time she'd felt the same about the man standing beside her, before everything personal between them had gone sour.

Ten minutes later Nikki was munching a BLT sandwich – having decided that meat wasn't murder – and playing a game on Calum's computer while Rio and her former lover whispered to each other.

'Whatever happens,' he said, 'you're still going to have to

explain why you nabbed the girl and you'll be lucky to end up with your pension rights.'

'The only thing I care about that's at stake here is the life of that girl.'

'So what are you planning to do next?'

'Jack Strong is going to keep an eye on anything that might pop up at the house in Kent—'

'It's Jack now is it?' Calum was giving her one of those you-been-holding-out-on-me looks. 'Have you been banging him while claiming overtime?'

That caught Rio off-guard. Woo-hoo, was cool man Calum J.E.A.L.O.U.S? *What if he is? He gave up all rights to where you lay your head every night years back.*

'Who I've been screwing with is none of your concern,' she eventually answered him, sticking her chin defiantly into the air.

'What if I told you I haven't been sexing it up with anyone in the last three years?'

Rio scoffed. 'Pull my other leg at the same time why don't you.'

That made Calum laugh so hard it left Rio bewildered; she didn't get where the joke was coming from. Then she clicked. She'd talked about pulling his leg – was this about his accident?

She dropped her chin slightly as she lowered her voice. 'One of these days you're going to tell me about what happened to you – but not now. Now we need to focus on this. Did you organise a flight for me?'

He nodded. 'It leaves at three from Stansted. How can you be sure that it's Samson Larkin in Northern Cyprus?'

Rio had asked him to organise a quick flight to Cyprus while she was in the car before setting off to see Cornelius Bell. Calum hadn't asked any questions, but now he was.

'His mugshot came through from Cyprus. It's baby-boy Larkin alright.'

'Still don't get why you need to see him—'

'Because whoever is pulling the strings in this case,' Rio cut in as she stood, 'thinks they've wiped out the gang, but there are two of them still left, if we're counting Terry Larkin. But I'm more concerned for his son. If Samson Larkin was part of that gang I need to get to him before someone else does.'

Calum gave it ten minutes after Rio left for the airport before he took out the mobile he only ever used for international calls.

When the call connected he said, 'I'm calling in that favour you owe me . . .'

forty-three

The Hit: Day 4
10:00 a.m. Northern Cyprus Time
8:00 a.m. London Time

Prisons, like gravesides, cast a chill over everything and as Rio was escorted from one security checkpoint to another, within the walls of the correctional facility in Cyprus, she began to shiver slightly. Nicosia was the dividing line between the Greek and Turkish sides of the island. As soon as she'd cleared immigration at the airport, Rio had alerted the Turkish authorities that she was acting as a legal adviser and wanted to pay a client a visit and they'd made the arrangements.

She'd had to wait until the morning, which had been a blow to her plans; she'd wanted to get everything done and dusted as soon as. But knowing there was nothing she could do about the time frame she'd booked a room in a pretty, self-catering three star affair. She'd carefully avoided doing anything that might have brought her to the attention of British representatives on the island because she didn't want word getting back to London that she was there.

The physical search of her person bought Rio back to the prison. The examination was thorough and forbidding.

'Which firm do you represent?' one of the two prison officers asked her.

Rio answered confidently. 'I'm a freelance solicitor for Stephen Foster in London and was in Cyprus to look after one of his client's interests.'

The female guard smiled and said, 'Ah yes, Mr Foster . . .'

It seemed everyone knew Stephen Foster. Rio had some fake paperwork, courtesy of Calum, but she froze briefly when the male guard reached for his phone. If he called Foster's London office, she was sunk and might be shoved in a prison cell herself. Turned out he was merely calling someone to escort her to an interview room.

The room was bare, even by the standards of such places, with whitewashed walls and a table that was bolted to the ground. Two functional chairs were the only other furniture and there was a red buzzer on the wall. Once Rio was seated, she didn't have long to wait before the door re-opened and a cuffed youth was escorted into the room. Despite the fading cuts and bruises on his faintly tanned face he had the look of the boy next door who was going to grow into a true heart-breaker. Short, deep-brown hair with a cluster of untamed strands licking his forehead, eyebrows and nose that seemed perfectly placed to fit the shape of his face and hazel eyes . . . It was his eyes that disconcerted Rio the most; they looked too alert.

As he was placed in the chair he acknowledged Rio by narrowing those eyes that were already getting her to rethink her strategy. Just before the guard uncuffed him and left, he made a gesture at Rio, which the youth couldn't see. He tapped the side of his head with his finger, in a gesture she took to mean that the kid was loco.

But Rio knew that already. This was Samson Larkin.

Larkin checked her over for a while, drumming his fingers against the table. Finally he said, 'So – who are you?'

'My name is Miss Filey. I'm a solicitor and I work for

Stephen Foster's law firm in London. He asked me to come and talk to you.'

The beat of his fingers against the table got louder. 'What's your first name?'

That took Rio by surprise. 'I think we need to keep this professional.'

'Foster?' He changed the rhythm of his fingers to a drum roll. 'But he's big time isn't he? I thought our family's brief was that Catley character?'

He tapped a new tune against the wood, one that sounded vaguely familiar to Rio.

'Know what this music is?'

'Mr Larkin, I don't think we've got times for games—'

'Beethoven's "Moonlight" Sonata. Otherwise known as his piano sonata No. 14 in C-sharp minor. Graceful. Beautiful. Lures you into thinking everything in the world is good and fine.' He tapped away some more. Then stopped. Shuffled back in his chair. 'Some say that Beethoven had African ancestry, like you. Think it's true?'

The unsettling effect this youth was having on her grew. He might not be as loco as everyone thought. Hadn't the information Jack Strong found out about him included a report from his psychiatrist that claimed he was a genius? Rio realised that Samson Larkin might be a completely different beast to the one she'd been expecting to deal with.

She got down to business. 'I'm not sure how much you know about what's been going on back home, Samson, but your Uncle Gary was arrested by the police on suspicion of being involved in, what the public are calling . . .' Rio made a big show of looking through her papers. 'Ah, yes.' She looked back up at him. 'The Greenbelt Gang.'

As soon as the word 'Greenbelt' was out in the open Rio

noticed the way Samson Larkin shifted in his chair as the muscles around his mouth tightened.

'Who said my name's Samson Larkin?'

'We both know who you really are.'

He pouted at her, but didn't deny the truth. But she didn't go in for the kill, kept it firm and professional as she carried on.

'Mr Foster appeared while your Uncle Gary was under arrest and decided he was going to represent him.'

'Now why would a big shot brief like him do that?'

Rio leaned across the table like she was about to tell him a secret. 'The police think you were involved in Greenbelt. He wants to find out what you know so he can defend your uncle.'

Samson wore the look of a cocky, older man. 'But, like I said Mizz-won't-tell-me-her-first-name, I don't know anything about nothing.'

'Gary told Foster that you do.'

The cockiness withered away. 'Why would he say that?'

'Because it's true?'

Samson shook his head as he too leaned forwards. 'Nah, you've got it all wrong, lady. I don't know anything about it and neither does my Uncle Gazza. I mean, be honest *Mizz* Filey – the Larkins aren't that kind of family. Raids on people's houses? Dousing people in petrol to find out where their valuables are? Gunning people down? That's not us—'

'For a man who doesn't know anything about the Greenbelt Gang you certainly seem to know a heck of a lot about what they did inside those houses.'

Samson swallowed.

Rio pressed on. 'So why did you flee the country after the fifth raid when the shooting started?'

He swept the unruly hair on his forehead into place. 'I don't know anything about any fifth raid, fourth raid or millionth raid, but I'll tell you exactly why I came to Cyprus.' He leaned so far across the table that Rio could feel the heat from his breath against her cheek. 'The courts back home sent me to see a shrink because of some trouble I was in. And you know what that shrink as good as said? That I was a nutter, and I should be banged up in a loony bin. So I decided to skip town before they locked me up with a bunch of bonkers people. So the family arranged for me to come here. Then I was framed for that ruck in the casino up the coast and here I am. So, I don't know anything about any Greenbelt crimes. Now then – are you going to help me persuade the local Johnnies that I'm innocent of the casino thing and to let me go? Or do I have to rely on that crap lawyer from downtown that the local Five-O have given me? Thought you Foster people are meant to be the best?'

Rio could hear the real question in the tone of his voice. Are you who you say you are? Or somebody else?

'I've got reason to believe that someone wants all the members of the Greenbelt Gang dead.'

Samson froze, his hands clutching into fists.

Rio kept the pressure on. 'If you were involved, that would include you too. And I've also got reason to believe that whoever that person or people might be has a very long reach. Perhaps even as far as a prison in Cyprus. If you know anything you need to tell me now.'

'Don't know shit, darling.' But the unsettled expression on his face told her different.

'In that fight in the casino, you were shouting, "I'm a gang-ster, I've killed people . . ."'

Samson unclenched his hand. Relaxed into his seat. 'You know what, Mizz Foley, I think I'm going to take my chances with that lousy local lawyer.'

Samson might be a psycho, but he was a clever psycho. Rio

knew her journey had been a total waste of time. Defeated, she got up from the table. As she turned to go, Samson looked up at her, 'Oh, when you get back to England, say hello to my Uncle Gazza for me . . .'

Rio gave him a half smile and went to press the red button to alert the guards that she wanted to leave. But as she raised her hand, she felt a strong arm squeezing hard around her neck. She was yanked backwards into a corner of the room. With his spare hand, Samson pressed something lethal and sharp against her face.

Hissed, 'You really must think I'm idiot? You don't think I know who you are? You don't think I know what went down back home? My uncle Gazza was killed by a cop.'

Rio started struggling, but he pressed the knife deeper into her skin.

'My dad told me there was a black, lady cop, with a cool momma afro, fronting the operation to catch my uncle, so I know who you are and I know why you're here. I might be mad but I'm not stupid. I'll tell you your first name and your last – Mizz Rio Wray.'

forty-four

Samson's hold on Rio grew stronger.

'Know where the word *shank* comes from?' he growled. 'From the word *shiv*. Some say it's a Roma word for knife and others say it's from *shive*, which was a razor.' His grip tightened. 'Know how easy it is to make a shank inside prison? A toothbrush with a razor blade in it; a filed-down piece of a bed frame ... Now I'm real proud of mine, Mizz Wray: wet toilet paper left to dry like papier mâché. Oh, don't worry, I didn't put any of my shit on it to cause you an infection as well. Mind you, what's an infection when your eyes have been stabbed clean through?'

The worst thing to do was to show fear, so Rio kept her face immobile and the emotions back. She had been trained to deal with violent confrontations. But that generally meant violent confrontations with criminals who could think rationally, even in extreme situations. This violent young man didn't know the meaning of the word rationality.

'This is all being played out on the security camera in here.'

He laughed softly. 'Ain't no cam in here, Mizz Wray, I checked it out as soon as I got in here, like you should've. Plus the way the guards chat about having lousy wages, ain't no way cash is going to be spent on a luxury item like plush security.'

'How do you know what the guards say; you speak Cypriot all of a sudden?'

His green-brown eyes lit up with relish. 'If you'd done you're homework *again* you'd know they speak Turkish this side of the island. And some of my closest friends back home are Turkish and I've always found it easy to pick up different lingos.' The makeshift knife pressed deeper, but didn't spill blood. 'Now stop stalling and start spilling.'

His angry breath fired up on her cheek. 'You're right. I'm Rio Wray. I shouldn't have lied to you. That was wrong and I'm sorry . . .' There was a very slight loosening in his grip while Samson gleamed with pleasure when he realised that he was right. 'And you're spot on again; your uncle Gary is dead. There was a police raid on the house, but I . . . we didn't kill him. It was a set-up. He was killed by someone else. I want to find out who killed him. That's why I'm here. I need your help.'

'Yeah? Well, don't worry about that at the moment, you've got a more pressing problem – how you're going to get me out of here.'

The prison guard was right; the boy was loco. 'I can't get you out of here. You know that. Think straight.'

His lips pressed up against her ear. 'You're lucky you're not dead already. If you don't get me out of here, you certainly will be. You won't believe what a slow, painful death I can deal out to you before the guards get in here. They'll be scraping bits of you off the floor and scooping them into bin bags. Trust me on this – I'm mad, Rio. You must have seen that report that calls me a potential psychopath. So it's official – I'm a nutter.'

As if to prove his point he jabbed his blade against her throat. Samson had inadvertently given her time to think while he explained his escape plan and Rio considered carefully what to do next. While Samson told her how they were going to overpower the guard, knock him out, steal his uniform and gun before walking out as calm as you like, Rio thought of another way of getting what she wanted. She let Samson finish off his ludicrous plan before saying to him, 'You've been watching too many B-movies in that cell of yours.'

'Well, you'd better think of another way to bust me out of here, otherwise someone in your family will be collecting your pension early.'

Rio knew she was probably becoming infected with Samson's madness but maybe getting him out of here wasn't such a bad idea.

'OK. But there's a price tag attached. If I get you out of here, you have to tell me all you know about Greenbelt.'

Samson let out that soft laugh again. 'Oh please. You're running the case and you want me to tell you all about it?'

'After your uncle was killed, I was suspended from duty. I'm supposed to be off the case. If I repeat what you tell me to anyone that would mean I've carried on investigating. I'll be in big trouble. Not as much as you, but big trouble nonetheless, which is not a place I want to be.'

Samson released the grip on her neck. He held his weapon in his hand close enough to be able to kill with it but he was clearly thinking about what Rio had said. 'It's still information though. You could use it against me later.'

'I know you were involved, Samson. I don't have any proof though and I don't suppose you'll be providing me with any.'

'How do I know you'll get me out?'

'I want the information you've got. I'll have to get you out if I want it, won't I? I don't care what you've got up to here.'

Samson took a step backwards and slipped his shank back down the back of his trousers. He gave her a broad but intimidating smile. 'OK. You get me out and I'll tell you what I know.'

Rio's hand rubbed against the last place the makeshift weapon had touched her skin. 'How about a down payment, to

prove your good faith? Half the payment now and half later
– that's how it works, isn't it?'

Samson's eyes became hooded. 'OK. You want a down
payment, how about this? Raid number six, where that Bell
family were whacked. You've been looking in the wrong place.
Get me out of here and I'll tell you the rest.'

forty-five

10:50 a.m.

Crazy, crazy, crazy.

Rio slumped back in the driver's seat of the hire car parked in the shade of a fig tree. Had she just agreed to get Samson Larkin out of prison? Was she losing her frigging mind? Wasn't it enough that she'd gone against orders to stay away from this case and now she was planning to do something that really crossed the line?

Not unless the way she did it didn't actually break the law. Rio's first thought was to go to the British High Commission. No, she couldn't do that; word would hightail it back and the top brass would know what she was up to. Damn, she needed to think of a way to get loco kid out. Whatever she decided, she had to make this happen overnight; she did not have the time to stay on this island another day.

She checked her mobile: a string of 'safe' texts from Calum. But for how long was the teenager going to be safe if she didn't get this fixed? Just as she was about to put her mobile away, it rang.

Rio recognised the ID – Strong.

'Have you found some evidence from the house?' Rio asked eagerly.

'Nope. Or that might be yes—'

'Just tell me.'

'Any members of your team, including me, are being kept well back. DI Paul Mayberry's squad are doing the honours, including anything to do with the hitman – although I think that's being completely scaled back. That guy's a real tight arse and the only people he's reporting back to are Newman and Tripple. If anything has been found, no one's saying. I'll keep my ear to the ground.'

'Thanks, Strong.'

'One of these days you might actually call me Jack.'

Then he disconnected the call.

Rio took out the car keys and leaned forwards to stick them in the ignition . . . and froze. The panel below the steering wheel was gone. No, she couldn't be seeing what she was seeing. Too much sun. Rio closed her eyes, shook her head, re-opened them. The ignition panel was definitely missing. Instantly she was on high alert. Unless this was some type of local novelty crime someone knew she was in Cyprus.

'Detective Inspector Wray?'

Startled Rio twisted her head to find a man leaning down, watching her through the driver's side of the car. His features were blunt, his nose broken more than once and his eyes hidden by shades.

He didn't wait for her to acknowledge what he'd said, just continued. 'You need to come with me.'

'And why would I do that?' Rio countered.

His answer was the opening of the passenger door by another man. From the slight bulge under the newcomer's jacket she could tell he was carrying hardwear. Surrounded on both sides Rio knew she didn't have a choice . . . yet. The man on the driver's side stepped back, giving her the space to get out. When she saw the size of the men her worries increased; both were well over six foot and packing a significant amount of muscle. Still, muscle might give you strength, but it could also slow you down.

'Don't think about running,' the man said, as if reading her thoughts, 'we will only find you.'

'What do you want with me? Who sent you?'

He extended his arm towards her with the curtsey of a gentleman taking his lady love for a stroll about town. But Rio wasn't moving until someone told her what the hell was going on.

'If a stranger came up to you on the street, told you to follow them without saying what was going on, would you do it?'

The men moved in on her. Rio tried to run, but she didn't get far. One of them grabbed her by the collar of her jacket and yanked her back. She almost tumbled, but was saved by both men taking one of her arms each and lifting her off the ground.

'Let me go,' Rio yelled, her feet kicking out.

But they took no notice as they carried her down the street, rounded a corner and headed straight to a gleaming Shogun Range Rover. One of the men took out his keys and popped the boot.

'Nooo . . .' Rio moaned.

But it was no use. Rio was dumped inside. The boot door slammed over her.

The four-by-four came to a stop about thirty minutes later, although Rio couldn't be sure because she couldn't see her watch in the dark. She wasn't afraid to admit that she was scared, but the only way she was going to be put down was after giving the fight of her life. Well, that's if they just didn't shoot her straight through the hood door.

With that sombre thought ringing around her head Rio heard the crunch of footsteps near the side of the car, then around the back. The boot clicked. Rio waited, and waited. Nothing. Cautiously she pushed the hood open. A strong stream of sunlight hit her in the face, making her squint. She couldn't see anyone, only gorgeous blue skies, so she scrambled out of the car onto a dirt road leading through row after row of stunning orange groves. She couldn't see the men but noticed a small, older man tending to an orange tree.

Looking around sharply she rushed over to him.

'Please help me.'

The man turned around, a pair of clippers in his hand and an orange in the other. He was a good four inches shorter than Rio, with the shrunken and spotted skin of the aged, and a cute Buddha belly. He wore a tattered straw hat.

'Some men kidnapped me,' Rio continued in a rush. 'Put me in the boot of a car—'

'In the boot of a car?' His voice was heavily accented, but sounded very different from those that Rio had encountered on the island. 'My men did that to you? That's certainly not very gentlemanly of them.'

Stunned Rio stepped back, the sweat pooling in a river down her back. 'Your men?'

He coughed, doubling over at the waist. Once he had the cough under control he slowly folded back up, the exertion of coughing leaving his face a brutal red in the heat. Then he smiled. 'Have you ever tasted an orange straight from the tree?' He held the fruit in his hand out to her. 'My groves are renowned for their succulent sweetness.'

Beethoven's 'Moonlight' Sonata? Where a shank got its name from? Sweet orange groves? If Rio did drugs she'd think she was tripping since hitting this island.

'Why did you kidnap me? How do you know who I am?'

He started peeling the orange. 'I make it my business to know most of the faces that come to this fair shore, but in your case that isn't strictly true. A friend asked me to watch your back.'

'A friend?'

He pulled the orange apart, held a segment out to her. 'Calum Burns.'

Midday

Rio wiped the orange juice from her lips as she lay back on a sun lounger by the extravagantly large swimming pool. The man, who still hadn't introduced himself – although Rio was in two minds whether she wanted him to or not, knowing the type of company Calum kept – had called his men back and they had driven to his home. The villa was situated on a hill with an eye-popping view of the coastline. The swimming pool area was shaded in places by palm trees and other trees with white and pink blossoms. It was idyllic – a true place in the sun, where relaxation was its number one job.

Except Rio didn't feel remotely calm. The problem with Samson Larkin hadn't gone away and she was the 'guest' of a man she suspected, if she had her badge, she definitely would not want to know.

'Ah, I see you've made yourself comfortable,' the man said as he reappeared outside. He had changed and was now dressed in loose-fitting linen pants and a matching top. His hat was gone, leaving the sun to mingle in his full head of short, iron-grey hair. He took the lounger beside Rio and settled back.

'Sometimes it's better to not know someone's name, it makes things easier. But it feels wrong in this case because I know who you are,' he said.

A bit of Rio told her not to ask, but curiosity got the better of her. 'Considering your home is on a hill, it suggests that you want to make sure you see anyone coming before they see you, so I suspect that you're someone I really shouldn't be sipping fruit juice with, on a terrace overlooking the sea.'

He heard her interest so supplied the answer. 'Khaled Zidane.'

There was no way that Rio could hide her surprise. Zidane was a notorious arms dealer who had stamped his name on the global map back in the 1970s, trading with well-known terrorist groups and outlaw armies. He was an illusive figure who had managed to evade capture from the many warrants out on his name.

'With your reputation, why tell me your name?'

He smiled, making him look more like a kindly granddad than an infamous crook. 'I don't have long for this world.' He said it with no sentiment. 'And Calum did me a good turn a year or so ago. Also I don't think you'll want anyone to know you've been associating with me.'

He was wrong; if she told anyone they wouldn't believe her in a million years.

'How can I help you?' he asked.

He was the only chance she had, so Rio put aside his deadly history and ran him through her dilemma with Samson.

' . . . But I need it to stay within the law,' she finished.

'Surely your need is to get this young man as quickly as possible.'

'I might be suspended, but that doesn't mean I have to start behaving like some out-of-control gangster.'

He frowned. 'Tell me the name of the owner of the casino where this Samson Larkin started behaving so badly.'

Rio pulled herself up and swung her legs to the side to face Zidane. 'A Mr Popescu.'

'Ah, yes.' He pulled himself up and called out a name.

One of the men, who had bundled Rio into the boot of the car, appeared. They spoke rapidly in a language Rio didn't understand. The man disappeared and came back with a mobile phone and a bottle of pills. Zidane swallowed two pills before taking the phone. He tapped in a number and started conversing quickly in Turkish. Less than five minutes later he was finished.

'Well that was easy,' he told Rio, lying back down.

'What did you do?'

'Mr Popescu agreed to drop all of the charges. He's been wanting to do some business with me for a little while—'

'Business?' Rio was horrified. 'I said nothing illegal—'

'Just some oranges, Detective Inspector. As I said earlier my groves have an exemplary reputation on the island, but I usually give most of the produce to the neighbouring villagers for free. Popescu has wanted to have a delivery for a long time. For his wife.'

'So what happens next?'

His voice sounded sleepy. 'Mr Larkin will be released at precisely nine tomorrow morning.'

Rio thought of the hitman probably still lurking in the shadows ready to pounce on Nikki. She didn't have time to sit around in Cyprus until another day dawned.

'Can't you get him out of there today?'

Zidane's voice was slow and breezy. 'Island life is much more relaxed and slow compared to London. Getting this Samson released tomorrow is considered quite fast by Northern Cyprus standards. Take this time to enjoy my hospitality.'

A plan stared forming in Rio's head. 'OK. Can I take your two men with me when I pick him up? I need them to help me with a little job.'

forty-six

The Hit: Day 5
9:00 a.m.

The next morning Rio waited outside the main entrance to the prison knowing she only had today and tomorrow to make sure Nikki was safe. She'd made a promise to the girl to get the job done in four days and by God she was going to keep it. Samson Larkin emerged, directing all her thoughts on to him, carrying a handful of possessions. Zidane's two heavies were in a new hire car in a street, a half a mile away, parked outside a café.

Samson Larkin grinned as he swaggered towards her. 'Well, well, well, if it isn't Mizz Wray with the magic touch. How did you swing it so I got out?'

'That you don't need to know,' Rio replied, noticing that the damage done to his face was fading fast. 'This better be worth all the effort I've put in.'

His grin widened. But he made no response, so Rio ploughed on. 'I'm taking you to a café where you had better start talking.'

The café was one of those that catered to British tourists, advertising different types of English breakfast. Before she went in, Rio checked that the car with one of Zidane's men stationed in it was where it was meant to be. The place was sunlit and empty. Rio chose a table in the middle of the room, but Samson stopped, pointing a finger at a table set in the corner. 'I like to make sure I can see who comes through the door,' was what he said by way of an explanation.

Rio shrugged; she didn't have a problem with that.

Samson grabbed his menu as soon as they sat down. 'Fancy something continental.'

'Thought you'd be after an old-fashioned fry-up.'

He patted his waist. 'A man has got to stay fit, especially when he's not sure what's around the corner.'

Before Rio could reply a balding, middle-aged man – who Rio assumed was the owner – came and took their order. She didn't need anything but a strong cup of coffee and Samson went for a flaky pastry cheese twist and homemade lemonade.

'You were saying, about the raid on the Bells' home . . .'

Samson ruffled his lips like a naughty school kid. 'Can't a man eat–?'

'Speak.'

He huffed and leaned his forearms on the table. 'Uncle Gazza and his crew never done raid number six.'

Rio had not been expecting that. She looked at him stunned. 'Are you saying that you have information to show the Greenbelt Gang–'

'The first five Greenbelt jobs were done by my Uncle Gazza and three blokes he knew – present company excluded, of course. Gary was trying to raise some dosh to buy into a stake in a drug trafficking racket. He was fed up with being small time, wanted his place in the sun. So he decided to identify nice places out in the sticks and then go in there and threaten the occupants to get his hands on their valuables. He knew that would make a stink and the cops would be after him big time, but he thought he'd only need to do a few, then lie low.' He shrugged. 'He thought the fifth job would be the last. It was bad luck for him that he took someone with him on that last job who was a bit trigger happy – a total nut job. He lost it and shot the woman of the house.'

Rio twisted her lips. 'And that trigger happy nut was you, was it?'

The food arrived. Samson tucked straight into his cheese twist.

He made a noise of utter pleasure as his eyes half-closed.

'Dee-lish. You ever had one of these?'

Rio almost snapped, but she held her temper back. 'Like I said, Samson, you were at those raids, weren't you? Of course you're going to try and blame the last raid on someone else because three people were murdered.'

For the first time Rio saw Samson really angry. His hazel eyes became more green than brown and a red blush crept up his neck. 'I'm telling you straight, they didn't do it. They did the first five and then cut out of the game.'

'They hired a hitman to kill—'

That made Samson laugh out loud. 'Reality check, Mizz Wray. They needed dosh quickly, which means they didn't have any spare dollars to give away and a hitman costs mega bucks. Whoever paid that hitman, it wasn't Uncle Gazza.'

'What type of masks did your uncle's gang wear?'

'Clown masks – so I hear—'

'They ever wear baggy cloth masks with a tube coming out of them?'

His face screwed up. 'Sounds like a gas mask, except the baggy cloth bit.' Then his face took on a shine like he'd won a prize. 'Wait a minute.' His eyes lit up. 'During World War One, The Great War—?'

Rio wasn't in the mood to play pub quiz with this annoying thug. His huge bank of general knowledge was starting to really pee her off. 'How do you know Gary and his people weren't involved in the sixth raid?'

But he didn't answer her; instead he started singing in a rousing low-toned voice. 'Pack up your troubles in your old kit bag and smile, smile, smile . . .'

Rio stared at the youngster as if he'd finally lost the plot. Genius? No the kid was a total nutcase. She'd had enough of this craziness. Rio thumped the table. His singing stopped.

'You listen to me,' Rio said, teeth almost clenched tight. 'And you listen good. You keep going with the Broadmoor routine and I'm going to march your crazy arse straight back to lockdown.'

He stared at her, his animation revving up into a cocksure smile. 'You're gonna wished you'd listened to me—'

'The only thing I want to hear is how you know your uncle and his mob didn't have anything to do with the Bell raid.'

He shrugged his shoulders before answering. 'My dad told me, and you'll have to ask yourself why he'd lie to me. Uncle Gazza didn't even know about the sixth raid. There's that rule, isn't there? You don't read the papers or watch the TV in case the cops are putting out false information intended to spook you and make you panic. He only found out about it later when he was interviewed by you.'

Rio's mind skidded back to the day she'd first interviewed Gary Larkin. He'd been dead calm until she'd mentioned the raid on the Bells'. Then he'd become so distressed with denial he'd had an asthma attack. But Nikki had said that one of the men had trouble with his breathing. If that hadn't been Gary Larkin, who was it?

'Uncle Gazza thought there was someone else, another crew, copying their MO,' Samson said, putting into words what Rio was just starting to realise. ''Course he couldn't tell your lot that because it meant admitting he'd done the other raids.'

'Which you didn't have anything to do with.'

Samson shoved his hands face up at her. 'You see any blood here? I'm no Lady Macbeth.'

Beethoven, the Great War, and now Shakespeare. Rio was starting to think that Samson had most people fooled with the full-blown psycho 'I'm a member of the dumb-ass Larkin family' routine. He was highly intelligent, clever and cunning, so no way was he ever going to admit to being part of the Greenbelt Gang. Just as well she had plan B all ready to rock 'n' roll.

'I didn't kill your uncle or the other men,' she repeated. Samson lifted his left eyebrow at that, then bit into the last of his twist. 'The house where Gary and the gang met their deaths – do you know anything about it or how they came to be there?'

Samson looked plain bored now. 'Nope. And I don't care either. I'm going to the john. That wasn't as nice as the cheesy twists you get in Lidl's; it's gone straight through me.' Catching Rio's dubious expression he added as he stood up. 'Don't worry, I'm not going to do a Michael Corleone, find a gun hidden in the toilet thingie and then waltz back and shoot you in the throat.'

He cocked his hand into the shape of a gun. Pointed it at her face. 'Pow! Pow!'

Chuckling he turned and swaggered to the back where the Gents was located. Rio immediately got onto her mobile and said, 'Detain'. She stood up and watched the man in the car get out. Then he talked into his phone, speed walking to the café.

Shouting came from the rear of the café, followed by a man screaming and what sounded like pots and pans being scattered. A woman let out a high-pitched howl. Rio raced to the back where she found the café owner sitting on the floor of the kitchen, his back resting against a cooker. He clutched his shoulder where his shirt was stained red. Blood oozed through his fingers. The man's wife was crouched over him, screaming uncontrollably.

Spotting Rio, the man said in halting English. 'He steal . . . knife.'

Rio didn't run, but took her time going out the back. She reached the narrow backyard just in time to see Zidane's other heavy, who'd been stationed out back, land a punch on Samson's face that had him flying backwards. Samson crashed into two stacked crates of empty bottles. Glass smashed and rolled against the cobbled ground.

Rio sighed as she moved towards him. As soon as she reached him she crouched down. Samson was blinking quickly and shaking his head.

'Why did you have to be so predictable?' Rio asked.

Samson opened an eye. 'Because you've given me a headache banging on your drum about me being involved with Uncle Gary.' He opened his other eye, with a wince this time. 'You might be suspended, but you're still a cop, which means you're going to try to take me in.' He had the nerve to grin. 'But, bad luck for you there's no extradition thingie this side of the island.'

Both of Zidane's men were now standing strong behind Rio.

'Oh yeah,' Rio innocently said, 'I forgot about that.'

Samson squinted his eyes at her. Then he jerked to a sitting position. 'No, you can't do this to me—'

Rio nodded to the men, who dragged Samson up by his arms. He had finally figured out what Rio was up to, but it was too late.

Rio asked one of the men, 'How long will it take to cross the border?'

forty-seven

They headed towards Ledra Street also known as Murder Mile because of the history of terrorist activities during the 1950s. It was only a ten-minute drive away, the main shopping area and the location of the Ledra Palace Crossing. Samson was in the back with the man who had decked him. A gun, with a silencer, kept him firmly in place. Once they crossed the border Rio intended to hand the youth over to the police with information that he was wanted for murder in England. By the time the authorities worked out that there was no international arrest warrant out for him, Rio intended to be back home to ensure that there was. Samson was right; it went against her principles to simply let him go.

'You can't prove anything and you know it,' Samson growled at her.

Rio ignored him. But he kept on trying to get under her skin.

'I'll tell them what I told you – I wasn't there.'

Rio kept her eyes to the front, her mouth firmly closed.

'I'll tell them you jacked me and then smuggled me back. Didn't you say you'd been suspended? You'll be the one facing a firing squad, lady, not me.'

Rio finally spoke, but didn't turn around. 'It's my friends here who'll be handing you over to the authorities not me.'

But she knew she was badly exposed. Of course Samson

was going to start yapping the first chance he got; he was right, it wouldn't take long for the top brass to hear her name mentioned in connection with this. But she'd deal with that when it happened; for now she was all about Samson. Rio's mind turned to the raid on the Bells' home and what Gary Larkin's nephew had told her. So if it wasn't the Greenbelt Gang, who was it? Another set of criminals jumping on another crew's MO? Or someone not connected to the underworld . . . like Cornelius Bell? The image of Cornelius hanging took over her mind.

I take the blame for everything.

By everything, had Cornelius meant the raid?

A mobile rang in the back of the car disrupting her thoughts. Rio shifted so that she could check out the back in the rearview mirror. The man with the gun pulled out his mobile. His expression changed to one of surprise as he listened, then he spoke in rapid Turkish and ended the call. He looked over at the driver and continued his stream of quick Turkish. Suddenly the driver swung the car around.

'Hey, hey. Hang on,' Rio said, her hands coming up. 'What's going on?'

'We have to go back,' the man behind her replied.

'No, we can't.' She twisted her upper body around to face him. 'We're almost there.'

'The old man has collapsed. We need to make sure that we're close.'

'I know he's sick—'

'He's dying.' He responded with no change of his expression, but leaned forwards.

Rio started pleading. 'Just drop us off inside the border. What's that going to take? Another couple of minutes?'

He shook his head. 'The old man pays our wages, not . . .'

Rio didn't even see it happen; the next thing she knew the

passenger's door on Samson's side of the car was flapping open and the youth was rolling in the dirt of the road. The car continued to accelerate forwards as Rio scrambled up on her seat, her gaze fixed on Samson who was growing smaller in the distance as he ran.

'Stop the car,' Rio demanded. But neither man listened to her as the vehicle continued to speed forwards.

She reached for the door, but the man behind her shot his arm forwards and grabbed her hand.

'We have to get back before he dies. There is much that needs to be done if God decides that this is his last day.'

Rio desperately looked back at where Samson was. She could still make him out. And then the cocky boy did something that made her loathe him for as long as she lived – he blew her a kiss. Then he was gone, disappearing into the secluded world of the trees and tiny side streets.

forty-eight

3:05 p.m. London Time

Rio's plane touched down at just after three in the afternoon London time. Zidane's men had dropped her off near the airport at Nicosia and headed back to the hills. Rio didn't usually do pity, but she hadn't been able to stop herself feeling like an orphan dumped in the baking sun with no mama or papa to protect her, not even a sun hat. There had been no point hiring another car to go in search of him; Samson was long gone. Rio had then flirted with the idea of hanging around town for one more day to see if he appeared, but knowing Samson he'd brazenly cross the border himself, mouth full of lies and then . . . puff, he'd have been eaten up into the stream of tourists.

Still, she hadn't come back empty-handed; the sixth raid was a copycat. And the one lead she had was a very dead Cornelius Bell.

Rio cruised through Stansted's immigration and then passed by the area, divided by glass, where passengers were gathering at the gate waiting to take them to Northern Cyprus. Probably going on the same plane that she'd disembarked from. Once she'd left the green channel she bypassed the crowd on the other side waiting for loved ones and pulled out her mobile to call Calum. She stopped near a crowded coffee house where a mounted TV was on the BBC 24 News Channel.

'I'm back,' she told Calum. 'Everything OK?'

'If it weren't I would have called you. Did you find baby Larkin?'

She turned in the direction of the television. 'Yep. Claims the raid on the Bells' wasn't his uncle's people. And that they wouldn't have the cash needed to secure a contract killer.'

'You believe him?'

'It fits with—'

Rio's words halted as a face came up on the TV screen.

Her tone changed to one of urgency. 'Is Nikki in the room with you?'

'No, she's—'

'Turn on the telly. BBC Twenty-four News Channel.'

She heard him moving because he put his mobile on speaker-phone. Her eyes never left the TV screen as she waited.

'Bollocks,' Calum said.

'Keep this news away from her. We don't need her tipping over the edge. I need to take care of a couple of things, then I'll be with you.'

Rio terminated the call as Adeyemi Ibraheem's face disappeared from the screen. But she read the breaking newsfeed at the bottom of the screen.

Body of student Adeyemi Ibraheem
found in the River Thames.

Passengers in rows 20 to 40 for the 4.00 p.m. flight to Northern Cyprus from Stansted airport started lining up for a final security check before they boarded the plane. First in line was a man wearing a waist-length leather jacket and shades. He curled his lip slightly when a soft request was made for him to take off his sunglasses. But he took them off and handed over his passport. The airline employee opened it and looked at the name.

The employee looked at him, back at the photo, then handed the passport back to him.

'Have a good trip.'

Terry Larkin smiled as he took back his passport.

4:10 p.m.

Rio walked into the coroner's office. Harsh memories of accompanying families to identify bodies of loved ones swept over her, and she thought of the bodies of those who were never claimed by anyone. Over the years she'd learned how to push her emotions down deep and get on with the job of consoling, lending a temporary shoulder to lean on, but ultimately reserving all her energy for solving the case.

She would never forget her first one. A nine-year-old boy found lying at the foot of a snake-shaped slide in a community playground. The only evidence of violence had been a bruise to his right temple. Her superior had told her the way to deal with it was to imagine the person was in a deep sleep; she hadn't been able to do that with the boy. All she'd seen when she'd gazed at his still body, his mum sobbing beside her, was the life that had been ready for him to live – maybe university, maybe a career that helped other people, maybe the father of another little boy. That was the last time she let any feelings sit on her shoulder when entering a coroner's.

Until now ... The night of the raid, Adeyemi's mum had turned up at The Fort desperate to speak to her about his disappearance and what had she done? Ignored her because she was preoccupied with the raid. And now a young man was dead. Rio hadn't even known Adeyemi, but she'd never forget the genuine protective emotions that glazed his dark eyes when he stared at Nikki Bell.

She shook the memories away as she headed for the partially

opened office at the start of the corridor. A young woman, hair
tied back into a practical ponytail, was working at the desk.
Her head came up as she heard Rio push the door further back.

'I'm looking for the Ibraheem family . . .'

The awful sound of wrenching from the corridor stopped
the rest of her words. Rio pulled away from the door and eased
slowly around to find Adeyemi's mother bent and sobbing,
being supported in the arms of a man she suspected was her
oldest son. They halted when they saw her, the hostile stare the
man sent Rio's way didn't stop her from approaching them.

'You're that pig that came to Mum's house.' It wasn't a question but a statement. A statement filled with bile and
over-flowing rage.

'I'm sorry—'

Mrs Ibraheem's head swung up, her bloodshot eyes bursting
with such grief she looked like she was facing death herself. 'I
came to see you . . . to plead for your help. This is all because
of that girl, isn't it? I told him to stay away from her, to keep
his head and mind in his books.' Her head moved from side to
side. 'But he wouldn't listen. Wouldn't . . .' Tears clogged her
throat stopping her from continuing.

'We don't know if this has anything to do with the case
surrounding Nikki—'

Chiwetel Ibraheem, well-known South London villain,
punched over her. 'I see that girl again, she's dead—'

'Don't be putting threats around that you may come to
regret.'

'Or what?' His question was belligerent and defiant. 'You
going to make sure my mum comes back here to view the body
of her other son as well?' He ended by sucking his teeth long
and hard.

They walked past Rio, never looking back. Rio stood there
for a good few minutes afterwards, the other woman's grief

still ringing in her head, thinking how a week ago a sixteen-year-old girl had been just like any other teen and now she had the corpses of the people she loved most in the world stacked up behind her.

Rio's phone pinged. Text. She pulled it out and read:

It's a long long way to Tipperary.

The strange message finished with a picture of a skull and crossbones. ☠

Rio couldn't make head nor tail of the message and decided that whoever had sent it must've have got their phone lines mixed up.

forty-nine

4:31 p.m.

'I want to see Stephen Foster. And I want to see him now.'

The look on the face of Foster's receptionist suggested to Rio that the idea that anyone could just blow into his suite of offices and demand to see her boss was a kind of crime in itself.

'I'm sorry but I don't think that's going to be possible – can I suggest you try and make an appointment?'

Rio loved the 'try'. She leaned over the desk. 'Just buzz your boss, babe – tell him it's Rio Wray and I want to talk about Greenbelt . . .'

The woman pursued her lips, then relaxed. 'One moment, please.' Then picked up her phone and spoke in a hushed voice to Foster.

Almost before she had replaced the receiver, Rio heard the great man himself coming down the stairs, so she left the receptionist's office to meet him. He stopped halfway down the staircase, his full head of sweeping black-grey hair looking like it had been freshly groomed. Rio was used to his two standard expressions – the blank one that told you nothing and his look of contempt, which told you everything. But this one was new: open curiosity.

'Detective . . .' He paused. 'I mean Ms Wray. What a surprise,

I hear that you are no longer part of an investigation, which I believe is no longer on-going.'

'We need to talk.'

He gestured with his hand for her to follow him upstairs. When they were seated in his spacious office, Foster ordered coffee before sitting in silence for a few moments. It seemed to Rio as if he was trying to work out on his own accord what the reason for her visit might be. But evidently he failed.

'So, Ms Wray – to what do I owe the honour of this visit?'

'I've got information that the Greenbelt Gang weren't responsible for the murder of the Bells and their cleaner. I need you to answer a few questions for me.'

'I see.'

Foster wore his blank expression now: a poker player with what might have been a very good or very bad hand. He sighed and leaned back. 'And what on earth makes you think the Bells weren't murdered by Gary Larkin and his group of amateur gunslingers?'

'A member of Larkin's gang–'

The lawyers shuffled in his chair. 'I thought all of the gang were dead?'

Rio had already made her mind up not to mention Samson Larkin's name. 'My source told me they did raids one to five, but didn't do number six. Also that fits in with the pattern of the gunmen at the Bells not wearing clown masks as the Greenbelt Gang did or expertly paint spraying all the security cameras. Plus no one spoke on the sixth raid unlike the other five raids.'

Foster seemed curious. 'And this member of the gang you've discovered – is he reliable?'

'I think he is. On this, yes.'

Foster frowned. 'It could make sense I suppose. A piggy back raid on the Greenbelt murders to get rid of Maurice Bell?'

Rio leaned forwards. 'Why would anyone want to get rid of Maurice Bell?'

Contempt crawled across the face of the man opposite her. 'Are you telling me you didn't look into Maurice Bell's affairs and background as a matter of course, as part of the investigation?'

Rio didn't like the finger pointing he was doing. 'If you've got something to say, Mr Foster, say it.'

He hesitated, straightening the cuff of his expensive look-ing powder-blue shirt over his wrist. 'I'm not saying Maurice Bell had enemies per se.' He reached into his drawer and produced a Cuban cigar, which he clipped and lit with an art deco cigarette lighter. 'But all successful men have enemies, Ms Wray. It's one of the key indicators of a well-lived life. Look at me for example – I've got plenty. It's only failures that everyone likes. Mr Bell was no different from any other man who's made something of himself.'

Rio pulled out her notebook and pen. 'Did you hear of any specific enemies he had? His daughter said she thinks he had a business partner when he started out?'

Foster blew cigar smoke upwards. 'Look, Ms Wray, I'm will-ing to help you here but not at the expense of my reputation. I'm afraid I can't divulge confidences that I've heard from my clients. I wouldn't have any if I did that.'

'Not even when they've been murdered?'

'Especially when they've been murdered.'

Rio knew better than to press the matter. But at least she had another potential piece of her puzzle – Maurice Bell might have been a target for some reason and that was worth investigating.

She moved on. 'You were one of the last people to see Gary Larkin before he went on the run to the place where he was killed. Did he give you any indication where he was going and why?'

Foster started laughing but it was a laugh without humour or warmth. 'Of course not; I advised him to go home and sit it out – he told me that's what he was going to do, but he either panicked or decided it was safe for him to do another job and relocated. Going on the run was the worst thing he could have done. In fact, in light of how it turned out, the very worst thing . . .'

'OK. The house in Kent, where the gang were holed up, was owned by a front company in the Caribbean. Did you know how Gary would have been able to arrange the hire of a place like that?'

Foster puffed more vigorously on his smoke. 'I've got no idea. Perhaps he knew some major league people who arranged it for him. I don't know. Perhaps he broke in and squatted.'

Rio remembered the chaos of the raid. It was indeed possible that Larkin and friends had broken in. 'I don't suppose there's any way you could find out who actually owns it? I'm not doing this for me, but to make Nikki's life safe as soon as possible.'

'No chance.' He saw the look of annoyance on her face. 'Front companies are fronts for a reason, Ms Wray. It's hard to trace who is the real person behind them. Even I couldn't do it.'

There was a long silence. But that was something Rio had noticed about Stephen Foster. He never used ten words where one would do and he never engaged in small talk. Like most lawyers he knew words were power. But then Rio was surprised that he was answering any questions at all. He usually didn't do so unless he was paid or had the opportunity to trip up the police. But Rio decided to take advantage while she could. 'What do you make of the two Bell kids?'

'You think they're suspects?' That was the great thing about Foster; he always cut to the chase. 'Two spoilt little rich kids I'm afraid. Shame that Cornelius committed suicide. I don't think either of those two is – was in his case – capable of tying their own shoelaces, never mind organising a murder. Although,' Foster flicked ash into the ashtray, 'my dealings with young Cornelius suggested that when he was under the influence of narcotics he'd be capable of anything. So perhaps . . .'

'You think he was capable of murder?'

'Maybe. He was a deeply troubled young man. The other one, the girl, I don't know her so well. She doesn't like me for some reason. But, of course, she's entitled to her opinion – however badly informed. But having seen her act on the TV, I'd say she can't even play a murderer properly, never mind actually be one. So no, I don't think they're your culprits.' He stubbed his cigar out on an ashtray. 'But then again, your source – this other member of the gang – might be lying and sending you on some wild goose chase.'

Abruptly Foster rose and checked his watch. 'I've got another client arriving soon.'

Knowing the interview was at an end, Rio got to her feet as well, but she had one more statement to make before leaving. 'I'm rather surprised actually.'

'About what?'

'You're not noted for helping the police, so why are you giving me a helping hand?'

There was a glint in Foster's eye. 'But you're not the police anymore, are you, Ms Wray? They've suspended you. I'm willing to bet your superiors don't want you poking your nose into a case they've decided has no loose ends. You need to watch your back, Ms Wray. If you poke the authorities in this country with a stick, they don't like it and they turn nasty. They're ruthless people. Believe me, I know.'

fifty

4:53 p.m.

'I'll let myself out,' Rio told Foster's PA.

They were both on the staircase – Rio going down, the other woman going up. Foster's PA carried a tray filled with the coffee he'd requested earlier.

'Sorry,' the woman apologised, 'the espresso machine was playing up – again.'

'No matter.' Rio smiled in an off-hand way as she passed her and was soon letting herself out of Foster's world, her mind preoccupied by what the lawyer had told her.

Or not told her. He hadn't told her anything really; his answers and talk full of mights and maybes. Typical lawyer – the act of spewing hot air down to an art form. Even the part about Maurice Bell was a maybe-maybe not scenario. But as Rio picked up her pace, she decided to go over their conversation, picking over everything . . .

Maurice Bell might have an enemy . . . but all businessmen had those.

The Greenbelt Gang didn't do the sixth raid . . . but was Samson Larkin telling the truth?

Cornelius Bell committed suicide, left a note with Nikki's name all over it blaming himself, was a troubled junkie . . .

All roads seemed to lead back to Connie Bell. But who was

his accomplice? And how was she going to find out? What about . . .?

'Ms Wray! Ms Wray!'

Hearing the frantic yelling of her name Rio turned around. Foster's PA stood just outside the house, her arms gesticulating wildly at Rio.

'What's the problem?' Rio asked quickly as she rushed over.

The woman's face was pale. 'There's someone in Mr Foster's private bathroom with him . . . I couldn't open the door . . . there's a lot of noise.' She grabbed Rio's arm tight. 'I think something very bad is happening . . .'

Rio rushed back into the house, remembering that Foster had an en-suite bathroom attached to his office. She took the stairs quickly and entered the office, reached the bathroom door to hear Foster shout out, 'Get off me!'

Then there was a loud bang as something inside the room hit the floor. A groan of pain rippled through the air. Rio slammed her shoulder against the door. The wood bowed, but not enough to free it from the prison of the lock. So she barrelled her body into it a second time. The door flew open.

Rio noticed two things at once: Stephen Foster lay on his knees on the floor and the frosted window was open.

'What happened?' She dropped to one knee by the injured lawyer, as her gaze cased the room; she couldn't see anyone else.

When her eyes snapped back to Foster she saw the blood streaming from his hand. He looked up at her, his face creased with pain. 'He got out through the window.'

Rio shot to her feet, rushed to the window, peered outside. She looked left, right, straight ahead . . . no one in sight. Whoever had been here would be long gone by the time she got outside. She turned to find Foster trying to struggle to his feet.

'Don't move,' Rio cautioned, as she knelt by him again. This time she saw the palm of his bleeding hand had two deep slash wounds across it.

'Take a deep breath and then tell me what happened.'

Stephen Foster made a scoffing sound. 'Being attacked is a hazard in my line of work.'

'Did you recognise your assailant?'

He shook his head. 'But I think I know who it was.' He looked deeply into her eyes. 'He asked me where Nicola Bell was.'

The hitman. So she was right: the gun for hire was still out there trying to get the job done.

'He was going to stab me, so I reached out to defend myself . . .' He looked down at his hand. 'Managed to grab the knife, but he cut me.' He looked back up at her. 'But when you arrived he hightailed it out of here.'

'Did you see his face?'

Once again he shook his head. 'I can't be certain, but he was wearing the same style of raincoat zipped over the lower half of his face as the man who tried to harm Nicola in the hospital.'

'Oh, Mr Foster,' his PA said fretfully from the doorway. 'I'll call an ambulance.'

'No,' he replied. 'I'm sure I just need a few stitches, so can you contact Doctor Purcell.' He turned back to Rio. 'An ambulance means being taken to a hospital and this unfortunate incident will become public news. I don't need that at the moment. You should go.'

Rio knew he was right. The last thing she needed was the top brass finding her footprints still all over this case.

5:45 p.m.

'Can you trust Samson Larkin?'

Rio let Calum's question soak in as she sat opposite him in his office above the butcher's shop in Brixton. Nikki was in the room next door, doing whatever it was teenage girls did when they had time on their hands.

'Trust him? Hell no,' Rio replied. 'Do I believe what he's telling me? Yes. There are just too many inconsistencies between the other raids and number six, including the gang having the money for a hitman. Someone is paying that hitter and we need to find out who that is. If he came gunning for Foster, he's still out to get Nikki too.'

Calum leaned forwards and pressed the space bar on his laptop. 'I think Foster had a point when he said he couldn't understand why you hadn't looked into Maurice Bell's background—'

'Come on, why would we have needed to do that? We believed that we were looking for a gang that had perpetrated crimes long before the Bell murders. The MO's were the same . . . Well, almost the same.'

'It's when you realised the "almost" part that you should have started to investigate other angles.'

Rio should have felt slightly irritated that he was chewing her up over her strategy, but all she felt was a wave of sadness. This man had been one of the best officers she'd ever known; really knew how to work a case.

'Don't go there, Ray Gun,' he said, reading her thoughts. 'I'm not in the mood for the razzamatazz of the good ole days.' He turned to his laptop. 'Come over here.'

Rio joined him, perching on the edge of the desk. 'I know you didn't ask me to, but I'd already started making enquiries into Maurice Bell's business dealings.' He typed away at the keyboard until Maurice Bell's photo came on screen. 'I checked him out: he was a respected businessman, no particular enemies. Actually for a businessman he did seem to be quite respected – none of the usual sociopathic, ruthless tendencies some of these guys use to forge their way to the top. Then I started wondering, how did he make his money?'

'His daughter, Ophelia, said that he was involved in all types of businesses, that diversification was the root of his success.'

'That still doesn't answer how he got his start-up.' Rio looked at him confused, so Calum explained, 'How he got his leg-up into the word of business. Was he from a well-to-do family who could send their son into the world with enough cash to prove himself? Or did he inherit a business? If he was neither one of those things, where did his start-up money come from? Poor boy makes good: there's always a story there. So I checked back and that's when I hit a brick wall. I couldn't find any mention of a Maurice Bell fitting his description before his thirtieth birthday.'

Calum pressed another button. Another photograph came up. Rio peered closer. 'Is that a young Maurice Bell?'

'No. That is Maurice Cloud.'

Rio caught on immediately. 'Why would Maurice Bell have changed his name . . .?' Abruptly she stopped. There was something familiar about that name.

Cloud. Cloud.

Clou.

Rio realised where she'd seen it before, or partially before. 'When Frank Bell filled in Nikki's adoption papers I think he mistakenly started writing Cloud and then scratched it out and put Bell instead.'

Calum shook his head as he tutted. 'Why didn't you tell me that before?'

That pissed her off; since when did she have to answer to him?

But Calum didn't give her an opportunity to vent her feelings as he carried on. 'People change their names for all kinds of reasons without there being anything suspicious going on. I had a mate who'd been abused by her father as a child and the first thing she did when she was eighteen was change her surname. Carrying her dad's name made her feel dirty. But our Maurice didn't have such an honourable reason for changing his. Your mother – if she was still with us – might have recognised him.'

Rio was baffled. 'What's this got to do with my mum?'

'Cloud and his partner were one of Notting Hill's notorious slum landlords back in the early 1970s. He was clever and managed to keep his face out of the press – like his partner, unlike some of the other landlords. I reckon he sold up and used the money to invest in other property and changed his ID at the same time. He must've persuaded his brother Frank to change his name as well, to ensure his new life looked legit. I couldn't track down any details about his partner, except for the nickname Slim. But Cloud and this Slim were implicated in the murder of a business rival, John MaCarry, in 1965–'

Rio threaded her fingers through her 'fro. 'John MaCarry? I'm sure he was the landlord who my mum told me about. A really nasty piece of work. When she first came to England she lived with a cousin in another house in Notting Hill. They shared a room on the ground floor. The landlord, John MaCarry, wanted them to leave, but they refused. You know what he did? He sent some heavies around to take off all of their windows and their front door. But they were tough ladies. Refused to budge, unlike the other residents. I don't know how they withstood the weather blowing into their room because it was a cold winter. In the end he shelled out some cash – they took it and got out of there; that's how mum got the deposit on her house.'

Rio stared hard at Calum. 'But what's this got to do with case? So the man changed his name – so what? He started his work life as a scum landlord, but appears to have redeemed himself with his cleaner-than-clean business dealings for the last couple of decades.'

Calum twisted his swingback chair away from the computer to fully face her. 'I'm not saying this has got anything to do with anything. Probably hasn't. But in my line of work I've seen how a man's past can come back to haunt him when he least expects it.'

Rio frowned. 'No. I think this is all about Cornelius Bell, not his dad's past.' Her frown deepened. 'When I described what the killers were wearing, Samson Larkin said it sounded like a gas mask, although the baggy cloth didn't fit . . .'

'Want me to Yahoo it?' Calum asked

He didn't wait for her response as he tapped a search on his computer.

Gas masks
Images

Eight photographs came up. The plastic eyeholes fit, but there was no baggy cloth or hose.

'Want me to use a different search engine?' Calum asked seeing the disappointed look on Rio's face.

She shook her head. 'No point wasting your time. But thanks for the info on Maurice Bell.'

Before Rio realised what she was doing, she was leaning down to drop a kiss on his cheek. His head moved in a way so that her lips hovered over his mouth.

'You going to kiss me?' he asked softly.

She wanted to throw back, 'Fuck, no.' But that's not what happened. Her lips touched his. No pressure, no tongues, just skin meeting skin. Rio pressed her hand down to his leg to make her position more secure ... Calum swung his whole body back away from her.

'Why did you stop smooching?'

They both turned to find Nikki standing just inside the doorway. She wore a pair of woollen, lime-green fingerless gloves that stretched to just below her elbow, resembling winter socks.

Rio scrambled to her feet, heat creeping up her face. 'How are you doing?'

The girl walked slowly into the room. 'Your time's running out. And I've decided that today's the last day–'

'You can't do that, Nikki. We've still got tomorrow. The hitman is still out there–'

'Yes I can. And I am. I'm going to stay with Ophelia first thing in the morning.'

fifty-one

'I say we clear out Connie's stuff and get the room ready for someone else,' said one of the four members of The Rebels' Collective, just before they snorted another line of coke.

They were sat downstairs at a round table scattered with an assortment of drugs and two bottles of vodka. Monica hadn't been happy when they decided not to accompany her to the demo, but they'd convinced her that someone needed to be looking after the place, especially after what had gone down with Connie. Truth be told, they couldn't wait for I'm-the-boss-woman Monica to sod off so they could indulge in a tote or two and get smashed.

'I don't think that Cookie would be best pleased if we shifted Connie's gear without talking to her first.' The man who spoke was wearing a red beanie hat and waving an elegantly rolled joint in the air.

'You'd think his famous actress sister would put in an appearance—'

'Get real,' another broke in. She pulled in some weed then passed the spliff on. 'Ophelia Bell isn't going to want to be seen dead around here. Can you imagine her fans' faces if they saw pap snaps of her underneath Che Guevara over there.'

They all looked across at the poster of the legendary

revolutionary posing in the spot where a framed picture of the Queen was once proudly displayed, back when the pub was in business. The four laughed as the booze and drugs flowed.

'Why do you think he topped himself?' The question was slurred.

'The guy was a royal mess. Without Cookie to lean on, I don't know where he'd have been.'

'That dad of his sounded like a first class c—'

The corrugated steel door shook as someone hammered against it. They all froze, looking at each other with apprehensive bloodshot eyes.

'Could be the cops,' one whispered.

'Or Monica, who'll be well pissed if she doesn't find us reading her revised Rebels' Collective manifesto.'

The banging started up again. This time the one with the red beanie hat – who told everyone his name was Santos, but whose birth name was William Farmington-Chandler – got up and approached the door.

'Santos, leave it,' one of the others called out, behind him.

But Santos didn't listen to the plea. Instead he shouted, 'What do you want?'

'Connie's expecting me.' American accent. Female.

Santos fiddled with the bolt and partially opened the door. He was surprised to see a woman wearing a combination of street clothes and African dress. There was a leather jacket and jeans on the one hand while her hair was bundled into an elaborate green and yellow head wrap. She wore dangly earrings in the shape of Africa and, despite the darkness, wore shades. But what stuck out most for Santos was that she was carrying a case for a double bass, which was nearly as tall as she was.

He checked the street behind her but couldn't see anyone else. 'Can I help?'

'Hey man – is Connie there?'

Santos was too embarrassed to tell her the truth, so he said, 'No, he's away. Sorry.'

He started closing the door, but the woman jammed her foot in the gap.

She was chewing gum. 'What do you mean he's not here? He only texted me a few days ago. Said I could come and stay. Are you sure he's not here?' She stretched up to check behind him.

'Look, I don't know to tell you this but I'm afraid Cornelius has passed away.'

'Passed away? You mean, as in, *dead*?'

'Yes.'

The woman stopped chewing, 'You're shittin' me?'

'I'm afraid not.'

The woman seemed to be choking up. 'Did he OD?'

Santos was embarrassed again. 'No, I'm afraid there was a family tragedy and, well, he didn't cope too well. It's our fault really, we should have noticed. Unfortunately, it all got too much and he took his own life.'

'No way . . .?'

'Yes, I'm afraid so.' He pulled back the door. 'Look, come inside for a second?'

The woman picked up her double bass but she was so upset Santos offered to carry it for her. He took her into the common room, past the curious and suspicious faces of the others and sat her down on a battered sofa. Lit a half-gone spliff for her when she said she'd prefer that to a drink. Santos asked her name. The woman took a long drag and said, 'Keisha. Keisha X. My folks were Panthers back in Chicago, so they got rid of the slave master's surname and put an X instead, in honour of our unknown African ancestors, you know like Malcolm X.'

Santos didn't have clue what she was talking about, but the

others were nodding their heads in approval, except Missy, whose expression was a cross between stoned and confused.

Keisha took another drag on the joint. 'Man, oh, man, it was bound to happen. Connie was a genuine artist, the real deal; he lived fast and died young. That's what happens to the real thing. It always has and it always will.'

Santos sat next to her and asked, 'Did you know him well?'

'Sure. Whenever I was over, we used to hook up. Used to jam and write songs together. Didn't he mention my name?'

She sounded rather hurt, so Santos told her, 'Yes, I'm sure he did.'

This seemed to cheer her up a little before Keisha looked downcast again. 'Only the good die young . . .'

She finished the spliff, stubbing it out on an old saucer. 'OK. Well, I guess I'd better be going. I haven't got much dough, so I'll have to find somewhere on the street for now until my gig tomorrow night.'

Santos looked over at the others, who eagerly nodded their heads, except Missy, whose face didn't look too happy. 'It's quite late; why don't you stay here tonight?'

'No, I couldn't . . .'

Missy got shakily to her feet, her gaze giving Keisha a not too polite once-over. 'We're a bit short of space at the moment.'

Keisha seemed to have changed her mind about staying. 'Hey, I'll stay in his room . . .'

Santos was quite shocked. 'You want to stay in Cornelius's room??'

'Sure. I'll pick up on the vibe in the room and feel his presence to write a tribute song about him.' Keisha shook her head sadly. 'Really going to miss the guy.'

Santos paused before saying, 'OK. Well, let me show you where his room is.'

While Keisha picked up her double bass, Missy hurried over

to Santos and hissed, 'Are you mad? She looks familiar. I've seen her somewhere before—'

'I look like another black woman?' Keisha said, her eyebrows raised in disgust. 'I guess us black folks all look the same to you, honey?'

That shut Missy up.

Santos took Keisha upstairs. As soon as they reached Cornelius's room, Keisha placed her double base case against the wall and started to rub her palms in the air in circles as she did a circuit of the room.

'He's really left a strong presence here,' she told Santos. 'Perfect for getting the right lyrics to remember him by.'

'Really sorry about Missy—'

'Don't worry about it man, I'm used to racist jerks like her. But you want to tell her to sort her shit out because if you folks don't cotton to black people and that gets around . . .'

She dumped herself on Cornelius's mattress on the floor. As soon as Keisha settled herself into a cross-legged position and started making circles in the air again Santos eagerly left the room. He didn't believe in none of that getting in touch with the dead vibe stuff; but he did feel guilty about the way Cornelius had died.

Keisha X kept up with the hand circles for half minute, then scrambled off the mattress. She took the solitary chair and rammed it under the door handle so no one could get in. She ripped off her head wrap, earrings and sunglasses. Then Rio Wray finger combed her 'fro.

fifty-two

Rio thought the game was up when that Missy character sowed a seed of doubt about who she was. During her last visit here, Miss Fluffy Pink Slippers Monica, and mostly everyone else, was clearly going out of town for a while for some type of demonstration, so Rio had gambled that they wouldn't be back yet and anyone left who decided they recognised her she'd just challenge back with all that 'Oh, so you think all black people look alike?' patter.

Rio was surprised that they hadn't found her out with that dubious American accent and all that 'sure', 'honey' and 'man, oh, man' gum-chewing stereotypical crap. The only person who could have really pointed the finger at her was Cookie, Cornelius's lady . . . But, thank God, she hadn't been here. With Nikki threatening to up and leave for her cousin's in the morning, Rio hadn't had much choice but to put this plan into action.

But they hadn't found her out and here she was, ready to search Cornelius Bell's small room upstairs. Then again, she wasn't sure what she was looking for. If Cornelius had had something to do with his parents' death – and that was a big *if* – what might she find in this room that would tell her? Rio sifted through his clothes. Nothing. Next she pulled off the bedding on the mattress. Nothing. Turned the mattress . . . the furniture . . . the three books . . . She stopped when she got to the small makeshift table. Something was missing ... what was it? Ah, yeah, the framed photograph of the small boy. Sometimes people locked their secrets behind the picture of a loved one; was that why the photo was gone? Cornelius had hidden something revealing in there?

Rio stored the info away and got back on with the search.

'Balls!' Rio let out ten minutes later, having turned up nothing of interest. It was a long shot anyway. Standing by the window, she stared outside, not really seeing anything, thinking about what excuse she could invent to leave. It had to be credible or the others would get suspicious – maybe Missy would start finger-jabbing again. As she turned away, her gaze caught something in the dark outside. Rio turned fully around again and realised that outside was the yard at the back and what had drawn her attention was as, at first glance, an old-fashioned style metallic outdoor rubbish bin, complete with lid. But what kept her attention was in the centre of the lid was a round chimney or flute. Maybe ...?

Rio shoved the window up, leaned out and saw a large, black downpipe attached to the wall. She placed half her body outside, reached and grabbed the pipe, then heaved completely out, throwing herself against the pipe. It shook slightly, so she remained immobile until it became still. Then she pushed her legs down, gripped the walk with the toe-end of her trainers and started to slide down, monkey-style. As she got halfway, Rio heard the distant chat and laughter of the others downstairs. A few inches from the ground, she let go and landed.

When she reached the bin, she worked out it was a garden incinerator. A circular band around the base which had a blackish-grey colour and polka-dot style ventilation holes covering it. The wall behind was thick with the same coloured residue. Rio poked the scum with her fingers; it had a slight spring to it. She scraped some off and smelt it. Carbonised rubber?

Rolling up her sleeves, she began sifting through the incinerator. It was mostly ash and scorched objects that had been expected to burn but hadn't. She laid the bin on its side as quietly as she could and let the contents spill out into the yard, then did an amateur's forensic search, putting anything of interest to one side. When she'd finished she scooped the ash back inside and placed the bin back on its feet. Crouching back down, she examined the two items she'd retrieved that now lay on the ground:

A blackened, long tube.

A pockmarked piece of oval Perspex.

They wore a piece of puffy cloth ... with two plastic things over the eyes. And a trunk or hose thing—'

Rio's heart raced as she remembered Nikki's description of the murderers' attire. Could the blackened tube be the hose/trunk that Nikki meant? Was the oval Perspex one of the plastic eyes?

That sounds like a gas mask, except the baggy cloth bit.

Rio heard Samson Larkin's smug words inside the café. Was the mask some type of gas mask? And were the rubber scrapings she'd felt the remains of a boiler suit? But why wear a homemade gas mask? It just didn't make any sense.

'What are you doing?'

Rio had been so wrapped up in her potential discovery she never heard the back door open. She turned to find the one person who could blow her cover.

Rio placed an ash-covered finger against her lips indicating the Cookie should remain silent. She beckoned the younger woman forwards with her hand. At first, Cookie didn't move, then the door swung closed behind her as she joined Rio.

Rio remained crouched down. Kept her voice quiet. 'I need to ask you some questions.'

'But I don't understand what you're doing here. The others said there was a friend of Connie's in his room. A black . . . is that you?' Her tone was now upset.

'I want to find out, just like you, why Cornelius is dead.'

'But I heard that you were suspended.'

Rio knew there was no point lying, plus she didn't want to treat this grieving woman as if she were a fool. 'I am. But I can't let it go.' She gazed up at the house, knowing she had to act quickly before someone else potentially arrived. 'I'm trying to get to the bottom of what happened with Cornelius's parents, so I blagged my way in here to have a look around.'

The young woman's voice was nearly a whisper. 'You want to blame Connie, don't you?'

'Should I?'

Cookie's voice was a whisper now. 'No.'

'Do you know if he burned anything in that incinerator out back? After his parents were murdered?'

'Everyone burns things here. In case the police raid the place again.'

'Did you see him burn anything made of rubber – like a boiler suit or something?'

Cookie blinked furiously 'I don't know.'

Rio pointed to the cylinder and the Perspex. 'Do you know what these might be?'

There was the sound of a car accelerating outside somewhere in the front.

Cookie looked angry now. 'Are you calling my Connie a murderer?'

Rio held up her palms. 'No. Three people were murdered inside his parents' home – including his mother and father – and the evidence is looking like it was not part of the Greenbelt

Gang raids. All I'm trying to find out is what happened in that house. Who did this? And I'll be honest – I need to find out if Cornelius had something to do with it.'

Cornelius's bereaved girlfriend took a step back. 'If you're not supposed to be here, Detective Sergeant Major, whatever you're called, you'd better go.'

The voices inside the house changed – became louder – but neither Rio nor Cookie noticed.

'If Cornelius murdered his parents, he didn't do it on his own. Is that what happened, Cookie, you did it together?'

The other woman's face went so white that Rio thought she was going to keel over. 'You're crazy. Fucking crazy. Connie couldn't do anything like that without getting a panic attack—'

'He had panic attacks? Did he have problems with his breathing when that happened?'

Cookie kept her mouth stubbornly shut, giving Rio her answer.

'Was it the money?'

'What money? I was with my little brother the whole day. You can ask anyone.'

'Was that your brother in the framed photo in Cornelius's room? What happened to it—?'

Cookie's anger burst forth as the words flew from her mouth like spit. 'Leave Tod out of this—'

The back door crashed open. Two uniformed police appeared.

One of them said, 'Both of you inside the building. We have a warrant to search the premises for drugs.'

Rio's heart sank. Of all the bad luck . . . She looked up at the wall, but it was way too high to make a run for it.

Seeing where her gaze went, the officer who had spoken walked forwards as he said, 'Don't even think about. We've got all exits and entrances covered.'

fifty-three

'What would you do with five hundred thousand pounds?'

Calum looked up from the playing cards in his hand at Nikki who sat opposite him. They were both on the floor. She sat crossed-legged, cards held tight between a pair of lime-green woolly fingerless gloves, while his were stretched out in front of him. He was teaching her Blackjack, which she'd taken to like a duck to water. He had a dud hand and from the happy smirk on her face Nikki was obviously pleased with her own.

'You wouldn't be trying to distract me, Miss Bell?'

Nikki's eyes gleamed as her shoulders wiggled like unheard music was being pumped up through the floor. 'Would you buy a house?' she continued. 'That's how much money auntie and uncle left me, until I reach twenty-five. Then I've got access to loads more.'

He picked up a card from the face-down pack. 'They probably wanted you to use it for your education and then yeah, maybe buy a cosy flat somewhere.'

'Have you met a hitman?'

He looked up at her. 'What kind of question is that for a half a million girl to ask?'

Nikki grinned shyly. 'Go on, tell me.'

'I might've met one or two in my time.'

'How do you find one?'

'And why would an innocent little girl like you want to know the answer to a dangerous question like that?'

The laughter on her face fell away. When Calum had first met the teen she'd use her hair to sometimes hide her emotions, but now everything she felt was laid stark and bare by her Ophelia-style hairdo. 'Just wondering how much someone is willing to pay to see me dead.'

'Don't think about bollocks like that. No one is getting to you while I'm around.'

'Tell me.'

Calum sighed. 'It varies depending on the job and what country it's in. I hear that in South Africa you can get that kind of job done way on the cheap because people are desperate for a bob or two. But in a country like this, you'd have to shell out a hell of a lot more.'

'Like half a million?'

'Rio wouldn't like me talking about this.'

'Fuck Rio.'

'Watch the tongue.'

'Why should I? You swear all the time.'

'Yeah, well, if you'd had some of the experiences I'd had you'd want to be cursing from morning till night.'

Nikki grinned as she lay down her cards triumphantly. 'Blackjack.'

Calum threw his cards down. 'Yeah, only because you distracted me.'

He leaned a hand against the chair he'd strategically placed next to him to help him get to his feet again.

'Time for you to have some of that pizza I ordered while I stretch my legs.'

'Can I watch the telly for a bit? I missed this week's episode of *The Wilcotts*. Cousin Lia is *so* good in it.'

He nodded, distracted by the pain shooting up his left leg. He walked slowly as he made his way out of the room to the bathroom along the corridor. As his hand reached for the handle his mobile went off. He pulled it out.

'It's Jack Strong.'

'What do you want?' Calum's tone was brusque. His leg was hurting like shit and he didn't have time for making new friends.

'I'm just checking that our girl's OK. I need to tell the boss that she's safe—'

'You haven't told him that Rio took—'

'Of course I didn't tell him what Rio did. All he knows is that she's with people who are taking care of her. So she safe or what?'

'Safe.'

Calum ended the call, sucked in his breath as the pain throbbed deeper in his leg.

Once inside he headed for the small twin-mirrored cabinet and took out a bottle of pills. He hated taking this stuff, but when the pain was bad he didn't have much choice. With the bottle in hand he moved across the room and dropped down onto the toilet seat, let out a long groan as his head flopped back. When the doctor told him that this pain might be a life-long thing he hadn't believed her. He hadn't wanted to believe her. His life had almost been destroyed and to have this pain flip him out anytime it chose was something he still couldn't deal with.

He pushed his head down as he used one hand to ease up the trousers over his left leg. He almost shifted his eyes away, still finding it hard to stare at himself, to deal with what had happened to him.

Suddenly the door pushed open and Nikki was standing in the doorway.

'Oops, sorry, I didn't realise . . .' Her voice trailed off as she saw his leg.

Calum's brain told him to push his trousers back in place but his hands wouldn't move.

'I didn't know . . .' Nikki's gaze left his leg and rose to his face. 'My mum's friend had one of those. She was in a car accident. Is that why you look uncomfortable sometimes – because you get those phantom pains?'

There was no pity in her stare, no question, no gasp of shock. None of the things that Calum knew twisted his own face when he looked at his leg. He looked down at it now: flesh and bone above the knee, but artificial leg below.

'Yeah,' he responded softly as he pulled his trousers back into place. 'Feels like my leg is really there.'

'My friend's mum hated people asking her all the time if she needed any help . . . but I'm here if you need me.' Nikki lifted her shoulders and closed the door.

Calum remained where he was, thinking he would be prepared to tell people if they would all react like that innocent girl. No forced questions, no 'you can hold my hand' crap or start chatting to him like he was a mouth-foaming imbecile. He hadn't told Mac, hadn't told Rio. He knew they assumed that it was nothing too major, just an injury taking its time to heal. What would they say if they knew part of his leg wasn't there anymore? Or how it had happened? That it had all been due to the job he loved so much – being a police officer.

When he'd confessed to Rio that he hadn't been with anyone since her and she'd told him to pull her other leg that had made him laugh so hard, but not with joy, just at the harsh reality of his situation. Pull her leg? She wanted to try pulling his non-existent one.

Calum checked his watch. Ten minutes to contact Rio to let her know that her witness was safe.

'Nooo! Nooo!'

Calum jumped up, hearing Nikki's hysterical voice, the pill bottle hitting the floor as he rocked unsteadily at the quick movement. He pulled out his semi-automatic Berretta and headed for the door – opened it – shouted, 'Nikki?'

The only response was the sound of her sobs. Gun ready for action, he stepped into his office, then lowered it when he found Nikki collapsed on the floor, her hands covering her face as she cried.

'What's going on?' he asked, his gaze wandering around the room. It stopped when it got to the small, flat-screen plasma television.

'Jee-sus,' he whispered as he saw what had set Nikki off.

On the screen was a photo of her boyfriend Ade. The voice of the newscaster was clear.

'Adeyemi Ibraheem was in his first year of an economics degree at Oxford University. The police are asking anyone who has information to call the number at the bottom of the screen . . .'

'They found him in the river.' Calum turned when he heard Nikki's voice. Her face was flushed and thick with tears. 'Someone cut his throat. Is he dead because of me?'

Calum winced as he eased down to the floor. He took the girl in his arms and let her cry.

8:05 p.m.

Rio paced inside the cell. Of course it wasn't the first time she'd been in one, but this time the door was shut and locked behind her. If drugs or anything else illegal had been found at The Rebels' Collective she was going to be held for a while and time was something she didn't have. As soon as they reached the local police station her fingerprints and picture were taken. The longer she stayed in here the more time they had to realise that she'd given them a bogus name and discover who she really was. Then her career would be over. The Assistant Commissioner and her DS would not be giving her any second chances. And no way could she be in here tomorrow morning when Nikki was determined to go to her cousin. Once the girl was back in the real world she was a naked target. She had to figure a way to get out of here. Now.

Rio stopped pacing. Sitting down on the makeshift bed, she started running through her options. She could claim to be sick – they'd pull the duty doctor in and maybe, just maybe, she could be taken to the hospital and then make a run for it. No. She shook her head; that was too much of a long shot. She could call Strong and get him to claim she was his CI and working an important case. But what if Strong wasn't available? Rio didn't have time to wait around for him. Calum was her third and final option. And how was he going to get her out of here? Plus if one of the other officers recognised him as the notorious ex-cop Calum Burns they'd probably bang him up as well. Anyway, she couldn't drag him down here because he was looking after Nikki.

Defeated and weary she laid her head back against the cold wall. It was over. She was out of exit routes to go down. Just when two and two was actually starting to make four . . . All this time she'd fingered Gary Larkin as being there because of his asthma, but it had probably been Cornelius having a panic attack. And who'd been his accomplice? Someone in the Collective? Cookie? And why had Cornelius murdered his parents?

The questions bounced inside her mind, her frustration at not being able to hit the street to get answers pumping her blood pressure higher and higher. She needed to get out of here. She needed ... The muscles in her body tightened. Her head jacked off the wall.

Of course. The one person who can get me out of here.

Rio strode over to the blue cell door, looked through the tiny observational window and shouted, 'Officer. Officer.'

She shouted until she heard footsteps echo in the corridor outside, then she stepped back as a lean face peered at her through the resistant glass.

'What?' The single word was laced with annoyance.

'I'm ready to make that phone call I'm entitled to.'

After she made her call Rio couldn't sit down because she was worried about Nikki.

fifty-four

Nikki eased off the mattress on the floor. With bare feet, she walked lightly to the door, pressed her ear against it and waited. No sounds. Quiet. Her hand formed around the round, brass handle. Gently turned. The door opened with a click that sounded like the accelerated thud of her heart. Once again she waited. Then she pushed the door out into the dark corridor. Waited. The left side of her head tilted slightly forwards to catch the sound of Calum moving. Quiet. She knew this wasn't going to be easy because there was only one other room here, so it must also be doubling up as the place that Calum slept in.

After finding out about Ade, Calum had decided it was best for both of them to call it an early night.

Ade, Ade, Ade.

His name twisted mournfully in her head as she remembered what had happened to him. Didn't matter what anyone else told her, she knew that he'd ended up dead in the river because of her. Nikki hurt so bad, but it also gave her the courage to do what she had to do. She crept out into the black beyond her room, kept going on tiptoes until she got to the door of the other room. Relief flooded her when she saw that the door was fully back against the wall, open. She slid her body against the wall on the opposite side to the door, took a deep breath, then poked her head around the corner to look inside the room.

It too was bathed in dark, and Calum was asleep on the chair behind the desk. His head was back, tilted to the side, a soft nasal beat of air moving in and out of his body. She suspected that he'd taken one of those pills from the bottle she'd seen him holding in the toilet earlier – probably something heavy-duty that took away the pain and made him drowsy.

Nikki saw what she wanted, sitting pretty on top of the filing cabinet against the wall. She moved quietly, but with an urgency to get this over and done. She got to the cabinet, sweat slicking the skin between her nose and mouth. Her hand shot out . . .

'What's up Nikki?'

Calum's voice made her jump, her hand dropping back. She turned to see him staring with hooded eyes at her. Apart from his eyes he didn't move, remaining relaxed and easy in the chair.

'I couldn't sleep – couldn't stop thinking about Ade.' He started to move, but she stretched her palm at him. 'No, please. Don't. I just needed to walk around, it's what I do sometimes to clear my head.'

Calum eased back into the chair. 'If you want to talk—'

'No. What's the point? He's not coming back.'

With her head hanging low, her hands folded in front of her, Nikki made her way back out into the corridor. Once back in the other room she laid down, hands clasped together, on top of the duvet. Alert she stayed on her back for fifteen minutes to give Calum enough time to either realise what she'd done or go back to sleep. He never came. That's when she looked down at what she held: one of the three mobile phones she'd observed Calum using.

Nikki quickly punched in a number. On the fourth ring the line connected.

'It's Nicola . . .'

9:07 p.m.

A full hour after making her call Rio's cell opened. The same officer who had appeared at the window stood in the doorway. His expression was even more surly than before. She was so tempted to give him a dressing down, infused with every regulation she remembered about how the police should interact with the public – including those housed within the four walls of a cell. So tempted . . .

'I take it I'm free to go.'

'Collect your stuff from the duty sergeant at the main desk.'

Minutes later, once she'd signed the necessary paperwork and collected her things from the desk sergeant, she allowed herself to turn to the man who had managed to get her out of there.

Stephen Foster.

He waited until they were outside before turning to her and saying, 'Never thought I'd see the day when you'd be calling on me for help.'

But Rio didn't have time to talk, only time to check her mobile. Her finger tapped the screen.

Password.

Activate screen.

No 'safe' text from Calum.

'Is everything alright?' the lawyer asked, but she ignored him.

Rio double-checked the phone. The last 'safe' text was at 8:00 p.m. Nothing for 9:00 p.m. Calum never missed a check-in.

Something was wrong. She called Calum. The phone rang and rang – six times – before connecting.

Voicemail.

Rio started running without thanking Stephen Foster.

fifty-five

10:03 p.m.

When Rio found the security door downstairs leading to Calum's office on the latch she knew that her gut instinct had been right – something was wrong. She didn't pause, didn't let herself think of the grisly scene that might be awaiting her upstairs if the professional killer had finally earned his blood money. Rio flicked the door further back with the tip of her shoe, swallowed a huge intake of air as she pushed inside. Her gaze swept the tunnel of darkness that was the staircase. Empty.

She took the steps one at a time. A noise came from out of nowhere, behind her. She swung around, keeping her footing balanced. No one there. She realised what the sound was – two people talking, their voices fading into the distance outside. Her chest rippled with the uneven air she was pulling in. She twisted back around, treading on a step that had no business creaking at a time like this.

Rio held back, waiting to see if there was any reaction from inside to the noise, but it remained eerily quiet. She held back again when she reached the top. Counted – *One. Two. Three.* – Shoved forwards ready to take on anything and everything that waited in the dark.

But there was no one there, which didn't mean that they

weren't concealed, ready to take her down. Cautiously she put one foot slowly in front of the other, towards the room where Nikki should be sleeping. The door was closed when she got there. Rio kicked the door and danced slightly to the side, but still with a view inside the room. No sounds. No one on the mattress. No Nikki.

This was bad. Really bad.

She got back into the corridor and picked up her pace as she reached Calum's office. Rio found it hard to keep the emotions away this time knowing what she might find inside. Someone who she'd once counted as one of her closest friends . . . No, he was so much more to her than that, probably dead because she'd brought a crap load of trouble to his door. Rio ditched the overwhelming feelings as she thrust the door back. Her heart hammered when she saw Calum tied to his chair lying on its side on the floor. She rushed over to him. His mouth was covered with metallic tape.

He wasn't moving.

Please God let him be alive.

She felt for the pulse in Calum's neck, sighed with relief when it beat against the pad of her finger. She pulled the tape from his mouth.

She shook his shoulders gently. 'Calum, wake up.'

No movement. She shook him harder – still no response. She slapped his cheek. He moaned. She slapped the other side of his face. He let out a groggy sound.

The volume in her voice grew. 'Calum, you have to get up. Now. Nikki's gone.'

His head moved, his dark hair clouding around and over his face. She raised her hand again as one of his green eyes popped open. Her hand dropped. She moved around the chair and untied his hands.

'Are you injured?'

He lay on the ground, both eyes now fully opened. He groaned as he shook his head. 'Don't know . . . how they got . . .' He sucked in much needed oxygen between words.

'What do you mean *they*?'

'I know you've been desperate to get me on my back, but can you help me up?'

It took Rio less than a minute to right the chair and have him sitting in it. Once he was upright she saw the blood at the back of his head.

'Have you got a towel or something—?'

'Forget that, I'm OK. They must've disabled the security system. One of them coshed me on the back of the head—'

'You keep saying *they*?'

'There were two of them, dressed from head to toe in black, wearing hoodies and scarves over their faces.'

Confusion pulled Rio's features. 'The hitman was working on his own as far as we know—'

'That's the usual MO, a lone pro who relies on no one but himself.'

Rio covered her mouth as her mind turned this way and that. If this wasn't the hitman . . . What the hell was going on here?

'Check the top of the cabinet for a mobile phone,' Calum said, as he gingerly rubbed his fingers into the blood on the back of his head.

'Nothing here,' she answered after she checked.

'Bollocks.' Calum cursed some more. 'Earlier I found Nikki in the room as I was sleeping. She'd just found out about her boyfriend.'

This was going from bad to worse.

'She said she was walking around because she was upset and needed to think and like I fool I believed her cock-and-bull story, but I suspect she came in to swipe one of my phones. Check next door.'

Less than a minute later Rio was back with the mobile. 'I found it amongst the bedding.' Rio punched it on and made a noise with disgust when it went straight to the home screen. 'I thought you were meant to be one of the best security consultants in the business, so why isn't this locked?'

Slowly he stood up. 'It's one of my back-up phones, so I don't use it very often.'

But Rio wasn't listening as she tapped the phone icon and checked out the recent calls history. The number she found made her breath catch in her throat.

She gazed over at Calum. 'This isn't good if this is what I think it is.'

'Who did she call?'

'I'll tell you on the way. We need to move now because there might not be much time.'

11:05 p.m.

There was no welcoming light on the porch of 20 Beacon House, Peckham, SE15 when Rio and Calum stood outside it this time.

'Let me do all the talking,' Rio instructed Calum.

The hallway light came on after Rio pressed the bell. The slap of backless slippers sounded inside, moving towards the door. It didn't open but Rio felt the eyes that observed her through the peephole.

'Move away from my home,' the voice inside commanded.

'I can't do that, Mrs Ibraheem. Nicola Bell is missing and I think that your son, Chiwetel, may have taken her. He was very angry when I saw him at the coroner's, threatening to kill Nicola.'

'My son would never do something like that—'

'We both know that Chiwetel is involved in all types of rough trade.'

The accusation pushed the other woman's voice higher. 'Go away and leave me alone to grieve for my boy.'

'If you don't open the door, how are you going to feel when your other son is back behind bars again? And believe me I'm going to make it my business to make sure that happens if he touches one grain of hair on that girl's head.'

Silence. Then a thud as a bolt was pulled back. Finally the door opened. Ade's mother looked drained, the flesh sagging on her face. She wore a green and white headscarf tied at the back and a caramel coloured dressing coat hugged her body.

As Rio stepped inside she turned to Calum. 'Wait for me here.'

'But—'

Rio quietly closed the door. The other woman stood her ground, not extending a welcome further into her home.

'Nikki phoned here earlier.'

Mrs Ibraheem's teeth twisted into her bottom lip. Then, 'I told her what I'm telling you; stay away, leave me alone. But she was so upset . . . The Quran says "Allah does not guide the wrongdoers", and it would have been wrong of me not to listen to her, so I listened, let her fill me with her words of love for my son.' Her hand swept up one side of her headscarf. 'But, Allah forgive me, I know that she is the cause of why I'm going to have to bury my Adeyemi.'

'Did she tell you where she was?'

'I never asked her to, she just told me. I repeated the address to her to make sure I had heard right. And Chiwetel was here—'

'Where do you think he took her?'

Tears formed in the bottom of her eyes and Rio felt an aching sympathy for her. 'He's not a bad boy. He just got so angry when his father left to stay in Nigeria. He felt abandoned . . . I did the best I could.'

Rio remembered hearing similar words spoken by her own mother to her auntie when her father had left.

'I swear if Nikki is unharmed we won't bring any charges against your son.'

The older woman breathed like a weight had been lifted from her head. 'He part owns a nightclub, about ten minutes from here. It's called The Delta Club. He works in the basement.' She took a deep breath before adding, 'I think the basement is soundproof.'

fifty-six

'No way am I letting you go in there Lone Ranger style,' Calum told Rio as she stopped the car's engine on the neighbouring road where the club was located.

The Delta Club was situated on the border with Peckham and Nunhead, not that far from Nunhead's Victorian cemetery.

Rio turned to him. 'You're in no fit state if things kick off. And I'm still pissed that you wouldn't go to the hospital.'

'It isn't happening, Rio. You go in, I go in.'

Rio didn't have time to fight what she knew was a losing battle. 'We can go through the front, but might not be allowed in by the bouncers. The last thing we need is to alert anyone that we're here.'

Calum pulled out his mobile. 'Let's see if there are any photos of the interior online which might give us a head start on the layout.'

He got the Internet running, put in a search for images of the club. Nothing came back. He looked at Rio. 'No images, which means there's a strict rule about taking snaps inside. That's not good; the only places that do that have got something to hide.' He put his phone away as he carried on speaking.

'Let's hope there's some way we can get in around the side or back.'

They hit the cooling night and turned into the street where the club was. Calum grabbed Rio's hand. She tried to pull out of his hold.

'What the effing hell are you doing?'

He tightened his hand. 'Let's appear to be a loving couple.' Their eyes caught and held. Rio was the first to turn away. 'That way we'll look like two people minding our own business.'

The club didn't have a neon sign or any other sign, just a group of young people standing outside, smoking and talking. Despite being a two-storey building, it appeared squat: oblong a better description for its shape than the more elegant rectangle. Painted a bland cream, it had two single lights at the front and a blue main door. Two, tall silhouettes stood in position beside the door. But their luck was in; one half of the building was detached.

'The place is probably covered by security cams,' Calum whispered as they walked past, 'although sometimes they are just a show of muscle and either no one is keeping an eye on them or they're not even on. Whatever the situation, we need to be quick.'

They played the hand-in-hand lovers routine until they got just past the alleyway at the side of the club. As Rio took another step she almost lost her balance when Calum jerked her close to his body and rushed into the narrow passageway. He wrapped his hand over her mouth and yanked her close to his chest as he backed into a wall.

'Quiet.' His voice was low, intense, blowing into her ear.

His hand dropped away as Rio did what she knew Calum was doing – her gaze scouted up and around. The environment appeared like it was up for a fight – razor wire stretched across the wall perimeter, brickwork that was broken, scarred and stubborn enough to take more abuse, and a ground that was dirty and hard. The one thing she couldn't see was . . .

'No cams,' Calum uttered the words in her head. 'Maybe this place isn't as rough and ready as we thought. Let's find the back door.'

They found it a few metres down, near a stack of bulging black bags. It was a thick block of rusting steel.

'How are we going to get past this?' Rio asked.

'Well if there aren't any cameras, maybe . . .' Calum didn't finish the sentence as his hand shot out towards the rusty, metal bar running along the width of the door. He pressed the bar down. Shoved. Click, the door groaned open.

Rio was the first to step inside. A long corridor with age-old white walls and boxes clumped together at one end. The muffled boom-bass of music playing somewhere on a dance floor vibrated against the walls.

'You go that way and I'll go down here.' She pointed to the opposite side of the corridor. 'Check out any doors that may lead to a way downstairs,' Rio said, taking charge.

Rio went left, bypassing a greasy-looking stain on the grey lino floor. She stopped when she came to a door – listened – nothing. She pulled it slowly open and peered inside what looked like a large kitchen. It was clean, tidy but with no evidence of any hidden stairwells. Rio carried on until she reached another door; this one pulled back slightly from its frame. She tucked it back – a cupboard filled with cleaning equipment.

'Think I've found it,' Calum called.

He was near the end of the corridor on his side standing near another opened door. Rio joined him and peered inside to find a set of wooden stairs leading downwards. A single bulb mounted on the side of the wall lit the way. Calum reached inside his jacket, but Rio snapped her hand around his wrist.

'No hard metal. We need to play this one out carefully. This guy is full of grief, so I think I might be able to talk him down.'

Calum shrugged his shoulders. 'You're the boss lady for now, but if things get dicey in there we may have to do this another way.'

Rio didn't bother to challenge his words; if Nikki was in a bad way they wouldn't have a choice. She took the lead as they went downstairs. The air was dank and dusty with a smell that told of a sewer nearby. As they got closer to the basement level there was the echo of sounds. At first, Rio couldn't grasp what she was hearing, but as she got closer she realised that it was voices. It was hard to make out what was being said. But at any rate, Chiwetel's mother had been wrong; the basement wasn't soundproof.

They reached the bottom of the stairs and immediately saw the black door up ahead. Now the voices were clearer and what Rio heard sent a chill through her.

'Don't play the fool, little girl.'

'I said don't touch me. Don't come near me.'

Both Rio and Calum belted towards the door at the same time. Calum got there first and bashed it open with an almighty shoulder. Rio froze on the threshold. Inside were Chiwetel Ibraheem and another young man. But that's not what made her stop. It was a long time since she'd been shaken by in-your-face-shock, but she was now at what she saw.

Nikki stood in the middle of the room, illuminated directly under the powerful light of the naked bulb above. One of her hands, still wearing lime-green fingerless gloves, held a knife pressed against her throat.

No one spoke. No one moved. They were the only inhabitants of a subterranean world with its own rules; well, that's how it felt to Rio. In this investigation she'd faced situations that she was well used to dealing with – murder gruesomely strewn in a domestic setting; being attacked with fists and weapons; a man hanging above drug paraphernalia that had only added more torture to his already tormented life . . . But a sixteen-year-old girl holding a knife to her own throat? Rio wasn't sure she knew how to deal with that. The one person she had never thought how to protect Nikki from was herself.

'She's off her head,' Chiwetel said, his voice breathless and frantic. 'I only brought her here to talk to her. Just wanted to find out why Ade—?'

Rio snapped into action. 'Shut up.' She didn't look at him, keeping her gaze pinned to the girl taking centre stage. 'Nikki you're worrying me. Please put the knife down.'

Nikki shifted slightly. The stark light above enhanced her paleness. The haunted and hurt emotions in her grey eyes. What worried Rio the most was that there were no tears in Nikki's eyes. The girl's voice was small when she finally spoke. 'Everyone I know just keeps dying around me, so I thought if I wasn't here anymore it would all stop.'

Rio dared to take another step. 'A few years back someone attacked me. They tied me to a bed and slit my wrists.' She held up a forearm, twisting it to show one of the scars. 'It was bloody and hurt so much the pain was ringing throughout my body. But worse than the physical pain was the agony of one of my team being murdered. He was young and I was meant to be looking after him and he died on my watch. I was eaten up with guilt – thought it was all my fault. But I started to realise that putting the blame squarely on me wasn't going to bring my friend back. And if you do something stupid now the only thing you're going to do is make more people feel guilty. How's Ophelia going to feel when she finds out?'

The girl's eyes widened. In that instant Rio realised what her hook was – Nikki's biological mother. Rio took another cautious step. 'She loves you. I see that clearly every time she looks at you. That's why you called your iPad Hamlet, wasn't it? Because you knew he was in love with Ophelia, just like you love *your* Ophelia. How am I going to tell her that one of the people she cares for most in the world is gone?' Rio saw the knife shaking in Nikki's hand. 'I'm close to shutting down this case, which means that you're going to be able to live with Ophelia if that's what you want.'

Rio didn't give the teenager more time to think. Just stepped forwards until she reached her and calmly took the knife from her hand. Instantly Nikki threw herself into Rio's arms, hugged her tight and started sobbing.

Rio ran her hand over her short, rich chestnut hair. 'You're OK now. Safe.'

Rio caught Calum's gaze over her head. He moved towards them and took Nikki from her arms and led her from the room. Rio immediately turned her fierce gaze on Ade's brother and his associate.

'What the fuck were you thinking?'

Chiwetel stood his ground, his stance defiant. 'I needed to find out the truth—'

'By terrorising some grief-stricken girl? A girl who your brother cared so much about? If you weren't trying to harm her, how did she manage to get a knife?'

His tone was now equally as fierce. 'She already had the knife on her. I never searched her because I didn't think some teen from the suburbs would be armed.'

Nikki had a knife? Where the hell did she get that . . .? Rio's mouth tightened as the answer fell into place: the reason none of her team could find the hitman's knife at the hospital was because Nikki had taken it. The sixteen-year-old must have had it hidden all this time. Fuck!

'You know what I am, so you going to haul me into the cop shop?' Chiwetel threw at her.

Some of the fight went out of Rio. 'No. But let me give you a bit of advice; you're not the only one grieving. Your mum is too. Go home. Put your arms around her and make her think that the world isn't such a bad place.'

She started moving for the door. As she passed him he said, 'I'm going to find out who killed my brother and when I find him . . .'

Rio shut the door on his vengeful words.

fifty-seven

12:46 a.m.

'Have you seen a knife like this before?' Rio passed the blade to Calum.

They stood beside her car in the dark a good ten-minute drive away from The Delta Club. Nikki was exhausted and asleep in the back of the car.

Calum held it up as he carefully examined it. 'The handle's soft; rubber. Now this part of the handle,' he held the knife out for Rio to see more closely, 'they're finger grooves. More deep that your average kitchen knife. Whatever job it's meant to be used for involves giving the user a tight enough grip.' He ran his thumb lightly along the blade edge that was slim and curved into a point at the end. Then he used his thumb and forefinger to try to move the blade; it moved. 'It's flexible, slim, tipped.'

'Have you seen one of these before?'

Calum tilted his head at her to emphasise the question he was about to ask. 'Why are you so interested in the knife?'

Rio explained whom it had belonged to and how Nikki had got it. 'If she had only left it where it was we might have been able to pull off some prints and find this killer a lot sooner.'

Calum turned his attention back to the knife. 'I think this is a specialist knife that is created for a particular job.'

Without waiting for Rio's response he handed the blade back to her and took out his phone, started up the Internet and got searching. Less than a minute later he passed the mobile to Rio. On the screen was a photograph of an identical knife, except this one had a navy-blue handle.

'A fisherman's filleting knife . . . Some contract killers have a speciality – a way of killing their victims. Maybe our bounty hunter is known for gutting his with a fish knife.'

Rio's mouth turned down in disgust at the image his words left in her head. 'Do you think you might be able to find out?'

Before he could answer Rio's phone pinged. Text.

Your country needs YOU

The message finished with a skull and crossbones like the other message she had received yesterday. What the hell was going on? She scrolled up and found the other message.

It's a long long way to Tipperary.

'What's up?' Calum asked.

'Someone keeps sending me these weird texts.' She held out her phone to him.

Calum considered the messages. Then looked at her. 'World War One.'

Rio gave him a blank look so he continued. '"A Long Long Way To Tipperary" was a popular song during the Great War and the other–'

'Is a strapline from a much-used recruitment poster. Why is someone sending me this–' Samson Larkin. His name slammed into Rio's mind as her words stopped. He'd been singing another World War One song as they sat in the café in Northern

Cyprus. A song that had an upbeat chorus that included the words 'Smile, smile, smile.' Well she wasn't smiling.

Without answering Calum took her phone from her. He flicked his thumb against the buttons a few times and then, with a sigh, passed it back to her. 'Whoever it is doesn't want to be found because the Caller ID is unknown.'

'I know who it is,' Rio said. 'Mad boy Samson Larkin. I suspect it's his way of letting me know he's still around.'

'That's a strange way of pressing your buttons.' Calum switched the conversation. 'I'll try to find out more about the knife.' He turned back to the car and watched Nikki. 'Are we sure that this is going to be a safe place to take her to?'

Rio let out a huge punch of air as if the enormity of keeping this girl alive had just hit her. 'I can't think of anywhere else to take her. We don't have a choice.'

1:16 p.m.

Rio cut the engine of her car outside Ophelia Bell's home. Nikki was still asleep in the back.

'What happened three years ago?' Rio asked Calum. 'Why did you get kicked out of the service?'

His green eyes became icy. Rio noticed the way his hand drifted to his leg.

'Is that how you hurt yourself?' she quietly asked.

His mouth twisted into a cynical smile, no dimple, as his hand snapped away from his leg. 'One day we'll talk, but not now.'

If he didn't want to talk, so be it. Rio killed the past dead as she turned to gaze at the sleeping teenager. Nikki's head was slumped to the side, her hair a mass of fussing short strands cupping her head. Her small chest rose and fell, but no sound came out of her parted lips. Peaceful. The slumber of the innocent.

Calum's hand reached for the door. 'You take her inside and I'll get back to the office—'

Rio's hand reached across and touched his arm. 'You should go home and get some rest.'

'Nah. I'm a big boy now, Doctor Rio. I've just got a hunch about something . . .'

'You can't go and leave me hanging like that. Is this something about Maurice Bell?'

Calum lowered his voice. 'This is just a hunch, OK? We know that he had a partner in his early days, someone we can't find anything about, except the name Slim. Who else do we know who once had a partner?'

Rio frowned as her brain ticked away. Her eyes widened slightly. 'You think it's Terry Larkin?'

'He might have been young back in the seventies, but remember he was a good ten years older than his brother. What if he was Bell's partner during those slum landlord days? We know that Terry dabbled in property when he first started out and it ended badly. What if both men reconnected and Bell was meant to put up the money for Terry's drugs deal, but maybe he bailed out once he knew what the money was going to be used for. Revenge is the only thing on Terry's mind. Maybe he killed Bell with an accomplice.'

Rio sank back into her seat trying to take it all in. 'But what about Cornelius—'

'Cornelius lived a life on the edge. He could've been in debt to Terry and this was the only way out?'

Rio let out a long, uneven breath. It made sense. And Cornelius hadn't worked on his own.

'We need to go after him—'

But Calum placed a finger on her lip. 'I might have this all wrong. I've got some information that I hope will be coming in to me when I get back to the office. Let me figure this out before we do anything else.'

Rio cupped Calum's face. 'I wish we could've just worked this all out.'

He knew that *this* had nothing to do with the case.

'Take care of our girl in the meantime. Make sure you get some sleep; it's been one hell of a long day for you.'

Then he was gone.

A few minutes later a groggy and mentally numb Nikki stood with Rio in front of Ophelia Bell's front door. Rio was surprised at where the other woman lived. She'd been expecting somewhere plush and yeah expensive, not this maisonette-style ground and upper floor flat, with black railings around it. Weren't those actors on the box paid big bucks?

A pasty and tousled Ophelia pulled the door back. As soon as she saw Nikki she went into concerned cousin mode; or was that concerned mummy mode, Rio thought?

Ophelia reached out and pulled her blood daughter into her arms and squeezed tight. The girl clung onto her with the fierceness of finally finding her safe harbour.

Ophelia gazed at Rio with daggers in her eyes. 'She told me she was staying with a friend. She looks like she's been to hell and back.'

'Let's take this inside.'

The inside of the flat was more like what Rio was expecting – minimalist style, white walls and even whiter floorboards off-set by black furniture and a large, shiny-blue exercise ball in a corner of the main room. There was the touch of other humans in the room, but only as still lifes – a framed photo of two children sat neatly next to a hefty looking black stone carving of what Rio assumed depicted a mother and child touching hands. It was what Rio didn't see that surprised her – no TV.

'What you're thinking now is what everyone thinks when they first come here,' the other woman told Rio as she settled Nikki onto a chair that looked more suited to an office than a lounge. 'That, because I'm an actor, there should be a telly. I'm sure you don't take your work home with you; nor do I. I watch what I need to online on my laptop.' Ophelia gave the teenager her full attention. 'Go and freshen up. Then lie down and I'll be in in a bit. Later on we'll watch more episodes of *The Wilcotts*. I've got advanced copies on DVD.'

She whispered in the girl's ear, but Rio heard, 'Lord Freddy has finally gone back to the trenches.'

As Ophelia's knuckles grazed gently against one of Nikki's cheeks Rio couldn't help but notice the bones jutting harshly against her skin. It couldn't be easy for her, Rio thought sympathetically – all this anorexia and eating disorder business.

As soon as the youngster had left the room Rio got down to business and told the other woman what had happened, including Nikki and the knife.

That made Ophelia drop to the two-seater leather sofa. Her palms cupped her lower face as her sad gaze stared at Rio. 'I feel like I've failed her. I should have insisted she come stay with me–'

'There's no point looking back,' Rio interrupted quickly as she sat by the distressed woman. 'What we need to do now is just keep looking forwards. I'll be upfront with you. I'm no longer on this case. I'm suspended–'

Ophelia's hands dropped from her face. 'What?'

Rio didn't answer immediately; she needed to think very carefully about what she was going to say next. 'It's my belief that your parents and their cleaner were deliberately murdered in a way that made it look like the Greenbelt Gang did it–'

Ophelia staggered to her feet. 'I don't understand—'

Rio joined her on her feet. 'I think that your brother was involved in this.'

The other woman just stared, her eyes blinking rapidly. 'Connie.' It wasn't a question, but a flat, monotone statement. Instead of continuing she strode across the room to a small-framed photograph that Rio had noticed next to the stone carving.

She came back and, with the sadness increasing in her gaze, displayed the photo to Rio. It showed a boy and a girl, anywhere between the ages of nine and twelve. The girl's head was tilted ever so slightly, like she knew her way around a camera, while the boy's expression was softer, almost shy.

'That was me and Connie at our Auntie Patsy and Uncle Frank's. Auntie was always reluctant to let him go home because he was the boy any mother would want.' Rio let her speak. 'Helpful, funny – he adored laughing – hard working.' She pulled the photograph back and placed it face down on the arm of the sofa. 'But as soon as he became a teen some-thing changed; it was like he woke up one day and decided he was part of the wrong family. Got expelled from two good schools . . . Dad tried everything to set him up with jobs, but Connie just never lasted long. I had to turn my back on him when he started stealing from me—'

'So he needed money?'

Ophelia lifted her finely shaped eyebrows. 'He took drugs like they were ready-meals. I wouldn't let him stay with me anymore because all he wanted to do was rip me off.' A shud-der passed through her. 'I had no alternative but to cut him off.'

'He didn't do the crime on his own; he had help. Do you know if he ever mentioned a man called Terry Larkin?'

Ophelia shook her head. 'I've been out of his life for a long time.' Her face turned red. 'What a bastard. All Mum and Dad wanted to do was help and how does he repay them . . .?' She heaved in a heavy breath. 'Connie needed money for drugs and God knows what else. Even with what I now know about him I can't stop thinking of him as my kind, little brother.'

'I can't give you a protection unit because – like I said – I'm not meant to be anywhere near this case. As far as the police are concerned the case is closed. I might be putting you in danger–'

'What I don't understand–' Ophelia frowned. 'If there is someone after Nikki, how would Connie have any money to pay them?'

'Maybe he didn't, but his accomplice does.' Yes, Terry Larkin was a man who mixed with the type of people who would give him a down payment. 'That's why I can't stay with you myself; I'm going to need to find out as much as I can.'

The other woman straightened her back. 'If there's one person in this world I'll kill to keep safe, it's Nikki.'

Before Rio could answer her mobile rang.

'Excuse me,' she told Ophelia and walked across the room as she pulled out her phone.

'Yes?'

'It's Cookie, Connie's . . .' Her voice was breathless. 'I need to see you. I'm the one who killed his parents, not him.'

fifty-eight

1:15 a.m.

Calum tapped away at his computer inside his office. The only light he had was from the single lamp on his desk. The information that he sought came up on his screen: information about Maurice Bell's former business partner. His mouth tightened as he read. Instantly he reached for his mobile to contact Rio, but just as his hand touched his mobile he stopped. Priority number one was getting the info printed and then he'd call her. His hands went back to the computer, pressed print.

It took two minutes. He grabbed his rucksack, put the papers inside, set the security system and then headed out. The cold chill in the early morning air gripped his face as Calum strode, as fast as his leg would allow him, to his car. He popped the lock, got inside, chucked the rucksack on the passenger seat. Pulling his mobile out, he got Rio's number up on the screen and started texting

Terry Larkin is . . .

Calum's eyes punched up at the noise he unexpectedly heard behind him, the heat of someone else. He moved – his finger accidentally pressing the 'send' button on the text – but was too late. Black gloved hands thrust from behind, over his face, and something sharp and slim snapped into the skin over his windpipe. Instinctively his hands came up, away from his mobile, as his head was yanked back. His fingers fought with what he suspected was wire around his throat. His legs kicked out. He savagely twisted and turned, but the pressure and pain in his neck only grew worse.

'All I want is the girl,' a voice hissed behind him.

Calum didn't even try to talk, what he did do was try to recall how to act in this type of situation. His legs stopped moving. He loosened all the muscles in his body. He tried desperately to get his restricted breathing under control. But the pressure tightened around his throat.

'If you don't tell me, you know what's going to happen.'

Screw. You.

Relax.

Relax.

His tongue started drying out. Some type of pressure inside his eyes was making them grow wider. And wider . . . If a blood vessel popped he knew he was in major league trouble.

Relax.

Relax.

'You've got five seconds or I'm going to snap your neck.'

One.

Two.

Three.

Calum stopped relaxing. Bundled up all the energy he could muster, muscles taunt and powerful, ready to strike. As he slammed to the side a searing pain ripped through his back, above his kidneys.

I'm not going to make it.

Make it.

Make . . .

Calum slumped to the side, onto his rucksack, the wire still strapped tight around his throat.

2:00 a.m.

Rio ignored the ping of the new text on her mobile for a third time as she faced Cornelius's girlfriend Cookie. The younger woman had been waiting for her in a North-East London council flat that was totally empty – just walls, doors, windows, a fussy orange and brown patterned carpet and a woman who had confessed to murder. They stood in the narrow, tiny hallway, midway between the main door and a room that Rio suspected was designated on the flat's floor plan as a bedroom. The woman in front of Rio still looked like a little lost girl, but with the imprint of a bad world on the ashen skin of her face.

'Is Cookie your real name?' Rio asked.

She stared back at Rio with those big, troubled eyes. 'It's Samantha Goodwill. But I liked to eat those big, fat Maryland biscuits when I was little so everyone started calling me Cookie.'

Rio didn't move, keeping the space tight around them like that of an interview room. 'And how old are you?'

'Nineteen.'

'Why and how did you murder Mr and Mrs Bell?'

The younger woman's shoulders lifted and tightened. 'That's why I wanted you to come here, so that you'd understand.'

'Is this where you planned it all?'

Cookie shook her head, her face twisting in sudden annoyance. 'No . . . I . . .'

'Take your time. I've come here because I want to understand.'

Cookie folded her arms tight around her middle like she

needed the support to keep herself upright. The angry cries of a baby came from one of the neighbouring properties.

'I've got a little brother. His name's Tod, we call him Toddy—'

Rio's mind spanned quickly back to being in Cornelius's room. 'Is he the boy in the photo—'

'In Cornelius's room,' the other woman finished and nodded. 'Our home life was shit, so I skipped out when I was fifteen. I heard later that they put Tod in one of them group homes . . .'

The ring of Rio's mobile cut through the thick atmosphere. Cookie took a half step back. Rio didn't answer it, but let it ring, never taking her gaze from the other woman. Finally the mobile stopped. The sound of the child's cries were gone as well. Rio said nothing, letting Cookie have the time she needed.

'I wanted to get Tod out of there, but they said I couldn't have him because I had no fixed address. So that's all I needed: some place to stay, a place that we could call our own. I put my name on the housing list, but they said I wasn't a priority case.' She took a deep breath that widened her eyes even more. 'I kept trying to tell them about my brother, but they didn't care. I'd be on the housing list for years and I couldn't wait that long, so Connie . . .' Her voice cracked. 'He said we'd find somewhere with a private landlord. We found a place but we needed a deposit—'

Rio finally allowed herself to move, taking a single step forwards. And she said what she'd suspected all along.

'You didn't kill Cornelius's parents did you?'

Cookie's head swung wildly from side to side. 'But I did, don't you see? If it wasn't for me Connie wouldn't have needed to get his hands on some cash really quickly.'

'From what his sister says he needed to get money pretty lively for his drugs and he probably owed the wrong type of people money.'

'That's a fucking lie.' Her voice bounced and echoed against the walls. 'Sure he took a tote every now and again, but he wasn't in over his head. He didn't owe nothing to no one and you know how I know? Because he always warned me to never get myself into a situation that gave other people power over my life. And that sister of his is evil. She was always bullying him and putting him down as a kid. He used to call her and know what she'd do? Slam the phone down on him. Bitch.'

Rio didn't even remember moving forwards, all she knew was that she had her arms around the young woman who was sliding to the floor. Rio let them collapse in a heap, Cookie crying openly by now.

'And do you know what the stupid thing is?' Cookie let out, 'The Council called me up yesterday and said they found a place for me. Gave me the keys for here. Why didn't they give them to me sooner? Connie wouldn't be dead if they had.'

'This isn't your fault.'

'I should've realised he was going to do something mad to help me. He said he loved me every day, every night. Told me how he was going to be the best big brother Toddy ever had.' Her voice ended in a flood of appalling sounding tears and grief.

Rio just held her. She was pleased that Cookie hadn't been involved in the murders. Rarely did she allow emotions to enter into her job, but this woman – who should have been enjoying the final year of her time as a teenager – deserved a chance: a chance to not only put her own life right but also that of her brother's.

Rio grabbed Cookie's chin and made her deliberately look at her. 'Cornelius did a bad thing to make something else right, but that doesn't come back to your door or make you bad. Think about Tod and the wonderful and safe place you can make for him here. Do you hear me?'

The other woman gave Rio a shaky nod. 'I don't care what

anyone says about him. I'll never forget him and I'll tell Toddy what a good man he was until my dying day.'

Rio's mobile went off again. A feeling of unease travelled up her spine. What if the hitman had caught up with Nikki at Ophelia's? Quickly she pulled out the phone.

Jack Strong.

'What's up?' she asked him.

'It's . . .um . . .'

Rio let go of Cookie and stood up. She couldn't understand it but her legs were trembling.

'Is it Nikki?'

'No. You need to get here. It's Calum Burns.'

As Rio urgently ended the call that's when she noticed the text message.

From Calum.

Terry Larkin is . . .

fifty-nine

2:47 a.m.

Rio rushed through the on-edge quiet of ICU on the first floor of Mission Hill Hospital. She knew she wasn't thinking, just moving on autopilot. Only when she spotted Jack Strong just beyond the nurses' bay did Rio realise that she wasn't even breathing right: chest pinching in pain with a frantic, quick-quick inhale-exhale motion.

'Where is he?' Rio asked as soon as she reached him, her dark eyes darting madly around.

Strong's hand caught the top of her arm. 'Take it easy.'

Rio shook his hand off with such force that the socket of her right shoulder started to ache. Fuck the pain, she had to see Calum. She started striding down the corridor, determined to fling open doors.

'Rio, stop it.'

She heard Strong, but his voice was distant, like he was in another room and she was stuck inside a set of revolving doors destined to go around and around forever. The pain in her chest was now pulling inside her throat. Her hand reached for the first door she came to, but she never opened it because Strong twisted her around. Slamming her up against the wall, he gripped both her arms and pinned her there.

'You're going to be no good to him this way.'

That made her stop, except in her head, where one thought kept racing and racing.

'Is he dead?'

The pressure of his hands deepened. 'I've just told you he needs you, so he can't be dead—'

'But he's in a bad way?'

Rio's head shot sideways to find a grave Doctor Melissa Green looking at her. Strong finally released her. Rio remained against the hard wall, her head flopping back.

'We don't know what happened, Rio,' Strong explained. 'He was found in his car near his office in Brixton. Looks like someone tried to strangle him and he's got a stab wound in his back.'

'He's critical,' Doctor Green softly added.

Strangle . . . Stab wound . . . Critical.

The words were like fire inside Rio's head. She couldn't move off the wall; she was scared that if she did she'd be like Cookie, on the floor in some empty space where no one could reach her.

'We need his next-of-kin details,' Doctor Green continued.

'That's easy,' Strong supplied, 'Maggie Burns. Dame Maggie Burns is his mother—'

Doctor Green's face showed surprise. 'She sits on the board of the hospital's Trust—'

'You're both wrong,' Rio cut in, pulling herself off the wall. 'His next of kin is standing right here.'

The other two looked at her as if she was really losing her mind.

'I'm his wife.'

'It was a mistake. Getting married. No, it was really an impulse.'

Rio's words were strained, but strangely calm as she faced Strong. Melissa Green had tactfully left them alone.

'You don't have to tell me—'

But she didn't let him finish. Couldn't let him finish. It was like the moment a suspect finally breaks and knows that the only way to escape the constant interrogation, the artillery of questions, the unrelenting, 'What the fuck have I done to my life?' is to tell the truth.

'Of course at the time it didn't feel like an impulse,' she continued softly. 'It felt like the most amazing thing in the world. Him and Mac were my best mates. I should've kept it like that, but then my dad died.' She took a huge breath. 'Dad left my mum when I was young. He was a charmer – selfish as hell, lady friends around every street corner. But I loved him. When he passed there was this hole inside of me; I needed something to make me feel whole again. And being with Calum – wow – it sure did the trick. He made me feel so fucking good.

'I proposed to him one day as we were eating toast in my bed. And the stupid idiot said yes. A week later we're holding hands like a pair of goofy teenagers, me in this over-kill cream dress, taking vows that were meant to last a lifetime.'

Rio's head fell back slightly as she let out a tiny ripple of laughter. 'We didn't tell anyone – decided to have a little gathering in a week's time to spill the beans. But we never got that far because the shit hit the fan and Calum's out on his ear.' Her face screwed up. 'Everyone's calling him dirty. No one's telling me what the hell's going on. Calum wouldn't take my calls. Then I hear he's been in an accident. I went to that hospital three fucking times, but he refused to see me. I was worried out of my head about him. Then he was moved and I didn't know where he was.'

'Rio—' Strong took a step closer but she violently shook her head, making him stop.

'Then he has the nerve – the bloody nerve – to send me a

letter telling me to stay the hell away from him. He didn't have the guts to say it to my face. What a coward. A total coward. Coward—'

It was only when she felt the detective's strong arms around her that she realised how hard she was sobbing – so badly she needed the support of the wall to stay on her feet.

'I keep calling him a coward,' she stuttered out. 'But's he's not. He's one of the bravest men I know.'

'Why didn't you divorce him?'

'Because it would've been like losing my dad all over again.' Rio pushed herself back from Strong, looked steadily into his understanding blue eyes. 'And he owes me. There's something he's not telling me. Call it the policewoman in me; I can't let go until I know the truth. When he tells me why he pushed me away and had to leave the force, then maybe it's my turn to serve him a piece of paper that makes sure he stays the hell away from me.'

Someone discreetly coughed. Rio snapped her gaze away from Strong to find Melissa Green hovering uncomfortably in the background.

'Sorry to interrupt, but I thought I should give you Mr Burns' belongings.'

She handed Rio a black wallet, ballpoint, black pen, a half eaten pack of mints. And a gun. Rio instantly recognised it from her days in the firearms unit. A semi-automatic FN Five-Seven: lightweight, low recoil and large magazine capacity. Two features upped it on the lethal scale – equal right and left hand controls and the ability to use cartridges that could pierce body armour. Calum hadn't been fucking around when he decided to pack this monster. Shame he hadn't been able to use it on the monster who'd attacked him.

'I should take that in as evidence, DI,' Strong said.

But Rio shook her head. 'No. It stays with me for now. You

know he could get into some serious trouble if he doesn't have the paperwork to go with this.'

Rio was thankful that the older detective didn't push it. She placed the gun in her pocket.

'Was this all you found on him?' Rio addressed the doctor.

'There's a rucksack—'

Rio frowned. 'Did you find a phone in his bag?'

Doctor Green lifted her shoulders. 'No, just—'

'He never goes anywhere without one of his phones. I know he had one because he sent me a text.'

'Maybe he knew he was just stepping into his car for a minute,' Strong rationalised, 'and then going back to the office—'

'No way,' Rio interrupted. 'He always has a phone . . .' Abruptly she stopped talking. Then Rio was striding away, pulling her mobile out at the same time, her mind ticking. When the line was connected she didn't hear Doctor Green ask what she wanted her to do with Calum's rucksack.

All Rio could think about was Calum's phone.

sixty

3:49 a.m.

The mobile phone pinged. The contract killer smiled. He picked it up from its resting place on the car passenger seat beside him. It was the only object he had taken off the security consultant – all he needed to hopefully find the girl. He knew that eventually the information he needed to lead him straight to her would come in. He read the text message.

And here it was.

> Thanks for looking after me. Ophelia is taking good care of me at her home. You were so good to me.
> lol Nikki ☺

Silly girl. He hoped he was bringing up his girl not to be such a dimwit. He smiled. His daughter's birthday was in a few days. And what a surprise he had in store for her.

He ditched thoughts of his family as he turned the ignition. It took him just under thirty minutes to reach his target's cousin's home. He parked up on an adjacent road, pulled out his mobile, made the call that he hoped would get this job done and get him back to his family.

'I've located her.'

'Why are you calling me? You know what to do.'

'She's at the actress's place.' His orders were not to go anywhere near the cousin.

Maybe his contact had a soft spot for the character the actress played in that appalling period drama.

'But,' he added, 'let me be clear. If I don't go into the actress's home and finish this I won't be here come the morning light. I've already changed my plans – which I never like doing – and have given you an extra day–'

'Which you're getting paid for–'

'True. But this job doesn't feel so lucky anymore.'

'Unlucky is being tossed out on the street after leaving the army. Don't forget who gave you a helping hand and brought luck back into your life.'

He swallowed. He didn't like thinking back to those days.

'Am I going in?'

Silence. Then, 'Do it.'

He disconnected the call, zipped his midnight-black wind-breaker to just over the bump in his nose, flicked his hood until it hung low over his face, and got out. Heading around the back to the boot of the car, he pooped the lid. Inside a large holdall bag were the tools of his trade – guns, wire, string, tape and a variety of sedatives and deadlier meds. And his beloved knives: knives, never derogatory names like blade, cutter, pig sticker, Tottenham toothpick. Those terms were disrespectful and you didn't diss things that were part of your family. He chose one of his larger filleting knives – one that was real easy to get close to the bone.

Finally he looked up at the small building, black railing set around it. He counted ten maisonette-style apartments. The actress's home took up a space on the ground and first floors. No security cams or alarms in sight. Good. He walked over until he stood directly opposite her front door. The place was dark downstairs, but there was the glow of a light behind the drawn curtains of a window upstairs. Was the room the shit actress's or the girl's? He shrugged as he took out his picklock. Didn't matter really; both were dead already.

Ten seconds later he was inside a hallway bathed in black. He immediately caught his reflection in the oval mirror that faced him at the far end of the hallway. He smiled tightly. He liked what he saw; the visual image of a shadowed beast, with only eyes for a face and black gloves for hands. He looked away from the mirror. Didn't bother checking any of the rooms downstairs; the light upstairs told its own story of where the residents of this home were. He took the stairs carefully, slowly, his covered hand gripping the bannister to keep his tread quiet and light. He counted the steps as he went.

One.

Two.

Three.

Four.

On number five he saw through the bannister which room the light was coming from. The second room on a short landing. Probably a bedroom.

Six.

Seven.

On number eight he pulled the knife into his hand.

Final step. His feet touched the landing. He took his time moving, the light from the room almost drawing him in. His hand tightened on the flexible knife handle. He took another step. And another. He reached the edge of the room. The door was partially opened into the room. He pushed the door slowly back with an expert, quiet ease as he entered the room.

And there she was, with her back to him, sitting on a stool at a dressing table. He could feel his cock getting hard. It was always the same with him. Just before the kill, he felt this power so strong, so engulfing, every nerve ending inside him fired up, pushing adrenaline to the four corners of his body until he thought he was going to blow and come. She hadn't heard him yet. That made the feeling so much sweeter. Him, so much harder.

He got himself back under control. His cock started shrinking as he finally moved towards her, knife rising wickedly high.

A female voice announced behind him, 'You take another step mister and you're a dead man.'

4:42 a.m.

'Drop it,' Rio said as she held Calum's gun steady.

She could feel the tremble in her finger; she so wanted to pull the hammer back and blast this man away for all the damage he had done.

'You shoot me and you know what's going to happen?' the professional killer said as he half-turned, his voice no way as steady as the last time they'd met in the hospital. 'All I've got to do is throw this knife straight into the girl.'

'No, you're just going to drop straight to the floor like the sack of sorry humanity you are. And, oh yeah, that isn't the girl.'

He turned his head slightly as the person on the stool turned. Not his target but the actress.

Rio saw the muscles contract in the gunman's shoulder. Only confronted by the possibility of Calum's death had she figured out she'd been playing the hitman all wrong. Instead of waiting for him to strike, Rio had flipped it around so that she was now the hunter. But it would only play out if Ophelia was willing to play the part of Nikki. Rio had explained the danger involved, but the other woman had immediately risen to the challenge, saying she'd do what it took to keep her daughter safe. Plus, she'd added, wasn't she an actress? Ophelia Bell had guts.

Rio took a step closer as she spoke. 'You should've figured out that this was all too easy. The only reason you took Calum's phone was the hope that the girl would contact you. But it wasn't her, it was me. By taking his phone you left yourself wide open for a set-up. Don't they teach you better than that in hitman school? You're cornered so let's not do the whole "I'm going to count to three" routine,' Rio said. 'Just let the knife go.'

Rio read the indecision in his eyes. Then his hand came down as his finger loosened around the knife. But instead of the weapon falling, with a quick flick of his wrist and a twist of his body he threw the knife at Rio. She did a quick side step, the knife missing her by inches and hitting the wall behind her. He rushed forwards as Ophelia scrambled down onto the floor. Rio levelled the gun onto his moving figure. Her finger twitched against the trigger. Twitched.

Go on do it.

Pull the trigger back.

Do it.

DO. IT.

But she couldn't do it – couldn't fire a gun that wasn't official issue, especially after what had happened on the raid. She wasn't willing to cross that line. So she ran after him, but it was too late. He hurled his body at the drawn curtains. Went crashing through the window.

Rio heard a piercing scream from outside. Reaching the broken window, she looked down to see the killer impaled on the iron railings below, two vicious-looking spikes jutting out of his back.

'Make sure Nikki remains in the sitting room,' Rio yelled at Ophelia as she ran out of the room, rushed down the stairs, flung open the front door. Gun still in her hand, the cold air twisting around her, she ran over to him. His face was flopped forwards as blood leaked down his back. Rio bent down, shoving her face close to his. Laboured breathing and blood oozed from his mouth.

'Tell me who sent you.'

No response.

'Who ordered you to kill Nicola Bell? Did you murder the gang as well?'

He shifted his head slightly to gaze at her. Rio could already see death in his eyes.

'You need to tell me . . .'

A nasty choking sound bubbled up from his throat.

'Tell me . . .' she shouted.

The choking sound stopped as his body relaxed.

'Shit,' Rio savagely swore.

She knew he was dead as she watched a line of blood stream from his mouth and tumble thickly to the ground.

'You need to get away from here.'

Rio looked up to find Strong nearby. She pulled herself straight, shaking her head.

'The bastard didn't tell me a thing.'

Strong scanned the body. 'I'd say one of those spikes probably went into his heart, if a man like him possessed one.'

'How did you know I was here?'

'Newman told me to keep this,' he pointed to his eye, 'squarely on you. You need to be gone before I call this in. I'll say this was my operation.'

They turned to find Ophelia and her blood daughter huddled in each other's arms in the doorway. Both their faces were frozen in shock as they stared at the dead body of the man.

'Find out everything you can about him,' Rio ordered as if

she were still in charge of the case. 'We still need to confirm who was pulling his strings, although I think I know who it is.'

'Who?' Strong asked.

'Terry Larkin.'

Strong swore. 'That's going to be a big major deal problem.'

The skin on Rio's forehead scrunched together. 'What haven't you told me?'

'Terry Larkin is in Northern Cyprus.'

'What?' Her voice rose. 'How the hell could he have gone there? Wasn't anyone—'

'He travelled using his own name because he knows we don't have any evidence to hold him. If we confirm Larkin is behind it all we'll haul him back from Cyprus.'

'Do you know how long an extradition can take? Bloody years in some cases.' She looked Strong square in the eye. 'I'm going to get on a flight and get that murdering dickhead myself if I have to.' Rio held up her hand when Strong opened his mouth. 'I've got to find out how Calum's doing before I do anything else.'

Then she turned and walked away, rocking with tiredness before she found a steady rhythm as she was swallowed up by the shadows of the street.

sixty-one

6:00 a.m.

Rio was dazed and bone weary as she walked slowly back into the hospital. She needed to be thinking straight if she was going to hit back at Terry Larkin. All she wanted to do now was to finally see Calum. As Rio got midway to the first landing her phone pinged.

Text message.

She almost swore but didn't when she saw it was another message from Skull and Crossbones, AKA Samson Larkin. She scanned the message. No writing, but a photo and a link. The photo was a large red poppy – another reference to World War One. Rio still couldn't understand the reference. Curiosity made her press the link.

It was a YouTube video with a painting of Beethoven on it. She recognised the face of the composer because she'd attended a murder scene once where a music teacher had been stabbed to death at home with the bow of her own violin. One of the paintings on the wall, someone had pointed out to Rio, was Beethoven.

The music video started playing: Beethoven's 'Moonlight' Sonata. The tune Samson had tapped out on the table in the prison. Rio didn't get why he was taunting her and she didn't have time to get it. She put the phone away and focused on what she had to finally do – see Calum.

The inside of ICU held almost the peace of a religious retreat, except for the occasional beep and blare of a machine that was a reminder that people were fighting for their lives. She nodded to the solitary nurse at the medical bay and proceeded to Calum's room, stopping at the door for a moment to focus on straightening out her breathing.

She finger-combed her 'fro. One more breath – in – out.

She entered. And locked the instinctive gasp in her airways as she saw the medical paraphernalia coming out of Calum and beside him. Her husband was pale, his dark hair swept neatly back as if someone had combed it.

She picked up his rucksack from the chair and gently placed it on the floor; pushed the chair close to the bed and sat down. Then her hand stretched out to grasp his fingers that lay limp against the pale blue bed cover. Just as she touched his cold flesh the door opened. Her hand flew back and she placed it in her lap as she turned to the doorway. Doctor Green stood there holding a manila folder.

'Have you told anyone that we're married?' Rio asked

The doctor shook her head. 'That's not my business to tell.' Her eyes drifted to Calum's body. 'We're taking care of his limb.'

Confusion stamped Rio's face. 'Limb?'

'Yes. His leg. You know . . .' The doctor abruptly closed her mouth.

'He won't tell me how he hurt it, not that we've spoken to each other since after the day we got hitched a couple of years back.'

The doctor placed her arms behind her back, looking very professional. 'Ah . . . Yes, his leg.' She frowned. 'Patient confidentiality and all that, I can't discuss this further with you I'm afraid. I asked the nurse on duty to alert me if you arrived because there's something I think may interest you.'

Rio stood up and moved to stand next to the doctor.

The doctor opened the file in her hand. 'When Nicola Bell

was first admitted here I requested to see her medical records. We've got this new nationwide computerised patients' record database that has proved to be a real pain in the posterior – a flipping waste of good money if you ask me – so her records have only just arrived.'

She handed the file, opened at a particular page, to Rio. 'I don't really need it now – I mean she's no longer under my care – but curiosity got the better of me. You'll see that the girl is no stranger to hospitals. I don't want to make assumptions, so read this and tell me if you notice anything.'

It was a standard medical history form: Name; D.O.B.; Address. Past medical history – a tick-box of the usual suspects – diabetes, high blood pressure, heart problems ... The only box that was ticked was allergies. Further information was provided below:

Peanut allergy.

Rio flicked her gaze back up at the doctor. 'Her allergy is common knowledge. Her mother told you about it if you remember. Nikki's usually very careful about it–'

'That's what worried me. Her mother did tell me about it and when I spoke to Nicola she seemed really aware, which is why the medical history just doesn't make sense.'

Rio read the papers again.

Personal medical treatment: three entries older than Nikki's recent stay at Mission Hill Hospital. All recorded at St Theresa's private hospital.

June 8th 2010: Type one hypersensitivity – allergy to peanuts.

June 8th 2011: Type one hypersensitivity – allergy to peanuts.

June 8th 2012: Type one hypersensitivity – allergy to peanuts.

Why were they all on the same date? And that date rang a bell in Rio's head. Where had she heard it? Where had she . . .? Rio quickly flipped the pages backwards until she was again on the front page with Nikki's main details.

DOB: June 8th 1999.

'Yes, that's exactly what I thought,' the doctor said. 'Why was she admitted to hospital for three consecutive years on her birthday?'

Rio didn't answer; her mind was buzzing, trying to capture all the conversations she'd had with Nikki. Then it clicked. She heard Nikki's words:

'Mum and Dad let me stay with Ophelia on a few of my birthdays. Then they stopped me going around to see her anymore.'

Rio quickly took out her notebook, rushed through the pages until she got to the interview she'd done with Nikki in the hospital. She stopped at the page she was after; the one where Nikki said that one of the killer's voices had been high. At first Nikki had said that it might be a woman and then she changed her mind and said she didn't know. Then claimed it was definitely a man. Rio had written down, then scratched out, the one piece of evidence she had immediately discounted. She gazed at the word now in her notebook.

Woman

The file dropped from Rio's hands. Calum was wrong – this had nothing to do with Terry Larkin. Rio ran out of the room thinking she might already be too late. That she had given the girl's safekeeping into the hands of a killer.

sixty-two

Rio hit every speed camera on the frantic journey back to Ophelia Bell's home. She didn't let herself think about the actress helping her a few hours ago; didn't let herself think about Ophelia being Nikki's biological mother; didn't let any kind of emotional attachment get in the way. Only the evidence got a say. Rio didn't even lock the car as she ran towards the front door of the flat. The place was dark. Rio raised her hand to pull back the knocker, then hesitated. No, she couldn't alert Ophelia if something dreadful had happened inside. Instead she shifted sideways to the lounge window. The blind was still up, so Rio peered in. The light from a laptop on a table illuminated the room. No one inside, everything appeared to be in place. Rio's blood pounded through her body when she caught sight of the half-eaten plate of food on the wooden floor.

There was no entrance point around the back of the flat she could get access to, so she was going to have to get in via the front.

She used her elbow, protected by the material of her jacket, to punch in the bottom right pane of the window. The glass shattered inside, but a few shards glided Rio's way. Carefully she pushed her arm through, running her fingers along the frame, seeking the lock – found it – twisted the catch. With steady and slow hands she hiked the window up. Then, bracing herself against the outer ledge, she pushed her way inside.

The warmth from the room enveloped her immediately. There was silence all around. Rio made her way straight to the plate of food on the floor. It was right in the light coming from the laptop on the table, which was showing an episode of *The Wilcotts*. She recalled that Ophelia said she would set it up so that Nikki could watch advanced editions of the show. The volume must be on mute because there was no sound coming from the computer. Rio took no notice of the programme as she dropped to her knees beside the plate. She didn't pick it up, just tried to catalogue the type of food she saw. Mashed-up food, well that's what Rio called the type of fare she saw on the plate: a little bit of this, a dollop of that. In this instance – although she couldn't be sure – it looked like hummus, some pink stuff she suspected was taramasalata, and some type of grain. The ideal cuisine to slip in a trace of peanut. But maybe she was wrong and Nikki was snoozing away, comfy and safe, in bed?

Yeah, but what if she wasn't? Rio scrambled to her feet, her gaze fleetingly catching the scene from *The Wilcotts* on the laptop screen. She froze, transfixed by the scene playing out on the computer screen: men in trenches; an officer was speaking to a crowd of muddy and disheartened looking soldiers. It was what the officer held in his hand that gripped her attention. Was it a gas mask? Of course – it was an earlier model, the kind that soldiers had used in World War One. Old-fashioned, large, made with cloth and a hose. Just the way Nikki had described the gunmen's disguise in the Bell's house. Ophelia must have borrowed them from the show's props department. That's what Samson Larkin had been tauntingly trying to tell her. *Gas masks from World War One.* Samson's words in the café in Cyprus came back to haunt her with a vengeance.

'*Sounds like a gas mask, except the baggy cloth bit . . . Wait a minute. During World War One, The Great War—?*'

'*You're gonna wished you'd listened to me—*'

He was right. She did. A thug with a genius for general knowledge facts had been prepared to tell her what she needed. And what had she done? Told him to shut up.

A triangular ray of light abruptly invaded the room making Rio slam her gaze up.

Standing by the side lamp that she'd just put on was Ophelia Bell.

'What are you doing here?' the other woman asked.

The faint light wiped out all the surface beauty of Ophelia's face laying bare the skeletal outline of her head, the ravages of a disease that, Rio suspected, she'd never truly been able to beat.

Rio got to her feet. 'I need to see Nikki now.'

Ophelia didn't move, but her eyes coolly darted over Rio. 'She's in bed—'

Rio strode towards the door as she spoke. 'Well, I'd just like to see that for my—'

She didn't even see the other woman's hand move; all Rio felt was a powerful pressure to the side of her head. Pain carved deep inside her, as black stole her vision, making her fall to the floor. She knew she wasn't unconscious because she could hear her own laboured breathing. She lifted the lids of her eyes, pain creeping and numbing the side of her face. Ophelia stood over her, the stone carving of a woman and child that Rio remembered seeing during her first visit to the maisonette, clasped tight in her palm. The other woman's face was cold, the beat of new blood deepening the colour of her cheeks.

'Why couldn't you just leave us alone?'

Then, with no hesitation, she bashed the sculpture against Rio's right knee. Rio bit back the scream of pain so bad it tore through her whole body.

But pain wasn't going to stop her from doing her job. 'It was you and Cornelius who killed your parents.'

The actress straightened up, staring down dispassionately at Rio. 'They stopped giving me money. Demanded that I should find a real job—'

'But you're a well-known actress in one of the most popular shows on television.' Rio's voice was strained and full of pain.

Ophelia scoffed. 'That's what everyone thinks, that we get paid bundles. I couldn't even afford to buy a flat in London. All they had to do was give me enough for the deposit on a mortgage—'

'So you decided to murder them, wearing gas masks you got from the costume department on the show. Once they were dead you and your brother would be in line to inherit their millions.'

Anger swept the other woman's face. With fury she licked the sculpture against Rio's other knee. This time there was a cracking sound and Rio couldn't help the high-pitched groan that punched out of her mouth. The pain was so strong now she didn't think she could utter another word.

'*Their* money?' the other woman continued. 'It was *our* money as well because they were going to leave it to us anyway. So what, we were going to take our inheritance early. Big fucking deal – we were entitled to it.'

Rio didn't know where she was getting the strength from, but somehow she was able to speak. 'But your plans went all wrong because you didn't factor in Nikki being a witness to the killing and that your parents would leave all their money to their only grandchild.'

That made Ophelia tremble as her mouth twisted with the impact of inhaling a nasty smell. 'I. Loathe. That. Kid.'

'How ... can ... you ... hate ... your ... own ... daughter?' Every word Rio said was punctuated with agony and feeling that a heavy weight was on her chest.

The expression on Nikki's natural mother's face was savage. 'She was the cause of every problem I had.' Ophelia was yelling now, bitterness sparking her every word. 'When I was fourteen I thought I was getting fat; I couldn't understand it, but I knew how to deal with it because some of the other girls at school told me what to do. Eat and then sick it up. But it wouldn't work, my tummy just kept getting bigger and bigger. So I stopped eating altogether. One day I fainted so mummy called the doctor ...' She drew in a shaking breath. 'He told her that I was pregnant. All the time I thought I was putting on weight it was that kid inside of me. If it wasn't for her I would never have struggled my whole life with this anorexia and bulimia shit. Every time I start putting on weight I get frightened of what's happening to my body. What if there's something growing inside me again?'

The shock of her story shook Rio up. 'Is that why you started trying to kill her on her birthdays?'

Ophelia stabbed a finger against her chest. 'The bitch deserved it after everything she put me through. She even had the nerve to cut her hair to look like me—'

'Did you bully Cornelius into helping, just like you bullied him as a child? But he couldn't live with what he'd done, so he killed himself. Did you know that he left me a letter asking me to save Nikki.' Rio saw that she had the other woman on the back foot. 'He knew about you trying to kill Nikki on her birthdays, didn't he? He knew you were planning to try and do it all again. So you got a hitman to try to silence Nikki about the killings and to make sure she was out of your life for good.'

Suddenly the other woman relaxed, her voice came under control and lowered. 'You may think you're smart, with all

your years of policing, but you still haven't figured it all out.
The one thing I learned about being on *The Wilcotts* is there's
always another twist to the story—'

'Are you saying . . . that you didn't contract a hitman? That
someone else did?'

Ophelia shook her shoulders back and settled her body into
a pose, like she was about to take the stage. 'Everyone will
believe me, you know. When I tell them how I thought you
were an intruder who terrified me in my own home.' She placed
a hand dramatically over her heart. 'How shocked I was to find
that you were that nice detective who had helped Nicola so
much . . . But Detective Wray was suspended, so what was she
doing in my home?'

Ophelia strode past Rio and walked towards the attached
kitchen. Rio knew she had to get away. Pain lacing through
her, she started wriggling her body against the floor towards
the doorway.

Rio heard something being thrust open, like a drawer.

She tried to pick up the speed of her movements, but the
burning in her leg made that impossible.

She groaned.

Footsteps headed back towards her.

Rio frantically shifted her shoulders and back from side to
side.

But it was too late. Ophelia was standing over her with a
large kitchen knife.

'Don't do this, you'll never get away with it,' Rio said
breathlessly.

'She's probably dead already. As soon as she'd eaten the
meal I gave her she went upstairs. I'll check on her after I've
finished with you.'

Ophelia bent over Rio. The knife came up as Rio raised her
hands to fight for her life. But Ophelia let out an outraged

scream as another pair of hands clamped and tightened around her wrist. Rio and Ophelia looked at the newcomer at the same time – Nikki.

'Let go!' Ophelia shouted.

But Nikki wouldn't. Instead, with her whole might, she twisted her biological mother around. Then leaned her weight onto the older woman. They tumbled to the floor. Ophelia's lips parted and a strange gurgling sound left her mouth.

Then silence.

Everyone remained frozen: Rio flat on her back by the door and Nikki on top of the woman she adored so much. Finally Nikki scrambled off the other woman on to her knees, giving Rio a view of Ophelia – the knife was sticking out of her stomach. Blood was growing against her long T-shirt. Nikki twisted towards Rio. The front of her night clothes were stained with blood.

A banging noise sounded from the hallway. Footsteps ran towards the room. Jack Strong appeared in the doorway.

His blue eyes took in the scene. 'Bloody hell.' He rushed over to Rio. 'I went over to check on Burns and Doctor Green told me what she told you so I figured you'd be here.'

But Rio didn't answer him because Nikki's sobs tore up the room. The teenager was bent over Ophelia, holding her hand.

Rocking she said, 'I didn't eat the food she gave me because I wasn't hungry. I didn't want to disappoint her so I threw some of it in the bin to make it look like I ate some. I loved her so much. I didn't know she was my real mum. Why couldn't she just love me back?'

Ophelia's eyes suddenly opened. With her last dying breath she viciously spat blood into her daughter's face.

sixty-three

8:15 a.m.

Rio gritted her teeth as the bandage was wrapped tight around her left knee inside the hospital room. DSI Newman looked at her with a measure of sympathy. The Assistant Commissioner did not. Jack Strong stood near the closed door, arms folded, wearing a neutral expression.

Once the nurse had left the room AC Pauline Tripple said, 'Give me one good reason why I shouldn't take your badge from you for good?'

Rio didn't hesitate with her answer. 'Because I was trained to find out the truth, which meant saving the life of a sixteen-year-old girl.'

The AC turned around and paced. Then turned back. 'The truth, as far as the public are concerned, is that the Greenbelt Gang committed those raids and murders.'

Rio jacked up from the pillow, wincing in pain. 'You can't mean that—'

'If it's ever found out that a suspended police officer *disobeyed* orders and was tearing around this city do you know what additional scrutiny that would bring to the Met—?'

'Bullshit.'

'Rio,' DSI Newman warned softly.

But Rio was having none of it. 'What about Nicola Bell?

Don't you think she deserves for everyone to know the truth – to have an opportunity to live a smooth life?'

'You think that girl is going to ever be able to live a normal life after killing her own mother, albeit in self-defence? There's nothing *smooth* about your whole family and boyfriend being murdered. Plus, do you want to face the possibility of Nicola Bell facing a trial?'

Rio knew that her superior was right. How was a teenager going to come back from all of this?

Rio leaned back into the pillow. 'How is she?'

Strong answered. 'She's OK and was checked over a little while back. I think they'll discharge her soon. She'll be in the care of one of her friend's family. We didn't tell them what happened, just that Nikki had met with a little accident.' He let his arms drop to his side. 'The hitman was thirty-one-year-old Ronald Miller. Former Para who left the army after he was put out of action in the Iraq War. He was part of a class action, with four other soldiers, who were preparing to take the MoD to court because they said that they weren't provided with adequate and safe equipment while on duty during the war. Their lawyer managed to negotiate an out-of-court settlement. Miller returned to his native Cornwall and became a fisherman. And obviously used what he'd learned in the army to become a gun for hire.'

Rio remembered what Calum had said about the knife Nikki had taken. 'Fisherman. That probably explains the specialist knives he used. Thank God he didn't have a chance to use them on Nikki.'

'You need to stop thinking of that girl,' the AC said quickly, 'and start thinking of your own career. You start talking about this and any chance you have for promotion is off the cards.'

'So I'm still in the running for a promotion?'

'Let's put it this way,' the AC answered, 'you're still one of the best officers I've ever known. As of now your suspension is over and you can return to duty any time you like. We still need to investigate what happened on the raid so it's going to have to be desk duty for you until the investigation is complete.'

Rio felt the weight of the world lift from her shoulders. 'Thank you.'

'There's someone to see you,' Strong's voice broke in.

Rio looked over to find Nikki standing nervously next to him in the doorway.

'We'll give you some privacy,' Assistant Commissioner Tripple said.

As the others filed out of the room Nikki stepped inside and moved towards the bed.

'Hey, how are you doing, kid?' Rio's tone was soft and gentle. This girl had been through so much.

Nikki was still pale and the expression in her eyes was wary and sad. 'I just wanted to come and say thank you for everything you did for me.'

Rio smiled. 'All part of my job. I hear you're going to be staying with a friend's family.'

Nikki nodded. 'My friend Muriel's parents. They're nice people.' There was a hitch in her voice. 'I hope that Calum's going to be alright.'

'He'll be fine. It's going to take a lot more than that to keep him down.' She hoped that her words would come true.

'I should go; they're waiting for me.'

They continued to gaze at each other for a few seconds. Then Rio said, 'If you should ever need me, just give me a call. Anytime.'

Nikki nodded and then turned and left the room. As soon as she was gone Rio leaned back and let out a long punch of air. The last six days had been a roller-coaster ride that she hoped never to repeat in her life. She truly prayed that Nikki was able to take up the reins of her life and put all this behind her. She knew that wasn't going to be easy, but the young are resilient and have the energy needed to bounce back. There was still one part of the investigation that troubled her – what had Ophelia Bell meant by another twist in the story? Was there some part of the puzzle that she had missed or was it the ramblings of a woman who hated her parents and her child?

Her mobile pinged. She leaned across and found her bag and took out her mobile.

> You figure it our yet Mizz Wray. Help me!!! I'm being attacked by mustard gas. hehehe

Samson Larkin. No skull and crossbones this time. If only she'd let the psychotic genius say what he'd had to say in Cyprus. She renewed her vow of a reckoning when she caught up with him.

'Detective Inspector Wray.'

Rio pushed up to see Strong standing in the doorway. It felt good to hear her official title again.

'I thought you'd like to know that Burns has regained consciousness and is calling for you. He's really agitated.'

9:02 a.m.

Neither Strong nor the nurse were pleased that Rio had decided to walk instead of using a wheelchair to visit Calum. The pain in her legs was persistent, but not too bad; she wasn't the type of person who resisted standing on her own two feet. But she didn't care about any of that; all she wanted was to make sure Calum was going to make it.

He looked weak, his eyes a mixture of liquid green and bloodshot white. A bandage circled his neck, hiding and healing where the wire had wrapped around his skin. As soon as he saw her he tried to lift himself off the bed.

Rio rushed forwards, despite the shooting pain in her legs. 'What the heck are you trying to do?' she let out crossly as she eased him back down.

His fingers clawed into her shoulder. 'No time to talk.' His breathing was laboured. 'Maurice ... Bell ... partner ... Slim—'

'It's OK,' Rio soothed. 'It had nothing to do with Terry Larkin. I know that the text you sent me said it was him—'

Calum furiously shook his head. 'Didn't manage ... to finish ... text. Was writing ... Terry Larkin ... isn't partner.' He swallowed. 'My ... bag ... rucksack.'

Strong stepped forwards and retrieved it from the floor, and handed it to Rio. She unzipped it and inside saw sheets of printed white paper.

'Read,' was all Calum said.

Rio made herself comfortable on the edge of the bed as she pulled the pages out and started reading. The air pulsing in her chest got rougher and rougher as she read page after page, not able to quite believe what she was reading. But there it was in black and white. Finally she turned to gaze dumbstruck at her husband.

'Maurice Bell's partner,' Calum said more clearly.

Determination and old-fashioned anger gripped Rio as she turned to Strong. 'Get the nurse to find me some painkillers that will keep me on my feet. We're going to make one final visit. Now I understand what Ophelia Bell meant by the last twist in the story.'

sixty-four

Rio and Strong strode into the Old Bailey as if they owned the place. Any attempt to interrupt Rio's progress was met with a withering look and a flash of her warrant card. When the two detectives arrived at the entrance to court number two, an usher barred their way. 'I'm sorry, you can't come through; the court is in session . . .'

Rio showed her card. 'I'm in charge of a murder investigation, so you need to step out of my way.'

'I'm sorry, madam, you'll have to wait until the court has—'

Rio, followed by Strong, pushed past him, leaving his outraged protests behind. They entered the court. The chamber was packed. The two made their way down the aisle. A witness was in the box being expertly grilled by a lawyer.

'Miss Jamieson, you are lying,' the lawyer proclaimed. 'Admit to these twelve honest and good people of the jury that you have been lying since the beginning—'

'No I haven't.'

But the lawyer wouldn't let up. 'Admit that your motivation in bringing these very serious allegations against my client are fraudulent. That your motivation is greed, pure and—'

The judge banged his gravel when he finally saw Rio and Strong. 'What is going on here?'

Rio called across the silent court. 'I beg your pardon, my lord, but I'm Detective Inspector Wray and I'm here to detain a suspect in a murder inquiry. I promise this won't take a moment.'

The lawyer turned around.

Stephen Foster.

Rio couldn't help herself – she enjoyed the expression on his face. It was one she had never seen before. Foster looked like a patient who'd just been given some seriously bad news by a doctor. He looked at Rio, then at Strong, then back at Rio. He looked over to the judge, the witness, the jury and the other lawyer as if expecting their support. When his gaze finally settled back on Rio his expression was the professional blank face he so often wore.

In a firm voice that was audible to the whole court, Rio said, 'Stephen Foster, I'm arresting you in connection with the murders of Maurice Bell, Linda Bell, Frank Bell, Patsy Bell, Adeyemi Ibraheem, Ania Brown and the attempted murder of Nicola Bell and Calum Burns.'

Strong immediately handcuffed him. As Rio read him his rights there was uproar in the courtroom as astonished onlookers started talking at the same time, and the three journalists in court raced outside to be the first to break the shocking news.

Rio gently took Foster's arm and escorted him, without resistance, towards the exit. As they left the court, Rio heard the judge behind her say, 'Stephen Foster? Murder? What the hell's going on . . .?'

News had already filtered through by the time they got Foster to The Fort. The desk sergeant told Rio that Assistant Commissioner Tripple was waiting in Newman's office for her.

When she got upstairs her mentor was alone.

'Judge Patel is not a happy man. He claims that the Met have brought his court into disrepute. You were specifically told that you're restricted to desk duty.'

Here we go, Rio thought, she's going to fire my arse.

Pauline Tripple leaned forwards. 'You've got forty-eight hours to squash that bastard. Make sure you do.'

sixty-five

48 Hours

'It was you pulling the strings all along wasn't it, Mr Foster?' Rio said in Interview Room Two.

But Rio had left it too late. In the interval between his arrest and her first question, Foster had recovered and re-inflated himself with his own diamond-edged and bomb-proof persona. He was so confident he waived having legal representation. He was no longer the shocked and bewildered suspect she'd detained at the Bailey.

He was Stephen Foster.

He took a half-smoked cigar she'd permitted him to keep, lit it carefully and blew pungent smoke across the table. 'I'm only too happy to answer any questions you may have, Detective Inspector – however ludicrous they might turn out to be – but I'm afraid you'll have to be more specific.'

It was too late. She should have hit him with questions when he was reeling with shock. He might have made a mistake then. That was the brief moment when the untouchable Stephen Foster had crashed into the brick wall of reality and been arrested.

'We know that you were Maurice Bell's elusive partner, Slim, back in the days when he was Maurice Cloud, slum landlord.'

He took another slow puff of his cigar. 'It's not a crime to have had a life before I came to the bar, which is not an admission of having known Maurice Bell during, what you so delicately called, his "slum landlord" days.'

'But it is a crime if you used that association to plan his murder. You were younger than him – his sidekick; he took advantage of you in a big property deal and never paid you your cut. It was hard to find people to talk to because people were either already now long dead or too frightened. But we found one person who would talk. And they gave you up – identified you.'

Foster smoothed back his mane of black-grey hair with one hand. 'If that's true why would Maurice Bell have employed me as his lawyer?'

'Because you duped him into thinking that the past was long gone, but it wasn't. The only thing you had in your heart was raging revenge. And what was the best and most twisted way of doing that? Getting his two, poor, deluded rich kid-children to do it for you. You organised the murder of Maurice and Linda Bell in cahoots with Cornelius and Ophelia, who wanted their parents' estate. You got the details of the Greenbelt raids and made the Bell murders look like a Greenbelt job. Except you never counted on them taking shortcuts and using gas mask props from Ophelia's show rather than clown masks.'

He made no comment so she pressed on. 'It was you who organised a killer to take care of Nikki Bell when you discovered, to your horror, that she was a witness. You even represented Gary Larkin and organised for him to take his gang to a secret hideout. Once you had them where you wanted them, you got your hired gun to wipe them out. No more gang alive meant they couldn't tell the tale of not committing the raid on the Bells' home. That's the truth, isn't it, Mr Foster?'

Foster sat back, examined his cigar and then took another

puff. 'Wow, that's quite a speech, detective – you do say the funniest things . . .'

'We'll see if you're still laughing when you're on trial for murder.'

Foster carefully tapped ash into the remnants of a cup of coffee before looking up again. This time it wasn't a look of hate but a smile. 'I assume you've got some proof for these outlandish assertions? You're going to be in quite deep water if you haven't.' He sucked on his cigar. 'I expect you're looking for some evidence at the moment aren't you? I expect your team are trawling though my bank and phone records, interviewing my staff, colleagues and friends, ransacking my office and checking any CCTV footage you can get your hands on . . .'

He looked upwards and imagined the scene. 'Yes, I can see it now. Find me something on Foster – anything - so we can nail these crimes on him . . .' He looked back down and over at Rio. He shook his head and whispered, 'You naive girl . . .'

Rio stopped the interview and left the room. Exhausted, she fell back against the wall in the corridor. The wily bastard was dodging her every move; not giving an inch. They needed to find something on him – quickly.

Rio's mobile rang. As she pulled it out she walked further down the corridor.

'Did he kill everyone, including Ade? It's all over the news.' Nikki said.

Rio didn't answer immediately. What the hell was she going to say to this girl – that all her loved ones had been killed at the order of the man who was meant to be helping keep her safe?

'I'm sorry, Nikki, but I believe that Mr Foster was behind everything.'

'Why?' she cried.

'I can't discuss that with you.'

'You will get him won't you?'

'I promise you that when he leaves here, the only place he will be going is to face a jury in a court of law.'

Rio ended the call. Determined to nail this scumbag she took some more heavy-duty painkillers and then went back into the room and restarted the interview.

sixty-six

40 Hours

At first Rio was confident. But as the hours ticked away, she began to regret her rash promise to Nikki. Foster had answers for everything. He cheerfully admitted what couldn't do him any harm.

Yes, of course he'd once been an 'associate' of Maurice Bell; he'd never denied it.

'I took care of Maurice's legal issues for him in those days. But I don't think that constitutes a crime, Detective Inspector Wray . . .'

Perhaps Maurice and he had once 'had words' but that was a long time ago and long forgotten. Foster even had the effrontery to claim that he didn't bare grudges. To Rio's other questions, he either denied her accusations or claimed he 'couldn't recall' the occasions she was asking about.

The team didn't come up with anything that would stick. After four solid hours of questioning, Foster claimed he was too exhausted to go on. Rio saw what his tactic was – make sure that most of the forty-eight hours were spent out of the interview room. He knew the law inside out; he knew that she wouldn't be able to interview him anymore that day without facing the accusation of unreasonable physical and mental pressure during an interview. If they got him to trial he would use any legal loophole to shut the case down. So Rio played it safe and banged him up in a cell for the rest of the day.

sixty-seven

24 Hours

By the second day, Foster seemed to be enjoying himself. The
protective wall he'd built around himself was setting and hard-
ening. Every time Rio closed the interview and went to check on
what her team had uncovered, her people avoided her eyes or
shrugged their shoulders. But Strong discovered that there was
no CCTV evidence of any fugitive fleeing the scene of the
supposed attack on Foster. Rio suggested to Foster the attack
never happened. He'd faked it. Her suspect took it in his stride. 'I
would imagine a professional assailant would know how to
avoid CCTV, Ms Wray. He wouldn't get any commissions otherwise. Not that I know about these things, of course . . .'

Rio played another new piece of evidence. 'Our search of
Ophelia Bell's property has turned up a call on her phone
where you had a conversation with her. Now that's strange
because you both claimed to dislike each other. It was all an
act, wasn't it? A smokescreen to make the world think you
would never have contact with each other.'

'I never claimed to dislike anybody. If you recall all I ever
said about my relationship to that young woman was that she
appeared not to like me. Why that was, I – and you – will
never know. Did my conversation with her say anything
incriminating about us planning to murder her parents?'

Rio knew she was caught in her own trap; the telephone conversation revealed nothing.

There was a knock on the door. It opened and Strong walked in.

'DI, can I have a word?'

Rio terminated the interview and left the room.

'I found something interesting,' Strong said, opening up the folder in his hand.

Rio held back the curse forming in her mouth. 'I don't need interesting, I need something that's going to take Foster down permanently.'

'Read this.'

Strong passed her a piece of paper. A renewed energy grew in Rio as she read.

Face grim she looked at Strong. 'Thank you.'

Back in the interview room, Rio sat down and placed the paper in front of her. Then she flicked her gaze up at the man opposite her, hoping to find his eyes glued to the paper. They weren't. She wasn't surprised. Foster knew all the tricks of the interview room. Instead his gaze was steady on her face.

'Do you know a Ronald Miller?'

Foster eased back slightly in his chair. 'Can't say that the name means anything.'

'This paper,' Rio jabbed a finger against it, 'says that you represented Ronald Miller and four other soldiers in a case against the Ministry of Defence. Got them a good out-of-court settlement by all accounts.'

'I've represented many clients.' He added sarcastically, 'That's what I'm paid to do.'

Rio's finger stopped moving. 'Can't be many of your clients who also have a second job as a hitman. You paid Ronald Miller to try to murder Nicola Bell. You paid him to kill the very sad Gary Larkin and his doomed gang.'

Foster stretched his shoulders and leg like he was getting ready to do a relaxing Tai Chi move to centre his karma. 'You'll have to do better than that, Detective Inspector. What my clients do in their spare time is none of my business.' His shoulders eased back down. 'Check my bank accounts if I'm meant to have paid this Ronald Miller.'

Rio checked his financial accounts again: a money trail that ended nowhere.

sixty-eight

18 Hours

Rio knew it was slipping away. She could even guess what Foster's response would be to her questions. When she raised the subject of the initial attack on Nikki in the hospital, she reminded him that he'd insisted no one could talk to the teenager without him being present, and suggested he'd arranged the attack. She almost whispered his reply under her breath as he made it – he had also been a victim of the first assault on Nikki. Strange behaviour for someone who'd arranged her murder. As for her accusations that he had been the one to set up the murders of Nikki's parents by insisting they have no police protection – he had merely given them a range of legal advice and they had freely made their choice.

Every which way Rio turned he blocked her.

sixty-nine

10 Hours

Desperately Rio went back over old ground with Foster.

'Can you tell me why you decided to represent Gary Larkin when you heard he'd been arrested? And it was you who arranged for Gary Larkin and his gang to hide in that oast house in Kent, wasn't it? Once you had the gang cornered you arranged for them to be murdered so it would look like they were killed in our raid. Dead men tell no tales. That's what happened, isn't it, Mr Foster?'

Foster was smoking cigars that his secretary had brought in and left at the front desk. He looked pensive before replying, 'How's it going, DI Wray?'

'How's what going?'

'Your inquiry? Have your officers uncovered any actual evidence against me yet?'

'I've seen defendants convicted on less circumstantial evidence than I've got against you . . .'

Foster nodded with approval. 'Yes indeed. But that would be ordinary defendants, wouldn't it, Detective Inspector Wray?'

Rio refused to respond.

Foster sighed. 'As to your questions, of course there's the issue of client confidentiality but as the unfortunate Mr Larkin is dead, I can tell you that I advised Gary to go back to his flat and sit it out. I don't know anything about any oast houses in Kent . . . Unless of course you can prove otherwise?'

The door opened. It was Strong. Rio punched the tape off and left the room. She was surprised to see the Assistant Commissioner waiting in the corridor. Strong left them alone.

'Let him go.'

Rio was furious. 'He's a murderer. Worse than a murderer, he got other people to do his dirty work for him. We've still got at least nine hours—'

'If you haven't got anything by now he isn't going to crack. This man has been practising law for decades, so he knows which strings to pull and how to pull them. I've already had his friends on the phone complaining and you know how powerful they are . . .'

But Rio wasn't listening. Her superior's comment about Foster being a lawyer with years behind him took her mind to one of Foster's self-satisfied lines in the interview room.

'I took care of Maurice's legal issues for him in those days. But I don't think that constitutes a crime, Detective Inspector Wray . . .'

Foster. Maurice Bell. Suddenly Rio realised that she'd been looking in all the wrong places.

'Two hours. That's all I'm asking for,' Rio butted it over AC Tripple.

The older woman's eyes squinted as she gazed deeply at Rio. 'Am I going to regret saying yes?'

'No, ma'am. Two hours. Please.'

'You've got one hour.'

seventy

'Is the archive of evidence from London's cold cases still in the basement?' Rio urgently asked the desk sergeant. The blood flowed hot and hard through her body pumping a sheen of sweat to her face. This was the longest shot she'd ever played in her career. And the odds against her coming out on top were not strong.

'In the bunker,' the sergeant answered, using the name everyone who worked inside The Fort called the basement, since it had once been set up as a potential bunker during the paranoid days of the Cold War. 'Yes. Most of the stuff was left to rot down there after the new computer system was installed last year. It's going to be moved out to a storage facility but I think it's still there.'

'How far does it go back?'

'I think there's stuff going back to the Second World War and up until the mid-1960s. Later records – where there's still a slim chance that a case might get solved – have been logged and stored properly off-site. But most of the things in the basement are over fifty years old—'

'Have you got the key?'

'No. But I know a man who has.'

As Rio impatiently waited she couldn't help but look at the large, plain white clock on the wall. Time was counting down against her.

Fifty-nine minutes.

Fifty-seven minutes.

Fifty-six minutes.

The key was in her hand on the fifty-third minute. She took the stairs with the speed of an army cadet on a take-no-prisoners training course. Rio punched in the access code on the keypad, flicked the light switch and entered an underground world of harsh, fluorescent lighting, long corridors and blue doors. She followed the directions the Sergeant had given and soon found the padlock door of the archive, undid the lock and stepped inside. The door swung open, squeaking in protest.

She flicked an ancient switch and an old-fashioned bulb flashed a few times as if blinded by its own light before coming on. The archive was row after row of dusty shelving while shoeboxes of evidence from long-forgotten cases were scattered around on the floor as if the place had been burgled. On the shelving were stickers indicating which year the evidence had been collected. The final one was 1966. But there was nothing from 1966 on those shelves. On the next row was a sticker which had '1964' typed on it, to which had been added '–1965' in biro.

Rio walked along the shelves. There were boxes with faded writing on the side cataloguing different types of crimes – murder, kidnap, bank robbery. Rio opened a couple at random. In one was a balaclava and a plastic bag containing two spent bullets. There was no paperwork inside and it was impossible to decipher the writing on the box. She kicked several more boxes on the floor by accident as she walked intently along, her feverish hands examining everything she found which gave way to an angry gasp of disappointment when she didn't find what she was looking for.

She slowed down her search as the boxes for 1964 and 1965 began to trail off. She checked her watch.

Forty-one minutes.

'Fuck.' Rio kicked a shoebox across the floor in frustration.

She sucked in a heavy breath, pulling back her determination. Foster was not going to outfox her. She turned and went to the next row: '1963'.

Sixty-three had been a busy year – the shelves were jam-packed - but Rio soon realised that was because boxes from other years had been dumped on it at random. She found evidence from a bank robbery in '61 and a bloody jacket in a bag from a grisly murder in '62. Underneath these she found another box with no date and no name on the side. Rio picked it up. Its weight brought new hope to her. She opened the lid and found a polythene bag. Inside was a revolver from World War Two and three spent bullets. Tiny flakes of discoloured blood from the bullets were scattered inside the bag. And there was a brittle brown envelope.

It seemed at least one detective from those days of swinging London had managed to do his job to the carefully regulated standards that an officer like Rio was expected to meet in the present day. There was a series of carefully typed, dated and signed statements concerning the murder of John MaCarry on May 4th 1965. Shot dead as he left a fashionable restaurant in London's West End, there were numerous statements from witnesses who'd seen a masked man emerge from an alleyway before calmly firing six shots into the victim. He died in the arms of what onlookers thought was MaCarry's girlfriend but the police subsequently discovered was a high-end call girl. Then the killer had calmly walked off into the crowds.

But that hadn't been the end of the story. An off-duty soldier had given chase and attacked the murderer. In the subsequent struggle, the soldier had managed to wrest the killer's weapon from him before he managed to slip away and escape. Tests proved that there were no fingerprints on the gun. Gloves were worn and the weapon had been carefully wiped with a handkerchief or cloth before use. It was untraceable. There had been no arrests although the case team were certain that the hit was ordered by MaCarry's business rival Maurice Cloud after an argument about money. But he had a conveniently rock solid alibi for the evening of the murder.

Rio put the paperwork back in the envelope, picked up the bag containing the gun that the soldier had recovered and examined it as if it were a religious relic. There might be no fingerprints, but back in 1965 DNA had not revolutionised police work.

seventy-one

Rio rushed into the forensic unit on the third floor of The Fort with twenty-three minutes left. She scanned the open office trying to find the chief forensic officer, Charlie. Shit, Rio couldn't see Charlie anywhere.

'Where's Charlie?' she shouted, bringing the room to a standstill. But no one spoke, they all just gazed at her.

'I need her now.' Rio stepped into the centre of the room.

'She's in the lab—' a tall, thin man in his thirties started to answer.

'Where?'

The man frowned. 'You can't go in there. She's doing a closed test.'

Rio strode over to the man and got so deep in his space that he started regarding her as a crazy. 'Please.' Only then did Rio hear how breathless she sounded. 'I need her urgently. Can you get her?'

The wrinkles on his forehead deepened. 'This is highly irregular . . .' That's all she needed: a replica of herself, a man determined to play it by the book. But she let out a huge sigh when he nodded and said, 'I'll get her.'

As the forensic team buzzed back to work, Rio stood alone in the middle of the room. No, she wasn't alone; diminishing time stood right with her.

Twenty-one minutes.

Twenty minutes.

Come on, Charlie.

Nineteen minutes.

Charlie appeared halfway through the eighteenth minute. Rio didn't even give her time to speak; instead she thrust the polythene bag with the revolver in it into her hand.

'I need you to test the DNA on this against the DNA in this file.' She handed over the manila folder.

'It will have to wait—'

Rio savagely swung her head. 'No-can-do; I need this now.'

Charlie held the bag up and scrutinised the gun. 'This looks like a really old piece of evidence. Any DNA might have disintegrated with time, although the bag might have offered a layer of protection—'

'I don't have time for this. Can you test it for me?'

'It's going to cost you a pint on a Friday of my choosing. Come back in an hour—'

'I don't have that kind of time. I need it in fifteen minutes flat.'

Charlie twisted her lips. 'I'm a forensic specialist not forensic Superwoman—'

'Please, Charlie.'

'I'll do what I can, but I'm warning you that this isn't possible in that time frame.'

'I'll be downstairs near the interview rooms. A young girl's life depends on this.'

seventy-two

Fourteen minutes.

Thirteen minutes.

Twelve minutes.

Rio paced outside the Interview Room waiting for word from Charlie. Strong stood leaning up against the wall, arms folded across his chest, a short distance away. He didn't say a word, just kept a silent vigil with Rio.

Come on, Charlie. Rio chanted the words over and over with the power of a magic spell to make the forensic officer appear. But she didn't.

Eight minutes.

Seven minutes.

Six minutes.

Rio's brain was screaming. She couldn't let Foster go out of the main door because she knew she would never have this chance to nail him again. Life couldn't be this unfair, could it? Then she thought of all the murder victims she'd come across in her career who'd probably thought the same just before their lives were snuffed out. She wasn't going to add Nikki Bell to that list.

Four minutes.

Three.

Two.

Rio took up position in front of the interview-room door,

her whole body guarding it as if she was not going to let anyone past.

One minute.

No. No. NO.

The efficient, clean footsteps of the Assistant Commissioner broke through the air. The older woman reached Rio.

'Just ten more—'

'Cut. Him. Loose.'

Rio didn't bother pleading again. Her long shot hadn't paid off. Her time was up.

Rio stood there, feeling like the last person on this earth as her superior walked away. Just like she was going to have to let Foster walk away. She twisted around and raised her fist to slam it into the wall, but a larger palm closed over her balled hand.

'He's not worth it,' Strong said. The electric tension in her hand vibrated through his body. 'People like Foster always get what's coming to them in the end.'

He let her go, stepped back. Without looking at him Rio ran the hand that seconds ago had been a fist over her forehead.

'I need to make a call.'

Strong walked away as Rio pulled out her mobile.

'I'm sorry, Nikki, we're going to have to let him go.'

'Go? How can you let him go? He murdered them all.'

'I'm sorry,' Rio repeated. She couldn't even add the promise that she'd try to get him in the future; once Foster was out of the door he would never give her another chance to get anywhere near him.

'You did your best, Rio.'

And then she rang off.

When Rio returned to the interview room, Foster took one look at her face and smiled with triumph, 'We're finished here are we, Detective Inspector?'

'This isn't over, Foster.'

The solicitor confidently stood up. 'It's over for you, Ms Wray. By the time I'm finished with you, you won't be able to get a job cleaning this building, never mind detecting in it.'

Rio's whole team were waiting in the reception area. They stood in an ominous silence watching Stephen Foster with hard gazes. In that moment Rio was truly proud of her people – for their bravery and tenacity during this investigation.

Once he had collected his belongings Rio escorted him to the exit. The doors to the front of The Fort swung open, letting in soft afternoon sunshine. There was a large crowd of reporters waiting for him outside. There was shouting and the clicking of cameras as Rio remained at the top of the stairs, left on her own in a lonely and troubled place.

Rio watched as Stephen Foster descended into the middle of the media scrum. He held up his hands until everyone was quiet. The bastard was going to milk his triumph for all it was worth. She moved to the outer edges of the steps to see his lying face as he spoke.

Foster cleared his throat and announced, 'Ladies and gentleman, as you are no doubt aware, two days ago I was arrested by the police and questioned about a number of serious crimes. Of course, I fully answered the questions that were put to me and I'm pleased to say that I have now been released without charge. As you will know, over the years, I have always endeavoured to defend the innocent and stand up for justice, without fear or favour. Obviously my work has caused a lot of discomfort to the police.'

His voice dropped slightly. 'Perhaps it was too much to hope that they would respond in a professional way to my work, instead of pursuing a petty and vindictive vendetta against me. But I make no complaint about that. I've no doubt too that they are hoping that their campaign of intimidation will deter me from pursuing justice in the future. They are wrong, it will not . . .'

'Rio.' She left Foster's sickening words and turned to find Strong next to her. 'Charlie in forensics said to give you this. Said to tell you you owe her a fountain worth of pints for doing this in record time.'

Rio ripped the paper out of his hand. Read.

'Come with me,' she told Strong.

With a look of confusion he followed her as she pushed and struggled her way into the media ring.

'My legal career has been based on two founding principles – a love of the law and a love of justice . . .'

Abruptly Foster stopped speaking as Rio stood, legs braced apart, in front of him. The crowd fell silent, leaving an expectant, almost explosive hush in the air.

'Stephen Foster, I am arresting you for the murder of John MaCarry in 1965. You do not have to . . .'

As Strong cuffed a dazed and disbelieving Foster the crowd shifted and swelled into a crashing noise and flashing camera bulbs. As Strong led Foster away Rio looked at the man who had a few moments ago been speaking about justice; well justice had finally found him.

seventy-three

'I would just like to say a few words,' DSI Newman said to the crowd gathered in the pub.

Rio smiled because his words came out more like, 'I thood jus like to shay a phew wurds.' The DS was well on his way to being rip-roaring drunk; and he had the right to be. This was his retirement and farewell do: a celebration of his thirty-seven years on the force. The place was packed with officers, but no family or friends; this was *their* time to say goodbye to one of *their* own.

It was good to see everyone so outrageously happy, Rio thought, after the fallout from Stephen Foster's arrest. Even though details about Foster's past relationship with Maurice Bell had surfaced in the press, some of his glam-pack celeb clients were vowing to stick by him. More like he had dirt on them that they never wanted to come to light, Rio suspected. But she was determined that Foster was going down for life.

'Looks like the guv is going to fall flat on his face,' Detective Jack Strong whispered in Rio's ear.

They stood together, jammed with others at the back of the room near the bar.

Rio turned to him. 'You should be up there as well, Jack. This was your last day too.'

That's how she thought of him now – not Strong but Jack. His blue eyes twinkled. 'Nah. I'm not into big goodbyes. A couple of farewell pints will do me fine.'

They both looked back at the mini stage at the front as Newman addressed the crowd again.

'When I came into the service, policing was a much simpler game. Two cops pounding the beat together, you really got to know the community, understood their needs. And that's what this is all about – servicing the public. And, of course, taking the bad boys out of action. My dad wanted me to join him in the building trade, but I was interested in another type of building – keeping this glorious city of ours cemented and strong, making sure that its foundations withstood anything thrown at it. And I think that I did that. But I couldn't have done it without the help of all you good people.' Someone clapped and the room erupted into cheers and whistles.

When the applause died down, he spoke again; this time his voice was much more sober. 'I soon learned the importance of teamwork – that there was no way I was going to be able to do this job on my own. I was lucky because my first partner was the best cop there ever was. He walked the beat with me and put his arm around my shoulder when I needed support. It's his final day on the force as well, so I'd like everyone to give a solid hand to Detective Jack Strong.'

The crowd and Rio turned to stare at Jack. But no one clapped. There was an awkward silence as everyone looked at him. Rio knew that many hadn't forgotten that fatal trip-up he'd made four years back and the storm that had hit the Met because of it.

Rio tipped her head back defiantly and started to clap. It

was a lone sound for a few seconds, then someone else clapped, and another person. Soon the room was back pulsating with whistles and cheers. A few people patted Jack on the back. He turned to Rio and gave her a single nod of thanks.

'OK, OK, I'm not finished folks,' Newman shouted from the stage. The pub grew quiet again. 'I know you're all eager to find out who will be taking my place. The honour goes to . . .' A few people looked Rio's way, but she kept her face straight, the emotions back.

Newman gave them the name. 'Detective Inspector Paul Mayberry.'

The crowd clapped as Mayberry waved his hand in the air, but there was more than one person who sent Rio surprised looks.

'Now people,' Newman said, back in full merry-making mode, 'let's party!'

'I thought it was a done deal,' Jack whispered to her.

'It was. I turned it down.'

'Why the bloody hell did you do that?'

Rio didn't answer straight away; this had been one of the toughest decisions of her life. She'd thought AC Tripple was going to throttle her when she'd knocked the promotion back. The Assistant Commissioner had asked her why? Rio now gave Jack Strong the same answer.

'Simple; it's not my time yet. I don't want anyone to think this was handed to me because of my colour, gender—'

Jack seemed dismayed. 'Look all that stuff and nonsense I said to you—'

Rio placed her hand on his arm. 'It wasn't you; it was me. I like my job – love the thrill of the investigation,' she shrugged, 'and maybe I just can't see myself sitting all day in an office. When my time comes, I will know.'

Jack opened his mouth, but he never answered because

someone slung their arm around his shoulder and dragged him away for a drink. He twisted his head to stare back at Rio. She just smiled and mouthed, 'Good luck.'

Rio took that as her cue to leave the festivities behind and head for the quiet of home. The air outside was cold, but there was a warm thread in the current that held the promise of a good spring to come.

'Hey stranger,' a voice called.

Rio peered in the dark to find Calum sitting in his car, the driver's window wound down. She might have made a decision about her job, but she hadn't made one about him. Rio walked slowly towards him. She shoved her hands in her coat pocket when she reached him.

'You don't look bad for a man who was at Death's door not that long ago.'

Calum smiled, drawing Rio's gaze to the thin scar line around his neck, a permanent memento from the wire the hitman had tried to strangle him with.

'Nothing keeps me down, not for long.'

'Well it's good to see you up and about.' Suddenly her tone changed. 'Look if you want to discuss a divorce—'

His smile dropped away. 'No. Not now. Let's leave that for another time.'

That was the theme song for their personal life – let's leave it for another time.

'I love you,' Rio blurted out. 'I don't know what that really means, but I do know that I hurt when I know you're hurt. You are one of the best men I have ever known in my entire life. But if there's ever going to be a chance for a you-and-me you have to tell me why you were made to leave the Met. Why you wouldn't see me in the hospital after your accident. I'm not asking you to do that now, but sooner or later Calum you're going to have to bring the truth to my door.'

He stared back at her, the green in his eyes brightening. Finally he spoke. 'There are things that I don't want you to know —'

'What things?'

He shook his head. 'You're right. The time's not now.'

Calum turned away from her and got the engine in gear. A few seconds later Rio stood alone, the decreasing roar of his car the only sound in the distance. She finger-combed her 'fro and then walked towards her car. She had one more call to make before calling it a night.

seventy-four

When Rio saw the house she felt as if she'd come full circle –
another house in Surrey, imposing and high-end, just like the
Bells'. When she knocked, Mrs Harkins, the mother of Nikki's
friend, opened the door.

'Detective Inspector Wray,' the other woman said, a small
smile lighting up her face. 'Nikki has talked so much about
you.' She laughed. 'Made you sound like a superhero.'

'Is this a convenient time to see Nikki?'

Mrs Harkins opened the door wide. 'Of course.'

Rio stepped inside a house that was a home – warmth and
the presence of human life all around.

'I'll call her down—'

Rio waved her hand cutting off the other woman's words.
'I'll go up and see her, if that's OK?'

Less than a minute later Rio stood outside a partially opened
door, the mellow shade of lamplight seeping onto the landing
outside. She knocked.

'Come in.'

Rio walked in to find Nikki with her iPad, cross-legged on
the middle of the bed. She was pleased to see the teenager still
wore her fingerless gloves – this pair total black with no frills.
There had been a flirty freeness about the way the teen had

worn those fingerless gloves, like she was eager to touch and experience so many aspects of life. Rio was glad that at least the girl's traumatic life hadn't stopped her still wanting to do that.

'I just wanted to check that you were OK.'

Nikki twisted her teeth in her bottom lip. 'Yeah, I'm good. I started school again last Monday. Everyone is being really nice to me.'

'I meant it when I said that if there's ever anything you want, you know where to find me.'

'Is *he* going to go away for the rest of his life?'

'I'm going to do everything in my power to make sure that Stephen Foster remains inside the four walls of a prison.'

Nikki nodded. 'I just want to get on with my life.' Then her face almost crumbled. 'But I can't. I see it every day.' Nikki's finger touched a spot on her cheek. 'Can you see it?'

Rio was baffled. 'See what?'

'The red mark.' Rio's confusion increased; there was no mark. 'That's where she spat her blood on me. I see it every time I look in the mirror.'

Shocked, Rio realised what she was talking about – Ophelia spitting blood, with her last breath, on her daughter's face. *God, if only parents realised how their actions could screw up their children's lives.*

'Your real parents were Patsy and Frank Bell. They loved you. Ophelia Bell was a woman filled with spite and selfishness. Don't let her screw up your life. One day soon you're going to look in the mirror and you won't see that mark anymore. And do you know why? Because you're one of the bravest girls I know. You're too smart to let some evil woman destroy your life.'

Nikki just looked at her as her hand came up. A finger rubbed against the spot where she still saw her biological mother's blood. Then her hand fell away. 'I'm going to use Aunt and Uncle's money to make a good life. A life Mum and Dad would be proud of.'

Rio smiled and nodded. Then turned and was gone.

Nikki flipped up the lid of her iPad and turned back to her Yakkety-Yak conversation.

Madam B: My favourite music is urban stuff, not that crap about women being bitches & ho's.

Cheese Twist: Yeah. Totally get you there hun. OK to call u hun??? Women are goddesses ☺ Know what music I like

Madam B: Head banger rock.

Cheese Twist: Nope. Classical. All time fav is Beethoven's Moonlight Sonata. Graceful. Beautiful. Lures you into thinking everything in the world is fine . . .

Alternative ending

We rejoin the story with Rio in the final stages of her interrogation of Stephen Foster . . .

10 Hours

Desperately Rio went back over old ground with Foster.

'Can you tell me why you decided to represent Gary Larkin when you heard he'd been arrested? And it was you who arranged for Gary Larkin and his gang to hide in that oast house in Kent wasn't it? Once you had the gang cornered you arranged for them to be murdered so it would look like they were killed in our raid. Dead men tell no tales. That's what happened isn't it, Mr Foster?'

Foster was still smoking the cigars that his secretary had brought in and left at the front desk. Foster looked pensive before replying, 'How's it going, DI Wray?'

'How's what going?'

'Your inquiry? Have your officers uncovered any actual evidence against me yet?'

'I've seen defendants convicted on less circumstantial evidence than I've got against you . . .'

Foster nodded with approval. 'Yes indeed. But that would be ordinary defendants, wouldn't it, Detective Inspector Wray?'

Rio refused to respond.

Foster sighed. 'As to your questions, of course there's the issue of client confidentiality but as the unfortunate Mr Larkin is no longer with us, I can tell you that I advised Gary to go back to his flat and sit it out. I don't know anything about any oast houses in Kent . . . Unless of course you can prove otherwise?'

The door opened. It was Strong. Rio punched the tape off and left the room. She was surprised to see the Assistant Commissioner waiting in the corridor. Strong left them alone.

'Cut him loose.'

Rio was furious. 'He's a murderer. Worse than a murderer, he got other people to do his dirty work for him. We've still got at least nine hours—'

'If you haven't got anything by now he isn't going to crack. Let him go. I've already had his friends on the phone complaining and you know how powerful they are. We don't have an alternative.' The skin around her lips tightened. 'Don't worry about Mr Foster. People like him always get what's coming to them.'

Rio stood there, feeling like the last person on this earth as her superior walked away. Just like she was going to have to let Foster walk away. She twisted around and raised her fist to slam it into the wall, but managed to stop less than an inch from the hard brick. Instead she ran her palm over her forehead. She was so sure they would get him, so sure. But they hadn't and she needed to let a certain person know.

Rio walked well away from the interview room and took out her phone.

'I'm sorry, Nikki, we're going to have to let him go.'

'Go? How can you let him go? He murdered them all.'

'I'm sorry,' Rio repeated. She couldn't even add the promise that she'd try to get him in the future; once Foster was out of the door he would never give her another chance to get anywhere near him.

'You did your best, Rio.'

And then she rang off.

When Rio returned to the interview room, Foster took one look at her face and smiled with triumph. 'We're finished here are we, Detective Inspector?'

'This isn't over, Foster.'

The lawyer confidently stood up. 'It's over for you, Ms Wray. By the time I've finished with you, you won't be able to get a job cleaning this building, never mind detecting in it.'

Rio's whole team were waiting in the reception area. They stood in an ominous silence watching Stephen Foster with hard gazes. In that moment Rio was truly proud of her people for their bravery and tenacity during this investigation.

Once he had collected his belongings Rio escorted Foster to the exit. The doors to the front of The Fort swung open, letting in soft afternoon sunshine. There was a large crowd of reporters waiting for him outside. There was shouting and the clicks of cameras as Rio remained at the top of the stairs left on her own in a lonely and troubled place.

Rio watched as Stephen Foster descended into the middle of the media scrum. He held up his hands until everyone was quiet. The bastard was going to milk his triumph for all it was worth. She moved to the outer edges of the steps to see his lying face as he spoke and was so intent on watching him that she didn't notice Strong stand beside her, until he whispered, 'Our friend Foster's a big star and linking him with Greenbelt and the Bell murders was bound to be hot news. Hold on – looks like he going to speak. This will be some kind of revenge on us . . .'

Foster cleared his throat and announced, 'Ladies and gentleman, as you are no doubt aware, just under two days ago I was arrested by the police and questioned about a number of serious crimes. Of course, I fully answered the questions that were put to me and I'm pleased to say that I have now been released without charge. As you will know, over the years, I have always endeavoured to defend the innocent and stand up for justice, without fear or favour. Obviously my work has caused a lot of discomfort to the police.'

His voice dropped slightly. 'Perhaps it was too much to hope that they would respond in a professional way to my work instead of pursuing a petty and vindictive vendetta against me. But I make no complaint about that. I've no doubt too that they are hoping that their campaign of intimidation will deter me from pursuing justice in the future. They are wrong. It will not. My legal career has been based on two founding principles – a love of the law and a love of justice . . .'

Abruptly Foster's head jerked backwards until his body was nearly arched so that it seemed inevitable that he would tumble backwards. But instead he bounced forwards, regained his balance and stood erect again. Rio leaned towards him to get a better look at what was going on. And that's when she saw it – an inky red mark on his forehead.

Foster tumbled to the ground, blood streaming from his head as someone shouted, 'He's been shot!'

Rio and Strong raced forwards as the crowd ducked, yelled and scattered. Rio dropped down on her knees beside the fallen lawyer and felt his pulse.

A few seconds later she looked up at Strong. 'He's dead.'

Strong scanned the fleeing crowd and the neighbouring buildings. 'Where the hell did that come from? Did you hear a shot?'

'Looks like a high-powered rifle, probably from a roof top.'

'I'll get the area sealed off; we might still catch him . . .'

Rio looked back down at the dead man who had a few

moments ago been speaking about justice. Well justice had finally found him.

One Month Later
7.00 p.m.

'I would just like to say a few words,' DSI Newman said to the crowd gathered in the pub.

Rio smiled because his words came out more like, 'I thood jus like to shay a phew wurds.' The DS was well on his way to being rip-roaring drunk; and he had the right to be. This was his retirement and farewell do: a celebration of his thirty-seven years on the force. The place was packed with officers, but no family or friends; this was *their* time to say goodbye to one of *their* own.

It was good to see everyone so outrageously happy, Rio thought, after the fallout from Stephen Foster's death. Accusations of police involvement had initially spread like wildfire, especially as the gunman had never been found, but then, mysteriously, the details about Foster's past relationship with Maurice Bell had surfaced in the press. One of the news articles had included an interview with the witness who had been willing to talk about Foster's days as a co-slum landlord; the picture painted of the dead lawyer had not been pretty. The heat had fallen away from the Met and Stephen Foster had left this world with dirt splattered across his reputation.

Rio knew that the only way the press could have got their hands on such information was if someone inside the service had leaked it.

'Don't worry about Mr Foster. People like him always get what's coming to them.'

The reassurance that AC Tripple had given her put her superior officer at the top of Rio's list of insiders who had blabbed

to the media. Of course, she could never ask such a high-rank-
ing officer if it were true. But then again, she didn't care;
sometimes knowing the truth was not the right way.

'Looks like the guv is going to fall flat on his face,' Detective
Jack Strong whispered in Rio's ear.

They stood together, jammed with others at the back of the
room near the bar.

Rio turned to him. 'You should be up there as well, Jack.
This was your last day.'

That how she thought of him now – not Strong but Jack.
His blue eyes twinkled. 'Nah. I'm not into big goodbyes. A
couple of farewell pints will do me fine.'

They both looked back at the mini stage at the front as
Newman addressed the crowd again.

'When I came into the service, policing was a much simpler
game. Two cops pounding the beat together, you really got to
know the community, understood their needs. And that's what
this is all about – servicing the public. And, of course, taking
the bad boys out of action. My dad wanted me to join him in
the building trade, but I was interested in another type of
building – keeping this glorious city of ours cemented and
strong, making sure that its foundations withstood anything
thrown at it. And I think that I did that. But I couldn't have
done it without the help of all you good people.' Someone
clapped and the room erupted into cheers and whistles.

When the applause died down, he spoke again; this time his
voice was much more sober. 'I soon learned the importance of
teamwork – that there was no way I was going to be able to do
this job on my own. I was lucky because my first partner was
the best cop there ever was. He walked the beat with me and
put his arm around my shoulder when I needed support. It's
his final day on the force as well, so I'd like everyone to give
a solid hand to Detective Jack Strong.'

The crowd and Rio turned to stare at Jack. But no one clapped. There was an awkward silence as everyone looked at him. Rio knew that many hadn't forgotten that fatal trip-up he'd made fours years back and the storm that had hit the Met because of it.

Rio tipped her head back defiantly and started to clap. It was a lone sound for a few seconds, then someone else clapped, and another person. Soon the room was back pulsating with whistles and cheers. A few people patted Jack on the back. He turned to Rio and gave her a single nod of thanks.

'OK, OK, I'm not finished folks,' Newman shouted from the stage. The pub grew quiet again. 'I know you're all eager to find out who will be taking my place. The honour goes to . . .' A few people looked Rio's way, but she kept her face straight, the emotions back.

Newman gave them the name. 'Detective Inspector Paul Mayberry.'

People clapped as Mayberry waved his hand in the air, but there was more than one person who sent Rio surprised looks.

'Now people,' Newman said, back into full merry-making mode, 'let's party.'

'I thought it was a done deal,' Jack whispered to her.

'It was. I turned it down.'

'Why the bloody hell did you do that?'

Rio didn't answer straight away; this had been one of the toughest decisions of her life. She'd thought AC Tripple was going to throttle her when she'd knocked the promotion back. The Assistant Commissioner had asked her why? Rio now gave Jack Strong the same answer.

'Simple; it's not my time yet. I don't want anyone to think this was handed to me because of my colour, gender—'

Jack seemed dismayed. 'Look, all that stuff and nonsense I said to you—'

Rio placed her hand on his arm. 'It wasn't you; it was me. I like my job, love the thrill of the investigation,' she shrugged, 'and maybe I just can't see myself sitting all day in an office. When my time comes, I will know it.'

Jack opened his mouth, but he never answered because someone slung their arm around his shoulder and dragged him away for a drink. He twisted his head to stare back at Rio. She just smiled and mouthed, 'Good luck.'

Rio took that as her cue to leave the festivities behind and head for the quiet of home. The air outside was cold, but there was a warm thread in the current that held the promise of a good spring to come.

'Hey stranger,' a voice called.

Rio peered in the dark to find Calum sitting in his car, the driver's window wound down. She might have made a decision about her job, but she hadn't made one about him. She walked slowly towards him. She shoved her hands in her coat pocket when she reached him.

'You don't look bad for a man who was at Death's door not that long ago.'

Calum smiled, drawing Rio's gaze to the thin scar line around his neck, a permanent memento from the wire the hitman had tried to strangle him with.

'Nothing keeps me down, not for long.'

'Well it's good to see you up and about.' Suddenly her tone changed. 'Look if you want to discuss a divorce—'

His smile dropped away. 'No. Not now. Let's leave that for another time.'

That was the theme song for their personal life – let's leave it for another time.

'I dropped by to tell you about something I just found out,' Calum continued. 'Stephen Foster's death was definitely a hit. Someone was paid – get this – half a mill to take him out.'

Rio made a nasty sound. 'Five hundred thousand pounds. The same bounty he put on Nikki's head. What goes around, comes—'

Abruptly Rio caught the rest of the words back as her mind clicked into gear.

No, it couldn't be true what she was thinking. No way.

'You did say five hundred—'

'Grand,' Calum finished for her. From the look on his face Rio knew he was thinking the same thing that she was.

'I've already gone down that road,' Calum continued, with a single shake of his head. 'It can't be true. You're putting two and two together and coming up with something bigger than four.'

But she couldn't leave this; she had to know. Rio turned and started rapidly walking away.

'Leave it alone, Rio . . .' Calum called after her.

He above all people should know that the one thing she'd never been able to do was *leave it alone*.

8:28 p.m.

When Rio saw the house she felt as if she'd come full circle – another house in Surrey – imposing and high-end, just like the Bell's. Every step Rio took down the winding pathway seemed to reinforce the thoughts twisting through her mind:

Sometimes the truth is not the right way.

You don't have to do this.

Turn around and walk away.

But she couldn't do that. The policing instinct inside her demanded that she confront this head on.

And then what?

What are you planning to do if this is the truth?

Rio stood in front of the door. Maybe she had this all wrong;

no way in hell could this really have happened. Rio pressed the bell. A woman opened the door. This must be Mrs Harkins, the mother of the friend that Nikki was staying with.

'Detective Inspector Wray,' the other woman said, a small smile lighting up her face. 'Nikki has talked so much about you.' She laughed. 'Made you sound like a superhero.'

She pulled back the door, an invitation to step inside, but Rio shook her head. 'Do you mind if I speak with Nikki?'

'She'll like that.' Mrs Harkins leaned into Rio, her voice dropping to a 'just between us friends' whisper. 'She's getting ready upstairs. She's got a date.'

That made Rio feel even worse about what she was about to do. Nikki had obviously moved on with her life and here Rio was, planning to drag her back again.

A few minutes later Nikki appeared downstairs. She looked like a colourful mix of radiance – the glowing tone of her face, the above-the-knee mauve dress, the block-heeled peep-toed ankle boots and her skin that was creating its own definition of healthy colour.

'Rio,' the teen greeted softly, once she stood in front of her. 'I'm on my way out, so I don't have much time.'

Nikki anxiously looked over Rio's shoulder outside. *Probably wants me gone, so she can meet her date and forget about the past.* But what she had to ask wouldn't take too much time.

Rio took a step back. 'Let's talk outside.'

The happiness surrounding the teenager faltered and she hesitated for a few seconds before complying with Rio's instruction.

'I'm OK, you know, if that's what you're worried about,' Nikki jumped in first, the words coming out in a rush. Her eyes darted down the pathway, then came back to Rio's face again.

'You're right; I'm worried. What's worrying me is all that

money you've got and what you might have been doing with it.'

Nikki looked at her innocently, her grey eyes widening. 'I don't know what you mean.'

'You were left a significant trust fund that you can access when you reach twenty-one, but you were also given six hundred thousand pounds that you can dip into anytime you want.'

Nikki half-twisted around, reminding Rio of the kid she'd spent time with, who did a runner every time she was confronted with something she couldn't handle. 'I've got to go—'

But Rio grabbed her lower arm and spun her around. 'Why did you do it, Nikki?' Only after she'd spoken did Rio feel the real heartache she was carrying around about this.

'I don't know what you're—?'

Rio hardened her heart. 'Foster. You had him killed—'

'What?' Now Nikki fought to get free, but Rio only tightened her grip. 'No way.'

'You asked me to let you know if Stephen Foster was being released—'

'And so what?' The girl wrenched free. 'I had a right to know. And if Calum told you I asked him how to find a hitman, so what? We talked about a load of stuff.'

Calum, how could you?

'If I accessed your bank accountant now, are you telling me I wouldn't find five hundred thousand gone?'

'Do you know what that man did?' Nikki was furious. 'He had my grandparents killed, my mum and dad killed, got someone to snuff out Ade's life, Cousin Cornelius killed himself. And Ophelia . . .' The words choked in her throat as she wrapped her lips together and rolled her head. 'I've got no one left.'

Rio realised that what she saw on Nikki's face couldn't be described as mere pain: it was agony, heartbreak, a type of dying inside while still living. This was so hard for Rio to watch, so hard.

'He turned my own mother against me.' Nikki pulled in deep shots of oxygen as she got herself back under control. Her hand came up to touch her face and Rio realised that she was wearing her trademark gloves. But there was something different about this pair: black leather gloves that covered the fingers. There had been a flirty freeness about the way the teen had worn those fingerless gloves, like she was eager to touch and experience so many aspects of life. Now her touch was closed off. Inwardly Rio mourned the one thing she had wanted to protect for Nikki all along – the girl's innocence. Because that's what those dark gloves represented – a child approaching adulthood with a hardness she shouldn't possess.

Nikki's finger touched a spot on her cheek. 'Can you see it?'

Rio was baffled. 'See what?'

'The red mark.' Rio's confusion increased; there was no mark. 'That's where she spat her blood on me. I see it every time I look in the mirror.'

Shocked, Rio realised what she was talking about – Ophelia spitting blood, with her last breath, on her daughter's face. *God, if only parents realised how their actions could screw up their children's lives.*

'You can't let this take over your life, Nikki–'

'I'm not,' the girl answered, a smile so bright springing onto her face. 'You can check my account if you want to Rio; all the money's there.'

So the girl had covered her tracks, but Rio wasn't buying any of it.

'I know what you did it.'

'Then prove it.' The sound of a car coming into the driveway didn't make Rio turn around. 'I didn't kill Stephen Foster, but may he rot in hell.' Nikki looked over Rio's shoulder and her smile increased. 'Here he is.'

As Nikki ran past her, Rio eventually turned around to see a smart-looking car come to a halt.

'Got to go, Rio,' Nikki shouted as she practically skipped to the passenger side of the car and eased inside.

The driver's window rolled down and the face that appeared took Rio into a zone of shock she hadn't felt for a long time.

'Hi, Mizz Wray,' Samson Larkin greeted her, his face split into a cocky grin.

No, Rio's mind roared. No, she wasn't going to allow this to happen. Ignoring Samson, she raced around to the passenger side of the car.

'Nikki get out of the car. You don't know who this is.'

The girl wound the window down. Her face was emotionless. 'I know who Samson is. We've been doing a bit of work together. Then we sort of hooked up. Thanks for everything you did for me, Rio, but I don't think we'll need to see each other again.'

Grinning Samson Larkin leaned towards Nikki's side of the car. 'You can't arrest me for anything; I ain't done nothing wrong. Parole officer just put me back on the books when I turned up.' His voice dropped to a mock-whisper. 'Between you and me I think he was more worried about being made redundant—'

'Did you help find her a hitman?' Rio growled.

Samson just laughed as he revved up the engine.

'Bye, Mizz Wray,' Samson yelled.

The tyres squealed and rushed past Rio. She couldn't even move. Samson and Nikki. Is that how this once innocent girl had found a hitman? Quizzed Calum for information on the dangerous trade and then gone to Samson Larkin to find one? But there was nothing she could do about it; she had no proof.

Two teenagers with blood on their hands . . . Nikki had said that she wouldn't be seeing Rio again, but she was *so* wrong. A few years from becoming a woman, what this girl didn't realise was that once someone had the taste of blood in them they were liable to want more. Rio had seen it too many times in the past.

Nikki was wrong; they would be seeing each other again. And Rio suspected – feared – the girl would be facing her on the wrong side of a table inside a police interview room.

acknowledgements

So many people are as always to thank for helping to craft Rio and Nikki's story. First on our list are you the readers for your continued support; we wouldn't be writing without you. A big shout out to two very special ladies – our agent Amanda Preston (what a brain that woman has!) and Kate Howard, one of the best editors in the business. A massive thanks to all at the Hodder team who helped make *Death Trap* into the book it is. To Robert for all his police expertise. And to the Mason, Edwards and Joseph clans for being the best and most supportive families ever!